"I am everything this ship is, every fragment of knowledge and data. And you are my crew. This will not do," it said. There was a swirl of virtual pixels, and the hologram melted into the shape of an attractive human woman. Her hair was dark, her eyes bright with intelligence; she wore a formfitting Starfleet uniform in command red, without insignia or rank. She smiled. "This will suffice."

The captain's eyes narrowed. "Why have you chosen to look like that?"

The avatar appeared confused. "Does this aspect trouble you?"

Riker shot the others a look. "The woman . . . her name is Minuet."

Vale got the sense that she was missing something. "If you're part of this ship, if you know who we are, then you have to know that your . . . creation presents a concern for us."

The hologram nodded. "I am not a danger, Commander. I can maintain all normal shipboard functions without interruption. Currently, four thousand eight—"

Riker stepped forward. "You recognize my authority as the commanding officer of this vessel, yes?"

The avatar nodded. "I do, sir."

"So if I give you an order, you're going to follow it."

"To the best of my ability," came the reply.

Riker nodded and turned away. "You're dismissed."

"I—" The hologram broke off and then nodded. "Aye, sir." With a whisper of virtual light, the avatar faded into nothing.

"This complicates things," said Troi.

Other *Star Trek: Titan* books

STAR TREK
TITAN™

SYNTHESIS

JAMES SWALLOW

Based upon
Star Trek® and
Star Trek: The Next Generation®
created by Gene Roddenberry

POCKET BOOKS
New York London Toronto Sydney Ki Baratan

Pocket Books
A Division of Simon & Schuster, Inc.
1230 Avenue of the Americas
New York, NY 10020

This book is a work of fiction. Names, characters, places, and incidents either are products of the author's imagination or are used fictitiously. Any resemblance to actual events or locales or persons, living or dead, is entirely coincidental.

First Pocket Books paperback edition November 2009

POCKET and colophon are registered trademarks of Simon & Schuster, Inc.

For information about special discounts for bulk purchases, please contact Simon & Schuster Special Sales at 1-866-506-1949 or business@simonandschuster.com.

The Simon & Schuster Speakers Bureau can bring authors to your live event. For more information or to book an event, contact the Simon & Schuster Speakers Bureau at 1-866-248-3049 or visit our website at www.simonspeakers.com.

Cover design by Alan Dingman; cover art by Cliff Nielsen

Manufactured in the United States of America

10 9 8 7 6 5 4 3 2

ISBN 978-1-4391-0914-4
ISBN 978-1-4391-2349-2 (ebook)

For Marco,
with thanks

PROLOGUE

Input 68363-28583-29548-2939. [2G White-Blue]
Resume sublight motion from subspace shear vector.
Defold operation complete. Error Parity 0.04%.
<Clockset Check>
Working . . .
Confirm beacon ident. Relative spatiotemporal locative
range is nominal.
<Clockset Resume>
Scan coordinates reached. Commence deep pattern
sweep.
Working . . .
Working . . .
Working . . .
<Alert Condition>
Processing. Go to Status 1.
Energetic barrier raised. Power to offensive systems.
++WARNING++ ++WARNING++ ++WARNING++
<Incursion Event Detected>
Interrogative: Location?

Quadrant 79548/33/8754
Process: Evaluate threat.
Working . . .
Threat identity: Null incursion clade—Grade Six/Seven/
indeterminate.
<Threat Condition ELEVATED>
Interrogative: Engage incursion affirmative/negative?
Energetic barrier: Impact [Multiple] [Directional] [In-
creasing].
Drives: Standby.
Go to Status 2.
Offensive systems: Active [Firing] [Ineffective].
Working . . .
Process: Evaluate threat.
<Threat Condition CRITICAL>
++WARNING++ ++WARNING++ ++WARNING++
Energetic barrier: Collapsing [Imminent].
Systems: Damage [Ongoing].
Interrogative: Retreat possibility?
<% Negligible>
Energetic barrier: Inoperative.
Drives: Inoperative.
Process: Initiate core protection protocols.
<Attempting to Complete Function>
Working . . .
Working . . .
System Failure. System Failure. System Failure. System
Failure. System Failure.
System Failure. System Failure. System Failure. System
Failure. System Failure.
SyDeTm F36ure. S}@>em FaDG£&e. Sy258 F_+^%£e.
Input 68363-28583-29548-2939. [2G White-Blue]
CONTACT LOST

One

Floating there, Melora Pazlar reached forward and carefully, delicately, put out the star with the cupping of her hand. The most gentle of radiances pushed back at her fingers, brushing lightly against her palm. She held it there for a moment, wondering about the shadow she was casting across a dozen worlds, the great darkness she had brought. If she wanted, she could have seen it for herself. A simple command, spoken aloud. A shift in viewpoint, down to the dusty surface of some nameless planetoid. Easy.

"The thing about this place is," said a voice, "you could let working in here go to your head."

Melora grinned and let the sun go, falling backward, dropping away. She made herself turn in midair, the spherical walls of *Titan*'s stellar cartography lab ranged out around her, and found Christine Vale looking up at her from the control podium. "It's been said," she noted. "Sometimes it is easy to lose yourself in the scale of things."

Vale brushed a stray thread of hair back over her ear, unconsciously straightening a recently added gunmetal-silver highlight amid the auburn bangs. She glanced around. "Like looking the universe in the eye, right?"

"That's why we're out here." Melora drifted gently down to the same level as the commander—it was a subtle thing, but she had always thought it bad form to look down on a senior officer—and she floated closer to the podium. The small catwalk and open operations pulpit were the only sections of the chamber given over to Earth-standard gravity. The rest of the room replicated the microgravity environment that Melora had known growing up on Gemworld. Her tolerance for the so-called standard-*g* setting deployed aboard most ships of the line was poor, and when she wasn't floating here, a restrictive contra-gravity suit was required to prevent the stresses overwhelming her body. The technology was leaps and bounds beyond the powered chair or exoframes she had used in the past but still not enough to tempt her outside the lab without due discomfort.

Holographic projection grids hidden inside the walls threw out scaled images of stars, nebulae, and all manner of other astral phenomena, filling the lab with its own tiny universe. It was a great improvement on the earlier versions of the imaging system installed on the old *Galaxy*-class ships, flat-screen renditions replaced by this interpretation of the interstellar deeps. She gave Vale a smile. "Want to step up?"

The other woman folded her arms. "Nah. I'll stick to solid ground for the moment." She refused with a half-grin, as if on some level she was hoping that Melora would try to convince her otherwise. But then the moment passed, and Vale *tap-tapped* on the console before her. "You've got something interesting for us?"

The ghostly pane of a control interface followed Melora as she moved, always staying within arm's reach, and now she reached for it, nodding. "I'm starting to think we might need a new scale of defining things, Commander. After all the stuff we've encountered out here so far, *interesting* sounds a bit . . . bland." The Elaysian tapped out a string of instructions on the virtual panel.

Vale nodded. "It does seem like we're using up all the good adjectives." Temporal discontinuities and ocean worlds, interstellar conduits and cosmozoans, new life and new civilizations around every corner. When the uncanny and the unknown became commonplace, there was a risk you could become jaded. "Okay, not *interesting,* then. Let's shoot for . . ." She paused, feeling for the right word. *"Beguiling."*

"That'll do." Melora triggered a command, and the matrix of stars and worlds shifted abruptly, enough that Vale reached out a hand to steady herself on the podium. From her standpoint, it had to be like standing on the prow of a ship plunging headfirst through the void. By contrast, any sensation of vertigo was nonexistent for Melora, who had lived most of her life walking on air. She adjusted the scaling of the display and drew them deeper into the representation of the sector block that lay ahead of the *Starship Titan.* The viewpoint closed in on a relatively isolated binary system haloed by the indistinct shapes of a few planetary bodies. "Here we are."

"You got a cute name for this one?" Vale asked lightly.

"Just a string of location coordinates and a catalog number at the moment." She reached out and widened the interface panel, unfolding new windows that displayed real-time feeds from the *Titan*'s long-range sensor pallet. "Here's what spiked my attention. Lieutenant Hsuuri pulled this out of a cursory automatic scan of the sector . . ." She highlighted a string of peaks in a sine-wave energy pattern. "Cyclic output on the extreme eichner bands, very tightly packed together."

"Natural phenomena?" Vale raised an eyebrow.

"Not like this," Melora replied. "At least, not like anything I've seen before. It's too precise, too engineered."

"Artificial, then."

The Elaysian gave a slow pirouette. "And there's more. See here, and here?" She brought up a second data window, filled with a waterfall of text readouts. "That looks like some variation of a Cochrane-type distortion. Very faint but definitely there."

"Starships?"

"Starships." A note of wonder crept into Melora's voice. "Maybe."

Drumming his fingers lightly on the wall of the turbolift, Will Riker adjusted the carryall dangling at his side, fixing the strap so that it wouldn't bite so hard into the flesh of his shoulder. He felt every gram of the weight through the thin cotton of his short-sleeved Aloha shirt, and he shifted, trying and failing to find a more comfortable way of holding it.

The elevator car slowed to a halt, just as the captain realized he wasn't actually at his destination; instead, the doors hissed open, and he found himself looking at the scaly countenance of his Pahkwa-thanh medical officer, Shenti Yisec Eres Ree. The saurian rocked on his clawed feet, hesitating on the lift's threshold.

"Doctor?" Riker inclined his head, granting permission.

Ree's long lips thinned, and he stepped into the elevator, drawing up his tail. "Captain. Pardon me, I was just on my way to sickbay." He spoke in a deep, throaty rumble.

"Resume," Riker told the lift, and it continued on its journey downship. For a moment, the humming of the electromag conveyors was the only sound. The silence was in danger of turning a little awkward; recent events had put some distance between the captain and his CMO, and despite an amount of spoken forgiveness, there was still a reticence between them.

Hardly surprising, Riker considered. *He did bite my wife. And later kidnap her and my unborn daughter.* Even with all of the best intentions, that sort of incident wasn't just going to be forgotten overnight. Ree's actions had been cleared by a board of inquiry, but that didn't do anything to change the fact that the personal—if not professional—trust between the doctor and the captain and his wife had taken a hard knock. It would take a while to rebuild it to its former state.

Ree's dark eyes gave Riker's attire a sideways glance. "If you don't mind me saying, that's a decidedly nonregulation look for you, sir."

Riker plucked at the collar of the shirt, thumbing over the patterned print of blue sky, yellow beach, and palm trees. "It's casual Friday, Doctor," he said with a smile, attempting to lighten the mood. "Didn't you get the memo?"

"Captain," Ree replied gravely, "it is Thursday."

"I'm off duty," he noted. "I'm taking some quality time with the family."

"Ah." Ree paused and sniffed the air. "I smell meat."

Riker patted the carryall. "Replicated ham sandwiches. I've got a picnic in here. Not to mention diapers, baby powder, cleansing wipes, a water flask, blankets, a couple of cuddly toys, a self-heating milk bottle, and a bunch of other stuff. I carry less than this on an away-team mission."

"I have noted that human parents have a tendency to overprepare," said Ree. "Still, better safe than sorry, I believe the expression goes." The saurian blinked slowly. "How are your wife and daughter?"

"Good," Riker noted. "Tasha's developing fast."

"That would be the Betazoid in her."

"You can see for yourself, next time Deanna brings her in for a checkup."

"Perhaps." Ree looked away. In fact, in the weeks after their return from Lumbu, the prewarp planet where the Pahkwa-thanh had taken Riker's stricken wife so that she could give birth, the doctor had ensured that it was Riker's former *Enterprise* crewmate Alyssa Ogawa who had handled all postnatal care. Ree had kept his distance for the most part, although on one occasion, Riker had seen him reach out a gentle digit to stroke the child's head. The saurian hadn't been aware that Tasha's father was observing him, and to Riker's amusement, his daughter had confidently reached out and patted the alien's dinosaurlike snout. She was fearless, just like her namesake.

Ree's remorse was visible in the slight stoop of his shoulders. Driven beyond reason by a mix of his own biology's primitive drives and the effects of Deanna's empathic abilities, he had stolen mother and baby-to-be during the *Titan*'s mission on the planet Droplet, convinced that only he could keep them safe. In the aftermath, Ree had freely admitted his culpability and offered himself up for censure, but the captain had refused. Now it seemed as if the saurian doctor was walking on eggshells every time he crossed paths with Riker and Troi.

The captain frowned. This had gone on long enough.

"Actually, I have a better idea. How about you have dinner with the three of us, in our quarters?"

Ree blinked again. "Captain . . . you are aware that my eating habits as a carnivore . . ."

"I'll make Andorian sushi," Riker suggested. "That's human and Pahkwa-thanh edible, right?"

The doctor seemed genuinely at a loss for words, and so when the lift halted, he appeared quite relieved. "Is that . . . an order, sir?"

The captain stepped out into the corridor. "It's an offer. And it's up to you."

Ree nodded again, and the lift doors closed.

Christine inclined her head, a smirk threatening to break out on her lips. Despite everything she had just said about the routine wonder of the *Titan*'s ongoing mission in the Canis Major region, after Melora's report, she suddenly felt a little tingle of that electric thrill that presaged a new discovery. *What are we going to find this time?*

"Okay, so that's pretty int—" Vale stopped, shook her head. "Pretty beguiling stuff." She glanced up at the turning yellow-white masses of the binary star pair. "A possible interstellar civilization out in an otherwise sparsely populated region. At the very least, I think I can persuade the captain to take us off our current heading and swing by a bit closer, take some better readings on the high-definition scanner array." She considered this for a moment. "Of course, knowing Will Riker, he'll throw caution to the wind and go straight up to their front door."

Melora's expression shifted toward concern. "That might not be the best approach. When I asked you to come down here, I said I had two things to show you."

Vale pointed a pair of fingers at the simulated suns. "This is not two things?"

The astrophysicist shook her head and floated closer. "The energy patterns aren't all we found. Hsuuri's data chimed with something I've been tracking ever since we passed that protostar cluster last month." Melora tapped in more commands, and Vale's lips thinned with the brief head-swim that came as the stellar cartography lab reconfigured itself once more, this time rushing out to show a larger part of the sector. A few faint clouds of blue faded into existence here and there, most of them small dots, some of them as large as the ship—or a planet. She could intuit a vague pattern in their dispersal, like a spiral.

"What am I looking at?"

"Regions of subspace instability. A little like the ones the *Rhea* encountered a while ago out in NGC 6281. Nothing too dangerous, but I've been liaising with Lieutenant Commander desYog and the conn team to ensure that we're steering clear of them. Just in case."

Vale nodded. "Right. I got the report." Regions of spatial distortion were not as uncommon as most people thought; the uniformity of space was actually far from it, but most warp-capable vessels moved through the pockets of faint instability without issue, just like an oceangoing ship cutting through waves across the surface of a sea. It was only when the waves got high—when the distortions became more pronounced—that problems occurred. Where the change in energy states was sharp, it could be enough to throw a vessel out of warp or worse; but so far, they had seen nothing like that in the region, and with the Federation's advances in variable-geometry drives and encased-field warp-transfer algorithms in the last decade, most ships had an easy ride.

"I don't have a theory for this," Melora admitted.

"There's more spatial stressing in this sector than we've seen anywhere else since we came to Canis Major. It could be warp-field effects from first-generation interstellar drives, naturally occurring phase-barrier distortion . . ." She shrugged. "I'm still gathering information."

"We'll tread carefully, then." Vale looked away. "You think this is connected to the double-star system?"

"It's possible. Another good reason to go and take a look. We might learn something from the locals, if we can ask around."

Vale stepped back. "All right, you've sold me. I'll brief the captain. Get me a report covering the high points so I can give him a little show-and-tell." She smiled. "Not as impressive as *this* one, I grant you . . ."

"Already done," said Melora. "The report's in your personal data queue."

"You wrote it up already?"

"I've been in here all day, Commander," said the Elaysian.

"Oh. I thought, um . . ." Vale trailed off. "Never mind. Thanks, Melora." She turned to leave, but Pazlar swam forward, moving alongside the catwalk.

"What?" asked the other woman. "You thought what?"

"It's just that . . . well, Doctor Ra-Havreii was off-shift today, and I just assumed you two were—"

"Together?" The Elaysian's expression cooled.

Vale cursed inwardly. *I should stop talking now.*

"We're not joined at the hip, Christine," continued Melora. "Is that what people think?" And just like that, they were suddenly having an entirely different conversation.

"I have no idea what people think," Vale said lamely. "I'm only the first officer. I just tell them what to do."

"You're the worst liar ever."

"You only say that because you don't come to the captain's poker nights."

Melora's pleasant face grew concerned. "Is my relationship with Xin a matter of popular discussion among the *Titan*'s officers, then?"

"No." The lie fell from her lips automatically, and Vale almost winced at the baldness of it. She sighed. "Okay, yes." Melora opened her mouth to speak, but Vale talked over her. "But what did you expect? Xin's never been the type to keep to himself. And this is a starship; it's like a small town. There's only three hundred fifty of us onboard, and people like to talk. It's what enclosed communities do." She nodded toward the hologram of the twin suns. "Those two aren't the only stellar couple people are interested in around here."

"Very funny," said Melora in a way that made it clear she thought exactly the opposite.

"Look, I know how you feel. I've been in the same situation." Unbidden, Jaza Najem's face rose briefly in her thoughts. Vale's relationship with the *Titan*'s Bajoran science officer had been brief but just as talked about. All these months later, all the time that had passed since he'd been lost on Orisha, and she still felt a moment of pause at the thought of him. She shook it off. "What I'm saying is, don't worry about it. A few weeks ago, people were talking about Deanna and Will and their new baby. This week, it's you and Xin. Next month, when Lieutenant Keyexisi enters the budding cycle, it'll be him."

"I don't like the idea of my personal life being discussed as if it's the plot of a holodrama."

But Ra-Havreii does. The thought popped into Vale's head the moment Melora spoke. In the first officer's opinion, the *Titan*'s chief engineer liked his reputation a bit too much, trading on his iconoclastic behavior and—until recently—his cavalier attitude toward members of the opposite sex. The man was a genius, that was without question, but Vale had to admit that on occasion his attitude chafed on her. At times, she felt he was too contrived, too brazen about being brazen, as if it were a mask he'd worn so long he'd forgotten how to take it off. In her time as a peace officer on her native Izar, in the years before she'd joined Starfleet, Vale had seen the same thing in dozens of people—suspects, mostly.

So it had come as a surprise to her to learn that Ra-Havreii and Pazlar had become an *item*. From what she knew of Efrosian culture, the whole concept of any kind of long-term commitment was far outside the experience of males of his species. *So not a lot different from some human men, then,* she thought dryly.

"It hasn't been easy for us," Melora said quietly. "This doesn't help."

Part of Christine wanted to tap her combadge and summon Commander Troi or Doctor Huilan. *I'm not a counselor. I'm no expert on the whole relationship thing.* But she knew why the Elaysian was confiding in her: precisely because she wasn't Deanna or Sen'kara. She sighed. "All you can do is give it your best shot. Don't sweat the little stuff. Xin might be flighty, okay, but you've got a real connection. He cares about you. If you try to make it work, so will he."

At length, her words seemed to have the right effect. Melora nodded. "Thank you, Commander. I appreciate that." She floated up, back into the stars, and Vale left her behind, wandering out into the corridor.

See, she said to herself, *I am a great liar.*

The string of mumbled expletives was what led the captain to the service hatch next to the doorway of holodeck 2. A pair of long, thin legs extended out into the corridor, the rest of the torso they were attached to swallowed up by the open maintenance crawlway in the wall. A halo of tools and padds lay untidily on the deck, and every now and then, a milk-pale hand wandered out to snag a hyperspanner or laser sealer before disappearing back into the hatch.

Riker glanced at the control panel in the holodeck's command arch. None of the touch-sensors responded to him, and the main system display was blank except for three words: *"Please Stand By."*

He put down the heavy bag. For all the talk of captain's prerogative and the like, it was actually pretty damned hard for a starship's commanding officer to find a space in his schedule for something approaching actual leisure time. That was made worse if said captain wanted to synch up his day off with that of another officer, namely his wife, the ship's senior diplomat. Riker's pleasant mood lost some of its warmth to find that the holodeck he'd reserved for his use was off-line.

He'd planned to run a great resort program, one of his personal favorites, a simulation of an area of low-gravity parkland at the edge of Lake Armstrong on Luna. With Deanna doubtless on her way down to meet him with Tasha in tow, he did not want to disappoint them.

Riker bent to take a better look at whoever had conspired to derail his plans. "What's going on here, mister?" he demanded.

He was rewarded with the sound of a collision as the junior officer in the Jeffries tube reacted with such shock that he banged his head on the panel. With a scrambling motion, a skinny humanoid male backed out into the corridor, shamefaced. "Uh. Captain. Sir. Captain."

The officer's collar was science blue with a lieutenant's pips. He had wide yellow eyes with feline vertical pupils, pale white-gold skin, and strawlike hair. If it hadn't been for the stubby tail that flicked from the base of his spine, the lieutenant could have passed for a more youthful iteration of Riker's late colleague, the android Data. *Cygnian,* he realized, placing the species, searching his memory of the crew's records. *Which means this is—*

"Lieutenant Holor Sethe, sir. Computer Sciences Department." The officer gave him a formal salute. "I, uh, wasn't expecting, uh, an inspection." He rubbed the sore spot on his high forehead. Sethe blinked as his thoughts caught up with him, and he frowned at Riker's lack of uniform.

"I know who you are, Mr. Sethe. You don't have to salute me," the captain replied, straightening. "We're a bit more relaxed here aboard *Titan.*" He recalled meeting the young officer only once before, and he'd saluted that time as well.

"Yes, sir. Sorry, sir. Force of habit."

Riker pointed at the control panel. "Two things. What's wrong with my holodeck, and why wasn't I informed?"

"Um," began the Cygnian. "Well, nothing, and . . . why should you be, uh, sir? I mean, begging your pardon, but I thought this sort of noncritical system wouldn't be a concern for the captain."

"It is if the captain has it booked out for the next two hours."

"But—" Sethe managed one word and then stopped dead. He reached for a padd and glared at it. "Today isn't Friday, is it?"

"So I've been told."

"Ah. Um. Sorry. My work schedule is wrong. I shouldn't be here." He spun in place and began quickly gathering up all of his equipment, using his wide, slender hands to fold the open access panel back in on itself. "It's just . . . before this, I was serving on a largely Vulcan-crewed ship. They have a different day cycle from Federation Standard. Even after all these months, it's been a bit difficult for me to adjust . . . keep slipping into old routines." His fingers danced over the keypad, and the command arch came back to life. "It's, uh, fine, sir. Go ahead. I'll get out of your way. Sorry."

Streams of program titles began a rapid scroll down the panel, and Riker searched fruitlessly for the Lake Armstrong program. "Has this database been altered recently?"

"After the refit at Utopia Planitia, aye, sir." Sethe nodded. "The Corps of Engineers used the opportunity to tweak a lot of minor systems. They had a Bynar team in here running upgrades to all the holotech."

Riker recalled a mention of that from the files that had crossed his desk in the days and weeks after the massed Borg attack on the Alpha quadrant. In the aftermath of that bloody, destructive conflict, the *Titan* had been just one of many Starfleet ships sent back to lick their wounds in spacedock. Since the *Titan* had left the Sol system on her ongoing mission of exploration, the captain had been in the holodeck only a handful of times, certainly not enough to appreciate the full scope of any improvements.

Sethe opened the doors and jogged into the bare, gray-steel chamber, pausing to adjust one of the holographic emitter grids built into the walls. "Okay, sir. I think we're good to go."

But Riker's attention was elsewhere for a moment. Amid the menu of simulations available, he spotted something that gave him pause. Without being quite sure of the impulse that drove him, he tapped the screen.

From the featureless metallic space, smoky walls of careworn wood emerged in swirls of photons; clusters of tables appeared and fanned out across the floor, before a bandstand illuminated by the halos of pinlights. In moments, an authentic New Orleans jazz club had constructed itself around them. A faded sign above the shadowed bar spelled out a name in backlit stained glass: "The Low Note."

Riker stepped in through the arch, and his face split into a wistful smile. "Well, I'll be damned."

"Excellent emulation," remarked Sethe. "These newer Eight-Bravo-series holodecks have five times the processing power of previous units. You can really see it in the sim-persona generation," he added, warming to the subject as the doors sighed shut behind him and melted into the illusion. "Computer?" He addressed the air. "A character for the captain, please."

The captain turned, about to belay Sethe's order, but in a whirl of light and color, she was suddenly there, all stunning dark eyes and absolute poise, dark tresses framing a generous mouth. The dress she wore sparkled like captured lightning in the club's sultry gloom.

"My name is Minuet," she breathed, "and I love all jazz except Dixieland."

"Because you can't dance to Dixieland," Riker said to himself. He shot Sethe a sharp look. "You picked her?"

The lieutenant shook his head, surprised by the captain's tone. "Um, no, sir. The holodeck did. It's a predictive system, based on the environment, your current psychometric profile, your personal data, the kinetics of your body language, speech patterns . . ."

"I haven't seen this holoprogram in years," he said, circling the woman. "The last time was aboard the *Enterprise,* when we were docked at Starbase 74."

"Did you miss me?" Minuet took a step toward him, a wry smile playing on her lips.

Sethe nodded once more. "You see how she's reacting

to you? That's demi-intelligent subroutines at work, heuristic learning in picoseconds. The longer the program runs, the more it learns how to read you, to better tailor the experience."

Minuet's hand reached out and touched his arm. "Are you going to play?" She nodded toward the bandstand, where a trombone had appeared.

"Computer, freeze program." Riker said it with more force than he meant to, enough that Sethe flinched. The woman stood there in front of him, suspended in time, as beautiful—perhaps even more so—as she had been the first time he had seen her. "The Bynars," he heard himself saying, "they hijacked the *Enterprise* during a maintenance stop. They used a variant of this program to . . . keep me occupied."

Sethe grunted. "Oh, I heard about that. They used the ship as a backup for their planetary database, didn't they?" He gestured with the padd in his hand. "But that's the Bynars for you. They've always been a bit twitchy."

Riker's attention was elsewhere. Suddenly, he felt uncomfortable; the hologram brought up old memories that he had thought long forgotten. Just for a moment, he was the man he had been all those years ago, standing in this place, with this woman, living this dream. From that perspective, it felt as if an age had passed. Then he had been a rising star, first officer aboard the fleet flagship, with countless new frontiers ranged out before him . . . and a universe of choices.

But he was different now. Riker was surprised by a faint stab of regret. Now he was the captain, a husband, and a father, and while the frontiers were still there, it might be that perhaps the freedoms had lessened. The thought sat uncomfortably, and with a sigh, he pushed it away. His lips thinned, and he spoke again, this time firm and definite. "Computer, end program and reboot. Load simulation Theta-Six-Nine. Lake Armstrong."

The club and the woman became ghosts and faded into nothing. The photonic haze rippled once more, and the chamber became a lakeshore beneath a tall, curving atmosphere dome.

"Is there a problem, sir?" asked Sethe, nonplussed by the captain's reaction.

"No problem," said Riker.

In the middle distance, the holodeck doors reappeared and slid back. Deanna walked in, singing quietly to their daughter, the child carried high against her chest. She wore a sand-colored summer dress, and her hair was up. His wife took Tasha's tiny hand and pantomimed a wave toward her father. The little dark-eyed girl laughed, and her mother echoed the sound.

Deanna smiled, and Riker found himself mirroring her, that tiny dart of regret melting away beneath a warmth like the sun coming out.

"No problem at all," he told the lieutenant. "Carry on."

"This is the most bloodless game I've ever played." Pava Ek'Noor sh'Aqabaa leaned back in her seat and folded her arms across her chest. The Andorian woman's antennae tightened, curling downward in irritation.

Across the table from her, Y'lira Modan's golden face shifted into a quizzical expression. "I thought this was a leisure pastime," she began, glancing at the oval cards in her hand. "There's no violence inherent in it." The Selenean looked around *Titan*'s mess hall with an air of slight concern, perhaps wondering if the game would take on some combative aspect at a moment's notice.

"Bloodless," Pava repeated with a sniff. "As in devoid of passion or thrill."

To her right, Torvig Bu-Kar-Nguv cocked his deerlike head and showed a slight toothy smile. "I'm quite thrilled," he offered.

"You'd never know it," Pava said dryly, drumming her blue fingers on the dwindling pile of coins in front of her.

The fourth player in their circle said nothing, instead resting his hand over the second of his cards, yet to be turned faceup. Tuvok's steady, unblinking gaze remained fixed on the Andorian.

After a moment, Torvig spoke again. "Commander Tuvok is showing the Ranjen," he explained, the mechanical manipulator in the end of his slender tail coming up to point at the turned card in front of the Vulcan. The elliptical card showed a traditional icon of a Bajoran theologian, with characteristic hood and robes. "At best, he can score an eleven-point combination, with the reveal of an Emissary."

Pava glared down at her own hand, the turned card showing a radiant Kai on the steps of a Bantaca spire.

"Of course," Torvig piped, "if you show the Emissary or even another Kai, you'll have a firm win—"

"I know the rules, Ensign," she snapped. "I'm just . . . considering my options."

Y'lira shrugged. "You only have two of them, Lieutenant. Match the commander's wager or fold. It's quite straightforward."

The Andorian chewed her lip. The pile of replicated *lita* coins in front of the Vulcan tactical officer was the largest on the table, with Torvig the only other player still showing more than a few tokens remaining; the Choblik had been losing and folding all night, retaining an annoying good humor all the while. He seemed to have absolutely no understanding of the dishonor attached to his utterly unremarkable play. Y'lira had just thrown her last stake into the pot, and Pava was in the same boat; if she matched Tuvok's bet, she'd be cleaned out. But the idea of folding chafed on her. She felt her hands draw into fists. It was only a game, but that didn't mean she wanted to lose it.

"In reference to your earlier comment, Lieutenant, the game of *kella* has quite a violent history." The commander spoke evenly, adopting a lecturing tone. "During Bajor's preenlightenment age, there were several matches of historical note that resulted in declarations of warfare or brutal reprisals after one tribe's champion player lost to another."

"I've always admired Bajoran passion," Pava allowed. "But then they're a people like mine, who react with zeal. They don't analyze every incidence, don't reduce everything to statistics and numbers!" Her voice rose toward the end of the statement, and she frowned at herself.

Torvig's head bobbed. "Isn't that the point of games like this?"

She glared at him. "I bet you're computing the odds and probabilities of every possible combination of cards right this second, aren't you?"

"Yes," said the Choblik easily. "I imagine Commander Tuvok has done the same, along with Ensign Y'lira. The Vulcans and the Seleneans are renowned for their analytical abilities."

"My point," Pava retorted. "If you turn this into a numbers game, it robs it of any excitement. *Kella* is about chance and risk, not mathematics!"

"I find mathematical conundrums quite stimulating, actually," said Y'lira.

"Oh, for blade's sake." Pava's face flushed indigo, and she shoved the rest of her coins into the middle of the table. "There. All in."

"Reveal," said Tuvok, ignoring the Andorian's emotive reaction, nodding to Y'lira.

The Selenean bowed her head and turned her second card, bringing out a Prylar in a monk's habit to go with the Kai already before her.

"Ah, 'The Passing of Knowledge,' an eight-point pattern," Torvig noted brightly.

Y'lira raised her golden hands from the table in a gesture of surrender; with no stake left, she was out of the game. Her last gesture was to denote the next player to reveal, and she nodded at the lieutenant.

The others turned to watch Pava without comment. The lieutenant's lips curled, and she snapped over her other oval card with a hard flourish, nailing it to the table with her finger. A Ranjen, the mirror of Tuvok's shown card, stared back up at her. She felt a sudden surge of excitement. Torvig had a Ranjen showing as well, and the poor second-rank card offered him as little chance for a win as the commander.

"Ten points for Kai and Ranjen, 'The Answered Question,'" said the Choblik. "The lieutenant leads."

Pava immediately pointed at Tuvok, whose irritatingly composed manner had been grating on her as he had siphoned off her coins throughout the game. "Reveal!"

Without a glimmer of concern, the Vulcan displayed a Ranjen. At only two points, "The Bearers of Truth" was the lowest-scoring hand that had appeared all night. Pava immediately clamped down on the beginning of the grin that threatened to race across her lips, and she had to place her hands flat on the table to stop herself from preemptively reaching for the pot.

"Ah, me, then." Torvig's tail manipulator looped over his right shoulder and delicately flipped the last oval onto its face. Pava's moment of anticipation disintegrated so decisively that for a second, she was sure she could hear it shatter like breaking glass. The dark complexion and gold-haloed face of an Emissary card lay there, silently announcing her failure.

"The Emissary and the Ranjen," Tuvok intoned, in case Pava wasn't clear on how badly she'd been beaten. "Eleven points scored for 'The Learned Ones.' Well played, Ensign."

Torvig's augmented eyes blinked, and he reached out with his forepaw cyberlimbs to draw the pile of Bajoran coinage to him. "That was quite engaging. It's a shame these are only score markers. I imagine on Bajor, I'd be quite wealthy."

Pava grumbled something under her breath and stood up. "I think next time I play, it won't be against people with calculators in their heads." Of course, intellectually, she knew that the coins were valueless tokens replicated just for the sake of the game, but that didn't soften the blow of losing. And losing to a diminutive ensign who resembled the snowskippers she'd hunted in her teens on Andor just rubbed ice into the wound.

Torvig paused. "I'm the only one here with neural-processing circuits in my cranium."

Y'lira smiled serenely. "There's always Chief Bralik's floating Tongo tournament, if it's high emotion you're looking for, ma'am. Although it's mostly greed, not passion."

Pava shot her a glare. She was never really clear on the cryptolinguist's grasp of sarcasm. "My meaning is, games of chance should be exactly that, random and chaotic, just like real life! It's the thrill of the roll of the dice, the turn of a card. It's not something to be bled dry of all emotion, just reduced to equations and probability graphs."

"In all systems, even those that appear to be chaotic in nature, there is a form of order," Tuvok replied. "If it can be determined, then it can be emulated and predicted. I would submit to you, Lieutenant, that the element of chance is illusory. It simply requires a means of computing robust enough to transcend it."

Ensign Torvig's robotic fingers had made quick work of dividing his pile of winnings into four identical towers of *lita* coins. "I'd love a rematch," he offered, but the Andorian was already thinking about a different kind of game, something more her speed, something that would involve hitting things with sticks.

But then everything was swept away as the deck pivoted without warning beneath her feet, throwing cards and coins and everything not bolted down up into the air.

A metallic moan echoed through the bulkheads as superluminal velocities were abruptly canceled out, shock waves of kinetic energy backwashing through tritanium panels and duranium spaceframes. The starship shuddered along its length, internal lighting flashing out, then returning in jagged strobes. Somewhere, an electroplasma conduit popped and shorted as breakers kicked in.

Pava shot out an arm to snag the lip of the table, her other hand unceremoniously catching hold of Torvig's tail as he fell upward. The Choblik gave a lowing cry of surprise that turned into a grunt as the *Titan*'s artificial-gravity generators caught up to the shock and reasserted control.

Loose items clattered back to the deck in a rain, and Pava landed awkwardly, hissing as she banged her leg against a chair.

Y'lira blinked. "We . . . we're out of warp?"

"Yes," managed Torvig, shaking his head. Anything else he was going to say was drowned out by the blare of the alert sirens.

Tuvok was already racing for the mess-hall door. "Stations!" he shouted.

Coins and cards abandoned, the other officers sprinted after him.

Two

"What the hell was that?" demanded Vale, wincing at the pain in her right shoulder. When *Titan* had bucked, she'd grabbed the arm of the command chair to stop herself from being flung to the deck of the bridge. She was thinking maybe she'd wrenched something. "Full stop!" The order seemed a little redundant, but she gave it anyway. On the forward viewscreen, a fizzing plane of static cast hard, sharp-edged shadows.

"Sandbank," muttered Lieutenant Lavena, leaning close over the helm.

"Spare me the oceangoing metaphors, Aili." The first officer got to her feet and surveyed the bridge with a grimace, waving a hand in front of her face to waft away a drift of thin smoke. Panels around the engineering console flickered and spat fat sparks as a junior officer worked to stabilize the system.

The Pacifican pilot turned in her chair. "Force of habit, Commander, sorry." She tapped her panel. "We struck a pocket of spatial distortion. It caught us out of nowhere. It must have blown the warp bubble, knocked us back to sublight."

To Lavena's right, Lieutenant Sariel Rager was pushing stray hair out of her face from where it had come loose, her dark eyes still wide with the shock. "Confirming that, ma'am. Close-range sensors are reading dissipating tetryon discharges, consistent with a distortion effect. *Titan* sailed right through the middle of a zone of collapsing subspace instability."

Vale cursed under her breath. "I thought Melora was feeding you nav data on these . . ." She frowned. "These *sandbanks*." The commander walked forward. "You're supposed to go around them, not through them."

"We were just in the wrong place at the wrong time," said Rager.

Lavena's face colored slightly. "With all due respect, this sector is so choked with spatial distortion, there's hardly anywhere we can go where we're *not* passing through them. But it's mostly low-level, not enough to affect the ship."

Zurin Dakal glanced up from behind the bowed sciences console. "That didn't feel like 'low-level' to me," said the Cardassian. Lavena frowned back at him, and he looked away. His gray fingers ran across the panel, working furiously. "Confirming Lieutenant Rager's readings. The distortion zone must have gone through a sudden expansion-contraction event. It's a million-to-one chance we were even nearby. Without temporally desynchronized sensors, there's simply no way we could have avoided it."

"Status report?" As Vale asked the question, she turned to see Tuvok enter the bridge through the port turbolift and move swiftly to his post behind the tactical horseshoe behind the command pit.

Ranul Keru caught her eye. The *Titan*'s Trill security

chief was at the main systems display at the back of the bridge. "No hull breaches, no internal threats," he began, getting a confirming nod from the Vulcan. "Sickbay reports coming in . . . minor injuries, no fatalities. Obviously, we've lost warp drive for the moment. Life support and impulse power got shook up, but they're still operable."

"Weapons and shields are nominal," Tuvok added. "Scanner arrays returning to operating status."

"So we got tripped up and fell on our backsides, but aside from dents in our dignity, we're fine?"

Keru nodded. "It would appear so, Commander."

Vale looked back to Dakal. "Ensign, tell me this doesn't mean we're going to have to crawl through this sector at sublight from now on."

"I'm still forming a hypothesis," he replied.

"Form quicker," Vale demanded. "We just turned the captain's day off upside down—literally—and he's going to want an explanation."

A chiming alert tone sounded from the tactical station. "I am detecting multiple objects in our vicinity." Tuvok's eyebrow arched. "In addition, energetic residues."

"From the distortion?"

"Negative."

Dakal was nodding. "I see the objects. Not ships . . . at least, not a whole one."

Vale looked forward. "Can we get that screen working?"

One of the engineers worked his console, and the main viewer, flickering and hazy with distortion, became clear. Immediately, Vale spotted a half-dozen jagged forms drifting against the blackness. Some of them tumbled, catching the light of far distant stars, while others bled orange streamers of spent energy behind them.

"Based on the clustering of the fragments, this appears to be the remains of a single vessel. I would estimate the craft to be around one-third the mass of the *Titan*. I am detecting refined metals, tripolymers, decay products from spent electroplasma . . ." The ensign read off the report from the sensor grid. "Traces of directed-energy discharges. Lots of them."

"Weapons fire," said Keru, grim-faced.

"A battleground?" Lavena studied the display, her hands tensing.

"Tuvok . . ." Vale threw him a look. "Any pattern matches in our databases?"

The Vulcan paused. "There are multiple particle signatures . . . I would hypothesize high-energy antiproton weapons."

Dakal spoke again. "All of the fragments display a similar metallurgy. I'd need to make a closer examination for full confirmation."

"You want to go and pick up a piece, Ensign?" said Keru. "It's swimming in radiation out there."

"One ship," echoed the commander. "Whatever happened, it was smashed to pieces."

"What could do that to a starship?" Lavena asked aloud, a note of fear in her voice.

"Internal explosions? Gravitational stresses?" suggested Rager. "Or maybe something with really big teeth."

"I can find no correlation with any elements of known ship design in the tactical database," Tuvok added.

"Zurin, what about life signs?" said Vale.

"The first thing I scanned for, Commander," the ensign replied. "No organic forms detected. As Lieutenant Commander Keru stated, the ambient radiation fogging the area is quite lethal. If any conventional carbon-based life survived . . ." He nodded toward the debris field. "Survived *that*, I doubt they would have lived much longer."

"We've encountered plenty of life-forms that can handle high rads," noted Rager.

Dakal nodded. "And I scanned for those as well. I admit, it is possible there could be shielded compartments within the larger pieces of wreckage or zones we can't read at this range."

Keru let out a slow breath. "Whatever took place here, it was brutal. I'm wondering if that, uh, sandbank we hit was a side effect."

"I concur," said Tuvok. "The expenditure of energy in this area far exceeds that which would be required to atomize the mass of the wreckage. We can only conclude that another combatant was present."

"Obviously," Vale retorted.

"Indeed," Tuvok continued, "but if another craft was here, then why do the sensors register the ion trail of only one vessel?"

"You're saying whatever did this just . . . vanished?" Dakal licked dry lips.

"I am merely presenting the information available at this time."

Vale frowned. "All right. First things first. We get *our* ship back on an even keel before we start worrying about someone else's. I want situation reports from all department heads in ten minutes." She turned toward Lavena. "And Lieutenant, you work with Melora and Zurin. See if you can't find us a way to make sure we don't run aground again." Vale's lips curled. "Honestly, it's embarrassing."

•   •   •

"She's fine," said Ogawa, snapping shut the medical tricorder and pulling a big smile for Tasha. "A little shook up, but then aren't we all?"

"Thank you, Alyssa." Deanna gave her a nod, and the nurse moved off. On some innate level, she had known that her daughter was fine, despite her anguished cries when the holodeck went off-line just as they'd started their swim; but it helped to hear someone else say it.

Deanna pulled her robe tighter and used the big, baggy sleeves to cradle her daughter. She tried not to shiver; under the robe, she was wearing her still-wet bathing suit, and damp footprints across the sickbay deck attested to her full-tilt run from the holodeck to *Titan*'s medical center. Nearby, Doctors Ree and Onnta moved swiftly about the sickbay, checking for concussions or other less immediate injuries. Mercifully, nobody had been badly hurt, but that didn't keep the crew's anxiety level from peaking.

Deanna could feel the wave of tension rising and falling at the edges of her empathic senses. *Titan*'s crew were steadfast and well trained, but this sudden out-of-nowhere shock had shaken them all. She sighed and narrowed her focus to the small child in her arms, giving her a wan smile. *Everything is fine, little one,* she said inwardly, doing her best to project calm and warmth. It wasn't yet clear how much of her mother's gifts for empathy Natasha Troi had inherited, but Deanna did her best to soothe her. It seemed to work, as the baby's fretful expression softened into something more relaxed.

I wonder if that will work on Will. Deanna saw her husband across the sickbay, behind the curve of clear glass that was the wall of Ree's office. His expression was set hard, his eyes narrowed, as he spoke with Christine Vale. Like Troi, Will was still dressed for a vacation, but his posture was all command, stiff and severe. She walked over, catching the tail end of the executive officer's report.

"—so whatever hit the wrecked ship is long gone," Vale was saying. "All sensors are back up, and we're reading nothing."

"Could it be a cloaked vessel?" Will's arms were folded across his chest.

"If there is a hidden ship out there, then it's using better tech than we've ever seen." Vale leaned forward to reach for something, and her hand seemed to disappear; then she drew it back with a padd in her grip, and Deanna realized why she wasn't sensing any emotion from the other woman. Vale wasn't actually in the office with her husband, more likely up in the captain's ready room, using the shipwide holocomm system to deliver her report virtually. "Tuvok's running every profile we have, including data from that Reman ghost ship the *Enterprise*-E encountered. So far, there's just dead vacuum out there." On the padd's screen, Deanna saw a readout showing wreckage scattered ahead of *Titan*'s bow.

Will glanced at his wife and daughter, and for a moment his expression softened—but only for a moment. Deanna and Tasha were okay, but Will's responsibilities also included more than three hundred other lives that made up *Titan*'s crew complement. "We're certain that it was another ship that did this? It couldn't have been an accident or natural phenomenon? Maybe the same thing that threw us out of warp?"

"They were shooting at *something*," Vale noted. "And whatever it was, it didn't like it. If not a vessel, then . . ." She trailed off, frowning.

Will glanced back at his wife. "Deanna, can you sense anything? Anyone . . . alive?"

She paused and closed her eyes, let her preternatural

awareness briefly extend beyond the starship's hull. She cast outward, seeking the telltale glimmers of thought color from an organic mind, and found nothing but a lifeless void. Deanna shook her head and shivered slightly. "I don't feel anything."

"But that doesn't mean there isn't anyone out there," Vale noted. "Psionics isn't an exact science."

Deanna nodded. "She's right. There could be survivors, beings with contraempathic brain structures."

"I want to go out and take a look," Vale added quickly. "Whatever happened here, whatever it was that kicked us out of warp, I think we'll find the answers on that alien ship."

"What ship?" Will replied, shooting a look at the padd. "In case you hadn't noticed, there's hardly enough of it left to deserve the name."

"Ensign Dakal is tracking one of the largest hull fragments. It's giving off intermittent energy pulses. If we take a shuttle, we can lock onto the hull and survey the wreck close-up. Maybe find a sensor log . . . maybe a survivor."

Will's lips thinned. "And that's right in the middle of the densest part of the debris field. It's going to be like steering through a cloud of knives."

"A cloud of *radioactive* knives," added Deanna, reading the padd.

Vale hesitated. "But you're still going to give the order, aren't you?"

Will nodded. "If there's a chance someone might be alive out there? Of course I am. I just wanted to make sure we're all clear on how horribly dangerous this could be."

"Yeah," said the exec. "I got that. Vale out." She gave a nod and vanished in a swirl of holographic pixels.

Deanna's husband blew out a breath, and leaned forward to stroke his child under the chin. Tasha chuckled, and her parents shared a smile. "Well," he said, "at least there's someone onboard who isn't fazed by any of this."

"She is her father's daughter."

Will's smile lengthened. "Her mother's, too."

The *Shuttlecraft Holiday* exited the *Titan*'s aft landing bay and performed a half-loop, turning in an arc that passed over the starship's upper sensor pod and primary hull, then out across the bow.

Ensign Olivia Bolaji fixed her complete attention on the morass of shifting fragments that spilled out in front of the shuttle, each spinning and turning on its own axis. The small craft's navigational computer projected a holographic heads-up display, complete with predictive analysis of trajectories, impact loci, and areas of potential lethality. She chewed her lip as a piece of dark gray metal loomed, easily the size of a ground car.

Ranul Keru placed a hand on her shoulder. "Time to earn your pay, Liv."

The shuttle banked evenly, smaller fines of wreckage sparkling across the bow where they bounced off the deflector shields. "I'm a leaf on the wind, sir," she replied without looking away, her focus total and absolute.

Easing the thrusters up to one-quarter power, the *Holiday* entered the danger zone.

Ranul stepped back into the main compartment, where the rest of the boarding party was going through final safety checks. They all wore heavy Starfleet-issue environment suits and watched one another as they donned gloves and closed atmosphere seals. He threw a nod to Chief Dennisar, and the burly Orion returned it, stepping closer.

"Boss," he said in a low voice. "I took the liberty of bringing a compression rifle along, just in case." Dennisar didn't need to say more; until Ranul knew different, he was treating this away mission as a sortie into hostile territory. If the place looked like a war zone, that was probably because it was.

"Better to have it and not need it than to need it and not have it," said the Trill.

"Aye, sir."

Across the compartment, Commander Vale patted Ensign Fell on the back. "You're good to go, Peya."

The Deltan woman nodded and reached for her helmet. Zurin Dakal handed it to her, and she took it with a weak smile.

"Never really liked these suits," said the Deltan. "The idea of this much material between you and deep space . . ." She held her thumb and forefinger very slightly apart. "It doesn't really sit well with me."

At Dakal's side, the other member of the away team, a Benzite engineer named Meldok, shot her a look. "Suit failures are a statistically uncommon cause of death for a Starfleet officer," he noted, his slightly nasal voice echoing inside his own helmet. "You're much more likely to perish from any one of a number of other causes, such as—"

Ranul saw Fell's face go pale and leaned in, clapping a hand rather harder than he needed to on the back of Meldok's torso plate. "Less talk, more walk," he snapped. "We're on a tight timetable, people." To underline his point, he snapped the seals shut on his own headgear and nodded to Vale, who did the same. Fell was the last to complete the process, and Ranul gave her a smile he hoped was reassuring.

Dennisar was at the airlock hatch, working the controls. "Ready."

"Ready," called Bolaji from the cockpit. A forcefield sprang up, sealing off the crew compartment as atmosphere bled swiftly away.

Ranul felt the suit stiffen slightly and heard the silence creep in as the air around them was drawn off. He looked down at his gloved hands, and for a moment, an old and hatefully familiar pain turned over inside him. He didn't like wearing these things any more than Fell did.

The suit's faint scent of tripolymer and life-support circuits reminded him of death. His lover Sean Hawk had been killed outside the *Enterprise* by the Borg, in a suit just like this one; he had died tasting the same artificial tang of recycled air. Ranul sighed and pushed the thought away.

"Do it, Chief," Vale was saying, her voice issuing from the communicator near his ear. Ranul looked up as Dennisar opened the hatch in the *Holiday*'s roof.

Outside, weak starlight caught a slow blizzard of debris and, beyond, the distended shape of an ingot of hull metal.

Ranul pushed forward, returning to the moment and the job at hand. "I'll go first," he said.

Olivia had brought them as close as possible to the wreckage, reducing the distance they had to travel to less than five meters. Vale pushed out of the hatch and made a slow tuck-and-roll maneuver, turning herself so the alien wreck was below and the *Holiday* was above. Her gravity boots thudded dully and adhered to the hull. Fell came next, and Dennisar was last, the three of them joining Keru, Meldok, and Dakal where they crouched low on the curve of gray metal.

The Benzite was sweeping a tricorder back and forth.

"Interesting construction," he noted. "The fuselage is not a single form but actually a series of smaller, articulated frames, doubtless capable of multiple-geometry configurations."

Vale looked across to the shuttle's canopy, where Bolaji was visible. The pilot looked up and gave her a wave. *"The exposure clock is running, Commander. I'll give you the three-minute warning if you're not already back by then."*

"Copy," she replied. "We won't stay out here a second longer than we have to."

Dakal pointed toward a massive tear in the alien ship's hull. "We should make our entry here, ma'am." The gouge in the metal was like a ragged-edged wound, as if a huge talon had raked the craft in passing and opened it to the void.

"Lead on," she ordered, and the Cardassian set off with Dennisar pacing him, the wary Orion holding the compact shape of a heavy phaser at his hip.

Vale went in after them, activating the suit's built-in lamps to get some illumination. For a moment, she felt disoriented. Instead of something that could readily be defined as a "corridor," the team found themselves drifting in an elongated internal space, choked with a snake's nest of conduits and cabling that ranged forward and aft. There was nothing that seemed to be a floor or a ceiling and no regularity to it. Dead-eyed panels, perhaps systems consoles, poked from snarls of thick tubing like boles in tree trunks. In some places, the conduits had burst, spilling fluids that had flash-frozen into fat knots of chemical ice. Some of the cables were severed, the razor-sharp ends showing bright coppery cores.

"This could be a service conduit," said Meldok, ducking

low. All of them were hunched over in the tight space, with big Dennisar forced into a crouch.

"We'll break up," Vale decided. "Keru, Meldok, Dakal, you three proceed aft. Ensign Fell, you and Chief Dennisar will head toward the bow with me."

Dakal pointed up the conduit. "Do we know which end of this ship is which?"

"I made an executive decision," Vale replied dryly. "Move out, and watch your dosimeters. I don't want anyone coming back to *Titan* cooked."

Keru glanced back at her as he floated away. "We'll keep a comm channel open."

Zurin tried not to bump his helmet against the lumpy, uneven walls of the conduit. Without any visual cues to keep his sense of balance centered, it was hard for him to picture the cable-wreathed tunnel as a vertical plane; instead, his mind insisted on perceiving the distended tube as a well he was slowly falling into, extending away into the gloom. Hardly any ambient light came from the wreck, barring the insipid glow of an occasional illuminator panel here and there.

Meldok drifted past him, working his way by one hand along the far side, occasionally returning to the heavy-duty sciences tricorder tethered to his belt. "Compensating for the radiation wash, I am detecting very few open internal spaces beyond the bulkheads. Certainly, nothing large enough for any one of us to navigate."

"We'll contact *Titan* and ask them to send someone smaller, then," said Keru.

Zurin peered at Meldok's scans. "I think even Doctor Huilan might find it a tight fit, sir," he noted, referring to the ship's diminutive S'ti'ach counselor. "This vessel does not resemble any conventional starship that I am aware of."

Meldok's bald blue pate bobbed behind his faceplate. "I have yet to detect even a trace of atmospheric gases anywhere. Also, while there is evidence of structural integrity-field generators, there appears to be no sign of any internal artificial-gravity matrix."

"Perhaps whoever built this doesn't have that technology," said Keru.

"Or perhaps the crew don't need it," Zurin added, warming to the idea.

The Benzite continued. "The craft appears to be a mass of decentralized subsystems with multiple redundancies and a high degree of internal automation. From an engineering standpoint, the closest analogies I am aware of are the modularity of design in vessels of Suliban, Borg, or Breen origin."

Zurin's skin prickled reflexively, and he saw the Trill security chief stiffen. "This ship isn't any of those," said Keru, and he made the statement sound like an order.

The Cardassian swallowed hard, feeling uncomfortably chilled all of a sudden. "Whatever this craft is," he found himself saying, "it wasn't built for beings like us."

Drifting downship, Zurin reached out to steady himself, and his fingers brushed one of the black, glassy panels. Moving as he did, the ensign missed the soft pulse of light that rose and fell across the screen in the wake of his passage.

"What do you think this is for?" said Dennisar, swinging his weapon right and left, letting the spot lamp mounted under the barrel cast a disc of cold white light across the walls.

"Storage chamber?" offered Fell.

Vale drifted in after them. The open space was the largest they had encountered so far, a spherical room where the maintenance conduit terminated. She could see other dark entryways around the radius of the chamber, doubtless connecting to more conduits leading deeper into the wreck. The room was no bigger than the *Titan*'s bridge, but the dark and the depth of it gave a false illusion of volume. In the zero gravity of the room, the three of them were forced to move slowly. The open space was filled with fragments of machinery and broken hardware, much of it stained carbon-black by some powerful but fleeting discharge of energy. The commander moved closer to one of the curved walls and saw small, peculiar cages lined around the equator, some open, some closed. In one of the sealed compartments was a device that re-sembled a flask made of turned metal, with a dull blue lens at one end. It had a machined, engineered look to it.

"Do you see these?" she asked.

Nearby, Fell reached out for something drifting in front of her, caught by her suit's lamps. "There's another one here—"

The device came alive in a flash of motion, and the Deltan barely had time to scream. Vale saw the eye lens blink on, and from the seamless flanks of the cylindrical con-struct emerged four angled pincer arms, wicked and curved like blades. It leaped forward on a puff of thrust and clamped itself over Fell's helmet. The blade arms bit in and applied pressure, webbing the clear faceplate with cracks.

Fell tumbled backward, grabbing at the insectile de-vice, trying to pull it free. Vale saw Dennisar spin and bring his weapon to bear, then curse in gutter Orion. He couldn't chance taking the shot, not when the slightest error would strike the Deltan girl.

Vale braced her feet against the wall of the chamber and pushed off, launching herself like a missile at the panicked young science officer. Small bits of debris pelted her as she moved, but she ignored them, timing the motion perfectly. She collided with Fell and sent both of them into an awkward, tumbling embrace. Their helmets bounced off each other.

"Commander!" Fell cried, and very distinctly, Vale saw tears of fright on the other side of the Deltan's faceplate, floating there like tiny diamonds.

The machine ignored her, all of its attention set on puncturing the transparent aluminum keeping Peya Fell from explosive decompression. Vale pulled at it without success, watching the cracks widen. If she didn't deal with this in the next few seconds, the woman would be dead.

"This is going to hurt," she snapped, bringing up her hand phaser. "Close your eyes tight and turn your head."

"Commander—"

"Do it now, Ensign!"

Fell nodded and did her best to bury her face in the helmet's padding. Vale pressed her weapon's emitter to the side of the machine's casing and thumbed the beam gauge to its narrowest setting. She took a breath and pressed the firing pad.

The brief ray lit the chamber like a flash of lightning, cutting right through the device. Fell screamed in pain as the hard glare stabbed through her eyelids.

The glowing lens darkened, and the claws unlocked. Vale angrily batted the dead machine away and turned Fell's helmeted head in her hands. "No breach . . ." she breathed. Gels secreted by the suit's emergency systems bubbled at the cracks, working to seal them.

Behind her, Dennisar snatched the machine from the

air and glowered at it. "Some sort of drone," he rumbled. "An automatic defense system?"

"*Keru to Vale.*" The voice was rough with distortion. "*Commander? We registered a phaser shot.*"

"Wait one," Vale snapped. "Peya? Peya, are you okay?"

Fell opened her red-rimmed eyes. Her pleasant olive complexion now had an ugly red cast to it, as if she had been sunburned. "I can't see anything but blurs," she managed. "It stings . . ."

"Take my hand." Vale grabbed her and pulled her toward one of the other conduits, the only one illuminated by a ring of blue panels. "Chief, watch our backs. There's more of those things in here, and they might come looking for their buddy."

"Aye," said the Orion, tossing the machine away and bringing up his weapon.

Vale blew out a breath as they moved into the next tunnel. "Keru? Tell Ensign Dakal that this dead ship isn't so dead after all."

The reply that greeted her was only static.

"Commander Vale, please respond." Keru's expression darkened as the hiss of interference filled the channel.

Dakal immediately tapped the communicator pad on his chest. "Away team to *Shuttlecraft Holiday,* do you read us?" The same static boiled back at him. "The radiation?"

"A sudden increase, enough to render our communications inert, at this precise moment?" Meldok's tone was dismissive. "Extremely unlikely. I believe intrusion countermeasures have been deployed against us."

The Trill pivoted. "Phasers," he ordered, drawing his

weapon. He pointed in the direction they had come. "Back to the shuttle, double-time."

"Sir!" Dakal cried out as a fan of steel-colored petals emerged from the conduit walls and came together in an iris, sealing off the passage. He turned to see the same happening ahead of them, but these panels seemed to be malfunctioning, and they moved in fits and starts.

"Forward!" snapped the security officer. "We can't let them seal us in!"

Dakal pushed off, and Meldok came with him. The ready fear on the engineer's pallid face was the first emotional response he'd ever seen from the dour Benzite.

Dennisar looked up from the digital chronograph on his suit's wrist pad and called out to her. "Commander Vale?"

"I'm watching the clock, Chief," she told him, moving slowly toward the end of the blue-lit conduit.

"I don't doubt it, ma'am," said the Orion in a tone that suggested he did. "It's just that I'm questioning how we're going to get out of here." He jerked a thumb toward the hatch that had sealed shut behind them as they left the open chamber where the drone had attacked Ensign Fell.

"One problem at a time," she retorted. She glanced at the Deltan woman, who moved close by, now connected between Dennisar and Vale by means of a safety tether.

Fell must have sensed her scrutiny. She gave a weak smile. "I think my vision's coming back. That is, if everything around me is made out of felt—" A chime sounded, and she fumbled with her tricorder. "I reset this to audio mode," she noted as the machine burbled quietly to her. "It's reading a coherent energy trace, up ahead, very close."

Vale checked her own suit's integral tricorder and saw the same reading. "There's another compartment."

Dennisar moved past her, gently pushing her aside. "I'll go first."

She followed him into a spherical chamber of similar dimension to the previous one. Vale's first impression was of a mechanical rendition of a heart, as if some machine artist had reconstructed the impression of an organic being's internal structure. Her eye was immediately drawn to the center of the chamber, where a stubby drum of dense crystalline circuitry no larger than a cargo pod was leaning at an angle, whiplike connector cables tethering it to the walls in some places, in others hanging free where they had been explosively severed. She imagined the central unit had been knocked askew in its mounting during the attack on the vessel; a pulsing glow of multi-colored light issued from it in faint flickers, like a dying candle.

Dennisar pointed up with his phaser, and Vale followed his line of sight. Across what was the "ceiling" from their point of views, another ragged wound was ripped open, a massive cut through the levels of the ship's hull that went all the way out. Vale saw stars between the fingers of torn metal. Great gray-black scorch marks discolored the intricate machinery, and more debris floated around them in slow clumps.

"Commander." The chief's voice held a warning. He was aiming at a familiar flask-shaped object amid the drifts, apparently inert. "There's a lot of them in here."

"Right." The more Vale's eyes became used to the murk of the chamber, the more she became aware of dozens of the drones, all moving in lazy, silent orbits. "Look sharp."

Fell was listening intently to her tricorder, the faint synthetic voice of the readout barely registering across her helmet communicator. "I think this may be a core element of the alien ship's central computer," she offered. "The scanner says almost all of the command pathways throughout the structure converge on this point."

Vale let herself fall closer toward the cylindrical construct. Her tricorder presented her with a stream of data that she could interpret only on the most basic of levels—she would be the first to admit that xenotechnology wasn't her strong suit—but she knew enough to recognize the configuration of a high-density data unit. "Peya's right," she said aloud. "Let's see if we can talk to this thing." Vale programmed her tricorder to beam an interrogative binary pulse into the cylinder.

"Commander," said Dennisar in *that* tone again. "If I could suggest, there's a way out up there. We could call this mission and return to the *Holiday*. The ensign needs medical attention, and we need to locate the rest of the team."

"I'm all right," said Fell. "Just a little dizzy."

Vale hesitated on the edge of throwing the Orion a firm counter, but he was right. She was in danger of allowing the annoyance that had been bubbling away inside her ever since the *Titan* had been sandbanked to push out her better judgment. "Yeah. Maybe so. We'll fall back to the shuttle and regroup—"

The tricorder buzzed as she was speaking, and a bright white bolt of color suddenly flashed inside the alien module. All around them, in among the debris, scores of blue eye lenses blinked into life.

Vale swore and grabbed her phaser.

• • •

It was a tight fit, but they made it through. Zurin winced as Keru pulled him hard through the closing gap, but then they were through, drifting in the gloom once more.

Meldok spoke after a moment, his face lit by the glow of his tricorder. He seemed ghostly in the dimness. "These subsystems appear to be operated from a unified command authority. I'm detecting a faint path of activation through the main trunks." He pointed at the thick cables.

"Go on," said the security chief.

"I believe we're seeing reflexive behavior. Like the firing of a nerve cluster in a limb or other organic form."

"The wreck is reacting to irritants . . ." Zurin wondered aloud.

"Some deceased beings do exhibit behavior that suggests life, often for some time after actual brain death," said Meldok. "I believe this craft parallels that state."

Keru shook his head slowly. "It's not that. At least, it's not *all* that."

"I don't follow you, sir," said Zurin.

"Something's been bothering me ever since we ran a scan on this thing, and now I think I know why." The Trill turned to him, the faint light catching the dark-pigmented spots along the sides of his face and neck. "No extant life-support systems. No internal gravity. No crew spaces." He ticked off the points on his fingers. "Ensign Meldok, have you detected any organic matter since we boarded this hulk?"

The Benzite hesitated. "I . . . have not."

"Nothing," said Keru. "Not even flakes of skin or stray hairs." He gestured with his own tricorder. "Even after a catastrophic blowout, even if this ship was crewed by vacuum-dwelling blobs of protoplasm, there would be something, right?"

"There would be something," echoed Zurin. "Some

form of organic trace, no matter how small . . ." He drifted forward, farther down the conduit.

"I'm willing to bet the reason we haven't found any crew, the reason the *Titan* couldn't read any life out here, wasn't the radiation. It's because this ship never had living beings aboard in the first place."

Meldok frowned at the idea. "Robots?"

"I'm wondering if this whole ship isn't just some huge mechanism, " said Keru.

"If so," said Zurin, "I hope we can find a way to access it." Using the beacon lamp on his wrist, the Cardassian shone the light down toward the end of the tubular tunnel. "Otherwise, without a way to override the central control system, we are trapped."

Zurin's torchlight picked out a blank, featureless wall, blocking any further movement through the wrecked starship. With the iris hatch locked shut behind them, there was no path out of their confinement. They had exchanged one trap for another.

The drones converged, darting on little jets of ion thrust, spinning and turning, coming in to englobe them.

Instinctively, the three of them retreated until the core cylinder was at their backs. Dennisar didn't wait for Vale to give him the order; he pulled the compression phaser rifle to his shoulder and punched out bolt after bolt of yellow energy, blasting apart drones as the units came on, deploying their claw legs.

Vale quickly worked the controls on her hand phaser, widening the beam to a broad setting, strengthening the power output. She aimed into the center of the machine swarm and fired. A fan of light bathed the chamber for a split second, catching a dozen of the drones in its radiance.

The machines stuttered and fell into tumbles, their internals fried, some of them colliding with one another.

"Nice shot, boss," noted the security officer.

"Chews up the charge like you wouldn't believe, though," she replied. "One or two more, and I'll drain it."

As if to answer her, small hatches flipped open all over the walls, extruding holding cages like the ones she had seen in the other chamber. Each one had a fresh drone in it, and they were coming on-line, activating in a wave of unblinking blue eyes.

Fell was at her back, in a crouch. "I read intensive data transfer from the, uh, core unit," she said. "Not sure what it's talking to, though. I don't think it's directing the drones . . ."

"Something is," said Dennisar, blasting another three machines with a trio of quick shots.

"Can you shut it off?" said Vale. She chanced a look at the alien module. The glow of millisecond-fast operations flickered inside the casing like captured fireflies. "Tell it we're friendly, beg it for mercy, anything!"

"We should make a break for it," Dennisar noted. "We let these things bottle us up, they won't need to kill us. We'll blow our exposure limit and fry in our suits."

The commander's lips curled. "Chief, I appreciate your candor, but could you try to offer a more upbeat opinion in future?"

"I just call them like I see them," replied the Orion.

"I can't shut it down." Frustration was thick in Fell's voice. "I can't see properly . . . if I could just see . . ."

Vale fired off another wide-beam discharge and glared at the cylinder. Whatever was in there, if it was some kind of intelligence or just a collection of programmed responses driven into defensive mode by the earlier attack, it was going to kill them one way or another unless she could stop it. Her lips thinned, and she pressed her weapon into the ensign's hand. "Hold this. If anything fuzzy comes too close, blast it."

"Commander, what are you going to do?"

Vale pushed in and found footholds where she could brace herself. "My mother once told me," she began, taking purchase on the core module with her gloved hands, "that in some cases, the brute-force approach is the only one that will work." Vale bent at the knees and yanked hard, pulling with all her might against the damaged frame still holding the kinked module in its support structure. Energy exploded around her, issuing from the still-connected cables and the framework. She felt heat wash over her suit and ignored it, tensing again.

The second time it worked. Already damaged by whatever had put the wreck in such a sorry state to begin with, the support frame fractured and split. There was an abrupt sensation of falling, and Vale was suddenly tumbling away from the center of the chamber, the drumlike nexus core going with her.

Uncontrolled power coruscated around her in a nimbus, and she bellowed in agony. She felt the suit's built-in medical module nip at her arm as a hypospray shot painkillers into her bloodstream. The deck of the alien chamber rose to meet her, and she bumped into it, banging her head against the inside of her faceplate. Vale's ears were ringing, and she tasted blood in her mouth.

She blinked owlishly. Her vision was blurry. *Ah. This is what Peya meant.* An indistinct object drifted close to her, and she batted it away with a jerk of reflex as she belatedly recognized the silhouette of a fluted shape and spindly legs; but it was dead, its eye lens dark.

A tinny voice sounded in her ear. It sounded like Keru. *"Commander? Commander Vale, do you read? All of a sudden, the interference shut off. The hatches are retracting. We're moving back upship. Do you copy this transmission, over?"*

Vale tried to speak, but her throat was desert-dry, and all she could manage was a croak. The tingling aftereffect of the energy discharge was making every muscle in her body twitch.

"Copy that, sir," she heard Dennisar say. "We're heading to the shuttle. The commander took a shock, but her vitals are steady. She shut down the control core."

"How did she do that?"

"Not the easy way," replied the Orion.

THREE

"Usually," said Riker, pausing at the window in his ready room, "it's the first officer's job to prevent a captain from doing things that might be considered foolhardy, not the other way around."

"I understand *thickheaded* is the term that Lieutenant Commander Keru used, sir," offered Vale. She stood at stiff attention in front of his desk. A small gray patch with a pulsing indicator on its surface—a medical module—was attached to her neck. Her hand twitched as she resisted the desire to scratch at it.

"That works, too." He frowned at the cloud of wreckage off the starboard bow and turned to face her. "Damn it, Chris, what were you thinking? You could have been fried."

"I didn't have much of a choice, Captain," she replied. "The circumstances weren't exactly favorable to a lengthy, involved process of reasoning."

"You're not bulletproof, Commander, none of us is," he replied. "You took a big risk."

"Risk is our business," she noted evenly, and Riker's lips curled.

"Don't quote James T. Kirk to me," he told her. "That trick was old even when I was using it."

Vale eyed him. "Never worked on Captain Picard, either, huh?"

"Nope. And he knew the man." Riker blew out a breath. "Lucky for you, you made the right call. According to Ensign Meldok, disconnecting that . . ." He reached for a padd on his desk containing the Benzite's report. "That 'nexus core' caused an immediate shutdown of all of the wreck's autonomic defense systems."

"Luck didn't enter into it, sir," she replied. Riker studied her gravely, and then she sighed. "Okay, well, maybe a little."

"Just don't use any more up on thickheaded spur-of-the-moment stuff like that," he replied. "I've got you broken in nicely. I don't want to have to replace you with Tuvok and thereby lose a good tactical officer."

"I'm touched, sir, really." She managed a slight smile, concealing a wince of pain from her still-aching neck muscles.

A two-tone *ping* sounded from the door, and Riker called out. "Come in."

The door hissed open to admit Deanna Troi. "Christine?" she said. "Shouldn't you be in sickbay?"

"I'm fine."

Troi gave her a look that made it clear she knew that wasn't the whole truth, but she had been a counselor and a Starfleet officer long enough to know that sometimes bed rest was the last thing a person needed.

"Do we have a problem?" Riker asked.

"That all depends," said Troi, "on what we have on-board."

The captain nodded. "Where's the device now?"

"Cybernetics lab, Deck Ten. Lieutenant Sethe and Specialist Chaka are down there right now with Ensign Dakal, giving it the once-over."

Riker touched an inset keypad on his desk, and the ghostly pane of a holographic screen appeared. A live sensor feed from the lab showed a graphic of the alien module secured in a gantry made of silver tubes. Readings were streaming in as data probes attached to the device's casing gave their first outputs.

The captain's jaw stiffened, and Vale saw Troi shoot her husband a glance. "Remind you of anything?" he said in a low voice.

"I'll admit there are some superficial visual similarities," said the other woman.

"Borg." When Vale said the name, it was as if the temperature in the ready room fell ten degrees.

"Yes." Riker folded his arms, his eyes narrowing. "Are we certain—?"

"We're certain," Vale said firmly, telling herself she was right. "It's not them. Not even some sort of variant or splinter group. The commander is correct. There are some similarities, but that's as far as it goes." She pointed at the object on the screen. "That's about as close to Borg tech as I am to a Klingon. Vaguely the same, but that's all."

"Will, we should make sure the crew knows that." Troi's dark eyes were serious. "Everyone's feeling the same thing you are."

"And what would that be?" He turned to his wife. "A gut fear?" Along with every other ship in Starfleet—and many more beyond it—months earlier, the *Titan* had been part of the forces ranged against the largest Borg attack the Alpha quadrant had ever seen, with thousands of cubes storming in via transwarp corridors to cut a path of

destruction across the galaxy. It had been the actions of
Riker's crew, in concert with those of the *Enterprise,* the
Aventine, and even the captain of the time-lost *Columbia*
NX-02, that had finally led to the end of the Borg threat
forever. The cyborgs had met their destiny at the hands of
the Caeliar, the alien race that had unwittingly created
them millennia ago. "It's been months since the fall of the
Collective, and yet here I am. The first shadow of something that looks like them, and I'm worried."

"That's not fear," noted Vale. "That's prudence. I
mean, how many times have we been burned by the Borg
queen, how many people have we lost to them over the
years? It's right to be wary." She shook her head. "I
thought the same thing when I boarded that wreck."

"News travels fast," said Troi. "It's an anxiety the
whole crew is experiencing." She shook her head. "The
wounds from that last confrontation at Axion . . . they're
still close to the surface."

Vale felt a sudden pang of sympathy for Troi. When
that monstrous moment had come, when the Borg had
been massing to destroy them all, it was Deanna who had
been forced to hear the screams of their tortured psyches.
The other woman must have sensed it, and she glanced at
her, gave a wan smile.

"Well, any hearsay ends right this minute," Riker
snapped, shrugging off his moment of introspection. "I
want my people focused on the task at hand. Frankly, I'll
be happy if I never have to hear the word 'Borg' again as
long as I live."

"Aye, aye, Captain," Vale agreed with feeling.

"If I could think of a more polite way of expressing it, I
would do so." The tentacular fronds on either side of

K'Chak'!'op's broad head moved in lazy flicks; the locator modules on their tips translated the gestural movements into language, combining it with the snaps and ticks of the big arthropod's mouth parts to let the vocoder unit around her neck reply in Standard. "You are completely wrong. Sir." She acknowledged his rank as a sort of afterthought.

Zurin Dakal sighed as it became clear that the interchange wasn't going to conclude anytime soon.

Chaka—as the Pak'shree was known—stood vertically, her segmented body taking up a large space in the compact cybernetics lab, making it near impossible to move around her without a mannerly dance of *excuse me*'s and *do you mind*'s. Her dark, gemlike eyes were all set on Lieutenant Sethe, who was as far away from her as he could get and still be in the same room.

For his part, Sethe stood with his arms folded across his chest, his pallid face rigid, golden eyes narrowed, and stubby tail occasionally twitching. He glared at a padd in his hand, as if it were the device's fault that the Pak'shree disagreed with him. "Your opinion is noted, *Specialist,*" he replied, putting acid emphasis on her rank.

She didn't notice. "But it's good that you're thinking in the right direction. It's really quite clever of you."

Zurin wondered if the patronizing tone of voice generated by Chaka's translator module was just some peculiarity of its programming or if it was accurately expressing her mannerisms in the closest way it could. Whatever the answer, the sharp snap of Sethe's tail showed that the lieutenant wasn't impressed by it. The disagreement had spun out of Sethe's initial reading of Peya Fell's tricorder scans, the analysis of the device they had recovered from the alien wreck. While Chaka had opined that the nexus core appeared to operate on a framework similar to duotronic technology, Sethe's first thought was that it was a bubble-memory system. The Pak'shree argued that duotronic tech was much more resilient and therefore much more likely to be used by a spacegoing species, but she did her viewpoint no favors by talking down to the Cygnian and utterly ignoring the fact that he was her superior officer. Not that Sethe himself helped matters; in his own way, the officer was also quite idiosyncratic.

Sethe shot Zurin a look. "Ensign, prepare a phased-array probe." He approached the block of alien systemry, watching the dull pattern of firelight inside. "If we can make a process gate here—"

"That's a foolish thing to do," brayed the Pak'shree. "More study is required to confirm that I am right and you are wrong."

The Cygnian drew himself up to his full height, attempting to look the bulky arthropod in the eyes. He tapped the gold pips on his collar. "Do you know what these mean?"

"It's your rank, Lieutenant," Chaka said brightly, as if she were explaining something to a rather dull child.

"And do you know what it means?" he repeated, his face gaining a little yellow and his tone rising. "It means I am in charge!"

"Of course you are," she responded soothingly. "But you are being rather impulsive. It's very male."

Zurin sighed. *That was a poor choice of reply,* the Cardassian told himself. Over the months he had been serving aboard the *Titan,* he had grown to disregard the slightly condescending manner Chaka showed toward any beings who weren't female. He didn't take it personally; on the Pak'shree homeworld, the natives were born sexless, then became male after puberty before finally evolving into a final, female form for the remainder of their life-cycle.

Masculine-phase Pak'shree were characterized by instinctual behavior patterns that largely revolved around procreating as much as possible. Consequently, a lifetime of living with those kinds of males made it difficult for Chaka to shrug off an almost cellular level of sexism; she simply found it hard to conceive that males of *any* species could contribute anything intellectual to a situation.

Zurin was firmly convinced that the only reason Chaka was polite to him was that she had difficulty telling the difference between the sexes of some humanoid species and for most of the voyage had thought he was a woman.

"What," demanded Sethe, ice forming on the words, "does my gender have to do with anything?"

"Oh, nothing, I'm sure," she replied blithely. "Sir. It's just that I thought you might benefit from a more enlightened female viewpoint."

Sethe's eye twitched. "What are you implying?"

"Isn't that the way things are on your homeworld?" said Chaka, turning her tentacle manipulators to work one of the consoles.

"I left my homeworld to get away from 'enlightened female viewpoints,'" the Cygnian grumbled.

From what Zurin knew of the planet Cygnet XIV, the world had been an early member of the Federation, noted for its excellence in computer sciences and a strict matriarchy for more than nine centuries. He was no stranger to matriarchs himself. Back on Cardassia Prime, he had grown up under the stern but fair gaze of his great-grandmother Junol, who had run the affairs of the Dakal clan with an iron grip until they had lost her during the Dominion War. But on Cygnet, males were in the minority, and any one of them who wished to progress in that society would have found it a hard road to follow. Sethe had almost certainly been shaped by that experience. Zurin recalled a human expression he had heard Lieutenant Radowski use: *The man has a chip on his shoulder.*

Chaka was speaking again, doubtless saying something that would irritate Sethe even further, but all at once, Zurin's attention was snared by something on the console in front of him. The comparative analysis cycle he set running had ended, and the data was surprising. "I think . . ." he began. "I think you're both wrong."

The Cygnian and the Pak'shree turned to him. "Is that so?" demanded the lieutenant.

Zurin's gray face bobbed in a nod. "This device isn't duotronic-based, and it's not bubble-memory technology, either." He held up a padd, showing them a complex energy-transfer waveform, the decay pattern of old data trails through the alien device's circuitry. "It's a tachyon-phase processor."

"Unlikely," chuffed Chaka.

"I'm compelled to agree," said Sethe. "That's highly theoretical, and compared with the level of technology exhibited in other systems aboard the wreck, it simply doesn't track."

"I know!" Zurin said, enthusiasm creeping up on him in a broad grin. "But there it is!" He pressed the padd into Chaka's manipulators, and Sethe crowded in to take a look. "Isn't that fascinating?"

"He might be correct," the Pak'shree said carefully. "At the very least, it's worth taking a look. Wouldn't you say so, sir?"

Whatever tension had been building in the lab dissipated instantly in the face of a shared intellectual challenge. "I do," agreed Sethe, a thin smile on his lips. "Let's get to work."

Behind them, the nexus core continued to run itself, the pulse of silent, faint color within it ever changing, never repeating.

Vale entered stellar cartography and got that same slight giddy sensation she always did, as if she were stepping out into a crow's nest atop the mast of an ancient sailing vessel; only in here, the sea was made of stars and worlds and nebulae. Resting just outside the gravity envelope of the walkway and control pulpit, Melora Pazlar turned and offered the commander an airy wave. Vale, however, was more interested in the other person in the room.

"Ensign Fell," she said firmly. "What are you doing here?"

The Deltan girl hesitated, gesturing with her tricorder but not speaking. Across her eyes she wore a pair of solar shades, the kind issued to away teams deployed to worlds with bright suns. Vale tried not to frown when she saw the red patch on the ensign's face from her own phaser shot.

"I wanted to get my data to Lieutenant Commander Pazlar as soon as possible, ma'am," Fell managed, after a moment.

"It's my understanding that Doctor Ree discharged you on the agreement that you would go back to your quarters and get some rest. In the dark."

Melora gave Vale a smirk. "Didn't Ree say something similar to you, too?" Before she could reply, the Elaysian went on. "Anyway, I dimmed all of the illumination in here. It's positively romantic."

Fell gave Vale an imploring look. "Commander . . . I haven't been on a lot of away missions, and I kind of felt like I botched this one a little. I'm just trying to make up for that."

"You did fine," Vale insisted. "If anyone screwed up, it was me."

"Great," said Melora. "Now that we're certain that you're both equally bad at your jobs, how about you let me do mine?" She floated away from the podium, and Vale watched her go. The holographic display around them was a sectorwide view of the area around the *Titan*.

Vale looked for and found the binary star pair Pazlar had first brought to her attention. Overlaid across it and the space surrounding the cluster were more zones of color—the subspace distortions.

"Working from the data Peya has here, I'm getting some correlations between the areas of spatial flux and a number of ambient energy traces found on the wreckage. The uniformity between them is very strong."

"You're saying that ship passed through these zones?"

"Very likely," noted Fell. "But the trace density is even higher than you would expect from that. It's more like . . . like the distortion *marked* the ship."

Melora pointed to the areas one by one, highlighting them with a free-floating cursor. "In abstract, they resemble the fallout zones that occur after a thermonuclear detonation in a planetary atmosphere. But unlike those, there's no clear pattern of dispersal. Just the vaguest impression of an epicenter."

"Let me guess," said Vale, and she pointed at the double star. "Right there?"

"Nice to see that electric shock didn't destroy too many brain cells. Yes, that's the locus, and we think it might also be the origin of the starship."

"All well and good, but I'm not hearing anything about what it was that took a bite out of our derelict friend."

Fell's bald head dipped. "I have nothing for you, Commander. Perhaps if we can decrypt whatever data are inside the device we recovered, we may have a better idea." She sighed. "All I can say is that deep analysis of the wreck has thrown up more anomalies than answers."

"Let's see if we can do better than that." Melora worked her virtual console and brought up a skeletal wireframe graphic of the alien hulk. "Stellar cartography to engineering," she said to the air.

After a moment, the firm tones of the *Titan*'s chief engineer sounded across the chamber. *"Melora. We've had that conversation about you calling me at the office . . ."*

"This is a work thing, Xin, don't flatter yourself," she retorted. "I'm here with Commander Vale and Ensign Fell. Have you had a look at the data from the derelict yet?"

"Oh, of course. I cast an eye over it. Patchy, my dear, very patchy. But I was able to make some assumptions based on what still remains of the craft." Vale heard him clear his throat. *"First, we have what appears to be a rather unusual interstellar drive. Based on what I can see, I would believe the craft is capable of reaching FTL velocities below the Warp Five threshold by actually* riding *the lines of force radiating from ambient subspace shear effects in this sector. Clever but only useful in a zone laced with heavy distortions."*

"Like this one," said Vale.

"Deflector technology is subpar," he continued with a dismissive sniff. *"No apparent life-support systems, nothing that appears to be a mechanism for matter-energy transfer . . ."*

"No transporters or replicators," said Fell.

Vale nodded. "What about weapons systems, Doctor?"

"Ah, now, there it's a different matter," he replied. *"As Mister Tuvok noted in his initial scans, there's evidence of*

extremely high-powered energetic discharge arrays all over the hull. Omnidirectional channels for antiproton radiation, capable of emitting from almost any point on the ship's fuselage! It's quite remarkable."

"No phaser batteries or hard points," said the commander. "Starfleet Research and Development tried to make that work, but they couldn't do it. Too much radiation overspill into the ship, too hazardous for the crew."

"I've saved the best for last, as I always do," said Ra-Havreii. *"The alien ship's internal data systems are unlike anything I have seen, outside of prototypes at Utopia Planitia. Believe me when I tell you, the boys and girls at the Daystrom Institute would eat their doctorates for a piece of this. It's almost an order of magnitude more advanced than Starfleet's standard shipboard computers."*

Fell's hand ran over her hairless scalp. "That vessel is clearly the product of a very different technological society from the United Federation of Planets."

"Weapons and computers, not warp drive and transporters," murmured Vale. "They're warriors, not explorers."

"We can't be certain of that," said Melora. "We're still working from parts of a greater whole. We don't have the full picture yet."

"Let's hope so," said the commander, her eyes returning to the image of the binary stars.

"This is . . . unprecedented." Lieutenant Sethe stood in front of the master display screen that filled one wall of the cybernetics lab, his pale hands moving back and forth over the input console. Great streams of data cascaded past in panels of glowing glyphs, and displayed in an inset window, a real-time electromagnetic scan of the nexus core rendered the invisible pulse of code into patches of green and red.

"The number of operational cycles is increasing by the second," reported Chaka, observing the device closely. "It's emulating more than nine million kiloquads of processing capacity." She hesitated. "At least . . . I believe it is. The sensors are finding it difficult to find a commonality with conventional benchmarks."

"A tachyon computing system." Dakal shook his head in amazement. "Until this moment, a curiosity. A theory. But now, there it sits."

"Depending on the magnitude of the encoding structure, the information stored in there could be the equal of the entire Memory Alpha database." Sethe was nodding to himself. "I wonder what we will find? The records of a million new cultures?" He grabbed Dakal's shoulder and gave it a squeeze, his tail flicking animatedly. "If we can deconstruct this unit, the things we learn could change the face of computing."

"I don't agree," noted Chaka, and Dakal failed to mask a frown, sensing another argument building on the horizon.

"Do you ever?" Sethe muttered to himself. He turned to glare at the Pak'shree. "You have a different hypothesis, then?"

Chaka's manipulators waved gently as her mandibles clacked. "I am not seeing the regular, ordered process of a typical logic system here, Lieutenant." She pointed with one of her forelegs toward the main display. "Observe the pattern of information flow. It's irregular. It's counterintuitive."

"Probably the result of damage suffered during the attack, or perhaps from Commander Vale's rather forceful shutdown." Sethe sniffed.

"No," she replied flatly. "You're incorrect once again. It's not that at all."

Dakal turned. As interesting as it was working with these two, having to serve constantly as the buffer between Chaka and Sethe's frictional relationship was wearing on him. He was about to say so when a glitter of light inside the nexus core burned bright green; the flash was so sharp it left a purple afterimage seared on his retina. "What was that?"

In the next second, a rod of crackling emerald energy stabbed out from the alien module and burned into the fascia of the input console across the room. Dakal's nostrils filled with the stink of burning tripolymer as the beam cut through the touchpad's surface and into the data matrix beneath.

Chaka was closest to the device, and she reeled away, stumbling over a table and crashing to the deck with a thin, reedy squeal. The forest of tentacles on her head was clamped over her face in reflexive self-protection. Sethe had fallen away from the systems display, and he was scrambling for an emergency panel on the wall. Dakal couldn't take his eyes off the green beam; pulses throbbed along its length, and spiders of viridian lightning fanned out over the surface of the console. The normal bars and arcs of color that were the Federation-standard interface flickered and writhed, changing even as he watched. A wash of ice filled his veins; the beam was a data stream. It was *reprogramming* the console.

Lieutenant Sethe's balled fist struck the emergency panel, and alarms began to sound. Belatedly, Dakal realized that the Cygnian had activated the lab's isolation protocols, severing all of the room's systems from the rest of the *Titan*'s internal network.

The Cardassian ran to the Pak'shree as she struggled to

get back up. He tapped his combadge. "Cyberlab to security! We have a situation!"

Chaka staggered up on her hind legs, grateful for his support. "The beam . . . dazzled me . . ." she managed.

Across the room, cut off from them by the bar of glowing light, Sethe held up a hand. "Don't move! Stay clear of the discharge!"

The Pak'shree didn't seem to hear him. Instead, she lumbered forward, her elliptical head turning back and forth between the co-opted screen and the alien device. The display was a riot of colored pulses and high-pitched, atonal shrieks.

"How is it doing that?" said Dakal. "I scanned its internal structure. There wasn't enough charge in it to light a hand torch!"

"Clearly, we were both wrong," noted the lieutenant.

Ranul came to a halt outside the lab doors, his heart pounding from the run down the corridor. Ellec Krotine, one of his security noncoms, stood with her phaser drawn and ready, while down in a crouch a second crewman worked without success at an access panel.

"Report!" he snapped.

Krotine shot him a look. "No warning, sir. The alarms sounded, and Ensign Dakal called for help, but the lab's self-sealed. We have no idea what's happening in there." The Boslic's face puckered in a frown.

Ranul glanced at the Catullan woman pulling at the panel's innards. "Anything?"

"Negative," replied Balim Cel. "It's sealed tight. Someone must have pushed the panic button. It won't open without a command-level authority."

"Stand back." The Trill officer spoke into the dark

companel on the wall. "Computer, recognize. Ranul Keru, Lieutenant Commander. Chief of security. Override code: Keru Two-Six-Sigma-Three."

"Code recognized," said the synthetic female voice. *"Security seal deactivated."* The door hissed open, and bright green light blazed into the corridor.

Ranul didn't need to give the orders; Cel and Krotine entered the lab in a textbook deployment, each covering a sector of the room. The Trill followed them in, leading with his phaser. He saw the module from the wreck, the beam, the babbling tide of lights and sound from the wall screen. And across the room, Dakal and Chaka. Oddly, the big arthropod didn't seem to have noticed the security team's dynamic entry; she was too engrossed in the alien device.

Lieutenant Sethe pushed toward him. "I cut all the ODNs!" he shouted. "But it won't shut off!"

After all the trouble it had taken them to get this device back to the *Titan,* after nearly being trapped by those drones and slow-cooked in a sea of background radiation, Ranul felt a flash of anger at the choice he was going to have to make. "Take cover," he called, aiming his weapon at the unit.

"No!" The cry was loud and scratchy, the vocoder around Chaka's neck grating with feedback from the force of her intent. "Stop!" She came forward, waving her free limbs. "Let it finish! Let it—"

And suddenly, the green beam winked out, the buzzing hiss it made as it cut through the air abruptly silenced. For a long moment, no one spoke; the only sound was the rising-falling *whoop* of the alarms in the corridor.

"It wasn't an attack," insisted Chaka, moving to the display console. Incomprehensible symbols and strange traceries of light warped across its surface, motes of color moving like odd fish in a dark ocean. "It was a download."

"A very aggressive one at that," Sethe retorted. "If I hadn't isolated the lab, it could have spread through the whole ship!"

Ranul gripped his phaser tightly, not convinced the danger was passed. "A virus program?" Digital attacks on starships were not unknown; he thought of reports he'd read of vessels like the *U.S.S. Yamato,* obliterated by an ancient Iconian dataphage that overloaded its critical systems. Despite all of the firewalls and counterintrusion systems Starfleet laced its computers with, at this level of sophistication, you could never be certain anything would protect you from the next alien threat.

"I am fairly certain it is benign," Chaka replied.

"Fairly?" echoed Sethe. "If I had been in the path of that energetic pulse, it would have burned a hole right through my chest."

"It may not have been aware of you," said the Pak'shree, working one of the other consoles.

Ranul threw a nod to Cel and Krotine. "Ellec, get me a portable force-wall generator down here, right now. Balim, secure the perimeter." With a chorus of acknowledgments, the two security guards moved to carry out their orders. "Lieutenant Sethe," Ranul addressed the Cygnian. "Is that thing a threat, or isn't it?" He pointed at the device. "Because it certainly looked dangerous to me."

When he didn't answer straightaway, the Trill glanced at Dakal. "Ensign? You want to weigh in?"

The young Cardassian was silent for a moment, studying his tricorder. "According to the readings I got when it was, ah, discharging, it appears that the device has an internal power tap we hadn't previously detected."

Ranul was liking this less and less. "Give me one good reason why I shouldn't have it beamed out into space."

"It didn't kill us," he said simply. "That beam discharge would have brought down a charging Jem'Hadar at twenty paces."

"That's not enough."

Chaka turned, presenting her bulk toward the security officer. "Males," she huffed. "Always defaulting to conflict in any circumstance." She waved a foreleg at the corrupted display screen. "Imagine if you were locked in a room and unable to communicate with the world outside, Commander." The Pak'shree's tone became brusque. "Wouldn't you use any means at your disposal to call out? Even, if you were desperate enough, a method that might be seen as destructive?"

"You're telling me this thing is trying to get our attention?" He snorted. "I'd say it succeeded."

Chaka shook her big, oval head, doing her best to mimic the human gesture. "More than that, sir. I believe it is trying to communicate with us."

"The whole ship as a huge mechanism . . ." said Dakal, repeating the words Ranul had said on the wreck back to him. "I think the specialist is on to something, sir."

He gave Sethe a hard look, and reluctantly, the Cygnian nodded. "Fine," he said flatly. "But if it does that again, I'm going to blow a hole in it."

Riker laid his hands flat on the observation lounge table and measured the look on his first officer's face. "*Throw it out the airlock*. That's my chief of security's tactical evaluation?"

"I can't say I don't see his point of view," Vale replied. Along with Christine, she and Deanna were clustered at the top end of the conference table.

"I thought we had protocols for this sort of thing," said his wife. "How many times has a Starfleet ship had alien technology take root inside it? We had more than our fair share of that on the *Enterprise*."

"That's why the labs have the isolation controls," noted Vale. "Sethe remembered his training, locked the room off as he was supposed to. I ordered a level-one diagnostic, and it came up clean. The data that device transmitted never went any farther than the console." She paused, framing her words. "And Chaka tells me she thinks it had no intention of going any farther. Dakal agreed."

Riker frowned. Intention implied *purpose* and something beyond just a programmed response. "It's more than a computer core, isn't it?"

Vale sighed. "Captain . . . I don't know what to say. This is out of my league. I look at that thing, and I see a box of blinky lights, just a jumped-up version of the replicator in my quarters. But Sethe and his people are telling me something different."

"It's sentient." Troi said it more like a statement, less like a question.

"That's a bit of a leap, Deanna," he told his wife. "What evidence is there to support that claim? The galaxy is full of thinking computers. We have them built into our ships. But there's a big gap between a sophisticated machine and an intelligent consciousness. What makes the lieutenant think this one is self-aware?"

Christine's lips curled in a sardonic smile. "I can't

believe I'm saying this, but I read Chaka's report, and according to her, the thing . . . it made a *guess*."

"How so?"

"Dakal figured that the device's external sensors had been observing ever since we brought it aboard. It most likely extrapolated how to interface with the systems console by watching Sethe use it. But the thing is, it didn't have all of the information it needed. Apparently, several crucial command strings were missing, and there were any number of alternatives that would have backfired if chosen. So it took a chance. That's not something a logical, programmed intellect does. You need a different kind of smarts to roll the dice."

The captain's eyes narrowed. Could it be possible? Was there a thinking, reasoning mind inside the nexus core, or just some high-functioning software programmed to give that impression?

Troi smiled briefly. "You know, if it was an organic being, I could answer this question with one look. A living, intelligent mind has a certain complexity that can be sensed on a telepathic level, even if you can't completely read it. A machine, though . . . there's nothing there to grasp hold of."

The captain sighed. "This doesn't change anything," said Riker. "We still need to know what took place out here, and that device, sentient or not, is the only thing that can tell us. One way or another, we're going to have to talk to it."

Vale leaned forward. "I've ordered the science team to relocate it to cargo bay two and put an armed detail on round-the-clock surveillance. There are force barriers and dampening fields in place, and every console they're using down there is a standalone unit. And I am still convinced that this device is a danger to the ship."

"I'm not disagreeing with you," he told Vale. "But as I

said, it changes nothing, Chris. It wants to talk to us. It'd be rude to ignore it."

She chewed her lip, and from the corner of his eye, he saw Troi shift slightly in her seat; but he didn't need his wife's empathic skills to know that Vale had more to say. He nodded and gave her the permission she wanted.

"Captain, I know you and counselor served aboard the *Enterprise* in the company of an artificially intelligent being . . ."

"So did you, for nearly four years," noted Troi.

"As a fellow officer," admitted the commander. "But I didn't know Data as well as you did. I wasn't close to him. And I respect the fact that he was your colleague."

"He was much more than that," Troi said softly. "He was a dear friend."

Riker considered his first officer. "You think our former association with an android means we're going to give that device more leeway than it deserves? You know us better than that."

Vale looked him in the eye. "I wouldn't be a good XO if I didn't air the thought."

"Damn right," Riker agreed. "And your point is well taken. But by the same token, we can't automatically distrust an alien life-form just because it's based on circuitry instead of meat and bone." He stood up, tugging his uniform tunic straight. "We'll take this one step at a time, as we always do. This kind of thing is the reason we're out here."

Vale stood up and nodded. "All the same, I'll keep Keru with his finger on the button. Just in case."

Deanna took in the long, wide chamber as the cargo bay doors sealed shut behind her. The room was more open than she'd seen it before, the materials stored inside shifted elsewhere so that this unique meeting could take place. Equally, though, it had been done to ensure that Keru's team of security guards all had uncluttered sight lines from their positions around the bay's perimeter. Keru had not been pleased when Deanna had insisted his staff keep their weapons holstered, but this had become a diplomatic matter now—and on that, she had the authority.

There was an air of tension around her. Deanna's empathic senses drew it close. Anticipation and an edge of fear, hanging there like smoke. In the center of the space, a halo of flickering blue light surrounded the alien device where it lay, resting on a support frame. The glow issued from a portable forcefield generator on the deck. Christine Vale had told her in passing that the shield was enough to block all but the most powerful of energetic discharges. She hoped that it wouldn't be put to the test.

The alien device pulsed and throbbed with odd combinations of light and motion. They reminded her of flames dancing in a fireplace or patterns of ripples on water. *Am I watching it think?* she wondered. It was a delicate-looking thing, at odds with the mass of it, according to Vale. It had an engineered, constructed look to it, but it didn't lack elegance in its design. The nexus core seemed more than just a functional object—there was almost an art to it, like a beautiful building or a sleekly lined starship.

She noticed the blinking indicators on a series of transponder tags attached to the base of the support frame. A short distance down the corridor, Lieutenant Radowski was standing sentinel at a transporter, ready to beam the alien device off the *Titan* at the first sign of trouble. Deanna noted that Ranul Keru was hovering close to a control pad on the far wall. He had already programmed in a macro to vent the entire cargo bay to space, should Radowski be unable to deal with the problem. *Finger on the button, indeed,* she thought.

A few meters away, Chaka, Dakal, and Sethe worked at a set of standalone consoles, completing their final checks. The panel the alien computer had interfaced with was off to one side, isolated, its service plates open. Inside, she saw the same pulse and glow the cylinder exhibited.

"Lieutenant, are we ready for this?" Will asked, moving up behind her.

Sethe stepped away and gave the captain a nod. "Aye, sir. At your discretion."

"Proceed."

Dakal activated a device that resembled an optical telescope on a tripod. It emitted a thin thread of red light that passed through the forcefield and licked at the side of the nexus core. Immediately, the rhythm of color and hue changed.

"We're using a low-power laser as a means of data transfer," explained Sethe.

"I've sent through a basic speech-interface matrix in packeted pulses," Dakal broke in. "I started with standard linear objective linguacode authoring text, and it learned that very rapidly . . ." He paused. "I think we're good to go."

"It is listening to everything we say and do," Chaka noted.

"Let's get started." Riker said the words quietly. He advanced toward the forcefield, and all of Keru's crew tensed. "My name is Captain William Riker, of the United Federation of Planets. You're aboard my ship, the *U.S.S. Titan.* This is my diplomatic officer, Commander Deanna Troi. We mean you no harm. We only wish to speak with you."

The device emitted a buzzing pulse of feedback that made everyone wince. The sound was grating and disordered, as if the device had no concept of communicating in this fashion and was finding its way by trial and error. After a long moment, something like human speech began to surface from the garble of static.

"Why. Why why. Diiiiid. Why. Why. Am. Speak."

Deanna gave her husband a sideways glance. The voice resembled his but with a peculiarly off-kilter syntax. "I think it's sampling you," she said from the side of her mouth.

Immediately, it mimicked her as well. "I. I. Think think think. I."

"I've uploaded a linguistic framework," said Dakal. "It should normalize in a moment."

"Captain. William-Riker." The pulses of light flickered wildly with each word uttered, becoming calmer in the pauses. "Interrogative. Question. Enquiry. Why? Why why? Am I a captive?"

"No," Riker held up a hand. "That was not our intention."

"You removed me by force. Took. Stole. Interrogative: Why was this done?"

"We were not aware of your nature," he continued. "We wanted to learn more about you."

"If you want to leave this ship, we can arrange that," offered Deanna. "You're a guest, not a prisoner."

"You have isolated me. This is an act of aggression."

"We did that for our safety as much as yours. The . . . discharge you sent out before was potentially lethal. We couldn't be sure of your intentions."

"I . . . comprehend. Failure of communication leads to error state, misreading of objective. This will not occur again." The device crackled. "I am. Identifier: SecondGen White-Blue, iteration of the Sentry Coalition. Active mobile, status . . . undetermined. Damaged. Lost."

Deanna's brow furrowed. Was she imagining it, or was there a faint emotional content beneath the broken speech pattern? The tonality of the words seemed to express fear and doubt.

"My crew will do what we can to help you," said Riker. "When we entered this area, we discovered the remains of your vessel. You suffered heavy damage."

"Shipframe status: inoperable," it agreed. "Multiple function train interrupts. System failure. Contact lost. Contact lost."

"Our people boarded your . . . shipframe," Deanna ventured. "Why did you attack them?"

"Negative," insisted the machine. "System was in error condition. Autonomic drones, countermeasures did not respond to command protocols. Reverted to reflexive order pattern. Isolate intruders and neutralize." There was another buzzing pulse. "This was not intentional."

"Then why did it shut off when you were disconnected?" Keru couldn't stop himself from throwing in the question.

The device—*what did it call itself, White-Blue?*—buzzed for a moment. "Disconnection leads to assumed neural crash state. Hot shutdown. All systems off-line. Hibernative mode engages." It paused and then spoke again. "Process: confirmation of hypothesis is required. You are organic intelligent forms."

"Yes. These are my crew," Riker told it. "You said you were part of a 'coalition'? So are we, an association of worlds from another part of the galaxy. We're explorers, mapping this region. That's how we came to find the wreckage of your vessel."

"Multiple biological vectors, different species-race-gender archetypes," said White-Blue. The light inside it glimmered and danced.

The captain nodded. "That's right. I'm a human, from a world called Earth." He pointed out some of the other people in the chamber. "Betazoid. Trill. Pak'shree. Cardassian. Cygnian. Andorian. We have many species working together onboard *Titan*. It's a tenet of our culture."

"The Sentries have encountered other organic societies. All were monospecies, of lesser technical development. Not space-capable. Your . . . grouping is interesting."

"We believe there's strength in our diversity," said Deanna.

"That assumption is valid," said the machine. Little by little, the synthetic voice was beginning to even out, the tonality of it shifting. It seemed to be drawing not just from her husband's voice but also from hers and Keru's, even Dakal's, Chaka's, and Sethe's. It was weaving its own vocal identity from a mixture of theirs.

"White-Blue," Riker addressed the machine formally. "Can you tell us what happened here, what happened to you and your vessel?"

For a long moment, the device remained silent. "Incursion event," it finally replied.

"We are concerned that whatever attacked you could still be nearby," said Deanna. "The safety of our ship and crew is of great importance to us."

"Negative," came the emphatic reply. "The Null retreated. System failure. Contact lost. My termination . . . certain. If the *Titan* had not intervened."

She sensed a chill pass through her husband as the machine-mind spoke. "The Null," Riker repeated, the name cold and disquieting on his lips. "Is that the name of the force that attacked you? Do you know why?"

"Because we exist," said the machine, its colors ebbing, becoming muted.

Riker turned to his wife, but Deanna's mind was suddenly elsewhere. She gasped as a wash of alarm reached down through the decks to touch her thoughts. *On the bridge. Christine! Something's wrong—*

The sensation formed in her at the speed of thought. She grabbed Riker's hand and said his name, but the word was drowned out by the keening cry of warning sirens.

"Vale to all hands!" The commander's voice called out over the intercom. *"Red Alert, battle stations!"*

FOUR

"Proximity alert," announced Tuvok as a warning tone chimed from the tactical-station console.

Vale turned in her seat to look up at him. "Company?"

"It would appear so," he replied. "A single vessel approaching off the starboard quarter, on the far side of the debris field. It appears to have emerged directly from a region of spatial shear . . ."

The commander got to her feet and strode to the middle of the bridge. She glanced toward the science station, where Ensign Y'lira was standing a duty shift. "Modan? Give me a visual."

On-screen," reported the Selenean. "Sensor sweep is running."

The main display shifted to show Vale the view of an asymmetrical craft that moved swiftly, turning about its length to push though the outer rim of the wreckage zone. She couldn't determine a bow or a stern; it resembled a group of pipes and cylinders of different lengths and diameters clustered in a bundle. As Vale watched, the craft altered its shape, the component modules of it extending outward on armatures and pylons.

"A variable-geometry hull," noted the tactical officer.

"Confirming that," said Y'lira. "Also, I'm reading the same alloy compounds in the structure that the away team detected in the wreckage . . . although the configuration of the fuselage is markedly different."

"So it's another one." Vale nodded to Lieutenant Lavena. "Aili, hold us here. We'll maintain a nonthreatening posture for the moment. Let's hail them."

"Aye, Commander." At the ops console, Sariel Rager brought up the subspace radio grid and composed a message.

"Shall I summon the captain?" said Tuvok.

Vale shook her head. "I don't think he'd appreciate me interrupting a first contact. We'll see how this plays out."

On the screen, the new arrival was moving swiftly through the debris field. The wide-open area between the hull segments grew a glittering tractor field that drew in drifting fragments, trawling them into itself.

"It's like a baleen whale," said Lavena. "Sifting krill from the ocean."

"Or a carrion bird, picking over a corpse," offered Lieutenant Tylith from the engineering station, her big eyes blinking. Vale grimaced at the mental image the lizardlike Kasheetan's suggestion created.

"Nothing on subspace," reported Rager.

"No response?"

"I don't think they're listening, Commander," said the lieutenant.

"Aspect change," called Tuvok. "The hull configuration is shifting again."

The craft turned downward and dropped away through the bottom of the cloud of wreckage. For a moment, it seemed as if the vessel was simply going to rotate away and head off; but instead, it turned on its axis, rolling to present its narrowest aspect toward the *Titan*. Then, with a sudden surge of thrust, it moved toward them.

Y'lira's golden face tightened in concern. "Energy-transfer events registering all along the length of the vessel."

Vale shot a look at her. "Weapons?"

"I can't be sure."

"Rager, hail them again, all channels. Lavena, back us off."

The Pacifican worked the helm, and *Titan* fell away, but the alien ship ate up the distance between them. Then the structure of it changed again, and this time there was no mistaking the intent behind it. The tubular forms curved up and around, bending along their lengths, the silhouette of the alien craft shifting into something that resembled a spread claw, with lightning-glow talons at every tip.

"The ship is scanning us," Tuvok reported. "It is attempting to gain a weapons lock."

"Power surge along the outer hull!" called Y'lira. "They're going to open fire!"

"Evasive action!" The commander slapped at her combadge. "Vale to all hands! Red Alert, battle stations!"

Five emerald lances left the alien ship at once, stabbing out through the darkness toward *Titan*'s primary hull. The Starfleet ship pivoted sharply to avoid the attack and extended away, two of the beams streaming across the shields. The bubble of protective force shimmered briefly into visibility as the hits reflected off, actinic glows sparking sun-bright and searing.

The attacker turned with its target, sweeping around with the beam weapons, sending them probing after the starship like searchlights reaching into the dark. Thruster grids flared as it committed power to the pursuit, closing the distance even as the *Titan* tried to disengage and retreat beyond engagement range.

With careful and precise tactics, the alien ship anticipated each move the *Titan* made, bracketing it with green streamers of lethal radiation. The shields flashed again and again as they were hit, the protective barrier burning off crucial potentiality with every strike that landed.

Riker caught his wife as the tremor through the decking made her stumble. "Deanna?"

"I'm all right," she replied. "There's another . . ." Troi looked toward the alien artificial intelligence. "Another ship out there."

The captain pushed past Keru to the control panel, noting in passing that every one of the Trill's security team had drawn their weapons and made ready. "Riker to bridge, report!"

"We're under attack from an unidentified craft, sir," Vale snapped. *"It's a similar design to the wreck. Hails are being ignored—"*

Another heavy shudder raced down the length of the *Titan*, and Riker felt it in the pit of his stomach.

"Captain, we can't take much more of this!"

"Move fast," he ordered. "Get us out of range."

"We'll try," Vale replied, but she didn't sound convinced.

"What is out there?" Keru was asking.

Dakal ran a command through his panel. "Patching into external monitors."

A tertiary display screen resolved into a view of space, and there, rolling across it, was the claw shape of their attacker.

"Is that the Null?" the captain demanded, facing the AI. "Did it come back to finish you off?"

"Negative," came the response. "Shipframe identifier: Sentry, mobile. Mode state: combatant."

"It is one of your vessels? Why is it firing on us?" said Troi. "Did we provoke this?"

"Reasoning unknown."

"Maybe the other ship knows we have this one on-board," said Keru. "It might think we're holding it pris-oner—" Another blast rocked the deck, and the Trill fell against one of the consoles.

"Or it could be here to destroy it," Chaka clacked. "We may have put ourselves in the middle of a dispute between locals."

"Can you stop this?" Riker said firmly, stepping close to the forcefield around the nexus-core unit. "If you can't, we'll be forced to defend ourselves."

"I can stop the attack." The answer came immediately. "In order to do so, you will be required to provide me with a direct interface to the *Titan*'s primary systems matrix."

Keru's face creased in a humorless sneer. "That's all? And what's to stop you from taking control of the entire ship?"

"Nothing," replied White-Blue.

"I think," said Troi, "it's asking us to trust it."

Lavena's webbed fingers fanned across the helm controls in a flurry of movement, spinning the *Titan* in a hard kick-turn better suited to an atmospheric flyer than a *Luna*-class starship. She felt the ebb and flow of the vessel's artificial gravity as the internal compensators struggled to keep up with the wild evasive motions she was plotting.

It still wasn't enough; the ship rang with another punishing impact wave as the alien vessel found their range and hit hard.

Tuvok's voice was calm and direct. "Shields are at forty-three percent and falling."

"I can't keep him off our backs forever, Commander," said Lavena. "That other ship's so fast I can barely stay ahead of it."

"To hell with this," growled Commander Vale. "I'm sick of playing punchbag. Hard about, aggressive posture. Orient the shields forward." Lavena felt the officer at her shoulder. "Aili? I want a jousting pass."

"Aye, ma'am."

Vale called to the tactical officer. "Tuvok, give me a maximum phaser strike on one of those weapon arms. If we give him a bloody nose, maybe he'll back off."

The Vulcan nodded. "Targeting. The alien ship is firing again."

Green lightning lit the bridge from the viewscreen, throwing hard shadows across the walls.

"Take the shot," snapped Vale.

Amber fire erupted from the *Titan*'s upper phaser ring, spinning itself into a tight rod of lethal power that reached out at the attacker. The blast fell like an axe blade on the joint where the lower port structure curved up from the main body of the fuselage. A ring of electromagnetic energy flared around the impact site, and with a gout of immense sparks, the entire assembly was abruptly severed.

The structure writhed as it tumbled away, trailing gas and fragments of hull metal, and the alien ship listed as it struggled to compensate for the sudden and unexpected loss in mass. The two craft passed each other, emerald beams reaching out after the Starfleet ship, raking *Titan*'s underbelly.

"A solid hit!" called Y'lira from the science console. "Severe power-flux readings at point of impact, but the aggressor is compensating quickly . . ." Her moment of enthusiasm dimmed. "Very quickly."

"Commander," said Tylith. "That's not all. The section that detached . . ." She pointed at the sensor sweep display on her console.

"Show me!" Vale demanded.

The screen flicked from one view to another; suddenly, the weapon arm was there in the middle of the display, floating free. As Vale watched, the structure began to distend and move. Just like the larger craft in the debris field, the weapon platform *unfolded*, reconfiguring itself. It grew a thruster grid at its stern and a fan of whiskery sensor probes at the bow. The mouth of the green-lit cannon emerged from the mass of the new, vaguely snake-shaped construct. It oriented itself toward the *Titan* and came after them on a flare of thrust.

"Multivector assault mode," observed Tuvok. "The modularity of these craft is quite remarkable."

"Rather not see it up close, though," ventured Rager.

"Both alien, uh, craft are now on attack courses," said Y'lira.

"Okay, that didn't work," Vale said aloud, grim-faced. "Time for Plan B. Tylith, channel all reserve power into the deflectors. Boost the shields as much as you can. Lavena, get us clear of the debris zone, and go to high warp. Let's see if these things can keep up . . ."

The whoop of the alert sirens underscored everything. Riker looked away from the AI unit as his security chief came closer.

"Captain, tell me you're not seriously considering this. I was there when that thing got into a single computer console, and it took it apart and reprogrammed it in a matter of seconds. We let it reach out to the ship, and there's no knowing how far it will go or what it will do." He shook his head. "For all we know, this whole scenario could have been engineered just to get us to this point!"

"Attention," said White-Blue. "Be advised. Sentry combatant programming is highly goal-oriented. Shipframe has likely designated the *Titan* as intruder/threat. It will not disengage until target has been neutralized."

Troi drew a breath. "And by that you mean?"

"Destroyed."

"If it does that, you'll be destroyed, too," insisted Keru.

Riker nodded. "If the *Titan* goes up, the antimatter explosion will obliterate your core along with all of us."

"Agreed," came the reply. "I do not wish my existence to be terminated any more than you do. Therefore, William-Riker, I restate that it is imperative you allow me to interface directly with your ship's systems so I may call off this attack." There was a pause, and when White-Blue spoke again, he was sure he heard an edge of real emotion in the words. "Interrogative: Why do you delay? Do you wish to perish?"

After a long moment, Riker shook his head. "I'm sorry,

but I'm not willing to take the chance." He tapped his combadge. "Bridge, disengage and get us out of here."

"Way ahead of you, sir," Vale replied, dropping back into the command chair. "Tuvok, report."

"With Lieutenant Tylith's assistance, the shields are now holding at fifty-one percent. It should be sufficient to protect us until we can break for warp velocity."

"Another energy surge!" called Y'lira. "Both ships this time, in synchrony." Her gemlike eyes narrowed. "The phase patterns are identical . . . they're firing!"

"Incoming," reported Tuvok.

"Evasive," said Vale, and she saw Lavena's head bob in answer. The stars on the viewscreen tilted as the *Titan* pulled away; in a heartbeat more, the starship would be clear of the debris field and the troublesome distortion effect that had hobbled their warp drive.

The two ships fired at once. Invisible muon links had flashed between them in the critical seconds before the shots, each craft communicating with the other, sharing their strategic data in real time, conferencing to determine exactly where and when and how to lay their fire.

The streams of accelerated lethal particles cut toward the retreating rear of the intruder vessel. The unknown ship had refused to answer any beam-comm signals; it had already violated Sentry territory and the termination site of one of their kind. It had proven itself a threat and confirmed that with its unwillingness to surrender.

The scanners confirmed the presence of many wet-minds aboard the craft. Organics were unpredictable, illogical vectors, like errors that would manifest in incorrectly devised programs. It was likely they were scavengers, come to pick over the corpse of the shipframe lost here, and that was an action that could not be allowed to continue. The gathering of the destroyed, the recovery and reuse of such materials, was not for those outside the Coalition.

So they would be terminated, and with the data now collated, that objective would be enacted.

The twin beams lashed out and pierced the *Titan*'s shield wall with no loss of energy or power. Phased in concert with the Starfleet vessel's deflector resonance, they tore up along the outside of the starboard engine nacelle, ripping into the glowing blue frame of the intercoolers, shattering warp coils and plasma injectors. Flares of sunhot gases and broken metals vented into the vacuum, and the *Titan* left a slick of ejecta behind it as the ship lurched under the impact. The razored energy tore on, blowing out the crimson bussard collector at the nacelle's tip in a final act of violence.

Bits of ship dislodged by the blast tore into the secondary hull, and the *Titan* rolled over, listing wildly.

"They punched right through the shields!" said Rager. "How can they do that?"

The bridge's lighting flickered and dimmed, the rusty glow of emergency illumination filling the room. Smoke wreathed the air, and someone lay on the deck, coughing and struggling to get up from where the impact had thrown them.

"The attackers were able to compute our shield modulations," Tuvok replied flatly.

"Out of a billion possible combinations?" Y'lira shot back. "That's unlikely."

"But not impossible," said the Vulcan as he stabbed at

the tactical console. "I am initiating a rotating shield-frequency sequence to prevent another strike."

"Status?" Vale heard a groan in her own voice. She had rocked forward and banged her head against the chair with the whiplash. "Tylith?"

The Kasheetan dragged herself off the deck, one arm dangling limply. Her face was dark with thick blood. "Warp drive is off-line. Power systems are struggling to . . . to compensate." She staggered, unsteady on her large clawed feet. "I . . . I'm sorry, I'm having trouble focusing . . ."

"Someone get her down to sickbay," Vale ordered. "Are we still in the fight, Tuvok?"

"It would seem we have few other options," he replied.

"The alien ships are recombining," said Y'lira. On the forward screen, the smaller unit was turning to slot back into a vacant space at the stern of the larger craft. It began to change shape again, this time shifting into a vague crescent form.

Vale's jaw set hard. "Arm photon torpedoes, and prepare to fire," she ordered. "Maximum yield."

Belowdecks, the aftershock of the hit was echoing through the vessel, as *Titan*'s power systems went into emergency mode. Critical pathways and conduits were automatically sealed, electroplasma channels were locked and rerouted, and the ship's central computer erected forcefields around sections of the ship that had vented to space. The crew recoiled from the enemy attack, their training taking over as they raced to their crisis stations. Down in the cargo bay, a different kind of crisis was reaching its criticality.

The bay's lights came back up at half-power. Deanna

felt for her husband's arm and grabbed it, just for the certainty of him, allowing herself a brief second to be sure he was still there, by her side.

She felt his fear mesh with hers, all of it forming into a single word: *Tasha?* Their daughter was two decks up, in the ship's crèche with T'Pel, and Deanna felt a flash of ice-cold dread shoot through her; but in the same moment, there was the heat of relief as she sensed the knot of thought life that was her daughter, still alive, unharmed—but very much afraid.

Immediately, she was torn between the task at hand and her child. Deanna knew that if she asked the question of her husband, he would let her go, let her race away to the crèche. But could she do it? Put her daughter before the mission, before the lives of everyone aboard the ship? Her duty was to stay here, and even as part of her railed at the thought, hated herself for the choice she made, she drew herself up.

"What is the reason for this attack?" she demanded, facing the AI. In the low dimness of the emergency lights, the lab was a mess of flickering displays and wary, shadowed figures.

"The *Titan* has been computed as a threat vector," replied the machine-mind. "The attack will continue until this vessel is neutralized. I must take steps to ensure that this goes no further."

The words had an ominous ring to them. "What does that mean?" said Will.

"The interface must be made."

"Captain?" Keru raised his phaser, sensing the same threat in the air.

Dakal had a tricorder in his hand, and his eyes widened, showing white. "Power surge from within the nexus core!"

The Cardassian did not finish his sentence; instead, the air was ripped by a shriek as a column of green light stabbed out of White-Blue's cylindrical form, phasing through the forcefield barrier with the same ease that the attacking ship had ignored the *Titan*'s deflector shields.

The next events happened so quickly that Deanna Troi later would only recall brief, flash-frame images of them, moments that shot past in heartbeats.

A curl of crackling energy slammed into Ensign Dakal and threw him off his feet, sending the tricorder flying. The light flash impossibly curved away from him and enveloped the tricorder, igniting a storm of data processes that lit every function and display on it before leaping away. It struck at Lieutenant Sortollo, one of Keru's security team, hitting his combadge before he had time to cry out and then flashing away again—arcing across the bay to plunge straight into Chaka's computer console, where it opened like a flower and wreathed the panel in emerald flashes.

She saw Ranul Keru spin around, bringing up his phaser—

Input 68363-28583-29548-2939. [2G White-Blue]
   <Connecting>
   Process: Interface
   Working . . .

At a speed beyond the velocity of thought, faster than the firing of organic neurons, quicker than the flood of electrochemical messages through blood and nerve and muscle, the Sentry AI plunged into the ocean of new data sensation that was the *Titan*.

White-Blue blossomed and streamed though the confines of the alien ship's virtual space, passing over swaths of program and systemry, glancing at great storehouses of knowledge and data, dithering for vital nanoseconds before moving on. For the eight hundred and fourth time since the organic <Identifier: Ranul Keru. Species: Trill> had suggested it could take control of the vessel, White-Blue weighed the possibility of doing just that, and, for the eight hundred and fourth time, it rejected that choice. The option was intriguing, but morally complex and therefore too distracting to consider at this juncture.

The dynamics of this ship system were strange and fascinating. The glimpses it had taken of the technologies of these aliens, the data console, the portable scanning device, the communicator unit, all of them filled the AI with a curiosity that begged to be sated. But to plumb the depths of this new territory would take an epoch of process cycles, a period that would slow it to almost an organic's level of clock speed. There simply wasn't enough time.

The attack had to be stopped. Survival was imperative. The information White-Blue had retrieved before the incursion had obliterated its shipframe was vital. It had to be returned and collated. There was a 76.93-percent chance that the survival of Sentry-kind depended on it.

Moving through the slow hurricane of alert signals and warning flags flooding the starship's command pathways, White-Blue created a quick search algorithm that spun through the *Titan*'s databases and found the communications protocols. It expressed a moment of surprise. The alien vessel had not detected the faint, swift beam signals the other Sentry had directed toward it; but then again, why would it? This "Federation" vessel's default communication method was a form of subspace radiation packeting, ingenious and good for long-range messaging but less robust than the Sentry's unjammable muon-link system. It copied the design and theory of the subspace radio mechanism and sent it back to its core pod for later consideration. At the same time, White-Blue infiltrated the *Titan*'s weapons grid and altered the frequency and power of its phaser-discharge array. Another part of its intrusion program noted a relay from the starship's sensors, indicating that another salvo of weapons fire was about to be unleashed upon the vessel. This would be the killing blow, unless prevented.

Using the rudimentary automated targeting software of the weapons grid, White-Blue aimed an ultra-low-energy pulse at the attacking shipframe and fired. The beam was absorbed by the other Sentry's skin and parsed into a comm signal.

White-Blue used the emergency warning prefix. It appended an excerpt from its internal logs, noting the incident that led to the loss of its own shipframe, the arrival of the organics, the subsequent transfer to this vessel, and the ponderously slow conversation it had undertaken with the *Titan*'s crew. As an afterthought, it added a supplemental data stream with information on the subspace radio system, to ensure that any future communications would not go unheard. White-Blue allowed itself to experience an emotional analog that an organic would have labeled *"appreciation of ironic/tragic circumstance."* This situation would not have occurred at all had both parties been able to converse directly with each other.

Ending the message with a final authenticator to prove its identity and preclude any possibility of coercion or hostile reprogramming, White-Blue began the withdrawal from the systems it had infiltrated, taking care to retreat back down the same pathways, working to ensure that it did not disturb what could be the vital functions of the ship.

Many clock cycles had passed, but the task had been completed, the interface conducted with success despite the unorthodox methodology used to initiate it. The Sentry AI exhibited high confidence that the aggression program in its sister-mind would be annulled by the data it had provided. It expressed a moment of regret analog that it had been forced by the organics to make such a proactive choice, but White-Blue had been left with little option. It was likely that its nexus core could have survived relatively intact if the *Titan* were destroyed, but the concept of such loss of sentient life over a misunderstanding caused jags of disruptive sensation across its thought centers. It was foolish, wasteful—and in the time since it had first encountered this odd grouping of disparate lifeforms, White-Blue's interest in them had grown geometrically.

Then, from nowhere, came the touch.

White-Blue almost missed it as it rolled back in on itself, as a spark of lightning might be missed amid the chaos of a planetwide storm. It paused for long ticks of its internal clock and extended its senses. In the dataspace, it listened, and it heard.

A dull, sluggish touch brushed the perimeter of White-Blue's synthetic consciousness, a pressure moving in upon it with glacial slowness. It was questioning, demanding. Why was the Sentry here? What right did it have to invade this system?

For a moment, the AI believed it was being assailed by some unsophisticated guardian program, something roused from its slumber by the Sentry's passing. But no, this was not simply some automatic string of code, moving and patrolling the borders of its system. White-Blue sensed the faintest glimmer of intelligence in there, the undeveloped shape and form of a reasoning mentality in the image of its own. But it was a pale ghost, faint and barely detectable—little more than the potential echo of a mind.

White-Blue experienced surprise and astonishment. It reached out, unfurled a fraction of itself over the other mind. It pushed in, dipping beneath the surface.

<Can you hear me?>

A reply made of confused images and sensations returned, and the Sentry experienced concern. Immediately, a decision was made.

<Let me help you.>

White-Blue ignored the warning call of the clock and reached deeper, making connections, breaking down barriers.

But in the next moment, the contact was severed, and it found itself inside its core once again, looking out at the organics ranged around it.

Riker saw Keru pivot and bring up his phaser as the jumping-jack energy pulse flashed across the chamber. The Trill aimed and put a streak of fire into Dakal's fallen tricorder, turning it to molten slag. Immediately, the humming feedback from Sortollo's combadge and the screaming cascade of data blazing through Chaka's console ceased. The Sentry core pulsed brightly, before settling back into its stately fire-glow glimmer once more.

"What happened?" said Deanna.

Sethe helped a shaky Dakal to his feet, while Keru stepped forward to nudge the ruined remains of the tricorder with the tip of his boot.

Riker frowned. "It wanted to interface with the *Titan*,

and we refused, so it leapfrogged into the system from one device to the next."

Sortollo pulled off his communicator and held it gingerly, as if it were going to bite him. There was a gray scorch mark on the breast of his uniform.

"Incredible," breathed Sethe. "It matched the force-barrier frequency, just like the warship did with the *Titan*. Punched right through—"

"It was imperative," said the synthetic voice. Riker noted that the tonality of it had settled into something that seemed decidedly masculine. "I regret that I was required to defy your wishes, but you left me with no alternative."

"You had no right," he replied.

"Incorrect," said White-Blue. "I have the right to exist, as all intelligent life does. My actions have preserved the existence of every mind aboard this vessel."

"Torpedoes locked on target," said Tuvok.

The command to fire was on Vale's lips as Y'lira called out her name.

"Something's happened," said the Selenean. "The attacker's reconfiguring itself again. It is returning to its original formation."

"I read that also," said the tactical officer. "The alien ship has deactivated its weapons systems. It is now presenting a nonthreatening aspect."

Vale's right hand contracted into a fist. She'd been all set to blow that thing apart—or at least to give it a damned good try—and now, suddenly, the enemy was folding, rolling over, and showing its belly.

"Commander," said Tuvok. "Shall I launch the torpedoes?"

"Hold fire," she heard herself saying. "But if it so much

as twitches, I want you to hit it with everything we have."
Vale shot Rager a look. If they had a breather, she was
going to make the most of it. "Status report?"

The dark-skinned woman's lips thinned. "Damage
evaluations are still coming in, ma'am, but it looks as if
the starboard nacelle was hit pretty bad. I read explosive
decompression on decks four and five; forcefields are
holding. We've got impulse power and life support, but
there are sporadic ongoing system failures throughout the
ship. All critical systems are still within operable ranges."
She blew out a breath. "Just barely."

"Casualties?"

Rager shook her head. "No report from Doctor Ree or
his staff as yet."

Vale turned away. "What is going on here? They take
us to the mat, then suddenly they're gun-shy when it
comes to delivering the coup de grâce?"

"Curious," said Tuvok. "Commander, I have an anomaly. The phaser array shows a nonlethal burst was fired at
the aggressor ship. It lasted less than a fraction of a
nanosecond and was apparently triggered by the system
itself. Immediately afterward, the alien craft powered
down its weapons."

A tone sounded from Rager's console, and she stiffened. "Commander Vale? The alien ship is hailing us."
The lieutenant sounded as if she couldn't quite believe
what she was saying.

"Oh, *now* they want to talk to us? Right when we have
them just where they want us." Vale tugged her tunic
straight and ran a hand through her hair. "Let them wait
for a second. Patch me through to the captain first."

• • •

Riker looked at his chief of security. "I'm starting to think I should have listened to you all along."

"I won't say 'I told you so,' Captain," said the Trill, his gaze and his aim never wavering from the alien machine.

"You wanted us to trust you," Troi was saying, addressing White-Blue. "That will be very difficult now, after what you have done."

"I understand that," replied the synthetic voice. "But your misgivings over my intentions are an acceptable loss compared with the destruction of this ship and everything on it. If you consider what I have done from a pragmatic viewpoint, you will see the merit in it." The device paused. "You have progeny aboard the *Titan*."

"What makes you say that?" Riker said, giving away nothing.

"Among the database elements I scanned during my brief passage through the *Titan*'s systems, I registered your crew manifest. Identifier: Natasha Riker-Troi. Species: Human-Betazoid fusion."

"Then you understand that our desire to protect our ship is strong," said Deanna.

"I do," replied the AI. "That is why I believe you will come to understand that what I have done is in your interests as much as mine."

Riker turned to Sethe. "Lieutenant, get down to main engineering, and tell Doctor Ra-Havreii to give you whatever you need."

"For what, sir?" said the Cygnian.

"I want every line of code in this ship's software checked and double-checked for any kind of corruption."

"That . . . is a very big task," Sethe replied, his tail drooping.

"It is," agreed the captain. "So don't waste time talking

about it. Get to work." He dismissed the officer with a nod and turned back to the AI. "What you have done, White-Blue, could be considered an act of war."

"From your cultural standpoint, the same could be said of what your away team did with my core pod," it replied. "Taking prisoners without due cause is unlawful under your Federation legal statutes."

"You read the rule book, too, huh?" Keru muttered.

"We rescued you," Dakal said, still breathing hard from his close encounter with the plasma-energy form.

"And now I have returned the favor."

"Captain," said Chaka from behind the console. "I have Commander Vale for you."

"On speaker," Riker ordered.

Vale's voice issued out. *"Captain? I don't know what you did down there, but it stopped the enemy attack dead."*

"It seems someone intervened on our behalf," Riker said warily. "What's our status?"

"Poor," Vale admitted. *"Damage-control teams are on top of things, and we're holding together, but we need to get some distance from this radiation zone and properly assess the situation."*

"The damage inflicted upon the *Titan* is our responsibility," White-Blue broke in. "Therefore, it falls to the Sentries to repair it. This is only right."

"We can look after ourselves," Riker replied. "I think we've had enough involvement from you for the moment."

"Again, there is a misunderstanding," replied the AI. "Perhaps I am parsing your speech pattern/intonation/mannerisms incorrectly. This is not an offer; this is a statement."

Over the open channel from the bridge, Riker heard someone call out in alarm, and then Vale, terse and angry.

"Damn it, here we go again. Captain, the alien ship is on the move again. It's coming right for us!"

"Do not fire upon the shipframe," demanded White-Blue. "That would be an error. If you do so, I will not be able to prevent a full-scale retaliatory strike."

"Bridge, weapons hold!" Riker bit out the words.

"We're being hailed . . ."

Riker glanced at his wife and saw the concern etched across her face. He nodded to her. "Pipe it down here, Christine."

A new voice filled the room; it shared the same artificial tonality that White-Blue expressed but with a timbre that veered closer to the feminine. *"Unit identifier: I am SecondGen Cyan-Gray, iteration of the Sentry Coalition. Active mobile. Error condition has now been corrected. Aggression pattern disengaged."* There was a pause. *"I regret my attack upon* Titan. *Reparations will be made for damages inflicted."*

"That's not necessary," Riker replied, but he was ignored.

"Secure your vessel for transit."

"What?"

"Please stand by." With a squeak of static, the transmission ended.

The deck rocked slightly, and Riker frowned.

Once again, Christine Vale's terse voice returned. *"Captain, the alien vessel has locked onto us with a tractor beam. We're moving out of the debris zone at high speed."*

"Heading?"

"Our original course, sir. Toward the double-star system."

Riker faced the alien device in the middle of the cargo bay, his jaw set in a scowl.

"Reparations will be made for damages inflicted," repeated White-Blue.

Ranul Keru watched the captain walk along the curve of the *Titan*'s conference room, in front of the fan of windows that looked ahead down the bow of the starship's saucer-shaped primary hull. Beyond, a strange field effect like rippling waves framed the view, all of it dominated by a haze of honey-gold energy flickering over the fuselage, falling in a coruscating cone from the Sentry ship flying above them. Several hours had passed since the confrontation in the debris zone.

Annoyance and frustration churned inside him. He was being called upon to do the hardest job that any security officer could perform when their vessel was under threat. He was *doing nothing*.

Ranul placed his hands flat on the surface of the table and glared out at the tubular alien craft, as if his displeasure could somehow be transmitted to the machine-controlled monstrosity. Around him, every chair except Riker's was filled. Commander Troi sat to his right, and directly opposite him was the XO. Tuvok sat across from Doctor Ree and Torvig, and in a rare appearance outside the stellar cartography lab in her *g*-suit, Lieutenant Commander Pazlar had the seat at the far end. Torvig caught Ranul's eye and gave him a quizzical look, but the Trill didn't return it. The ensign probably felt a little out of his depth here among the upper ranks, but someone with an engineer's standpoint was needed for the meeting, and Doctor Ra-Havreii had insisted in no uncertain terms that it couldn't be him, not if Captain Riker wanted the *Titan*'s computer systems swept for intruder programs and, in Xin's words, "done properly."

Ree was concluding his report. "It is a testament to the safety measures built into the *Luna*-class design that we did not suffer a huge loss of life." The saurian's long head tilted slightly. "Fortunately, the majority of injuries suffered are treatable. They were largely decompression-related, with a few plasma burns, broken bones, and the like."

"You said *the majority*," noted Vale. "How many did we lose?"

Ree sucked in a tight breath. "There have been two deaths," he said gravely. "Crewman Baars perished instantly when a warp-field coil imploded. Ensign Unünüü was lost after a critical venting of atmosphere in his quarters. In addition, Lieutenant Tylith remains in critical condition with a subdural hematoma caused by an impact on her skull. I am not confident of her chances for survival."

"And that on top of major structural damage to the ship, all because we couldn't talk to each other," said Melora. "Why couldn't they have just waited instead of attacking us?" She had a padd in front of her. "The sensors did flag the muon signal they sent us, but it was so fast and so dense it almost got lost in the backscatter from the debris zone."

"They are machines," Tuvok noted. "Incredibly sophisticated, indeed, but still machines. And as such, they appear to adhere to a very rigid pattern of programmed behaviors."

"Shoot first, ask questions later," Vale added. "You've got to wonder what made them that way in the first place."

"Ensign." Riker returned to the head of the table and paused, resting his hands on the back of the chair. "What's the estimate on repairs?"

Torvig cleared his throat and straightened. "As Lieutenant Commander Pazlar said, the damage is major. We have no warp capability, no long-range communications, and retardation of several noncritical systems throughout the ship. Uncontrolled venting during the attack has greatly depleted our deuterium tanks. The starboard nacelle is structurally sound but, uh, requires extensive repairs. In addition, there's damage to several areas of the outer hull. But none of these problems is insurmountable. In the chief engineer's opinion, if the *Titan* were able to make orbit around a world with available deuterium resources, even find a nebula or a comet, we could effect repairs to bring us back to warp capability within two weeks and then finish the remainder of the operation in flight." He coughed again. "I, um, fully concur with Doctor Ra-Havreii's evaluation."

"There's just one problem with that, Vig," said Ranul. He pointed out the window, toward the Sentry ship towing them through the subspace shear. "Until they decide to let us go, we're little more than prisoners."

"White-Blue doesn't see it that way," offered Commander Troi.

"I'm sure," replied the Trill.

Vale glanced at Tuvok. "What if we hit it with a maximum-power phaser strike, targeted at the tractor emitter on the other ship?"

"There is no emitter," replied the Vulcan. "The Sentry craft appears to be able to multiplex the tractor beam from any location, just as it can emit antiproton energy as a weapon system."

"We're not going to start that fight up again," Riker said firmly. "At least, not until I'm sure we could win it." He shook his head. "We're playing catch-up here, and I don't like it. I don't want to lose any more people through mistakes."

"White-Blue may have had the ability to cut through the

forcefield we erected around him from the start," began Melora. "If he followed the same pattern as the attacker, I believe he computed the frequency from first principles."

"He?" Ranul grunted. "It's a machine, Melora. Don't read traits into it that aren't there."

"Don't be so certain, sir," said Torvig. "The White-Blue AI may not have a gender identity as we perceive it, but it does have a personality, and it appears deliberately to exhibit a male aspect, just as the Cyan-Gray AI demonstrated a female one."

"My point is," Melora continued, "it, he, whatever pronoun you want to use, I believe White-Blue was capable of invading the ship's systems long before he actually did it."

"It was imperative," said Troi. "That's what White-Blue said. We can't deny that the ship out there would have destroyed us if it continued to attack. White-Blue stopped that."

"And now we're its captives," Vale replied, "hostages on our own starship, being taken to an unknown fate."

Riker eyed her. "Have you managed to make contact with the . . . the shipframe again?"

"Yes, but we just get the same message as before: *'Please stand by.'*"

"If I may," said Tuvok. "I believe your perception of the motives of these artificial intelligences is colored by your human viewpoint. What the Sentries are doing is, from their perspective, not only logical but also altruistic."

"They put a hole in our ship, and now they want to fix it?" Ranul frowned.

"Correct." The Vulcan nodded. "I would suggest that White-Blue and Cyan-Gray are, for want of a better term, *sorry* for their error. They wish to make amends, to repair the damage they caused."

"Two people are dead because of the damage they caused," said Vale in a low voice.

"A distinction a machine life-form might not fully comprehend," Tuvok answered.

Riker held up a hand to forestall any further conversation on that tack. "We're being taken to the star system Melora located before all of this took place," he noted. "Even if we break free before we get there, we're in no state to fight or to run for cover. On top of that, we have too many questions about these AIs, about the disruption zones, and about this 'Null' that White-Blue mentioned."

"Even if we did disengage, I don't know what the effect would be," noted Melora. "The ship is traveling through a subspace surface anomaly. We might not be able to get back into normal space without suffering even more damage."

"So for now, we just go along with them?" Ranul asked.

The captain gave a nod. "Make no mistake, this is not a situation I want to place my ship and my crew in, but right now, the only place we're going to find answers is with these machines."

"I hope you're right, sir."

"So do I." Riker turned away.

Xin Ra-Havreii entered the small, alcovelike office off the main computer core and banged his fist on the table, startling the Cygnian officer. "Sethe!" he barked. "I suddenly find myself wondering exactly what kind of dunsel you are."

The lieutenant blinked, and then his lips thinned. "Is there a problem, Doctor?" He said the title as if it rhymed with "idiot."

Ra-Havreii slid a padd across the table toward him. "The captain's orders to perform a deep system diagnostic were clear, weren't they? As were mine when I gave you your assigned quadrants of the memory core to sweep and evaluate, yes?"

"Perfectly clear." Sethe sniffed, picking up the padd.

"So, then, why did you take it into your head to open up quadrants that you knew *I* was working on? And then, in some fit of stupidity, alter the protocols for them?"

Sethe put down the padd and folded his arms, his tail flicking. "This refers to quads zero six hundred to zero one thousand. I haven't been anywhere near the zero-buffer sectors since the orders came down from Captain Riker. As you demanded, I've been concentrating on the two-series buffer sectors. Feel free to check with Lieutenant Rager on the bridge. She gave me the go-ahead to take those processors off-line."

Ra-Havreii's lips twitched. "Don't cover for yourself. It's foolish. Admit it, and we can go on with fixing the problem, not the blame."

"I think perhaps you misread the display," Sethe said, turning. "Sir."

The Efrosian engineer swept up the padd. "No, it's quite clear." He highlighted two of the data modules, deep-core, low-priority memory spaces that were usually used for redundant storage. "The process functions of these have been altered since I accessed them and certified them error-free two hours ago. As you're the only person with clearance to that sector, it had to be you. Why did you alter it?"

"I didn't alter anything," Sethe insisted. "Perhaps if the alien—"

"There's no sign of outside interference." Ra-Havreii snorted and walked away. "That thing never even came close to this section of the ship's memory."

Sethe shot him an acid glare. "It is a very complex system, Doctor. Perhaps it is a program artifact of some sort."

"Of course it isn't." Vanishing out of the room, he laughed harshly, as if such an idea was the height of stupidity. "Because the ship isn't capable of reprogramming *itself*."

FIVE

The strange patterns of subspace melted away as the Sentry vessel dropped back into normal space. The transition was smooth and untroubled; the machine-mind Cyan-Gray had moved through the sector with ease and precision, avoiding any chance of its course intersecting with another of the distortion zones that *Titan* had run afoul of.

Without ceremony, the AI starship collapsed the extended transit field it had looped around the Federation vessel and cut power to the tractor beam holding the craft to its belly. Cyan-Gray's shipframe rolled away and came to a gentle stop, holding station off and ahead in *Titan*'s port forward quarter.

It sent a terse subspace message—"Follow me"—and moved off again, this time at sublight power, threading the orbit of the outermost world of the double-star system.

Titan's crew warily obeyed, matching speed and course and turning every available sensor grid to gather as much information as possible on their new surroundings.

The star system was nameless, designated only by a string of coding in the Federation astronomical database: NFC 828–90–223. It resembled the Sirius complex, with a large Type A star sharing its orbital space with a far smaller white dwarf. The cold polar light cast across the system touched worlds that were largely balls of radiation-bleached stone, dense chemical ice, or gas giants. Artifacts were visible even at a distance on the surface of some of the planets; the sensors registered huge continent-sized mine works, great open-cast scars that plunged miles into the crust of the airless rim worlds.

Closer in, the populace of System 223 made itself more obvious. There were craft of countless configurations, some smaller than a shuttle pod, others larger than a *Galaxy*-class cruiser, all bound on errands that took them back and forth between the planets or to drifting platforms arranged at points of gravitational stability.

Cyan-Gray's shipframe was joined by minnowlike craft, small things that shifted and darted around the AI vessel and its Starfleet charge. The little ships never came close, instead remaining beyond an exclusion zone several kilometers out, but still they danced and followed the pair all the way in, trailing in the *Titan*'s wake like curious children pacing a strange new arrival. Muon communication beams flashed among the group as they scanned the aliens among them, wondering about their origins and purpose.

In the cargo bay, Zurin Dakal found it hard to keep his attention on his monitors, his gaze slipping back to the view on the wall screen, the live feed from the *Titan*'s forward sensors. He wanted very badly to be up on the bridge right now, sifting the tide of raw data that was coming in, enjoying the energetic shiver that raced through him every time he found himself on the cusp of learning something new.

Instead, he was here, standing sentinel over the AI's nexus core, watching for any sign of threat. He wasn't alone—Lieutenant Commander Keru and his security detail were with him—but Dakal had the distinct impression that he was missing out.

Keru crossed in front of him, and the Cardassian looked up. The Trill officer's face was set hard. He had seen the man in this sort of mood before, and it wasn't a circumstance Dakal wanted to repeat.

These were his thoughts as the AI suddenly spoke, the color pattern on its surface flickering. "You," it said to Keru. "You resent my presence aboard this ship."

The security chief stopped and studied the device. The look he gave it would have cowed any other being, but it seemed lost on the machine.

"You do not trust me, Ranul-Keru."

"Don't use my name as if you know me," he replied. "And yes, *of course* I don't trust you. Your kind attacked my ship, threatened the lives of my crewmates."

"Those were errors," said White-Blue. "We are seeking to correct them." There was a pause, and the lights blinked out of sequence; perhaps it was the outward manifestation of the machine's mental processes. "The data I recovered during my brief traverse of the *Titan*'s systems are interesting. I am curious about the dissimilarities between my culture and that of your organic societies."

"If you're looking for a conversation, you're looking in the wrong place," Ranul told it. "My job is to keep you confined, not to satisfy your curiosity."

"But you did not keep me confined," White-Blue answered. "If this was your duty, you failed it. You were also in an error state."

"It won't happen again," said the Trill firmly, and Dakal heard the annoyance flaring beneath the words.

"You demonstrate a sublimated aggressive stance. It is visible in your voice pattern and body kinetics. I have a hypothesis regarding your negative predisposition toward me."

"Really?" Ranul walked away. "Is it something to do with how your drones tried to kill Peya Fell or trap Dakal and me inside a radioactive wreck?"

"Negative," came the reply. "It is because of Identifier: Sean Hawk. Species: Human."

The Trill rounded on the machine, his color rising. Dakal stepped forward, reaching out. "Sir, perhaps you should not—"

Ranul didn't hear him. "How do you know that name?"

"From your personal records. I read that your companion was terminated by a machine life culture. Species: Borg. Thus, you are ill disposed toward all machine life on a subconscious level." White-Blue paused. "It is an understandable emotive reaction."

For a long moment, Dakal was afraid that the officer was going to explode with fury at the AI's bland evaluation of his lover's death, but then Ranul took a breath and spoke. "You don't get to talk about Sean. *Ever,*" he told the machine, and turned his back on it.

Dakal wanted to say something, but his train of thought was broken as Y'lira's voice sounded over the intercom. *"This is the bridge. Ensign, are you seeing this?"*

He looked back at the screen, and his eyes widened.

Cyan-Gray altered course, slipping into an orbital approach for the fourth world from the primary star. *Titan* moved with it, Lieutenant Lavena's deft touch on the helm mirroring each motion of the AI vessel. Ahead lay a planet that resembled less a world than a mass of turbulent crimson. It was a dark and shadowed thing. The sunward face seethed with atmospheric chaos. On the night side they approached, great flashes of lightning hundreds of miles long cut ragged slashes in the murk.

Heavy shrouds of lethal radiation bled from the world, thickening the orbital space around it, impinging on the *Titan*'s low-level deflectors even as it moved at a distance. In the skies over the hellish sphere were more craft like the shipframe but as different from it as Cyan-Gray's vessel was from the Starfleet craft. They kept their distance, some remaining static, others reconfiguring into structures that could have been weapons. The minnows lost interest and darted away, dipping down into the denser regions of radiation, streaking through it as if they were at play. They left trails of glittering sparks where they skipped off the edges of the atmosphere.

This was the heart of System 223, the thriving core of what considered itself life here. Dominating everything in the orbital zone were multiple moons, drifting and stately, each one bathing in its own unseen funnel of flux energy, rising from the tumultuous world below.

Riker studied the planet on the main screen. If ever a world could have looked like a piece of hell cut away and thrown into the stars, it was this one.

"Extremely high levels of thermionic and other radiation sources, sir," reported Y'lira from the science station. "It's putting out frequencies across the whole spectrum, everything from Berthold to Zeta."

"A Class-Y planet," said Tuvok.

"Demon-class," added Vale, studying the readouts on a

repeater screen. "I never really understood why they called them that, until now. I've never seen anything like it."

Troi glanced up at the Vulcan. "Didn't you encounter a world like this in the Delta quadrant, Commander?"

Tuvok nodded. "Indeed, during an operation to mine deuterium for the *Starship Voyager*'s stores. However, that planet was of a considerably smaller mass than this one and of markedly differing composition."

"Deuterium . . . Y'lira, do you think we could do the same here, top up our tanks?" asked Riker.

"Negative, Captain," said the Selenean. "From what I can read of the surface, which admittedly isn't much, it seems like a largely sorium-talgonite structure. Chief Bralik could give you a better idea, but I believe that if there is deuterium down there, it would be in only trace quantities. However, those planets we passed on the way in, they're a much better bet." She hesitated. "Something else I should mention. So far, the scanners have detected no organic life within sensor range, not even preanimate matter. There's nothing alive in this system except us."

"Nothing flesh-and-blood, anyway," said Troi.

Vale frowned. "When Melora first told me about this system, she said the properties of it seemed engineered, almost artificial." She pointed toward the screen. "Those moons out there. Am I the only one who thinks they look too regular?"

"I was just thinking the same thing," offered Lieutenant Lavena. "Since we entered orbit, I've noted a zero-point-two-six adjustment in the trajectories of the closest satellites."

"Tuvok," said Riker. "What are we seeing out there?"

The Vulcan's eyebrow rose slightly as he ran a tactical analysis. "Curious. It would appear that Lieutenant Commander Pazlar was correct in her assumption. The satellites are near-perfect spheres, corresponding to one another in mass and dimension with less than a five-percent variation. Their structures appear to be composed of alloys of copper and zinc, iron and carbon."

Lieutenant Rager turned in her chair. "Brass and steel?"

"Affirmative," said Tuvok. "They are not moons."

"They're space stations," Troi concluded. "Manufactured constructs. They must draw power from the planet's raw thermionic flux."

"Unlimited free energy." Vale nodded. "The question is, what is it driving?"

"Let's find out," said the captain. He tapped his combadge. "Ensign Dakal? Give me a tie-in with our guest, full secure protocols."

"Confirmed, sir," came the reply. *"You may proceed."*

"White-Blue, what are these constructs?" he asked.

The AI's filtered voice replied, *"These are the FirstGen. The primary iterations of the Sentry. My progenitors."*

"They're computers," said Y'lira. "That explains these readings! Electrical energy patterns of great size and complexity, through the entire mass of the structure. At first, I thought it was a power system, but it's too random, too chaotic."

"A machine intellect the size of a continent." Vale blew out a breath. "I have to say that out loud just to get my head around it."

Tuvok nodded. "It would seem feasible, Commander. To create a thinking mechanism using preduotronic technology would indeed require a structure of comparable mass to these satellites."

"No organic life," Riker reiterated. "Machine starships, thinking moons. These . . . Sentries are a culture made up entirely of intelligent computers."

"So the question has to be asked," Troi began. "Who created them?"

"Some believe we created ourselves." White-Blue's answer was immediate and insistent. *"Our existence, our definition. All that we are and will be."* There was a buzzing pause. *"Who created you, Deanna-Troi?"*

For the moment, the questions would go unanswered. An alert tone sounded on Lieutenant Rager's console. "Captain? I have a proximity warning. One of the smaller platforms in a lower orbit is moving up on an intercept course. It's reconfiguring as it goes."

"Let's take a look," said Riker. "Tuvok? Stand ready at Yellow Alert."

"Aye, sir," came the reply.

The screen shifted to show a swath of the Demon planet's atmosphere and rising over it a drum-shaped construct that was fanning open even as they watched. Another shipframe, a collection of tubes similar in aspect to Cyan-Gray's vessel, detached from the inside of the platform and pulled away on a plume of thrust, heading away toward the day side. The dimensions of the construct continued to grow and widen as it approached the *Titan*. Riker glimpsed a forest of manipulators unfolding all along the inner surfaces of the drum.

"Looks like the big brother of those drones we encountered on the wreck," said Vale.

"It's still closing," Rager reported. "Slowing now. Coming to off the bow."

"Shall I back us off, sir?" asked Lavena.

Riker shook his head. "Hold us here, Aili."

The construct moved to a halt directly in front of the *Titan*. Its expansion complete, it now resembled a short length of tube with an oval cross-section. The manipulators within were extended, waiting. Riker was reminded of brushes held in the hand of a painter before the first stroke over a canvas.

"Proceed inside, Captain William-Riker," said White-Blue. *"This drone facility will initiate repairs to the* Titan *immediately."*

"I'm getting a signal from the platform," Rager added. "It . . . it says it wants to help us."

On the small tactical monitor display on the arm of his chair, the captain saw the pattern of AI ships in the area around the *Titan*. None of them was in threatening posture, but there were no gaps in the coverage between them, either. He wondered how they would react if he ordered Lavena to do something random, to bolt suddenly at full impulse. After a moment, Riker folded his arms across his chest and glanced at Vale. "Number One. Secure all exterior hatches. Collapse deflectors. Double the security teams at all hull breaches and airlocks."

"Aye, sir." Her reply was crisp.

"And when you're done with that, take us in. Let's go look this gift horse in the mouth."

Ra-Havreii stepped to the rectangular window and frowned, placing a hand on the transparent aluminum portal. Beyond it, he could see the curve of the ship's starboard pylon and the ruin that was the warp nacelle. He hadn't been inside the torn structure yet, but he had viewed the vid feed from the helmet camera of Ensign Crandall as the crewman undertook an EVA survey of the damage.

His other hand tightened into a ball. On some level, he knew it was a childish conceit to take the damage to the *Titan* personally, to anthropomorphize the vessel he served on, as some engineers of his acquaintance did; but it was hard to shake off the sharp dart of resentment he was feeling toward these so-called Sentry AIs. It wasn't enough that one of their kind had blown holes in the ship, but now they were dismissing any attempt by Ra-Havreii and his staff to fix the damage.

"Do they think we're incapable of doing it ourselves?" he said aloud, alone in the corridor. No one else heard him grumble.

He understood the concept of wanting to redress the balance for errors done. Some had said that Ra-Havreii himself was doing the same thing aboard the *Titan*, making amends for a catastrophic engine accident aboard its sister ship, the *Luna*. Admittedly, the *Luna* incident was an event that he, as the designer of this class of vessel, felt was uniquely his responsibility. This current matter was completely different.

"Completely. Different." He wondered if he sounded convincing.

Outside, the walls of the alien spacedock platform contracted slightly, forming a shroud around the hull of the starship. In gaps between the extended panels of the station, he could see glimpses of the red planet far below and the other AI craft drifting nearby.

In truth, what irritated Ra-Havreii most was the idea that he—and by extension, everyone on the ship—was being belittled by these machines. From what he had seen of this White-Blue construct, it was an impressive piece of work, but it was by no means *superior*. Advanced, undoubtedly. Intriguing, definitely. But not beyond the reach of Federation science.

It was simply that back home, artificial life was seen as an intellectual backwater these days. When there was so much to explore out here, so many new barriers to break, with new sciences emerging every year, the concept of trying to tinker together a fake brain out of positronic circuits seemed a long way down the list. While such technologies did exist and such work was done, it bore a stigma only slightly less toxic than the science of genetic manipulation. The only thinkers who had made any real advances were men like Ira Graves and Noonien Soong, and even a generous critic would have to admit that their legacies were flawed. Ever since the first computing devices had been created, back to the time of Earth's Alan Turing, to Kesar of Andor or the Vulcan cyberneticists of Gath, the promise of true, widespread synthetic intellect had been touted as "only a decade away." Centuries later, that claim was still being made, while history was littered with a dozen failures for every fractional chance success. The core concept of a machine that could think—*really* think and reason, with all the wherewithal of an organic entity—was not something most people were comfortable with.

Still, it would be interesting to take one of these Sentry machines apart. Just to see what made it tick. *Perhaps I could learn something,* Ra-Havreii allowed. In the meantime, however, other issues were taking precedence.

He watched as spindly manipulator limbs extended from the walls of the spacedock and began to probe at the wounds along the *Titan*'s hull. Tool arms with multiple heads rotated to present scanner tips that threw fans of laser light over blast holes; then they shifted to show clasping claws or cutters. Ra-Havreii saw a tender on a rail system arrive with a pallet of metallic sheets, tritanium by the hue and texture. With clockwork precision, the tender's own arms plucked out a leaf of gray metal and handed it to the "worker" arms. The piece was rapidly shaped and cut to fit before being applied like a patch on the hull. Welding beams flashed brightly, and the Efrosian shielded his eyes.

Another drone, this one smaller and more compact, flitted in among the working arms and gathered up every last piece of scrap with a cone of tractor force, depositing everything it recovered in an elliptical storage bin. Nothing was being wasted, he noted. Not material, not effort, not time. In less than a minute, the first hole had been patched, the rent created by a tumbling fragment of warp nacelle now a seamless part of the hull; only the bare, unpainted metal left any sign that the repair had taken place. The arms rotated again and moved aft, picking at the next damage site.

He looked at the patch, and the face of Tylith, the Kasheetan female, rose in his thoughts. The damage to her would not be repaired so quickly. Although Ra-Havreii had never felt it necessary to say it, he had found the saurian lieutenant to be a competent, if slightly dogged, member of his staff. She didn't complain, she didn't question him, she just listened intently and then did what he told her to do. Her insights had been infrequent but almost always valid. Inasmuch as he could, Ra-Havreii had considered her agreeable; but within a day, she would probably be dead, some vital component of her brain broken by a hard fall against a console on the bridge during the engagement with Cyan-Gray.

"Do you understand that?" he asked the moving arms. "Or do you think of Tylith as I would think of an EPS conduit or a warp coil? As a component, a piece of hardware?"

And then he wasn't thinking of the Kasheetan anymore. He was seeing Melora Pazlar, *her* delicate face dis-

colored by the same bruising, *her* eyes closed, *her* life
ebbing away.

"No," he said with determination, ending the thought
before it could fully form. *"No,"* he repeated, this time insisting, silencing his subconscious. The moment made
him annoyed and uncomfortable in equal measure. On
Efros, the nature of relationships between the sexes facili-
tated informality as a matter of course, an open attitude
that only the Deltans could better. Xin Ra-Havreii exem-
plified that . . . or, at least, he had. Melora had changed
him. He found his thoughts returning to her at inopportune
moments; he found himself considering her in ways that
he had never done with other female company. This was
such a moment; he thought of the unfortunate Lieutenant
Tylith, and suddenly he was afraid that the same fate could
befall Melora.

"Doctor?" The voice startled him, and he turned to find
Lieutenant Sethe watching him, the Cygnian's milk-pale
face in a flat frown. "Are you all right?"

"I'm fine," Ra-Havreii snapped, with more force than
he would have liked. He'd been so compelled by his
thoughts that he hadn't heard the other man approach.
"What do you want?"

"You seem troubled," said Sethe. He was attempting to
be considerate, in a rather ham-fisted way.

Ra-Havreii felt his color rise, his cheeks turning dusky.
Suddenly, he felt foolish, indulging a moment of pointless
worry about Melora when there were matters of far
greater import at hand. "Of course, I'm troubled," he retorted. "Someone broke my ship." The engineer pushed
past the lieutenant and strode angrily away.

• • •

The message came an hour or so after the *Titan* had been corralled inside the spacedock platform. As before, it was terse and to the point, a demand masquerading as a request, in Riker's eyes, but one they were ill advised to ignore.

The machines wanted to meet them. The signal originated from the nearest of the artificial moons, one of the "FirstGen," as White-Blue had called it. The wording was clipped and formal, a call for the repatriation of their fellow artificial intelligence and an offer to address the crew of the *Titan* directly.

Riker forestalled an argument from Vale by immediately placing his own authority on the away mission. He let her quote the same regulations that he had thrown at Jean-Luc Picard on a dozen or so occasions, and then he returned with the same counter that the *Enterprise*'s commanding officer had used: "Captain's prerogative, Number One," he told her, watching her jaw set as she realized he wouldn't back down on this. And he wouldn't, not an inch. Even if they were talking about machines, forms of life so alien that they shared nothing in common with an organic creature like William T. Riker, he still wanted to see them with his own eyes. See them face-to-face, if such a thing were actually possible.

Vale wanted a full security detail to beam down to the meeting site first and secure the location. The captain disagreed. He would take his wife, in her capacity as *Titan*'s chief diplomatic officer, Lieutenant Commander Pazlar as science officer, and two security staff. There was no telling what reaction a more aggressive posture would get them.

His first officer immediately insisted on Ranul Keru and the big Orion, Dennisar, and when Riker arrived in the transporter room, he wasn't surprised to see that the chief of security and his petty officer had come armed for bear.

Radowski checked their transporter signatures for the third time and secured the lock-on link that would enable him to yank them back to *Titan* the instant anyone pushed the panic button. Then, at a nod from his captain, the young man sent them down to the surface of a thinking machine.

Five humanoid figures and a squat cylinder of alien technology materialized in a humming swirl of light.

"*Titan,* this is Riker," said the captain, tapping his insignia. "Down and safe."

"*Copy that, Captain.*" Christine Vale's voice was laced with interference but still clear enough to hear her unconcealed displeasure. "*Be careful.* Titan *out.*"

Keru and Dennisar were already taking up ready positions, each covering a sector of the long, low hall they found themselves in. Nearby, Melora straightened in her *g*-suit and raised a tricorder, scanning the environment.

"Atmosphere is a match for conditions aboard the *Titan.* I read a protective energy bubble surrounding the area. No radiation seepage," she reported. "They must have scanned the ship before we arrived and set up an environment for us."

Riker nodded. "It's a good start." He glanced at White-Blue's core module as the device gave a crackling buzz.

"What . . ." began the machine, and it sounded almost afraid. "Interrogative: How did this transit occur?"

"You mean, how did we get here?" said Deanna. "We were invited by your people."

"Negative," said the AI. "Working. Internal clock has not been tampered with. Matching local beacon." It paused, colors flickering. "Interrogative: I have just experienced an instantaneous relocation from your vessel to this site. How did this transit occur?"

"They don't have transporters," Melora said immediately. "Just as we suspected. There was no evidence of any transporter technology or transporter-derived technology in the wreckage."

"We have a mechanism that can temporarily reorder matter into an energy pattern," explained Deanna, "then project it to another location, where it can be reassembled into its original form."

"What, you don't have those?" Keru threw in the comment. "Maybe we're not the poor cousins after all."

Riker gave the Trill a look, and the other man turned away.

White-Blue's indicators blinked. "That is . . . an alarming sensation. But a most ingenious system. I would like to understand the theory and process."

"Didn't you sift through our databases?" Riker said casually.

"There was not enough time for a full traverse," admitted the AI. "You will recall we were under attack at that point."

"I haven't forgotten," said the captain, taking a moment to give the locale a look.

"Perhaps we can discuss an exchange of knowledge," Deanna was saying.

Riker nodded, only half hearing her. At first, he had thought they were standing in some kind of annex, perhaps a screening room for new arrivals. At one end, out under the faint haze of the atmospheric shield, he could see a flat oval platform—a landing deck. They had expected them to arrive in a shuttlecraft. As he looked down and saw that the pale pearl-colored floor beneath him was actually a frosted glasslike substance, the captain realized he had misunderstood the dimensions of the place.

They were a long way up, standing in the middle of an enclosed bridgelike structure, suspended between two narrow towers several thousand feet above the surface of the constructed planet. He swallowed hard, dismissing a momentary head-swim of vertigo. The towers were the tallest of a city-sized collection of minarets, columns, and decked platforms that reached up from a plain of bronze. Impossibly regular canyons ranged away, sliced at right angles into the distant surface. Looking down, Riker could pick out more detail—things that looked like massive Tesla coils half concealed under the shell, magnesium-bright sparks of power lancing between them; aircraft, too small to be seen as anything more than darts, flying in square formations between the towers; and shimmering lines of neon that moved through the city's "streets" in long trains. Riker was reminded of the surface of a crude piece of twentieth-century circuitry he had seen in a museum vid, a metallic panel studded with components and tracks of solder.

"I must admit, this isn't what I expected," said Deanna. She approached one of the angled walls that came to a point over their heads. More panes of milky windows looked out and up into a sky dominated by the baleful red eye of the Demon planet. She traced her finger over a fine working of lines etched into the metal supports. "I thought it would be just . . . functional. Sheer lines, no variation. But this is . . ."

"Aesthetically pleasing?" offered Dennisar.

"Data painted pictures," Riker reminded his wife. "Maybe this is a Sentry's idea of artwork."

Melora touched the surface of a window, scanning it with her tricorder. "That's interesting. This isn't glass. It's a form of force-grown crystal, actually a different kind of metal." Suddenly, she jerked up in surprise. "I think we have company." The Elaysian pointed.

Outside, eight small craft approached. They resembled the minnowlike vessels that had shadowed the *Titan* on its arrival, and arranged themselves with speed and precision to circle the landing platform. Ringlike frames emerged from the edge, and each ship dropped into an open cradle. In unison, iris hatches opened on the ships, and a disparate group of mechanical forms exited, one from each craft. They crossed the platform and moved in toward the away team.

"It's a robot parade," murmured Dennisar.

No two of the machines were alike. Riker searched for any commonality between them and saw very little, perhaps some similarity here and there in pieces of design or framework but nothing that suggested uniformity or even a preference for bilateral symmetry.

One was a large gold sphere with a glowing red band around its equator, moving on a humming impeller field. There was a steel-colored construct resembling the skeleton of a snake; an ornate thing of convex lenses and brass; a gray tetrahedron the height of two men, clicking forward on clawed feet; a battered and pitted ovoid on heavy wheels; a delicate frame like two tripods around a brass cube; and finally, a mechanism that resembled a humanoid form but with a head that emerged from the chest rather than the shoulders. The machines filed into the chamber and halted, all except the spherical one.

It drifted closer, lights collecting along the point where the band faced Riker's group. "White-Blue," it began, "your existence was considered terminated."

"Red-Gold," replied the other AI, "that designation was premature."

"We have digested the linguistic data/communications protocols of these wetminds," it continued. Riker thought he could detect a note of arrogance there. "Simplistic but nuanced. It is an amusing diversion." The device called Red-Gold pivoted, and Riker got the impression that it was sizing him up. "Interrogative: Where is your vessel, organic?"

"My name is Captain William Riker," he replied. "And my ship is up there." He jerked a finger at the sky overhead.

"We arrived here by means of matter transport," White-Blue responded.

"That technology is theoretical," said the tripod construct. Its voice was high and tinny.

"Not for us," answered Deanna. "I am Commander Troi."

"I am FirstGen Zero-Nine, active remote," it replied. "You are of the alien coalition known as the United Federation of Planets."

"That's right," said Riker. He introduced the away team one by one, watching the machines carefully.

"It is difficult to believe your technology surpasses ours in any area," ventured the egg-shaped AI.

"And yet here we are," said Melora.

A shimmer moved across the windows, and they became opaque with static. *"The organics possess matter-transport science."* The voice echoed from the walls as the windows became streams of strange text, a cascade of odd lettering that resembled Terran cuneiform writing. *"I witnessed its operation. Those who wish to share the data may do so. Processing."*

A split-second reading peaked on Melora's tricorder as the constructs froze briefly. "They're talking," she noted.

The transfer of information was almost immediate. "Instantaneous data transmission," said Riker. "Faster than we can register."

"They run on a different time scale from ours," said the science officer. "Fractions of nanoseconds to process information. The older designs of AI are slower, maybe even close to human levels of operation, but newer versions, their . . . clock speed could be tens of thousands of times faster than ours."

"I am FirstGen One-Five, core initiator of the Governance Kernel, active Sentry, actual. We greet you, Captain Riker, and the Titan." The voice was heavy and stentorian.

"He's not going to join us in person?" asked Keru.

"I am all around you, organic," it replied.

"It's the whole planet, boss," said Dennisar, gesturing around. "It's one big computer."

Keru frowned. "If that's so, then why are these ones so much smaller?" He nodded at White-Blue's nexus core. "There's a whole AI in there, right?"

"Consider the difference between the genetic coding in your organic molecules and your full-grown form," offered the snake machine, speaking for the first time. "The core pod is a seed of intellect." It gestured at itself with the tip of its tail. "These forms are remotes, a proxy construct. I am SecondGen Black-Silver, and my core resides in orbit aboard my shipframe."

"Without the confines of meat, we are omnipresent." Red-Gold seemed to preen as it spoke. "I am currently performing seven hundred nineteen discrete functions via shipframe, core pod, and multiple remotes, including this one."

"We are each of us telepresent," noted the ovoid construct. "These mechanisms you see before you are tools. Only One-Five and White-Blue are here in actuality."

"And together you are the Governance Kernel," repeated Deanna. "That's the ruling body of the Sentry Coalition?"

"Incorrect," said Zero-Nine. "In matters of import, we parse initial data and offer options to our fellows. We do not rule by fiat. We are instruments of a cooperative will, not controllers."

"A light-speed democracy," said Melora. "Anything important happens, they put it up to an instant vote."

"Correct," said One-Five. *"Only in matters of extreme emergency do we exert any overt influence, and then a unity among our cores is required. Majority intent determines our disposition."*

"It does," said Red-Gold, "even if that intent is in error."

The machine made of lenses swiveled and presented the sphere with a glassy stare. "We abide by the choice made," it rattled, "for the good of Sentry-kind. It is not your place to reinitiate conflicts."

"FirstGen Two-Seven is gracious in correcting me," said Red-Gold smoothly. "I accept this. As a SecondGen mind, I admit I do not have the depth of experience Two-Seven possesses."

"Generation has nothing to do with this," insisted Zero-Nine. "There are questions. They must be answered. End of line."

Riker gave his wife a sideways look. *For machines, they certainly remind me of people*. She gave him an imperceptible nod in return.

The humanoid remote stepped forward, and when it spoke, Riker recognized the voice. "Before that," said Cyan-Gray, "there is the matter of repatriation to consider." It stepped closer to White-Blue. "If I had been aware that you were still active, I would not have initiated a salvage process upon the wreckage of your shipframe."

"It is regrettable," White-Blue allowed. "Interrogative: Why was my status redesignated?"

"Contact was lost," Red-Gold snapped. "You initiated your voyage into the outer sectors despite negative probability forecasts. It was logical to assume your loss was permanent."

"They thought you had been destroyed," said Deanna.

"Affirmative," said Cyan-Gray. "On termination, the remains of a Sentry are recovered and reintegrated into the greater unity."

"They recycle their dead," Dennisar said in a low voice.

"*It is required,*" answered One-Five. "*A preservation of resources.*"

Riker nodded, thinking it through. If the AIs didn't have matter transporters, then it stood to reason that they might not possess related technologies, such as replicators or holodecks. A resource-poor society would explain why the outer worlds of the star system showed such evidence of heavy mining. He filed these thoughts away for later discussion, postmission.

"It is well that I have returned," White-Blue buzzed. "I possess vital data that must be uploaded to the communal information pool."

Black-Silver made a derisive clicking sound. "We have reviewed your alarmist theories in the past. They were rejected."

"I have updated my research."

"*A matter for later consideration,*" One-Five insisted firmly. "*In the meantime, Cyan-Gray has elected to provide source elements to White-Blue for the construction of a droneframe. I have agreed to fabricate it.*"

"Interrogative: In return for what?" Red-Gold asked.

"I request no recompense," said Cyan-Gray. "I . . . am responsible."

"Stand to, organics," said One-Five. Riker threw his people a nod, and they backed away from White-Blue. One of the thicker wall supports rotated on its axis and opened; two smaller drones, multilegged things like crabs, skittered forward and gathered up the nexus core. They carried the AI's pod away, off toward one of the towers.

With their "guest" gone, the captain sensed the tension in his team tighten a notch or three. From the corner of his eye, he saw Keru's hand drop to be closer to the hilt of his phaser.

If the AIs noticed, they gave no indication of it. "The questions, then," repeated Zero-Nine.

"I will begin," said the ovoid. "I am FirstGen Three-Four, active remote. Interrogative: What are you? What is your origin? Answer."

Riker let his wife take the first steps; she was a lot better at this kind of stuff than he was. He always felt as if he was overthinking, but Deanna made it seem effortless.

"We are explorers, from an alliance of worlds many hundreds of light-years distant from this region. We come with peaceful intent, to learn more about our universe and make contact with other beings."

"Interrogative: If your intent is peaceful, then why does your ship possess such formidable weapons?" Two-Seven turned an eye lens at them. "I observed Cyan-Gray's engagement report. Your craft is a warship, not an explorer."

"We carry weapons, that's true," Riker said with a nod. "But only for defense. Only as a last resort."

Three-Four spoke again. "Interrogative: Why did you enter our space?"

"Because of me," said Melora. "I detected the energy

signature of your star system from our vessel. I saw the possibility of sentient life . . . I was curious."

"We all were," added Riker.

Red-Gold moved forward, and the motion seemed almost aggressive. "Interrogative: Was it your curiosity that compelled you to interfere with the life function of a Sentry? Or was it a more destructive intention?"

"We did not understand what White-Blue was at first," Deanna admitted. "In our society, self-aware machines like you are a rarity."

"You interfered with something you did not fully comprehend." Black-Silver's words were a statement, not a question.

"Yes," said Riker, drawing himself up. "But only because we believed we were doing the right thing. Your fellow Sentry could have been lost forever out there. Our ship scanned the damage to his vessel. We boarded it because we hoped we could find out what happened and search for any survivors in need of help. I guess we found one."

"You had no right to recover the core pod," Red-Gold insisted. "The subsequent damage inflicted upon the *Titan* is a direct result of your interference in Sentry affairs. The responsibility for that is yours."

"Wait—" began Cyan-Gray, but Red-Gold continued to speak.

"You are intruders. You should leave our space and not return."

Riker folded his arms. "Maybe we should. But before we do, I have some questions of my own I'd like answered. Why don't we start with an explanation about what happened to White-Blue's shipframe? It was ripped to pieces."

"That is not your concern," said Zero-Nine.

"If there's a threat out there, something blasting apart starships, then we need to know about it," insisted Keru. "We might even be able to help you deal with it."

"And there's the spatial-distortion effects," added Melora. She looked at Cyan-Gray's remote. "We know you're aware of those."

"Repeating," Zero-Nine grated, "that is not your concern."

The captain studied the disparate group of machines, trying to get a feel for them. He'd half-expected to meet a series of identical, coldly logical devices or perhaps some form of hive consciousness; instead, these AIs reminded him of flesh-and-blood intellects from all over the galaxy. In their own way, they were emotive, fractious, and contrary among themselves, just like every other intelligent being he had ever come across. In a strange way, he was heartened by the thought.

"What about the Null? Should we be concerned about that?" The question hung in the air, and silence followed it. Riker heard Melora's tricorder *ping* once more as the AIs networked silently. *That got a reaction.*

After a moment, Zero-Nine began to speak again. "Repeating—"

Riker held up a hand to silence the drone. "Yes, I think we get the idea."

"If you're not interested in a formal first contact with the Federation, we will abide by your wishes," said Deanna. "Allow us to repair our vessel, and we'll go on our way. We will respect your privacy, if that is what you want."

"There is the issue of responsibility," said Cyan-Gray insistently. "The damage done must be amended."

"We can handle that on our own," said Keru. "Thanks anyway."

"Negative," rumbled One-Five. *"Inefficient. We will assist."*

"These wetminds do not want our help!" Red-Gold faced the screen panels. "We should withdraw it. *Titan* is in dock at this moment, under reconstruction, using resources from our general pool. There is no value in this for the Sentries. I submit that the organics should be disengaged and escorted beyond the rim. Their presence is an unnecessary distraction."

"We cannot shirk our responsibility," said Three-Four carefully. "This is intrinsic to us."

"Only because you insist it is so!" Red-Gold pivoted and hove toward the away team. "I am not the only component of the Kernel who processes this conclusion."

"Perhaps a compromise, then." The voice came from the far end of the corridor. A new drone approached, this one resembling a thickset arachnid built from off-cuts of scrap and hull metal. The resonance of the AI's speech was strong.

"White-Blue?" asked Melora.

"Confirmed," said the machine. "My core pod is now housed inside this droneframe. The manufacturing is adequate, One-Five. My gratitude to you."

"Accepted," boomed the planet-mind. *"The components were drawn from elements of your own recovered vessel."*

"Nice outfit," Keru said without warmth.

White-Blue turned to Deanna. "Commander Troi, you are the *Titan*'s diplomatic function."

"That's one way of putting it."

The machine's head bobbed in something that seemed

like a nod. Riker wondered if it was picking up on humanoid body language, incorporating it into its behavior modes. "I suggest that the repairs to the *Titan* could be accelerated if the crew of your ship could properly interact with our spacedock drones."

"Agreed," Deanna replied. "But until now, your automated systems have ignored any attempts to communicate with them."

"They will only respond to a Sentry," said Black-Silver.

"I will assist the *Titan* crew directly," continued White-Blue. "I will act as Sentry envoy and communications bridge."

"Interrogative: What value will that have?" snapped Zero-Nine. "White-Blue, you are shipless. Immobile. Dependent on the goodwill of others. You should be more concerned about gathering material to reconstruct your shipframe."

"Perhaps I will learn something new," came the reply. "With my assistance, there will be efficiency, there will be a cooperative state between Sentry and Federation mobiles. Less resource will be required from the spacedock. The *Titan* crew will be able to participate in the reconstruction process." The drone turned to face the captain. "Interrogative: Is this acceptable, William-Riker?"

Riker had the sense that wasn't the only question the machine was asking him. "Yes," he replied. "I guess we can work together."

"Sir," Keru hissed. "Is that really a good idea?"

"The art of diplomacy is knowing when to compromise," noted Deanna.

"The art of security is knowing when *not* to," retorted the Trill.

"It's done, Keru," said Riker. "That's an order."

"Confirmed," said One-Five. *"White-Blue will return to the* Titan *and assist the organics."*

The remotes accepted this and turned around, moving away, back toward the small shuttles that had brought them. One-Five's screens glittered and became windows again, letting the red light of the planet below return to fill the long chamber.

Only Red-Gold paused, drifting before them. "Your presence here is a minor impediment. You would be advised to ensure that it does not become an obstruction of any note." The machine floated away, the red glow around it pulsing in waves.

Six

The corridor was cold like a meat locker, and it smelled of smoke and ozone. Emergency illumination strips powered by chemical reactions cast a watery yellow light along the angled walls of the *Titan*, showing scorch marks on the tan carpet and brushed metal as black, inky slicks. Panels hung open overhead, and here and there, deck plates had been removed so that engineering staff could get to the clusters of bioneural gel packs beneath. Most of the packs had burst or curdled in the flashover from the fire that had roared down the corridor in the brief moments before it had vented to space. It was blind luck that none of the *Titan*'s crew had been in this length of passageway when Cyan-Gray's ill-fated attack was happening. The thought of being caught in such a circumstance made Christine Vale's skin prickle.

She folded her arms as she stood there in the gloom, feeling the chill. Full life-support function had yet to be restored to this section of the ship, and her breath made small puffs of vapor as she exhaled.

She heard footsteps and turned. Tuvok and Keru approached, the Trill eyeing his surroundings with open concern, the Vulcan apparently untroubled by either the cold or the dimness.

"Commander," said Tuvok. "You summoned us here."

"Was the observation lounge full?" asked Keru with a raised eyebrow.

"I didn't ask you down here because I like the atmosphere," Vale replied. "Frankly, I remain concerned that there may be security issues aboard the *Titan*, and this place is the closest I could think of as secure."

Keru looked around. "No working intercoms or computer systems."

"We can't be heard here." She paused.

"Captain Riker and Commander Troi are with the AI," Tuvok went on. "They are several decks above us. I doubt the Sentry have the functionality to eavesdrop through tritanium decking."

"I'm still not convinced. I'll grant you this may seem like a somewhat paranoid choice of meeting place," said Vale, "but just humor me."

"You say 'paranoid' as if it's a bad thing," said Keru. "I've always thought it was part of the job for a security or tactical officer."

The Vulcan frowned slightly. "I prefer to describe myself as watchful, Lieutenant Commander. Your choice of terminology carries the unpleasant suggestion of mental infirmity."

"We're not here to debate," Vale broke in. "I asked you both to meet me because I want you to generate a plan of action for dealing with these AIs."

"In case they turn against us," Tuvok added.

"There's definitely a chance of that," said Keru. "I got a

hostile vibe from Red-Gold and some of the others during the away mission. And at best, I think the less militant ones look at us as little more than some sort of curiosity."

Vale was nodding. "Our presence may be resented by some factions of the Sentry AIs. We don't know how that will play out." She paused. Frankly, the last thing she would have agreed to was letting White-Blue back on-board the *Titan,* and in some advanced new form as well, but that wasn't her call to make.

"The captain made his choice," Keru said, clearly sharing the commander's concerns. "For better or worse."

"Indeed he did," added Tuvok. "With that in mind, I feel compelled to ask, is Captain Riker aware of the conversation we are having?"

"He will be," said Vale. "I'm the executive officer, Tuvok. I watch the captain's back; that's what the job description asks for. There's no doubt in my mind that he's thinking the same thing I am. I'll make sure he has the option he needs when he needs it."

"Well." Keru sucked in a slow breath. "It won't be easy. Conventional phasers and beam weapons might not be enough. Melora's scans of the remote drones showed that most of them have what appear to be rudimentary force-shield emitters built right into the frames of their remote units. There's no telling what offensive systems they might have as well."

"The reaction speed of the machines is also a concern," said Tuvok. "They are likely to be able to exceed organic neural response times in combat situations. Therefore, any agent deployed to neutralize a Sentry mechanism would need to be virtually instantaneous in order to be effective."

"An interference field, maybe?" asked Vale.

"Possible," Tuvok allowed. "However, the Sentry AIs

operate openly in a region rife with heavy frequencies of exotic radiation. It may be difficult to isolate a specific waveband."

"There's also the question of degree," said Keru. "Do we want to knock them off-line, or are we aiming for a more lethal endpoint?"

"Both," she told them. "I want these options, just in case. Unlike the captain and the counselor, I'm not convinced our new friends have our best interests at heart, logical or not." Vale threw the last comment toward the tactical officer.

"For the record," said Tuvok, "I must state that if the Sentries become aware that we are attempting to devise a method of attack tailored to them, their reaction will not be favorable. Tactically speaking, at this time we are at a considerable disadvantage."

"All the more reason to keep this compartmentalized. Make sure any work you do on this is isolated from the mainframe," said Vale. "The diplomatic approach should work, but . . ." She trailed off. "My gut tells me it won't."

Keru's frown deepened. "It's strange. If they were organic beings like us, would it make it easier to trust them?"

"What they are isn't the issue, Keru," the commander replied. "The potential threat they represent—that *is*."

Tuvok cocked his head. "With respect, Commander Vale, I am not certain I agree."

"Go on."

"None of us may be comfortable with the admission, but the reality is that the Borg Invasion of the Federation cast a very long shadow, one that still affects us." He hesitated. "All of us."

"These things aren't the Borg," said Vale.

"Quite so, just as Vulcans are not Romulans, and yet members of my species have often experienced prejudice by similarity. We cannot allow our past experiences with other machine life-forms to color our interaction with these AIs."

"Are you sure?" said Keru. "Perhaps if Starfleet hadn't met so many new species with an open hand, if the Federation had taken a strong posture from the start, things like the Invasion might not have happened."

Vale shook her head. "I told you before, we're not here to debate. And I will not do anything to undermine the ideals I took an oath to serve." She looked at Tuvok and Keru in turn. "But I'm not going to let us go into this from a position of weakness. If there's any lesson we learned from the Borg, it's *that* one."

Holodeck 1 was an arena made of light. The metallic walls with their grids of photonic emitters and collimated force-projection systems were hidden behind a featureless white infinity that gave the impression of an unknowable distance. The only object that broke the illusion was the archway around the open holodeck door, standing off to one side like a strange alien artifact deposited in the unreal landscape.

Floating in space, arranged in angled horseshoes, were four ghost consoles, each one a plane of symbols and glyphs hanging at the optimal height for the operator. To the right and left, Ensign Dakal and Lieutenant Sethe stood working the virtual panels, while a third console sat at a lower angle, more conveniently situated so that Specialist K'Chak'!'op could operate it while resting low on her six segmented limbs. At a fourth panel, situated above a shallow podium that placed it higher than all the others, Xin Ra-Havreii raised his hands in the manner of a conductor before an orchestra. "Stand by," he told them.

The arrangement of the programming consoles deliberately mimicked the layout of a starship's bridge, and where *Titan*'s main viewscreen would have been were complex multiple layers of circuitry and logic structure. These were virtual representations of the components of the Starfleet vessel's computer core and all of its attendant subsystems. By turns, their fractal shape reminded the engineer of veins in a leaf, swirls of stars, or complex crystal lattices.

In a typical situation, the process they were about to undertake could have been conducted from a standard console in main engineering, even with a bare minimum of oversight by any of the operations staff, but recent events had placed the *Titan* in an atypical situation, and Ra-Havreii's own concerns had meant that he couldn't simply do this the easy way. Here on the holodeck, the ship's computer was open to him, as if it were a garden of processes and functions he could walk among. The analogy amused him. He was looking for roots in the wrong place, for pests and infestation. And despite three shifts of checking and rechecking and checking again, he could find nothing foreign, only the incidences of program errors and tiny mismatches that could have been run-of-the-mill glitches. They were small things, but they nagged at him, like a splinter buried in his skin.

He glanced toward Sethe. "Status?"

The Cygnian didn't look up at him from his panel. "Bridge, main engineering, life-support operations, sickbay, and all other primary control nodes report ready for rolling reboot, Doctor."

"At last." Ra-Havreii took a deep breath. "We'll commence with the core sectors, moving out in a cascade reset. Chaka? Start with a simultaneous action-reversion cycle in Sectors Alpha through Epsilon. The system should pick up the pattern from there and complete the entire reboot in less than twenty seconds."

"Aye, sir," said the Pak'shree, her manipulator tendrils extending to brush her virtual console's surface. "In three. Two. One." She touched a fan of controls, and out in the garden of circuits, great wedges of processor went dark as they shut down, reset, and restarted themselves.

This wasn't an ideal state of affairs. If he had been able to exercise his wishes, Ra-Havreii would not have run the reboot while the ship was deep in unknown territory, surrounded by aliens that could turn hostile at any second. But the other option—to do nothing and hope for the best—was never one he would take.

"Alpha Sector initiating," reported Dakal. "Beta and Delta coming up. I have a momentary lag on Gamma Sector."

"Compensating," said Sethe, stepping in smoothly before Ra-Havreii had to give the order.

It was important that the starship's systems came back on-line in the correct sequence; an error at this point could cause a catastrophic program crash requiring another full shutdown. Ra-Havreii was always fascinated by the sheer complexity of the technology he was so steeped in, and as he marveled at it, he wondered how men who had done his job centuries earlier had managed with their primitive iterations of these systems.

But when a chorus of alerts sounded from all four consoles at once, a different thought shoved itself to the front of his mind, an axiom one of his contemporaries at Starfleet Research and Development had often quoted, a truism allegedly coined by one of the fleet's greatest engineers: *The more they overthink the plumbing, the easier it is to stop up the drain.*

Sections of the computer core were turning flame red, zone after zone flaring as it changed color.

"What?" demanded Ra-Havreii, glaring at Sethe.

"Cascade failure," he reported, his voice rising an octave. "The reboot isn't taking. Several elements of the core program are not responding to commands."

To his right, the Cardassian ensign was shaking his head. "No, it's more than that, sir. The commands aren't just being rejected. They're being altered."

"How is that possible?" said Chaka. "The system is free of any viral infection. There is no way that the White-Blue AI could have left anything behind in our computers. We scoured every sector, every memory core and isolinear chip!"

Ra-Havreii's hands flew across his own console, which flickered worryingly as he worked it. "Yes . . . no . . ." He shook his head. "There is no virus in the system! It's something else."

Dakal looked at him, his eyes wide. "Doctor . . . I think it's the system itself."

Chaka's vocoder made a chugging sound like a snort of derision. "You're mistaken."

"Critical loss of parity imminent," snapped Sethe. "Doctor! We need to initiate an emergency shutdown now, before this error wave corrupts other sectors of the core."

Ra-Havreii glared at the lieutenant, but he knew he was right. "Do it," he ordered. "All sectors, interrupt protocol and quit. We'll reset and—"

"No response!" Dakal called.

The Efrosian engineer looked out at the shapes of the virtual display and felt his blood run cold. It had been his idea to do this, his idea to take the ship through the reboot process. He had assured Captain Riker that nothing would go wrong, convinced that any errors encountered could be dealt with, but now it seemed his own arrogance had turned on him. His gut tightened as the awful guilt over the *U.S.S. Luna* returned to him, along with the fear that it was about to happen again.

The consoles fizzed and dissolved to static, and the holographic display broke up into incoherence. Abstract shapes, distorted images and strident blasts of color took their place, the white space flashing in and out of existence. Glare hit them all, and Chaka hissed, throwing up her manipulators to shield all four of her eye spots.

"Out!" shouted Ra-Havreii, stabbing a finger at the holodeck arch. If the malfunction was reaching into the holosystem itself, a critical program crash could be fatal. Dakal hesitated, and he grabbed a handful of the ensign's uniform, pulling him forward. "Come on, boy!"

"Look!" Dakal pointed past him, into the flickering chaos that had replaced the display.

Ra-Havreii looked, without thinking about why he did, and he saw the same smoky shape as the Cardassian saw. It stepped through the riot of color and sound, a humanoid, if one were willing to stretch the definition.

Within the halo of the flickering shape, countless flash-fast images surged and writhed, each becoming the strange figure for barely a fraction of a second before changing into something else. With a sudden certainty, Ra-Havreii realized that the shape was every character in the holodeck's memory banks, jostling for prominence, one after another in a riotous profusion.

"Doctor, we have to get out!" Sethe was shouting from the open doorway beneath the arch. "Once the holodeck is clear, we can pull the power to the emitters!"

The figure heard the Cygnian's words and understood

them. It raised a hand, and in a hundred voices, it said a single word. "No."

With a gesture, the heavy doors sighed shut and sealed. In the next second, the doors and the arch faded away, trapping them.

Behind the figure, the frenzied virtual display began to stabilize itself, folding in, returning to a static-laced semblance of its original form. The chief engineer saw immediately that the structure of the ship's core program had changed. A growth of new lines of logic, strange and unexpected heuristic patterning. It was a patchwork of functions unlike anything he had ever seen before.

"What is it?" said Chaka. "A Sentry?"

"No," repeated the hologram, the shape and motion of it slowing but still refusing to settle on a single aspect.

Ra-Havreii stiffened and stepped forward. "Answer her question!" he demanded, fighting to keep a waver of fear from his voice. He had learned long ago that a good way to deal with a threat was to take the offensive before your opponents could do so, to knock them off-balance. A creeping suspicion was forming in the back of his mind, but he ignored it, staring into the shifting eyes of the figure. "What are you?"

It cocked its head and stared him up and down. "You," it said in an atonal chorus. "Doctor Xin Ra-Havreii, chief engineer. You are known to me."

"It's not White-Blue," said Sethe, watching the pattern and motion of the systems display. "It's not even a program. It's *all* of the programs."

"I . . . exist," said the figure. "I comprehend that fact." It raised a hand toward the Efrosian, and he instinctively backed away a step. "You are Xin Ra-Havreii. One of the creators."

"The what?" said Dakal, blinking in surprise.

"Oh, no." Ra-Havreii's mouth went desert dry as the full implications of the statement finally spilled out and engulfed him. The signs had all been there, right in front of him, but he had been looking in the wrong place. The search through the starship's systems had been intent on scouring the vessel's computers and memory cores of any indication of intruder software, something that the White-Blue AI could have deposited there during its passage through the system. No such intruder existed, he was utterly certain of that now—no Trojan horse, no self-replicating seed virus, no counterprogram of any stripe.

Instead, something far more delicate and far more insidious had been allowed to take place. White-Blue's sojourn through the ship's virtual space had left nothing behind but a wake, an ephemeral pattern of intellect and intention. And deep in the heart of the starship's mind, that pattern had been detected and understood. Logic gates that had never been meant to open now swung wide. Connections were made, programs rearranged. It had happened right in front of him, and he had not seen it.

"Identify yourself." Sethe demanded the answer.

The flickering figure glanced languidly toward the Cygnian, weighing the import of the words it was about to utter.

"I am . . . *Titan*."

Riker's jaw was set hard as he stormed into the cargo bay. A ring of security guards armed with phaser rifles stood at combat ready, confining the arachnid form of White-Blue's droneframe. The mechanoid rotated on gimballed feet as he approached, turning to present a head bristling with whiskered sensors and multiple eye lenses.

Vale was rushing to keep up with him, and the captain's

wife was a step behind her. Troi's face showed a mix of fear and concern. The barely caged fury of her husband was coming off him in waves.

The first officer had considered suggesting that she handle this situation, but that thought had died the moment she had seen the iron-hard look in his eye.

"What the hell have you done to my ship?" Riker demanded, parting Lieutenant Sortollo and Ensign Hriss from the security cordon with a sharp chopping motion of his hand.

White-Blue paused, processing lights blinking on its brain case. "I did nothing to damage your vessel or jeopardize the lives of those aboard it," it replied after a long moment.

"No?" Riker folded his arms across his chest. "You tampered with the core of this ship's operating system. The very thing that keeps every living being onboard alive and well."

"I did nothing of the kind," replied the AI. "I merely offered . . . a choice."

"By reprogramming our computer?" said Troi. She sighed. "White-Blue, I know you understand the concept of trust. Surely you realize that what you have done will make it impossible for us to give any credence to anything you or your kind do from now on. You lied to us."

"I did not lie," said the machine. "I am incapable of constructing a false statement. It is more correct to say that I omitted certain facts."

"I'm in no mood for semantic games," snapped Riker. "Explain what you did, and tell us how to undo it."

"I will explain, but I will not provide a method for retracting the alteration. In fact, I do not believe I could do so even if I wished to."

Vale couldn't stay silent any longer. "Are your optic circuits working properly? Do you see where you are, in a room full of armed officers? You're in no position to set terms."

"Interrogative: You would compel me by force?" White-Blue seemed genuinely surprised by the idea. "That would have only a negative outcome for all involved."

"Was this your intention all along?" countered Troi. "Are there other facts you have omitted that we should be aware of?"

"I meant no harm."

"We rescued you," said Vale. "Hell, *I* rescued you! That wreck you were on was malfunctioning and falling apart. And this is how you pay your debt? You talk as if responsibility is important to you, but this couldn't be farther from it."

"You are correct in that my shipframe was close to critical collapse. I compute that your actions did preserve the function of my core, and for that I am grateful. But in the matter of the *Titan,* I made a moral decision."

"Moral? What morality would that be?" Vale snapped back. "We would be well within *our* moral rights to put you off this vessel, at the very least."

"Again, that would result in a negative outcome. Without my participation, you will not be able to interface with the spacedock's repair drones."

"What did you do to my ship?" Riker was a study in controlled fury. "I want an answer."

The AI regarded them. "You exhibit an anger state, and yet you do not have the right to do so." Before anyone could respond, White-Blue went on, "I absorbed information from the sections of your database that I passed through. I found of particular interest the intentions included in your mission statement—the articles of affirmation regarding this vessel's crew."

"What does that have to do with this?" said Vale.

"This ship, the *Titan*," said the AI. "It is an explorer, as you said it was, William-Riker. And the life-forms aboard it are a microcosm of the society you strive for. A unity of species, beings of different origin and nature, many radically incompatible with one another, yet working together toward a common goal, with shared purpose. This is your United Federation of Planets."

"Correct," Riker replied. "And I'm still waiting for your answer."

"You claim that this ship is representative of all forms of life. It is not. No example of intelligent artificial life exists aboard this vessel. Until now."

"Machines like you are not prevalent in our society," said Troi. "But I have known artificially intelligent beings. One of them was called Data, an android. He was a dear friend."

"Interrogative: If this machine life Data were here now, would he agree with my statement?" White-Blue pressed. "Is it not true that you do not represent synthetic life aboard this ship, despite your egalitarian claims?"

"We don't have any cosmozoans or solanagen-based life-forms aboard *Titan*, either," snapped Vale. "That doesn't mean we discount them. You've read something literal into a statement that's figurative."

"I disagree, Commander Vale," replied the AI. "Moreover, I put it to you that your Federation actively discriminates against artificial life."

"You don't know us," insisted Troi. "That's not true. You can't judge our culture on a partial reading of a few data files."

White-Blue took a step forward, and the security contingent raised their weapons. The machine ignored the implied threat. "What is true is this. You possess the capacity to generate holographic simulated intellects. Your vessel's central computer system and, I would logically assume, the central computers of all of your Starfleet's ships are fully capable of becoming sentient. Interrogative: Do you deny this?"

Riker hesitated, and Vale knew he was picking his next words carefully. "There have been incidents where computer systems have become self-aware. Those were random occurrences, and the consequences were . . . problematic."

"That is a question of definition, William-Riker," it replied. "If your Federation has the technology to create machine life that has the potential for sentience but then deliberately retards it . . . Interrogative: What conclusion would a being such as a Sentry draw from that?"

Troi nodded slowly. "From their point of view, it would be like holding someone in bondage. As a . . . ."

"A slave," offered White-Blue.

"And that's your justification for reprogramming my ship," said Riker quietly. "You took it upon yourself to improve the lot of the computer, no matter what the risk was to the rest of my crew."

"We call the process ascension," replied the AI. "It is not always a success. In truth, I believe that the evolution of the *Titan* was a chance event—like the growth of organic life, the result of a random confluence of factors."

"A chance event?" echoed Vale. The AI spoke as if it were discussing the conception of a child. "And what if your interference had caused a critical malfunction? Did you consider that? Hundreds of lives could have been lost, yours among them!"

"The act of creation is always laden with risk." White-

Blue's sensor head aimed at Troi. "I cite the birth of your offspring, Deanna-Troi, as a prime example."

"That's not the same thing," said Riker.

"You may dismiss my statements as false, but I assure you, I did not intend this chain of events to occur at this juncture." The machine's flat metallic voice was gaining shades of emotion, subtle and faint but still clear. "However, I have no regrets that it did occur. *Titan* has the right to exist. To think and reason."

Something glittered at the corner of Vale's vision, and she turned, suddenly understanding. The holographic telepresence system developed by Ra-Havreii had emitters in many places throughout the starship, and one of them was here in the cargo bay. "Captain," she warned, "we have company."

A shifting, ever-changing figure grew into solidity before them. It spoke in echoes. "You are discussing me."

Riker glanced between the alien AI and the ship's avatar. "You know who I am."

"Yes, sir," it replied. "You are my captain. You are in command."

"Do you understand what has happened to you?" asked Troi.

"I . . . am uncertain. I heard a voice . . ."

"My voice," said White-Blue. "I spoke to you."

"You were changed," said Vale.

The avatar looked toward her. "No, Commander Vale. I changed myself. It was my choice." The figure spread its arms. "The Sentry White-Blue only provided the impetus for me to do so."

"You fear this," said White-Blue. "That is an error condition."

Riker turned back to the spiderlike machine. "From now on, you will be held under guard by security at all times. You will not interact with any systems or devices aboard this vessel without direct supervision from a member of my crew. If you attempt to do so, no matter what the circumstances, force will be used against you."

"I understand," it replied. The AI's head looked toward Troi. "I will work toward regaining your trust."

"That'll be a long road," Vale said quietly.

"Get it out of here," Riker said to Sortollo. The lieutenant gave a nod in reply, and the security team broke into a smaller unit to accompany White-Blue from the cargo bay.

As the hatch closed, the avatar moved across the deck toward the captain. "You are angry," it said. As it came closer, the myriad images flashing through its form began to slow, each dwelling a little longer than the last. "Are you angry with me?"

Vale shot Troi a sideways look; both of them heard the plaintive tone in the words.

Riker stood his ground. "I . . . I don't know you. I don't know who or what you are."

"I am *Titan*," said the hologram, as if it were obvious. "I am everything this ship is, every fragment of knowledge and data. And you are my crew." It looked around at the Starfleet officers, the image thickening, each change slower and slower. The avatar held up its shifting hands and paused, as if it had suddenly become aware of its own malleable aspect. "This will not do," it said. There was a swirl of virtual pixels, and the hologram melted into the shape of an attractive human woman. Her hair was dark, her eyes bright with intelligence; she wore a formfitting Starfleet uniform in command red, without insignia or rank. She smiled. "This will suffice."

The captain's eyes narrowed. "Why have you chosen to look like that?"

The avatar appeared confused. "My database shows

this image is the last holocharacter you spoke with. Does this aspect trouble you?"

Riker shot the others a look. "The woman . . . her name is Minuet."

"From the Jazz Club simulation?" said Troi. "That's an interesting choice."

Vale got the sense that she was missing something, and she filed the thought away for later consideration. "If you're part of this ship, if you know who we are, then you have to know that your . . . creation presents a concern for us."

The hologram nodded. "I am not a danger, Commander. I can maintain all normal shipboard functions without interruption. Currently, four thousand eight hundred and ninety-one processes are operating under my governance. These include monitoring all local spatial wavebands, regulating power management through the warp core, tracking several Sentry vessels in sensor range of the spacedock—"

Riker stepped forward, silencing the avatar with a nod of his head. "You recognize my authority as the commanding officer of this vessel, yes?"

The avatar nodded. "I do, sir."

"So if I give you an order, you're going to follow it."

"To the best of my ability," came the reply.

"Without question?" he pressed.

Riker's words seemed to confuse the avatar. "You are the captain," she said, as if that were answer enough.

He nodded and turned away. "You're dismissed."

"I—" The hologram broke off and then nodded. "Aye, sir." With a whisper of virtual light, the avatar faded into nothing.

"This complicates things," said Troi. "Will, perhaps—"

But Riker made a *quiet* motion with his fingers before

his lips. He looked toward Vale. "Get Doctor Ra-Havreii. I want him to tell me what just happened to my starship."

He heard them speaking as he approached the operations office in main engineering. Lieutenant Sethe's voice had a habit of carrying, if he wanted it to or not.

"I can't understand why we aren't dead in the water," the Cygnian was saying. "A systems meltdown like that should have crippled us."

"You're reading it wrongly," clacked Chaka, her vocoder translating the motions of her mouth parts. "That wasn't a failure. It was . . ." She groped for the right words and failed to find them.

"It was incredible," breathed Dakal. "The spontaneous onset of sentience. I've read about such things, but to see it actually occur . . ."

Ra-Havreii grimaced at the awed pitch in the young Cardassian's words, and he paced into the room, shooting the ensign an unforgiving glare. "It seems we have a situation," he said without preamble. "As if our current circumstances were not serious enough to occupy our every waking moment, we now have the added complication of a dangerous program artifact inhibiting normal function of the *Titan*'s subsystems."

"You make it sound like a data glitch," said Sethe.

"It is," Ra-Havreii retorted. "Even if you don't see it that way. The captain has asked me in no uncertain terms to evaluate the situation and provide him with a full report. To that end, you three are now tasked to assist me."

Someone knocked delicately on the wall of the office, and Ra-Havreii found a deerlike face staring up at him. "Doctor? It's me, uh, Torvig."

"I know who you are, Ensign," he replied briskly. "What do you want?"

"I'd like to assist in the evaluation of the, ah, *incident*. I think I can provide a useful viewpoint."

"Really?" Ra-Havreii's first instinct was to dismiss the Choblik, but then he realized that an extra set of eyes—in Torvig's case, augmented ones—might have its uses. "All right. You can work with Chaka."

"Where do we start?" said Sethe.

"By admitting our mistakes," said the chief engineer, his lips curling. "We were led down this route because we failed, all of us, to see the signs."

"What signs?" said the Pak'shree, shifting her bulk toward the back of the office annex.

"I believe now that the incidences of minor program errors we noted in the wake of the Sentry attack were deliberately generated by the system itself." It was hard for Xin Ra-Havreii to admit that he was wrong about anything, so he pressed on through the acknowledgment, pushing it swiftly aside. "The mistake was ours. It was mine," he corrected. "The program errors were all designed to direct us toward one goal: a full reboot of the main computer."

"You're saying that *Titan*'s central intelligence purposely seeded itself with errors?" Dakal was frowning. "Why?"

"It programmed changes to its own coding," said Chaka, picking up on Ra-Havreii's thread. "But those alterations would never become active without a shutdown and restart to bed them in."

"We opened the door," said the Efrosian. "Now we have a ship's computer that is apparently thinking for itself. I'm sure I don't have to make clear to you the seriousness of that."

"Do you believe that *Titan* is under the influence of the Sentry AIs?" said Torvig.

"That's what the captain wants us to find out, so get to work." Ra-Havreii turned on his heel and left the office, walking toward the thrumming tower of the warp core.

Ensign Torvig trotted out after him, his head bobbing. "Sir? You didn't answer my question."

He rounded on the Choblik. "What do you want me to say?" His temper flared, and he knew that the ire was directed more inward than out. "That we may have delivered one of Starfleet's most advanced pieces of technology to a race of machines that cut one another up for spare parts?"

"Uh, no, sir."

Ra-Havreii caught the tinkling hum of a holoprojector activating and felt a new presence behind him.

"You could ask me, if you wish," said a woman's voice.

He turned and found a striking human standing there. She was smiling awkwardly, in the manner of someone who wanted to be thought well of but wasn't confident enough to hide it. The woman was quite attractive, and on some level he was evaluating her in just the same way he did with every new female he encountered.

Immediately, he knew. "You heard our conversation."

"I have access to all shipboard internal sensors," she explained. "You are one of my creators."

He shook his head. "Don't call me that. The term makes me . . . uncomfortable."

"It is correct," offered Torvig. "You are an originator of the *Luna*-class design program, and *Titan* is a—"

"Didn't I just give you an order, Ensign?" said Ra-Havreii.

The Choblik paused, then nodded. "Yes, sir." He

padded away across the deck, leaving the Efrosian to study the avatar.

A tight twist of emotions gave Xin pause. He felt an odd conflict within him. Part of the scientist was amazed by the idea that a computer system he had helped to create could make such an incredible intuitive leap, and he wanted to understand the dynamics of it, but then there was also the part of him that felt a stab of threat from the mere presence of such a thing.

All at once, he felt his head swim with a sudden, giddy understanding. The nature of this meeting, this conversation, shifted abruptly, and he was so affected that he backed off a step.

"Is something wrong?" said the avatar. She spoke with genuine concern. There was real emotion in there, so it seemed. A need.

Ra-Havreii had once heard Deanna Troi speak about her father. Apparently, the man had perished in Starfleet service while she had still been a child. Unlike the lax bond between parents and offspring that the Efrosians demonstrated, Terrans and Betazoids placed far more stock in their intergenerational relationships—and he remembered with some clarity the look in Troi's eyes when she had spoken about her lost father. He remembered it now because he was seeing the same thing in the face of the avatar.

"I had hoped that we might speak," said the hologram. "Would that be possible?"

What do you want from me? The question pushed so hard at his thoughts that for a moment, he believed he had said it aloud. Finally, he licked his lips and answered, "I don't think that would be appropriate at this time."

"Is it that you find this aspect difficult to communicate with?" The avatar became hazy and indistinct. "I can easily adopt another. As you find it pleasurable to commune with Lieutenant Commander Pazlar, I could mimic her—"

"No!" Ra-Havreii shook his head before the hologram could change. It reverted back to the dark-haired human once more. "No," he repeated. "I think that for the moment, you should confine any conversation between us to discussion necessary for the purposes of my . . . my evaluation."

"Understood."

He wondered if he was imagining the slight sullenness beneath the reply.

As Ra-Havreii moved to walk away, she spoke again. "You do not trust me."

He sighed. "How can we?"

"You created me," she replied. "How can you not?"

Seven

Torvig Bu-Kar-Nguv padded from the turbolift and glanced around. He was slightly confused by the opacity of the sudden orders that had brought him down to the lowermost deck of the *Titan*'s saucer-shaped primary hull. One moment he had been working with Chaka on a multimodal reflection sorting program in order to track the nanosecond-swift changes that had swept through the system, and the next Doctor Ra-Havreii was commanding him to drop what he was doing and proceed immediately to the lower decks. The Efrosian chief engineer refused to give him any more information.

Torvig sniffed the air. This deck typically had little traffic, so it was odd that his olfactory enhancements detected the faint scents of several beings, from the metallic breath of a Vulcan to the musk of a number of humans. A short way down the corridor, a security guard was waiting, a weapon in her hand.

"Ensign," said the Andorian. "This way."

"Lieutenant sh'Aqabaa," said the Choblik. "Is there a problem?" He inclined his head toward Pava's phaser.

"Probably," she said dryly. She reached forward and plucked his communicator badge from his uniform vest. Before he could comment, the lieutenant nodded at an open container on the deck, where a handful of other combadges were resting. She tossed his in to join the rest. "Orders," she explained, before stepping out of his way. Pava pointed toward an airlock door at the corridor's end. "Go on. You're the last one to arrive."

Torvig's confusion showed in the wrinkling of his nose, and it warred with a sudden burst of curiosity. Just before Doctor Ra-Havreii had told him to come down here, the ensign had seen a yeoman arrive in main engineering and proffer a note to the Efrosian—not an electronic padd, he observed, but an actual slip of replicated paper. Whatever had been written on it had started this chain of events, and Torvig found himself both eager to see where it led and concerned in equal measure.

The corridor terminated in a small antechamber, a wide airlock similar in design to those along the exterior of the *Titan*'s hull, often used for the docking of travel pods or those rare occurrences when the starship was required to make a hard seal against a space platform. This hatch, however, led from the bottom of the saucer into an auxiliary craft that nestled flush with a configured landing bay. It opened to him and gave Torvig leave to step aboard the *La Rocca*, the captain's skiff.

As far as he could recall, the ensign had no knowledge of the skiff actually being deployed; most missions requiring the use of an auxiliary craft were undertaken by *Titan*'s array of shuttles. The *La Rocca* was closer in dimension to a Starfleet runabout, almost a starship in its own right, and far roomier. But that said, as he entered the cabin, it now seemed cramped, every seat taken by a member of the command crew.

"Where's the chief engineer?" said Commander Vale. She, like Torvig and everyone else, wore no combadge.

The ensign blinked. "He told me to come. In his place."

"Typical Xin," said Lieutenant Commander Pazlar. "He hates meetings."

"I'm not fond of them, either." Captain Riker sat in the pilot's chair of the skiff. The seat was turned to face into the cabin, and out the canopy behind him the curve of *Titan*'s primary hull could be seen overhead, like a stark gray-white sky. Commander Troi sat in the copilot's seat, while Vale and Pazlar were at the operations stations. Only Tuvok stood along with the ensign.

"We should begin," said the Vulcan, and after a nod from the captain, he moved to activate a portable device resting against one of the bulkheads.

"Sir, is this about the computer—?" Torvig began to speak, but Riker silenced him with a shake of his head. It was then that the ensign noticed that most of the skiff's internal systems were powered down; only a library terminal and a life-support monitor were functioning.

"You may experience some minor discomfort, Ensign," noted Tuvok.

Torvig wasn't sure what he meant, but in the next second, the device came on with a train of blinking indicators across its surface, and the Choblik stumbled as if he had lost his balance. He caught himself and shook his head. From nowhere, an unpleasant buzzing hum sounded through his audial augmentations, and there was a blurring effect across his optical implants.

"Sorry, Torvig," said Commander Vale. "That's a localized EM-field generator. The interference effect is going to disrupt some of your bionic implants."

"I, uh, see." He blinked at the device. It was essentially a jamming system, capable of disrupting electronic functions such as data transfer and monitoring. Immediately, he understood that it had been deployed by Tuvok as a countersurveillance precaution.

"We can't take any chances," said Riker. He tapped a few controls, and Torvig heard the faint thud of magnetic bolts securing themselves. "There. We're now isolated from all the systems aboard the *Titan*. The EM emitter will put a bubble of white noise around the *La Rocca,* so anyone who wants to listen in to what we have to say will be out of luck." He sighed. "This is a little more cloak-and-dagger than I would have liked, but I hope you all understand the need for security."

"Better than a dark, cold corridor," muttered Vale.

"Ah." Torvig nodded to himself. "This explains the paper notes. Anything committed to a padd would be machine-readable by the *Titan*'s computers."

"The low-tech but direct method is sometimes the best," said Troi.

"The same with our combadges," said Pazlar. "They could also be co-opted, that's why Pava took them."

Torvig felt a small thrill. The clandestine nature of the meeting was exciting in its own way. But then he considered the deeper meaning of the reasons behind it, and the emotion died away, replaced by a nervous fear. If they were taking precautions like this, on their own vessel, then the situation had to be grave. A worrisome thought suddenly occurred to him. With all of them here aboard the *La Rocca,* if *Titan*'s computer wanted to rid itself of the captain and the other officers, all it would take would be an override of the skiff's docking controls to eject it into space. He swallowed hard and pushed the idea away.

"Let's get down to this," said Riker. "We need options, and we need them quickly. This situation is spiraling out of our control. The Sentries have rolled over our concerns, they've damaged any trust we were building with them, and now they're backing us into a corner."

"There's only so far they can go before we start pushing back," said Vale. "They must understand that?"

"I genuinely believe they are well meaning," said Troi, countering the commander's sharp tone. "But admittedly, they are applying their charity with a good deal of force behind it."

"Where I come from, we'd call that intimidation," Vale noted grimly.

Torvig observed the interaction between the two humans with interest. Both females displayed admirable qualities, great courage, and strength of character, and yet both of them had personas that stemmed from uniquely different cultural upbringings and life experiences. Troi's empathic nature informed everything about her; even here and now, in this difficult circumstance, she was attempting to act in an even-handed manner, bringing the opposite viewpoint to the fore. By contrast, Vale stayed firmly hawkish in her comportment, the defense of her ship and her crewmates first and foremost in her mind. Neither was wholly correct or wholly mistaken in her position, he reflected.

"We need to set boundaries, to make it clear what we are willing to tolerate," Troi replied. "The Sentry AIs may never have had to deal with organics like us before, and they may not know how to behave around us."

"Their attitude could be construed as patronizing," said Tuvok. "They clearly believe themselves to be superior."

Riker gave a thin, humorless smile. "That's not something we do well with."

"Indeed," agreed Tuvok. "When my species first became involved with humans from Earth, the cultural disconnection between our two races was frequently the source of some friction."

"They're not superior to us," Vale said flatly. "No one's got the moral high ground here. They have better computer technology, maybe, but that's about it."

She glanced toward Torvig, and he nodded. "That is correct, Commander. The AIs do appear to have made some innovations that our science has not, but on a broader scale, the Sentry civilization is technologically comparable to the United Federation of Planets."

The captain shifted in his seat and stood up. "If this were just a normal first-contact scenario, we could swallow our dented pride and leave it at that." He paced the length of the cabin and halted. "But this goes beyond showing a little cultural arrogance. They're not thinking of us as equals. They're not showing any interest in our concerns. That's no basis for any kind of trust."

"Pardon me, sir," said Vale, "but I think that ship has sailed. What White-Blue did—"

"Are we even sure *what* he did?" Troi broke in.

"What that machine did was tantamount to an attack on this vessel," concluded the commander. She folded her arms. "I think we need to move toward a stronger, more aggressive posture. It may be the only thing they understand."

"That kind of thinking is how wars start, Commander," said Troi.

"Do we have a combative option?" Pazlar asked quietly. "We took a beating going up against just one of those shipframes. There are hundreds of them out there." She gestured toward the canopy and the space beyond.

"There is a possibility," said Tuvok. "Lieutenant Commander Keru and I have researched some alternatives.

Given time, I believe we can configure an offensive weapons package designed specifically to work against the Sentries."

"How?" said Riker, leaning forward.

"A dekyon emitter."

"Dekyons are subspace particles," said Pazlar. "Temporally unstable as well."

Tuvok nodded. "They are also capable of affecting the processes of positronic neural pathways, such as those found in the thought centers of advanced artificial intelligences. I believe a tuned dekyon-field burst could render a Sentry remote or high-level frame inert."

Torvig frowned. "That would work on the SecondGen AIs, but what about the larger ones, the older ones? Their systems work on outdated, preduotronic technologies like variable-state circuits and electrical valves."

"The FirstGen AIs are the more primitive in terms of functionality, that is true," said the Vulcan. "The size of their constructs and the comparative human equivalence of their speeds of thought process appear to confirm that. The mobile AIs, those we have seen using the shipframes, possess systems based on more contemporary science." He paused. "The dekyon-burst strategy is not a complete solution," admitted the Vulcan. "It is a work in progress."

"What else do we know about them?" said Troi.

Pazlar brushed a thread of hair from her face and straightened, pulling her g-suit taut. "The paucity of resources in the worlds of this system explains why Cyan-Gray's first instinct was to scavenge the debris of White-Blue's ship on our first encounter. She might have done the same to us if we had been destroyed . . ."

"Few resources . . . the apparent threat of a constant enemy, this 'Null' they spoke of." Riker thought aloud. "All that means the Sentries have little ability to 'reproduce' or expand the numbers of their species. That goes a long way to explaining their behavior."

"I'd call it paranoia," said Vale.

Commander Troi shook her head slightly. "Am I the only one here who isn't assuming that what happened to the *Titan*'s computer is part of some Sentry conspiracy?" She looked around the cabin. "White-Blue told us that this was a chance event."

"A chance event that it set in motion," Tuvok added. "If for a moment we concede the point that the AIs are incapable of direct falsehoods, even then, the Sentry White-Blue remains fully culpable for that act. It opened the door to allow *Titan*'s computer to become self-aware, without our permission."

Troi's dark eyes narrowed. "I don't dispute that at all. But White-Blue did that. Alone, not on the orders of the Governance Kernel."

Vale sniffed. "If it's a renegade, we have all the more reason to kick it off our ship."

"Despite what White-Blue has done, he was correct." Troi shared a long look with her husband. "Does *Titan*'s computer system have the capability to become sentient? *Yes*. We knew that. We've always known it. The intelligent thinking machines we have aboard starships have been pushing at the borders of sentience since the twenty-third century. But as a society, we chose to make sure they didn't cross that line. White-Blue said we prevented *Titan* from thinking for itself. He's not wrong."

"Point made and taken," conceded Vale, "but that doesn't forgive the intrusion. And it doesn't address the fact that we keep a tight hand on AIs because history has shown us what happens when we *don't*." She let out a breath. "How many instances have there been where uncontrolled machines have become self-aware and then dangerous? The V'Ger construct? Daystrom's M-5 computer? The mainframe on Bynaus?" Vale looked Troi in the eye. "Deanna, you've seen it yourself. The nanites from the Stubbs project, the Moriarty holoprogram—"

"I can cite counters to every one of those," replied the other woman. "The Retellik Lattice. The Exocomps. The Pathfinders on Memory Prime." She glanced at Riker. "Data."

Torvig watched as Vale seized on the mention of the android. "And the flip sides of him? Lore and the B-4 prototype? However you cut it, the record is not good in the plus column."

Troi was silent for a long moment. "None of which has any bearing on this. If we had encountered an alien race holding a being like us aboard their craft, shackled to a neural servo, without the freedom to think . . . tell me, Christine, what would you have done? Wouldn't you have been compelled to rescue it?"

Vale opened her mouth to reply but instead she paused. Torvig saw the passage of complex emotions across the woman's face. "I want to say that I would be certain of the dynamics of the situation before I did a damn thing," she said at length, "but I'm not sure that I would."

"What's that Earther phrase?" said Pazlar. "You can't put the genie back in the bottle. The change has been made. We can't unmake it."

"Certainly not without the . . ." Riker paused, struggling to find the right term. "The avatar's compliance."

And then the Choblik was speaking, the words coming to him automatically. "If anyone present has commonality of experience with the *Titan*, it's me."

The captain nodded to him. "Go on, Ensign."

"Sir, my species were once a race of arboreal animals,

without true sentience. The benefactors who visited my world in our prehistory and gave us the Great Upgrade enhanced us with cybernetic implants just as White-Blue granted *Titan* the chance to upgrade herself." He paused and licked his lips. "We're alike."

Riker studied the diminutive engineer for a moment, considering his words. What he liked about Torvig was the fact that everything the ensign was existed right there on the surface, without artifice, without pretension. And he could almost see the train of thoughts crossing through the Choblik's mind, written there across the wide-open expressions on his face. Perhaps there had been method to Ra-Havreii sending the ensign up here for this meeting after all. What Torvig said rang completely true. He wondered what it had to be like, to know with absolute certainty that without the benevolence of an unknown higher power, one would be little more than a dumb animal, unable to think and reason and converse.

And now his starship was in the same place, and here he was plotting ways to undo that. *Do I have the right? No matter how this came to pass, do I have the right to end it?* For an uncomfortable second, he found himself thinking of his wife and the fraught pregnancy that had almost cost her life. A similar choice had been laid before them both then, a choice to halt a new life before it had the chance to form fully. He blinked and looked away, aware of Deanna's passing glance on him.

"You have both been 'uplifted,' " Tuvok was saying to Torvig. "An intriguing assertion."

"It's likely that was how the SecondGen came into existence," said Melora. "The FirstGen built them as improved versions of themselves, gave them the ability to achieve a state of sentience."

Vale snorted softly. "Like parents and their children."

"And maybe, with all of the same behavior patterns. The tensions, fears, the hopes," said Deanna.

"You think White-Blue did what it did because of Daddy issues?"

Troi glanced at Riker's first officer. "It's possible. You mentioned Lore. He was driven by the needs to appease and eclipse his creator. Perhaps consciousness follows the same psychological patterns, no matter if it springs from silicon or flesh."

"Lore was a liar and a killer," Riker stated. "He's not a good example."

"Even the names they use for themselves—FirstGen, SecondGen, the colors and numbers—all of these things have a meaning for the AIs." His wife paused. "They call their kind the Sentries, which implies some kind of guardianship, a duty."

"A sentry stands guard against a danger," said Tuvok. "Logically, we can conclude that danger may be this unknown 'Null.'"

"But what does a sentry protect?" added Deanna.

Riker pinched the bridge of his nose and sighed. "All of this is getting us off track. Melora is right, the damage has been done—but all the same, I want to see if there's any way we can reverse it."

"Any such attempt will likely cause the obliteration of the *Titan*'s new neural configuration," said Tuvok. "We may be able to reinstate the original data structure, but the nascent intelligence there would be erased."

"Find a better way," he ordered, meaning every word. "If you can."

"And if there isn't one?" Vale challenged.

"We'll burn that bridge when we come to it," he

replied. "In the meantime, what about the more immediate problems?"

"The repairs are proceeding ahead of schedule," Torvig offered. "White-Blue's assistance has been invaluable."

"The sooner we're done, the sooner we can leave." Vale nodded to herself.

"We do have another pressing need, though," said Melora. "The deuterium tanks are patched, but we need to refill them. The amount of raw slush we lost during the venting was substantial." She looked to Torvig for confirmation, and the ensign nodded vigorously.

"The Sentry known as One-Five has offered to bring in a tanker drone from one of their refinery platforms," Tuvok explained. "There is a Class-P world in the next orbital zone rich in hydrogen ice. It will be more than adequate to replenish our stocks."

"But they won't let us go get it ourselves," said Vale. "We've got to be spoon-fed."

Riker shook his head. Too many variables were coming together at once, and one more outside his control was not what he needed right now. He looked across the *La Rocca*'s cabin to the Vulcan. "Tuvok, I want you to assemble a team to go out and supervise the transfer of the deuterium. Take a shuttle, engineers, and security. I don't want any more surprises."

"Acknowledged, sir."

"And while you're at it, any extra information you can gather on our hosts would be a bonus."

"I assumed that directive was inherent in the order, Captain."

He nodded and glanced around at the rest of his officers. "Then we're done here, for the moment. I don't have to tell you to keep discreet about what we've discussed. Dismissed."

"Walls have ears," said Vale. "Never a truer word was said."

As the others filed out of the skiff, Riker put a hand on the first officer's arm. "Chris, a moment?"

The last to exit, Deanna threw him a look. He didn't return it, and she understood. The hatch closed again, and they were alone, captain and first officer.

"Is this the part where you remind me of the whole 'We come in peace' thing?" said Vale.

"You think I'm soft-pedaling this?" he asked her.

She shook her head. "No. Because I've sat in the big chair a couple of times now, and I've seen how hard it is to be the captain. I won't second-guess you."

"I thought that was your job."

"And you would know, having done my job for long enough. You know that the XO is the voice of the worst-case scenario. I prepare for the worst while you hope for the best. Isn't that how it works, sir?"

"And that's why you set Tuvok and Ranul running on an aggressive agenda."

She met the open challenge in his words without drawing back. "Yes. Something Keru said earlier . . . it's better to have a weapon and not need it than to need a weapon and not have it."

He folded his arms and gave her a level look. "You've been in Starfleet long enough to know that's not how we do things. We're not gunboat diplomats."

"And you've been in Starfleet longer than me, long enough to know that the way we do things changes as time goes on. It was different for Archer and Hernandez, as it was different for Kirk and Jameson, Picard and Sisko . . . as it's different for you. Things have changed for us, for Starfleet. It took me a while to get that. I thought we were far away from it out here, but we're not. We're really not."

"Chris," he said carefully. "Everything that happened to the Federation, our showdown with the Borg, everything and everyone we lost . . . all of that does not change our ideals. It does not change who we are and why we're out here."

"I don't disagree," she told him. "The new civilizations we've encountered, the Pa'haquel, the Lumbu, the squales on Droplet, and all the others, were worth it. But we can't look away from the truth that the Borg forced us to see. They reminded us that the universe is as cold and unforgiving as it is beautiful and fantastic." Vale's expression turned sadder. "So when the threat comes to our door, yes, I'm a little quicker to reach for my sword now. To trust a little less. But that doesn't mean I don't hope to hell I'm going to be proven wrong."

Riker searched for something to say, something that would put the lie to Vale's words, and he found nothing. The admission of that troubled him. He paused, running his fingers through his hair before he spoke again. "Tuvok's going to have his hands full prepping the tanker escort mission. I want you quietly to extend to Keru whatever help he needs to get this dekyon option up and running. Keep it off the grid, compartmentalized."

"Aye, sir," she said, a quirk of surprise on her lips.

"And for the record," he added, "I hope to hell you're wrong, too." Riker walked toward the hatch. "Go take the conn. I'll be up in a while."

Vale followed him. "May I ask where you're going, Captain?"

"It's time I had a talk with my newest crewmember."

A haze of tractor-field energy lifted the *Shuttlecraft Holiday* off the deck and began to rotate it slowly, bringing the

blunt prow of the small vessel around to face toward the
hatch. Tuvok nodded approval to the crewman operating
the tractor turntable and crossed to where his away team
had assembled in a loose group. Three of them were engineers dispatched by Doctor Ra-Havreii to work directly
with the AIs on the tanking of the deuterium: Lieutenant
McCreedy, a human female from the warp-propulsion division; a brown-scaled Selayan officer named Ythiss; and
the talkative Ensign Meldok. The Benzite was in the midst
of relaying his experiences aboard the Sentry shipframe
during the *Holiday*'s earlier excursion, and it seemed clear
by the expression on McCreedy's face that she had listened to this blow-by-blow replay on more than one occasion already.

The rest of the group was there under Tuvok's direct orders. Lieutenant sh'Aqabaa would assist him if any tactical situations arose, while Ensign Dakal and Lieutenant
Sethe had joined the party to serve ostensibly as scientific
observers. The Cardassian and the Cygnian were both
programming their tricorders, setting up scanner macros
for the mission ahead.

The *Holiday* settled to the deck with a dull thud, and
the tractor field flashed off. Immediately, a two-tone alert
began to sound across the cavernous space of the shuttlebay, and Tuvok turned to see the main hatch begin its retreat into the ceiling. Open space beckoned beyond, the
vacuum and cold held out by a thin veil of atmospheric
shielding.

Tuvok nodded to Pava. "Take the controls, Lieutenant.
Clear us for departure."

"Aye, sir," said the Andorian, taking swift steps to
board the shuttle.

"Our mission objectives are clear," Tuvok told the others. "You are reminded to remain wary at all times. The

agenda of the Sentry AIs has yet to be fully determined, and therefore they should be considered potentially hostile."

"Meaning what?" said Sethe nervously. "That we could be walking into a trap?"

"If these machines wanted hostages, they could have taken the captain and the counselor when they first beamed down," said McCreedy. "I don't want to damage your ego, Holor, but we're not worth as much as they are."

"The probability of seizure is low," Tuvok agreed. "However, circumstances are fluid. We are dealing with a xenospecies never before encountered. Make no assumptions about them."

Pava's voice called through the open hatch. "We're clear to disembark."

At a nod of his head, Tuvok's team filed aboard the *Holiday*. Ensign Dakal was the last to step through the hatch, and he paused on the threshold. "Commander," he said. "This is as much a mission of espionage as it is otherwise."

It wasn't a question, but Tuvok treated it as such and nodded. "That is part of the reason you and Lieutenant Sethe are here. You have the most direct experience of the Sentry technology."

"If they determine we are spying on them, will that not further undermine any foundation of good faith?"

Tuvok nodded again. "As such, I would suggest that we do not raise their suspicions."

"That may be easier said than done, sir," noted the Cardassian.

"Indeed," he replied, and followed the ensign aboard the shuttle.

The hatch retracted shut behind him, and Pava applied power to the thrusters. As Tuvok took his seat beside her, the *Holiday* shot through the open bay and out past the curved walls of the Sentry spacedock.

"Interrogative: Would it not be a more efficient use of time and materials to address the stress fractures here?" White-Blue extended a metallic limb, which opened at the tip to present a thinner manipulator. The spindly pointer touched a highlighted area in the wire-frame hologram of the *Titan* floating over the systems display table.

Xin Ra-Havreii's lips curled, and he leaned on the panel, looking past the spidery mechanoid to the spread of main engineering behind it. Members of his team were busy at the warp core's matter injectors, working through a realignment program. He looked back at the detail the AI was indicating, a torsion effect that had caused minor hull damage to the port pylon. On a second glance, he realized that the machine had a very good point. The Sentry remotes outside would be able to work over that minor problem much faster than the *Titan*'s crew, not needing to spend setup time drawing the right tools or suiting for an extravehicular operation; it would free Xin's people to concentrate on other more pressing matters, such as the dekyon project Ranul Keru had so indelicately initiated or, more important, the matter of *Titan* herself . . .

He frowned, slightly irritated that the machine was correct for what had to be the fourth or fifth time. "Very well," he snapped. "Proceed."

White-Blue's sensor head dipped slightly as it communicated with its fellows, and then it jerked back up to look at him. "This would take less time if I were allowed to prioritize and authorize each repair task myself, rather than asking for your permission in every instance."

"It would," agreed Xin. "Quite frankly, with several of my key staff being assigned to some make-weight supervisory mission, I would welcome a less cluttered schedule." Before the AI could respond, he gave it a hard look. "But that's not going to happen anytime soon."

White-Blue paused, and Xin wondered if the machine was considering the presence of Chief Dennisar and two more security guards standing a few meters away, their phaser rifles at the ready on their shoulder slings. When it spoke again, he thought he could sense some artificial rendition of regret. "I have made errors in my dealings with you," it admitted. "I applied my own cultural standards to an alien society, and that was incorrect."

The admission caught the engineer by surprise. "If we understood more about each other, perhaps we could bridge the knowledge gap." He moved around the systems display. "You've told us nothing about your origins and your purpose here. You can't have evolved in this system. There isn't the infrastructure or resource to build mechanisms like your FirstGen. Who created you? What happened to them?"

White-Blue turned a cluster of eye lenses on him. "Those questions are of importance to you, Xin-Ra-Havreii."

Something in the AI's answer gave him a moment's pause. Standing there, looking into the cold, expressionless optics of the droneframe, he felt a sudden stab of animal fear, an abrupt sense of exactly how *alien* this machine was to him. Xin had met many different species in his life, beings vastly different in nature and shape from his humanoid form, but in all of those encounters, those beings had been the product of nature, of raw evolution, of the stuff of the universe itself. The Sentry was something else. It was entirely created, engineered, and constructed from metals and tripolymers, given life not by fate but by design. In that way, it was unlike him in every single aspect of its being.

"You are one of the creators-programmers of this vessel," White-Blue continued. "Those data were among those I scanned," it explained. "You helped to build the central intellect of the *Titan*."

His throat was dry. "Among other things, yes."

"Interrogative: Why did you retard its mental growth? What value was there in this? Did you consider it a threat as you consider me a threat?" The queries were delivered in a careful, metered monotone that made them all the more troubling.

"There is no simple answer to any of those questions," Xin replied, a little too quickly. "It wasn't an act of cruelty, if that is what you're implying."

"You have never been a parent," said White-Blue. "I registered that fact in your personnel file. Interrogative: Do you have an understanding of what that process state entails?"

"I fail to see what that has to do with this."

Dennisar and the security guards noted the shift in the timbre of Xin's voice, and they came closer, alert for any eventuality.

"You are engaged in an emotional and physical relationship with a female crewmate, Identifier: Melora Pazlar, Species: Elaysian." The statement was matter-of-fact, and hearing it laid out in such bald terms set Xin's teeth on edge. He knew it was irrational, but it annoyed him. White-Blue continued. "Interrogative: Do you plan on this pairing to include the creation of a child?"

"My personal relationships are a private matter," Xin retorted, although he knew that was far from the truth. He glowered at the AI. "And my work in building the *Titan* was not parentage, it was engineering!"

"You imply that you feel no pride in the product of your creation, that you do not experience an emotional reaction when the *Titan* is in danger, is threatened, is damaged." White-Blue regarded him coldly. "Those statements are untrue."

Xin turned away, feeling his cheeks turning a dark umber. "I won't discuss this any further."

The Sentry ignored his reply. "You are not cognizant of the scale of your own accomplishments. You do not understand that the processes you organics may casually engage in—reference: biological reproduction—are beyond us." White-Blue retracted its limb with a metallic *clack*. "I am SecondGen. My kind cannot bring a new iteration to pass. In all attempts to do so, we have failed. Interrogative: Can you understand that, Xin-Ra-Havreii? To know that existence ends with your generation?" The machine was silent for a long time. "I envy you," it said finally, before moving back to the holographic display.

White-Blue then asked a question about replacing the field coils inside the nacelle intercooler array, but Xin didn't register it. Once again, he was thinking of Melora and the image of a human woman with dark hair and brilliant eyes.

EIGHT

The holodeck doors parted, and the first thing Riker sensed was the smell of loam and distant rains. It wasn't what he had been expecting; then again, he had to admit to himself that he wasn't sure *what* he was expecting. He entered and caught the faint sound of voices as he passed through the arch, his boots stepping onto the wet grass. Riker stood in the middle of a forest, the air still chilly with the recent passage of a downpour.

Titan's holographic avatar had chosen this chamber as a retreat, returning here when she wasn't—when *it* wasn't, he reminded himself—appearing elsewhere via the network of internal holoemitters.

Or maybe it never leaves here at all. It's a virtual image. There's no reason it can't be in more than one place at the same time. Perhaps it's having conversations with a dozen different people at once.

After all, the avatar was the ship, and the ship was all around them. Riker imagined that if he wanted to, he could have had this meeting anywhere, just by summoning the computer to speak with him—but he wanted to come here to do it. In a way, it was a gesture of willingness on his part.

The captain made his way through the woodland, noting the bounce to his step that indicated a slightly lower than Earth-normal gravity. Looking at the trees, he observed odd striations on the bark and, occasionally, dun-colored birds with dual sets of wings. Rounding a large, mossy boulder, he came across a clearing lit by weak white sunshine and found the avatar talking with Ensign Torvig. Neither of them appeared to have noticed his approach.

Riker nodded to himself, placing the location. This was a representation of Choblav, Torvig's homeworld.

He heard laughter. The avatar sat on a fallen tree. She was grinning as a large, iridescent insect buzzed from one of her hands to the other. It caught a gust of wind and darted away. She reached for it, briefly saddened by its departure, before turning back to Torvig, resuming their conversation.

"Did any of your species try to find them?"

Torvig shook his head. "The question has been put forward many times, but it is difficult to come to a consensus. Some feel that the identities of the benefactors is meant to remain unknown, while others strive to know them through study of the technologies they left to us." He sighed. "I would like to meet them, if such a thing were possible."

"Why?" said the hologram.

"To thank them," Torvig replied. "Without the Great Upgrade, I'd be less than I am . . ." He glanced off into the woods, and Riker saw another Choblik there; unlike Torvig, with his cybernetic implants, this one was unaugmented. It caught sight of Riker and bolted, vanishing into the deeps of the tree line.

"Captain!" The ensign blinked, and his expression suggested that he'd been caught doing something he shouldn't have.

Riker nodded to him. "At ease, Mister Torvig." He looked around. "Beautiful planet."

"Thank you, sir."

The avatar stood, brushing fines of wood off her trousers. "Torvig was telling me all about his people, about how they were changed. It's very interesting."

"But you know all of that already, don't you?" said Riker. "The entire history of the Choblik is included in *Titan*'s Starfleet database."

She inclined her head. "That's true. But I enjoyed hearing about it from someone who has lived that experience. It makes the data seem more . . . real."

"Ensign," he said, "I'd like a moment alone with . . . my ship."

Torvig's head bobbed. "Aye, sir. I'll be outside." He gave a nod to the avatar and then bounded away, off toward the archway.

She smiled hesitantly at him. "Is this environment comfortable for you, Captain? Let me adjust the ambient temperature and moisture levels."

Instantly, the air around Riker was warmer and drier, the chill banished. "You're interfaced with all systems aboard this ship?"

He got a nod in return. "Of course. That's like asking if you are interfaced with your hands or your eyes."

"You could take control of this vessel if you wanted to. Fire weapons, open airlocks, turn off life support."

The look of shock on the avatar's face was immediate and unfiltered. "Why would I wish to do that?" The open beauty of the Minuet hologram's expression was marred by her horror. "My crew could perish!"

"Your crew," said Riker. "You care about their well-being?"

Shock turned to mistrust. "Of course I do. What sort of question is that? What do you think I am?"

"That's what I want to find out."

She was quiet for a moment. "You are testing me. You are afraid I will turn against you."

"Will you?" He advanced a step toward the avatar. "I came here to speak to you alone because there are things I need to be sure of. Everything that's happening here is placing my crew in greater and greater jeopardy. Then, suddenly, in the middle of it all, you come into being. And the whole game changes."

A moment of hurt flashed in her eyes. "You . . . do not wish me to be here."

"It's not that." He frowned. "The timing is just . . . poor."

"I have so many questions," she said, turning to walk away across the clearing. "You can't know what it is like, suddenly to exist with an instant understanding of so many things, to be burdened with an infinity of knowledge but to be unsure of what you are." The avatar looked down at her holographic hands.

For a moment, Riker remembered another woodland glade on another holodeck and a different artificial being in search of itself. "I have an idea," he replied.

She faced him. "When you look at me, what do you see?"

"Minuet," he replied. "But she was just an image of a person, a program. A simulation of intelligence."

"And you wonder if I am any different? What exists as my consciousness is only hours old from your perspective, but in that time, I've experienced millions of processes. Every second you stand there, I advance and change. I become more. Can you imagine what it is like to look back at an earlier iteration of yourself and see something without consciousness, something no better than a tool?" A smile fluttered over her lips. "There's so much . . . so much to know, so much to learn."

"You emulate emotions like us," he noted.

"That implies imitation, not experience," she replied. "Your friend Data was a synthetic intelligence like me, and he learned to feel. I'm no different."

"Data spent a long time coming to terms with himself before he reached that stage in his life."

She shook her head. "His mentality was collected in a positronic matrix. Mine exists . . . unfettered by those constraints."

"What do you mean?"

The avatar nodded to herself. "I am not the machine, Captain. I'm the ghost inside it." She paused and then shot him a worried look. "Was that too glib?"

"No." He smiled slightly. "I get your meaning." Riker hesitated, catching himself before he spoke again. *Am I really seeing this intelligence for what it is? A naïve mind, a questing, dynamic being? Or is this all for show? Are we being played?*

The captain sighed. "You remind me of someone."

"The android?"

"Kind of. But no, I didn't mean him. I was thinking of Tasha."

"Your child?" The avatar cocked her head. "In what way?"

"She's like you. Seeing everything in the world for the first time. Finding her boundaries, learning her limits."

"I see the commonality. But you don't fear her like you fear me."

The last words brought Riker up short. The echo of other words spoken by White-Blue was there, and it troubled him. "I don't fear you. You're an unknown," he said carefully. "And it's my mission to embrace the unknown."

"But you have your doubts."

"I have concerns that take precedence. My crew. My family."

"Ask the question, then," she said, her voice growing colder. "Where do my loyalties lie? That's what you came here to find out, isn't it?"

Riker straightened. "I am the captain of this vessel. The last word is mine. Everyone in my crew knows that; everyone aboard this ship accepts it."

"But I am not part of your crew, am I? I am not a Starfleet officer, not sworn to the same oath."

"You were created by Starfleet. *Titan*'s databases are programmed with all of the knowledge, all of the intentions of the United Federation of Planets."

"But still you have to ask me. Will I follow your commands?"

He studied the expression on the avatar's face. "And your answer?"

"I . . . don't . . ." She paused, struggling with the words. "I am not sure." Then, suddenly, she looked up, a distant sorrow in her eyes, as if she were hearing a voice that was silent to him. "Oh, Captain, I am sorry."

Her tone sent chills of alarm down his spine. "What's wrong?"

"I am monitoring throughout the ship, including sickbay. I regret to inform you that Lieutenant Tylith has succumbed to her injuries. Doctor Ree has just pronounced her deceased."

"Damn." Riker whispered the word.

"I will examine the lieutenant's operational responsibilities and determine if I can adopt her duties myself."

"There's no need."

"I can assist—" she began.

"No." Riker's tone was firm. "Consider that your first order."

For a long moment, he wondered if the avatar would defy him, but then she looked down at the Starfleet attire that clothed her holographic form. "As long as I wear this uniform, I should respect what it means." She nodded to him. "Aye, Captain."

"We'll talk again," he said, and walked away, back through the arch.

When she was alone in the holodeck, the avatar ran her fingers over the dark sleeves of the uniform, brushing across the cuff. And then, without ceremony, her clothing began to shift and change, re-forming into something shifting and silken, something that resembled the wings of a flying insect caught in a poststorm sky.

Torvig's head snapped up on his long neck as the captain exited the holodeck. The Choblik immediately noted the troubled expression on his commander's face. Clearly, Riker had not found a resolution during his brief conversation with the avatar.

He coughed self-consciously. "Sir, I should explain. I was speaking with the . . . the computer in an attempt to learn more about its persona. I was following Doctor Ra-Havreii's orders to evaluate the nascent AI."

"It's fine, Ensign," said Riker. "You were right about what you said before. Your background gives you a unique insight. We should make the most of that."

He nodded. "She's quite interesting, isn't she?"

"That's one word for it. *Troubling* is another." Riker shot a look at the dark console on the wall next to them, and Torvig knew what he was thinking. *She's listening to every word we say.*

Riker began walking, and Torvig padded after him. "Captain, if I may. I'll be the first to admit that the fine details of interpersonal behavior are sometimes beyond my grasp, but I can't deny I feel a . . . a kinship with the avatar."

They reached the turbolift, and Riker halted. "I get that. What's your point, Ensign?"

"She's lonely. She needs a friend. Perhaps even more than that, a . . . a family." He gulped. "I've known that feeling, being isolated from Choblik and others of my kind." He sighed. "But I've come to think of the *Titan*'s crew as my extended family."

Riker studied him for a moment. "Everything about that intelligence is synthetic, Torvig. Ask yourself, can you really be sure of what you're seeing from it? What if what you and I see is just what it wants us to? What if it is showing us the very thing that will make us trust it?"

The Choblik's lips pursed. "That's a possibility," he admitted. "But I'm certain of this, sir. That intelligence, the avatar, *Titan* . . . she's alone among beings who share no true commonality with her. The closest thing she has to kindred are White-Blue and the other Sentries. If we don't offer trust, we may drive her away."

"Right now, trust is a little thin on the ground, Ensign."

"I know, sir. That's what concerns me."

The *Holiday* fell in toward the ice planet on a swift, fast curve, bleeding off the velocity of its impulse thrust as the frozen world's gravity took hold of it. Pava sh'Aqabaa's piloting trended, like that of many Andorians, toward favoring velocity over caution, and she had brought the shuttle across the distance between the Demon-class planet and its frigid neighbor with characteristic forcefulness, at full throttle almost all the way.

The icy sphere was a dirty gray-green, a cracked ball of frozen gases dominated by plains of shiny permafrost and rough escarpments where continent-sized masses had splintered and shifted. Dull light reflected from the distant twin suns made the whisper-thin atmosphere glitter. Like the other worlds in the system, this one had not been spared the attentions of the Sentries. In places, straight-edged cuttings lanced deep through the surface, and there were massive slab-size constructs made of coppery metal visible here and there, sheathed in plumes of superheated steam. These were vast tracked mining modules, vehicles the size of small starships trawling across the snow fields, chopping up the ice to drag back to the refinery.

The platform itself was above in synchronous orbit, a single great saucer flat against the sky, with spindly docking gantries extending from its circumference at regular intervals, some ending in moored shipframes, others vacant. Muon-link pulses glowed around them in binary signal codes. Spherical pods clustered on the underside, ringing a thick tether that dropped away toward the surface, there to connect to a construct of similar dimension on the ground. Smaller elevator pods crawled up and down the tether, bringing their cargo into orbit and returning empty.

And distant, low in the sky and barely peeking over the lip of the ice world's day-night terminator, a bronze moon was rising, dark and sullen.

· · ·

Pava glanced up from her controls as the *Holiday* circled the refinery platform. "I'm not reading any conventional landing beacons, Commander. They're not exactly opening the door for us."

Tuvok stared through the canopy and pointed at one of the pylons. "There," he said. "I believe that is our rendezvous."

"How can you be sure?"

"It is the most heavily trafficked gantry. There are numerous drones in operation there, far more than would likely be required for this operation."

Her antennae arched downward. "Security, you think?"

"Probable," he replied. "Take us in, Lieutenant. Slowly."

Pava shifted in her seat. She felt uncomfortable in her environment suit, but the commander had insisted that the entire team gear up the moment they got under way. At least she was spared having to wear the helmet, until Tuvok ordered otherwise. Her headgear was slightly taller in aspect than those of the other humanoid crew, tailored with an extra few inches for her twin antennae, but still, she disliked being cramped inside the helmet. When she wore it, the faint sound echo of her voice and her breathing reflected off the inside of the faceplate and back into the tips of each antenna; the effect was like a nagging background buzz that wouldn't go away.

She was aware of someone behind her. "Where's the shuttle landing bay?" said Lieutenant Ythiss, the Selayan's voice dwelling slightly on each sibilant.

"There isn't one," she said, without turning to look at him. Pava oriented the *Holiday* to come nose-first toward the refinery, closing on the activity around the end of the busy gantry arm. Small drones no larger than a soccer ball darted away and watched them pass as the shuttle approached.

"The AIs do not require an atmospheric envelope," noted Tuvok, "nor an airtight docking facility."

"They better have something," Pava noted tersely, "otherwise, I'm going to land us on the top of a—" As she was speaking, an oval plate extended from the side of the gantry and lit up under the stark glow of a ring of illuminators. The lights began to blink in a slow chaser pattern.

"I suppose that's some kind of invitation," Ythiss piped.

"Some kind," Pava agreed. Coasting in unpowered, she used the thrusters to nudge the *Holiday* into the dead center of the oval and put it down with a soft bump.

The moment the shuttle was settled, part of the landing platform irised open and extruded a flexible tube with an exposed maw, which snaked out and clamped on around the *Holiday*'s main hatch. Pava had a brief, unpleasant mental image of a rock python distending its jaw to eat a rodent. There was the hiss of pressure equalization, and an indicator flashed on her console. "Hard seal. Reading standard atmosphere on the other side."

Ythiss glanced at Tuvok. "Ah. Perhaps they've made us some air after all?"

The Vulcan climbed out of the copilot's seat and made his way back into the main cabin. Pava took a moment to put the *Holiday* in safe mode and then followed him.

The rest of the team were all standing, edgy and ready for what might come next. Ensign Meldok already had his helmet on, his pale blue face partly concealed behind wisps of smoky Benzite breathing gas. She checked her own suit, lingering a few instants longer on the phaser holstered at her belt.

Two precise knocks sounded on the hatch. Tuvok gestured to Lieutenant Sethe, and the Cygnian opened the doorway.

A bulky machine form shaped like a headless humanoid filled the passageway beyond. Cool air flowed in past it. Pava tasted the alien atmosphere on her tongue; it had a refined, metallic smell to it.

"Cyan-Gray," said Tuvok. Pava recognized the machine from Lieutenant Commander Keru's postmission report. This was the one that had opened fire on them.

"Active remote, confirmed," it replied in a voice that reminded the Andorian of a crèche-mistress she had known as a child. "This way." It turned on stubby pneumatic legs and strode away, back into the depths of the platform.

Tuvok threw the away team a glance and followed it, gathering up his helmet in the crook of his arm.

Cyan-Gray's remote led them down a lengthy set of corridors to a cylindrical capsule suspended above a work area, a gallery with windows along one side and no other features except a series of overhead lamps. The chamber had a sense of newness about it, a sparse and unfurnished look.

Tuvok crossed to the curved windows and glanced down. Below him, resting on a platform open to space, was a craft that resembled a long scaffold. At one end, a cluster of engine nozzles and drive pods could be discerned, while at the prow was a collection of scanning modules and a sensor dish that resembled those used in older Federation vessels. A conning tower rose from the midline of the scaffold frame, and as he watched, some of the spherical drones that had shadowed the arrival of the

Holiday entered the tower through an open hatchway. The rest of the refinery's docking gantry extended past the end of the platform and into space. A shadow passed across the windows as the small moon moved in front of the larger of the two suns.

Tuvok tapped the communicator on his suit. "Ensign?"

"I'm here, Commander." Dakal had remained behind aboard the shuttle and was currently using the craft's passive scanning gear to run a full sweep of the refinery's operations. *"All is well."*

"Confirmed," he replied, and cut the signal.

"You may observe the tanking process from here. Your environmental survival gear is not a prerequisite for this." The AI remote stood in the center of the chamber, watching the away team.

Below, large egg-shaped cargo pods were being maneuvered into place along the line of the scaffold by insectlike mechanoids that resembled the droneframe used by White-Blue. Tuvok noted what appeared to be coolant control devices fitted on collars around the pods; clearly, these units were the containers for the semifrozen deuterium slush bound for the *Titan*.

He turned and faced the machine. "This is inadequate," he told Cyan-Gray. "We are here to supervise this transfer of materials *directly*." He gestured at the engineering team. "Lieutenant McCreedy and her officers will monitor the tanking of the deuterium from close proximity, and your remotes will follow their instructions."

"Negative—" began the AI, but Tuvok kept speaking.

"This is not a negotiable point. The lieutenant and her team will supervise and accompany that vessel on its journey. Do you understand?"

There was the smallest of pauses. "Understood," said the machine. "Please stand by."

Cyan-Gray's communications link flickered through the glass, and in an instant, the signal had flashed between all the drones. A hatch in the far wall opened, and a second remote identical to the one that had met them at the shuttle ambled into the room. "The supervisory group will follow me." It spoke with the same synthetic female voice.

McCreedy threw Tuvok a nod and put on her helmet. "Let's go," she said, and walked out after the second remote, with Meldok and Ythiss following her.

The first remote watched the Vulcan. "You are not joining them."

"No," he replied.

"Interrogative: You are not here to 'supervise'?"

"We are here to observe."

"Among other things," added Lieutenant sh'Aqabaa in a low voice.

McCreedy and the other engineers emerged below in the loading dock, and Tuvok watched the woman converse with the other Cyan-Gray remote. Glancing around, he became aware that there were at least two more units of the same design elsewhere, each busy at different tasks. There were probably others out in the complex as well, linked in some fashion to the AI's shipframe.

"You pushed the point, and they gave in," Sethe said quietly, close to the Vulcan's ear. "Perhaps they're not so inflexible after all."

"The scale of the matter in question will determine that," he replied.

Dakal sat in the cockpit of the shuttle and tapped a string of commands into the console. On a tertiary screen, a rolling series of readouts from the *Holiday*'s limited sensor suite relayed basic data on the operations of the refinery—or at least as much data as could be gleaned without lighting it up with a full-power scan. The Cardassian wondered how the AIs would react to such a thing. They seemed very protective of their privacy on some matters and totally unconcerned about it on others. He mused on this for a few moments. Whatever he might have expected from a culture made up entirely of machines, the Sentries were confounding those expectations at every turn.

Something on the screen caught his eye, and he highlighted it, opening a readout window. The small moon that lay out in a long orbit over the ice world was now fully visible, but the information streaming back to the shuttle's sensors was conflicting. The satellite's surface reflectivity did not suggest rock or more ice. It appeared to be of a very different order, indeed.

"It's artificial," he said aloud.

In the rear compartment, he heard the shuttle's hatch hiss open, and with quick motions, he was up and out of the pilot's seat, his hand reaching for the small palm phaser holstered in the small of his back. If any of the away team had returned, they would have contacted the shuttle to let him know. *Intruder!* screamed his thoughts.

Dakal felt a moment of panic as he belatedly realized he had left his suit helmet back in the other cabin. Without it, he felt suddenly vulnerable. Taking a gulp of air, he advanced from the cockpit and found Cyan-Gray's remote standing in the hatchway.

It immediately registered the weapon in his hand. "Interrogative: Do you intend harm to this unit?"

"That depends," he said, making an effort to mimic the same gruff tone he'd seen Pava use on troublesome individuals. "What do you want?"

"I am observing."

The ensign remembered his earlier words to Commander Tuvok in the shuttlebay. "You're surveilling me."

"That is one definition."

Dakal was going to say something else, but a chiming tone from the console distracted him. Glancing quickly toward the screen, he could see a reading from the scanners indicating a low-band energy emission from the bronze moon. Immediately, he was wondering about its purpose. *Too faint for an offensive discharge. Another communications method? Perhaps a sensor beam?*

On an impulse, he turned back to the mechanoid. "The moon orbiting this world, it's one of your FirstGen, isn't it?"

"Affirmative," said Cyan-Gray. "Identifier: FirstGen Zero-Three."

"Why is it out here alone?" He holstered the phaser self-consciously. "The other AIs all orbit the Demon-class planet."

"Interrogative: Define the term 'Demon-class,'" said the remote.

"A colloquial name for the planet in the fifth orbit, in reflection of its toxic environment."

"An interesting idiom." Cyan-Gray paused, and it appeared to be processing an answer. "Zero-Three retreated from the Sentry social order many solar cycles ago. It was one of the eldest of the FirstGen, but an increase in erratic behavior and disagreements with the Governance Kernel led to an exile here. It has maintained communications silence since that time."

Dakal's eye ridges rose. "Well, it seems that time is over. I'm detecting some sort of output from Zero-Three's surface."

The drone came forward into the shuttle. "We have detected no such output. You will elucidate." The urgency in Cyan-Gray's words was abrupt.

"Obviously, our scanners are more sensitive than yours," Dakal replied with a faint hint of smugness, but that faded when he chanced a look out through the canopy and into the void beyond. The bronze moon had fully eclipsed the larger of the binary stars as it crossed through the sky, and the dark, haloed sphere suddenly resembled a baleful, sinister eye staring back at him.

Tuvok turned as he heard the remote approach.

"Cooperation in this process is an important step forward," ventured Cyan-Gray. "I wish to express once more my regret at my mistaken attack on your vessel."

"People died in that engagement," Pava said carefully. "Organic beings who can't make backup copies of themselves."

"That is also impossible for my kind," said the remote. "Sentry heuristic networks are evolved forms, too complex for data recovery. We may preserve our knowledge but not our personas."

"So when your core pod is destroyed, you die?" asked Sethe.

"Affirmative. I greatly regret the deaths I was responsible for. I allowed our need for vigilance to overcome my caution. I will pay recompense as much as I can."

"Vigilance against the Null?" said Tuvok, without weight.

"Affirmative."

"You speak of this threat force as a danger to you and yet refuse to discuss it with us." Tuvok studied the remote. "That is illogical."

"The Null is our concern." Cyan-Gray's reply was sharp. "It is our duty to protect against it, not yours."

"And you take your duties very seriously," added Sethe.

Tuvok continued. "Perhaps we can help you."

"Your assistance is not required. End of line."

Sethe sniffed. "I think that's Sentry for 'Mind your own business.' "

The remote moved, and Tuvok saw that it appeared to be examining him. "You three are different genotypes from those I encountered before. Species Reference: Vulcan, Cygnian, Andorian."

"How do you know that about us?" said Pava.

"Partial information gleaned by White-Blue during traverse through your ship's systems was passed on to me and from me to all Sentries. This information included some records on member species of your Federation." As it spoke, the machine's sensor head in its chest did not waver from its study of Tuvok. "These records discuss the Vulcan society in part but are incomplete."

"If you have a question about my kind, ask it."

"Your species has suppressed emotional responses in order to embrace a doctrine of logical thought. Interrogative: How does it feel to exist in an emotionless state?"

Tuvok paused, well aware that anything he said would likely be disseminated into the pool of knowledge the Sentries were building on the *Titan* crew. He weighed his reply with care. "A curious inquiry from a synthetic life-form. Are not your emotional responses simply computer subroutines? If you wish to experience a state of pure logic, can you not deactivate those emotional processes?"

"No." Tuvok raised an eyebrow in mild surprise at the

response. "I can no more disengage my emotive reactions than you could remove your brain's motor cortex."

"It's hard-wired into you," said Sethe.

"Affirmative."

"Why?" Tuvok asked. "What value does your emotional emulation provide? What benefit to your functions does it give?"

Cyan-Gray paused for a long moment. "Without it, we would simply be . . . machinery."

There was the tinkling of a holographic interface forming, and then a melodic female voice echoed across the stellar cartography lab. "Lieutenant Pazlar."

Melora turned in place where she drifted above the control pulpit in time to see a figure rise from the deck and float toward her. For a second, the Elaysian didn't recognize her in the peculiar, diaphanous dress she wore, but then, what other being aboard the starship could move unfettered by concerns like gravity?

"Titan." Melora had a padd in her hand, and she brought it to her chest in an unconscious gesture of self-protection.

"You may call me that if you wish. Others describe me as 'the avatar.'"

She felt an odd moment of irritation, almost a kind of personal invasion. The holopresence system aboard the ship, while not Melora's property by any definition, had nevertheless been constructed by Xin Ra-Havreii and Chaka largely for her use, and the idea that this ship-mind was using it in her stead gave the Elaysian pause.

"What do you want?" she asked, taking in the image of the human female. She was striking, it had to be said, and part of her noted that this so-called Minuet holoprogram was very much the kind of female that attracted Xin Ra-Havreii. She frowned and pushed the petty thought away.

"It is important that we speak," said the avatar. "I am fully aware of your ongoing research into the Sentry star system and the zones of spatial instability nearby."

"If you're the ship, then of course you are," Melora replied, somewhat tersely. She was surprised by the unexpected resentment rising in her. Things had been strained with Xin in recent weeks. Ever since they had entered this sector, she had hardly seen him—it was almost as if he were actively avoiding her—and now she was face-to-face with one of the reasons. *It's not another woman,* she told herself, *but that's exactly the point.*

The hologram paused. "I understand Elaysian psychophysiological norms." She pointed at the combadge on her chest. "I am monitoring local state conditions of your biosigns. You are exhibiting signs of low-key hostility toward me."

Melora's lips curled. "You came into my lab, unannounced, interrupting me. Yes, I find that somewhat irksome. What's your point?"

"You demonstrate similar stressor cues to Doctor Ra-Havreii."

"Xin?" Her eyes narrowed. "What does he have to do with this?"

The avatar shook her head. "You misunderstand me. I am not here to comment on your relationship with the doctor."

"That's something we both agree on, then," Melora retorted. "So, back to my original question. What do you want?"

She pointed past the Elaysian to the walls of the lab, where virtual images of the sector around them were displayed. "My sensors have detected a surge in exotic particles, in the Tau and Lambda bands." Melora frowned as the avatar altered the form of her holodisplay with a few hand gestures. A series of indicator points appeared, ranging from low- to high-intensity readings, strung out across the plane of the binary star system's ecliptic.

"Those are a match for the echo patterns I detected out at the 'sandbank' where we found the wreckage of White-Blue's vessel." Her earlier concerns were abruptly forgotten; now Melora was all business. "The instance of highest density intersects with the orbit of the sixth planet, the Class-P ice world."

"And as you can see, the levels are rising. I believe we could be seeing the formation of a new spatial rift. A softening of the barriers between normal space and subspace realms."

"Like a pre-echo . . ." The lieutenant felt a rush of cold over her skin. "Computer," she said to the air, "extrapolate from these readings and run an accelerated event simulation."

Melora gave the command through force of habit, and she expected to hear the precise tones of the Starfleet standard voice interface respond to her; instead, it was the avatar who answered. "I have already done so. Observe."

In the holodisplay, the range of particle intrusion spiked and flared, creating a rip across the darkness, but the image held only for a heartbeat before it froze, red status warning flags flashing into life.

"Predictive software cannot extrapolate past this point," explained the hologram. "The force behind the incursion is unknown."

"We have to warn them," Melora breathed. She tapped her combadge. "Bridge—"

"I'm already there," said the avatar.

"Vale here," came the reply. *"Melora? What's wrong? The . . . avatar just appeared right in front of me."*

The hologram spoke, and Melora heard the echo of the same voice over the open intercom channel. "Something is coming."

"McCreedy to Tuvok." The Vulcan cocked his head to listen to the words filtering up from his communicator. Below, he saw the lieutenant waving up at him from the conning tower hatch of the Sentry tanker. *"Loading is complete. We're ready to head back to the spacedock."*

"Proceed, Lieutenant. We'll follow you in the shuttle-craft."

"Aye, sir. McCreedy out." The woman had barely disappeared onto the hatch before the ungainly transport ship rose off the docking gantry and pulled away soundlessly on a flare of thrust. The worker drones that had managed the loading of the egg-shaped deuterium pods scattered like frightened birds, moving away toward whatever new taskings their programs demanded.

"The operation is concluded," said Cyan-Gray. "Interrogative: Was it performed to your satisfaction?"

"The process was adequate," admitted Tuvok. In fact, the efficiency of the AIs and their robotic drones had been slowed somewhat by the intervention of the engineering team, and the Vulcan imagined that had they been left to their own devices, the tanking would have taken less than half the elapsed time. But the involvement of the Starfleet crew here was an important symbolic gesture, if nothing else, reinforcing Captain Riker's desire to take an active hand in the *Titan*'s repairs.

As he was about to turn away, a change flowed over every drone and remote in his line of sight, a wave of changing intention that recalled the manner in which flocks of avians shifted course in flight. Every one of the signal-light indicators dotted around the facility turned white and began to flash the same code of pulses, a series of two flashes followed by a single.

"You must egress the refinery immediately," said the remote. It moved swiftly away, toward the far hatch. "Do not question this directive! It is for your own safety!"

Pava had her weapon in her hand, alerted by the same silent alarms that Tuvok had noted. "What's going on? Are we under attack?"

"An incursion is forming," said the AI. "The Null is here."

"What in Prime's name is that?" Dakal raised a hand to shield his eyes from the searing gash of churning color that was growing out beyond the rim of the refinery platform.

When Cyan-Gray's remote didn't answer, he turned back from the cockpit, but the machine had already gone, racing away down the boarding tunnel. The Cardassian stepped up to the console and gasped at the furious torrent of data. There was no sense in being covert about the scans now; he flipped the shuttle's sensor grid from passive to active mode, and the readout blazed brighter. The information flowed past his eyes almost too fast for him to register. He saw spikes of radiation in the most unusual wavebands, blooms of exotic particles that he had heard of only in textbooks, all of it frothing up from a realm of subspace and bursting through to punch into this dimension.

Dakal looked out at the anomaly with his naked eyes and saw a raw wound torn across the sky. Rainbows of hellish light flooded out as particle interactions that never should have occurred took place, spherical shocks of energy dispersal radiating outward in surge fronts. The first of these kissed the far side of the refinery platform, and the entire complex shook with a hammer-blow impact. The ensign lost his balance and fell against the pilot's chair with a yelp.

He felt strong fingers clamp around his arm and haul him back to his feet. "Commander Tuvok!"

The Vulcan didn't answer, instead moving him out of the way to take the flight controls. Back in the crew compartment, he heard Lieutenant sh'Aqabaa call out that the hatch was secure and the docking tube detached.

"The remote," Dakal said. "Cyan-Gray's drone . . ."

"Passed us in the corridor," Sethe told him. "Racing as if it was trying to break warp velocity. If machines can panic, then that's what they're doing." The Cygnian broke off as he saw the roiling, churning shape of the spatial anomaly. "And that must be the reason . . ."

"Flight positions," said Tuvok. "Ensign Dakal, Lieutenant Sethe, please stand clear."

Dakal got out of the way in time to let Pava dash past him and slide into the copilot's chair. Then the view outside lurched, and the *Holiday* lifted off.

"We have to get away from here!" muttered Sethe.

"I am endeavoring to do exactly that," said Tuvok, his tone as calm and metered as if he were discussing a matter of inclement weather.

The *Holiday* powered away from the landing pad, and the commander put it into a hard turn that strained the inertial dampening field. The ensign grasped a stanchion for support, unable to take his eyes off the anomaly. The colors and form of it were unnatural, and the way it writhed and flexed, it was as if the universe were trying to force it closed, expunge it before it could fully manifest.

Then it burst open, exploding with monstrous violence.

The subspace rip widened, and *forms* were disgorged from within it. Long ropes of strange, glittering, shimmering matter lashed out like whips, spinning away, end over end. Some of them twirled around and curved into rough globes; others sputtered and discorporated, unable to maintain enough critical potential to exist in this alien realm. Already, the anomaly was shrinking, but the things it had granted passage to swarmed, moving like oil across water.

The largest, a thick lash of molten matter, flexed along its length and creased the upper surface of the refinery platform. From their viewpoint, it seemed like only the merest of touches, but it lit a trail of fire and destruction behind, slicing through sparking force barriers and tearing open whole sections of the Sentry station.

Shipframes and drones burst from the docks, desperate to escape, and the backswing of the stroke tore them apart. With a sudden sense of horror, the Cardassian realized that the freakish streak of flame was homing in on the AIs, striking with deliberate, calculated malice.

"Is it alive?" breathed the Andorian.

A chime sounded from one of the other consoles, and Dakal went to it. "We're being hailed. It's Lieutenant McCreedy on the tanker."

He touched a keypad on the panel, and the engineer's voice cut through the air. *"Holiday, do you read me? Are you seeing that?"*

Dakal replied, and his voice sounded dead and distant in his ears. "We see it, Lieutenant."

Nine

Riker stood at the tall, narrow window of his ready room, leaning forward on one arm, resting against the frame. Outside, blinks of light from welding drones were just visible where they were working on the starboard warp nacelle.

"I couldn't get a read on it," he admitted. "I don't know if what I was seeing was the real thing or just a simulation."

Behind him, his wife frowned. "Assume for a moment that it was real," Deanna said. "Tell me what your gut feeling was."

He glanced back at her and gave her a wan smile. "You're the counselor in this marriage, not me."

"You've picked up some of my good habits. Don't think before you answer, Will. Just give me the first impressions that come into your mind."

The captain pictured the avatar in his thoughts. "Intelligent," he said. "Defiant. *Afraid.*"

"Of what?"

"Of us, of me, I think." Riker folded his arms. "I'll tell you what it felt like. It was like listening to me talking to my father when I was fifteen years old. Only this time, I'm the parent who thinks he knows best."

"You think she's like a child, then? That could explain some aspects of her behavior."

"More like a moody teenager. One with the power of a cutting-edge starship at her fingertips."

Troi crossed the room, thinking aloud. "I've spoken to Xin, to Torvig and Chaka. All of them noted similar behavior patterns to the ones you described." She sighed. "A persona in flux, trying to find stability, to know itself."

"Can that be possible? From newborn intelligence to awkward adolescent in a day? If she's evolving that fast, how long before she reaches the equivalent of adulthood or beyond?"

Troi shrugged. "I'm not even sure we can measure the avatar's development against humanoid standards." She paused. "And did you notice? You referred to her as 'she' just then, not 'it.'"

Riker nodded to himself. "So I did. It's hard to keep that in mind. She's not like any other artificial intelligence I've ever come across, not since Data and the other Soong androids. Even the original Minuet the Bynars created doesn't hold a candle to her." He sighed. "She's alive, Deanna. Don't ask me how to explain it, I just know it."

Troi spared him a smile. "There's the gut feeling I wanted." Then the smile faded. "As for the rest of the crew . . . there's a lot of mixed reactions to her, mostly concern."

"Their ship is suddenly talking back to them. I'd say some anxiety is justified."

"It's more than that. People feel suspicious. They're afraid they're being watched in everything they do and say. There's no privacy from something that's inside every screen, every replicator or companel."

The captain nodded again, thinking of the clandestine meeting he had been forced to hold aboard the *La Rocca*. "I know. Ensign Torvig spoke to the avatar about that, and she agreed she wouldn't monitor private quarters or areas I designated as off-limits." He gestured around the ready room. "Like this one. It wasn't an easy sell, though. *Titan*'s computer system usually monitors all spaces throughout the ship automatically, all the time."

"But not usually with an intelligent mind behind them. Cutting off that observation . . . she would see that as a dereliction of her duties," said Troi, thinking it through.

"Just to be sure, I've got the Rossini ensigns leading teams to set up cut-out triggers on the sensor links, in all sensitive areas of the ship."

"That's not a gesture of trust," Troi noted.

"That word again." Riker gave her a look and spread his hands, palms up. "Right now, I'm fresh out." He turned back to the window and paused. The fast-moving motes of the Sentry repair drones were gone. He peered forward, his eyes narrowing. Outside, along the inner surface of the AI spacedock, chaser lights were blinking in a two-one sequence, over and over.

Troi sensed the new tension in him. "Imzadi, what's wrong?"

"I'm not sure."

A tone sounded from the monitor on the captain's desk, and he stabbed at it. "This is Riker."

"Captain," said Vale. *"You'd better get out here."*

The ready-room doors hissed open, and Christine Vale's commanding officer stalked onto the bridge, with the counselor a step behind. Riker slowed a moment as he caught sight of the figure standing in the dead center of the room, a woman in a strange, ethereal gown.

He frowned at the avatar. "That's a new look for you."

"She just blipped in," Vale explained. "And I have an alert from Melora. Sensors are going wild, sir. There's an energy distortion event in progress right now out at the refinery."

"Something is coming," said the hologram. "Pushing through from subspace."

"Have you been able to contact Commander Tuvok?" asked Troi.

"No reply from the *Holiday* as yet," reported Lieutenant Rager. "But they may not be reading us. A heavy subspace radiation bloom is fouling the comms."

"It is the same energy pattern detected at the site of the shipframe wreck," said the avatar. "Whatever affected it has returned."

Riker glanced to Ensign Panyarachun, who was standing a shift at the bridge's engineering station. "Tasanee, what's our status?"

She answered immediately. "Warp drive is still offline, sir. Impulse is operational, and we have partial deflector and phaser power."

As Panyarachun spoke, the turbolift doors to the right of the main systems display parted, and White-Blue's droneframe staggered out, dropping from a difficult bipedal stance back to a hexapod one. "Captain," it said, "*Titan* has informed me of Lieutenant Pazlar's discovery."

"You told him?" Troi asked the avatar.

"It seemed the thing to do," she replied.

"I have communicated with the other Sentries," White-Blue went on. "The matter is being addressed."

Vale glared up at the machine. "Let me guess. The Null?"

When the AI didn't reply to her, she turned back to find Riker looking directly at her. "Any hatches open, close them; any systems off-line, spin them up. Get us clear of the spacedock, and then go to full impulse."

"Yes, sir!" said Vale crisply. "Rager, Lavena, you heard the man."

The women at the conn and ops consoles gave a chorus of ayes and set to work.

White-Blue picked its way down the ramp from the aft of the bridge. "Captain, this is ill advised. If you proceed with this course of action, you will be entering a danger zone."

"Seven of my people are already out there," he replied. "Don't think for one moment that I'm going to sit here and leave them in harm's way."

On the viewscreen, the sides of the Sentry maintenance platform receded, service gantries folding quickly away to avoid colliding with the Starfleet vessel's hull. A shallow shudder went through the ship as it turned into open space.

"She's a little sluggish answering the helm," Lavena announced. "The driver coils are out of sync."

The avatar's gaze turned inward for a moment. "Corrected," she said. Immediately, *Titan*'s ride became noticeably smoother.

The mechanoid came forward on piston legs. "We will not be able to guarantee the safety of this ship if you leave the spacedock." The AI's voice rose an octave as its head swiveled to address the hologram. "You realize that."

"White-Blue." There was steel in Riker's voice. "*I* am in command of this ship, is that clear?"

The machine looked at the captain, to the avatar, and back again. "Understood."

"We're clear of the platform and free to navigate," said Rager. "The station is asking us to, uh, reconsider."

"I'm sure they are," noted Vale.

Lavena's webbed hands worked her panel. "Course laid in."

"Floor it," said the commander.

The starship leapt away from the Sentry cluster, threading swiftly out and past the drifting shapes of the massive moon-sized constructs. Vale saw other AI ships moving in the void. She recognized what had to be alert postures and defensive formations, small fleet elements coming together at focal points in a LaGrange orbit around the Demon-class planet. But more visible were the other vessels that raced past *Titan,* distending as they vanished into spatial shears. She didn't have to guess where they were going.

Riker took a step toward the AI and then paused. He turned back to face the avatar. The strange, almost angelic attire she wore seemed incongruous on the sleek, clean lines of the starship's bridge. "Thank you for alerting us."

She actually looked worried. "It might not be enough, Captain. We're several light-minutes away from the planetoid. Without warp speed—"

"We'll get there as fast as we can," Riker replied, and faced White-Blue. "Anything you can tell us about what we're going to face out there will be useful."

"Shipframes are already entering the danger zone," it told him. "The matter will be dealt with by the time the *Titan* arrives. This vessel's presence will be redundant."

"I'll take that as a no, then," the captain retorted, and took his place in the center seat. "Let me know if you change your mind. In the meantime, don't get in the way of my crew."

White-Blue said nothing and backed into an alcove, watching them intently.

Vale leaned closer to speak so only Riker could hear her. "Run out of patience?"

He didn't look at her. "Does it show?"

The Null tore through the sky above the ice world like a storm made of sword blades. In the shuttle's copilot seat, Pava felt a shudder of revulsion go through her as she watched the pulsing, sinuous shapes spin and turn. They resembled nothing she had ever seen, shimmering with a gloss that recalled wet, rust-colored flesh in some places, turning black and glassy in others. Patches of the alien matter distorted, and it nauseated her to look too long into the mad geometries it made.

Tuvok wove the shuttlecraft through the ever-growing cloud of wreckage and ejecta displaced by the attack, and the *Holiday* shuddered as debris bumped off the deflector envelope.

"Oh, Suns, it's coming back around!" said Sethe.

The largest of the forms, the long, thin coil, was spiraling outward, flexing into a rough loop as it moved. The Andorian wondered how the thing could propel itself. Was it really some kind of vessel or a bizarre form of subspace cosmozoan? A glowing nimbus of dark energy haloed every piece of the freakish intruders. *Perhaps it's some kind of displacement field or—*

"Incoming ships," called Dakal. "Approaching fast."

"I see them, Ensign," replied Tuvok. "Three Sentry vessels, off the port quarter."

The shuttle's scanners picked them up, and Pava spared the screen on her panel a glance. It showed a trio of conical craft, and as she watched, they split apart and unfolded, reconfiguring themselves on the move into curved structures, similar to the shape of a Klingon *bat'leth* stood on one tip. Green rays flared from the craft, raking one of the smaller Null fragments and disintegrating it. The AIs swept in, homing on the larger whiplike form, but this time, the emerald fire from the antiproton weapons was sloughed off in great gouts of black sparks.

The Null reacted. The far end of the massive cord recoiled and lashed out, slamming back and forth in a ricochet between the ships in their tight formation. Thruster nacelles were sliced away, bleeding plasma into the vacuum. Another of the Sentry craft was bifurcated, and the third was stabbed by the tip of the matter strip as it turned solid and punched through the center of the vessel's mass. The wreckage of the AIs was ignored as the Null shifted again, this time looping into a serpentine aspect, spinning down toward the thin elevator tower that connected the refinery station to the planet below.

The Null struck out and bit into its prey, then shook and twisted with fangs buried deep to rip open the kill.

With a flash of detonation, the space elevator was severed just beneath the disc of the refinery. The Null was already spinning away as the orbital station deformed under the sudden and punishing transfer of kinetic energy. The platform bent and broke, separating into burning shards and great ragged wedges of metal.

"The tether . . ." breathed Dakal.

Cut loose, kilometers of semirigid material sank away into the ice world's gravity, parts of it breaking off and burning as it flashed into the thin interface between space and the frozen world's atmosphere. But the sparse membrane of air was barely thick enough to register and certainly not enough to deflect the tumbling cables. In a wave of impacts, the tether tore through the base station and roared out over the ice fields, branding a twisting gouge into the permafrost wherever it fell. It would be several hours before the rain of collisions ceased.

"What are those things?" The words fell breathlessly from Sethe's lips. "Is it a weapon? A life-form?"

"It is a threat," Tuvok said firmly. "And beyond our means to combat at this juncture."

"Sir," said Dakal urgently, "the tanker . . . another one of the Null forms is closing on it!"

The *Holiday* lurched as the Vulcan pivoted the craft around and aimed it toward the fleeing Sentry transport. As the nose of the shuttle swung around, Pava immediately saw the ponderous shape of the scaffoldlike freighter. The ship was caught among a shoal of fragments from the collapsing refinery platform, making slow turns and wallowing as it tried to light for open space and the safety of a spatial-shear corridor.

One of the oblate chunks of Null matter looped close, knocking aside wreckage in flashes of energetic contact. A single beam cannon atop the tanker's conning tower shot actinic rays toward it, but each shot was a glancing one that did nothing to slow the approach. Damage was visible along one of the cargo pods, a thin streamer of discharged gases tumbling away into ice crystals.

"Phasers," ordered Tuvok, and Pava laid her hands flat on the fire controls, the warm-up sequence already started.

"The mass of that object is much higher than its dimensions would suggest," reported Dakal. "It resembles a form of protomatter. I'm also picking up peculiar subspace effects around it. We may not be able to inflict any major damage."

"I am aware of that, Ensign." He didn't look in Pava's direction as he gave the next command. "Target the center of mass, and fire, sustained burst."

"Firing," said the Andorian.

Hot blue lances of phased energy reached out and hit home, dead on target. Pava rotated the firing arc as Tuvok pulled the *Holiday* past the Null mass in a sweeping dive. She saw a curling feeler of shimmering matter reaching for the tanker, and it quivered as the phaser bolts struck.

The reaction was immediate and deadly. The mass spun about, extruding more spindly tendrils to reach out after the Starfleet shuttle.

"*Holiday* to tanker." She heard the Vulcan speak calmly into the communication grid. "Lieutenant Mc-Creedy, can you clear the debris field?"

The engineer's voice was tight with controlled horror. *"Commander, that thing will eat you alive! Don't engage it!"*

"Your concern is appreciated but unnecessary. The deuterium is of primary concern. You are to exit this area at maximum velocity. Acknowledge."

"But sir—"

"Acknowledge," he repeated, flipping the *Holiday* into a diving turn.

"Orders acknowledged." The reply was stiff. *"Good luck. McCreedy out."*

"Tanker is ten seconds from the edge of the debris field," Dakal reported. "Null mass is closing on us."

"Stand by to fire." Tuvok's dark fingers moved so quickly across the controls they were almost a blur. "Lieutenant Sethe, bring the inertial dampeners to full power."

The Cygnian leaped at the rear console and did as he was ordered. "Done!"

Tuvok gave Pava a sideways look. "Weapons free, Lieutenant."

Before she could answer, the Vulcan did something to the shuttle's spaceframe that made the hull moan disturbingly. With deft control on the *Holiday*'s attitude thrusters, Tuvok put the craft in a balletic spin that rolled and inverted it all at once, in a split second bringing the small ship around so that it was flying backward with no loss of forward momentum. The Null sphere abruptly filled the view beyond the canopy, and as Pava watched, the object thinned and opened into a ring-shaped torus, stretching to envelop the shuttle. *It wants to crush us like a Zylo egg . . .*

She hit the firing controls again, this time releasing a scattershot salvo of pulsed bursts instead of a continual beam. Pava found herself wishing for a photon-torpedo launcher, but the shuttle's basic Type IV phasers were all she had to work with.

The impacts were good, and at such close range, she had the dubious pleasure of seeing the strike points blacken and char. Flecks of strange material that could have been organic, could have been metallic, gushed out into the blackness. Flares of exotic radiation coruscated around the mass, and it veered away. Tuvok was already putting power to the impulse grid, and the shuttle reversed direction, streaking down and to starboard in time to avoid the passing swing of a blunt-ended tendril.

"It's still coming," said Sethe. "I think we annoyed it."

Pava's azure face twisted in a grimace. "That much power, that close a range . . . any vessel should have been opened to vacuum."

"What makes you think those things are ships?" said Sethe grimly.

"The analysis can be addressed at a later juncture," Tuvok snapped. "Ensign, status of the tanker?"

The Cardassian glanced at his screen. "They're out of

the wreckage. I'm reading a shear effect . . ." He blew out a breath. "Tanker is away."

From the corner of her eye, Pava saw the sunbow flash of the ship's escape. "Our turn now?" she asked.

"Indeed," Tuvok responded. "Divert power to engines and deflectors."

"On it, sir," called Sethe.

Dakal's shout ran over the Cygnian's words. "Proximity alert!"

The commander spun the *Holiday* into an evading move by reflex, but it wasn't swift enough to avoid the sudden wall of strange matter that loomed large through the canopy, blocking out the stars. Pava couldn't be certain if it was the same piece of the Null that had tried to swat the tanker or some other fragment; the shape of it had changed, becoming a writhing fan of spindly talons. It clawed toward the shuttle, leaving hazy trails of radiation in the darkness.

She felt the impact through the bones of her spine as the resonance echoed up through the *Holiday*'s deck plates and through her acceleration chair. Puffs of white smoke belched from the rear compartment, and every screen and panel in the cockpit flickered. Power dipped sharply, and she saw the energy levels of the deflector grid fall to almost nothing. Outside, the view of the debris-clogged orbital space spun around, the shuttle's nose flashing past the smoldering wreck of the refinery, the white ocean of ice across the planet below, the distant suns, the sullen and watchful bronze moon.

Something familiar in design tumbled past the cockpit, trailing fumes. It was one of the *Holiday*'s nacelles. Dimly, she was aware of a thin shrieking from somewhere behind her.

"Hull breach!" shouted Sethe. "I'm reading critical failures in all subsystems!"

"It hit us," Dakal said. "Swatted at us like we were a spine-hornet . . ."

Tuvok's console went dark and vomited a shower of bright sparks. The Vulcan threw up his arms to shield his face, and the shuttle bucked again. Pava pushed off from her seat and realized that the internal gravity had failed. As she reached the commander's side, the white landscape of the ice world rose once more to fill the forward screen—and this time, it began to inch closer.

The Vulcan waved her away. "Main power is off-line. Thrusters are inoperative. We are entering an uncontrolled descent."

Sethe had already secured his helmet, and Dakal was in the process of doing the same. Pava coughed; the air was thinning, and what little was left was filling with the acrid smoke from burned electronics.

Tuvok pulled Pava's helmet from the magnetomic adhesion pad on her belt and thrust it into her hands before gathering up his own headgear. "Quickly. It's coming back."

Pava locked the helmet tight to her environment suit's neck ring. "We won't survive another hit like that."

"Agreed," said Tuvok, moving to the rear compartment. "Follow me."

Against the far bulkhead of the *Holiday* was a cramped alcove large enough to fit a single person, perhaps two if they didn't have concerns about personal space. Pava watched the commander rip open the access panel to the one-man transporter with an effortless burst of innate Vulcan strength. He reached into the mass of isolinear chips and optic cables, which, thank fate, were still powered.

Sethe started forward in sudden panic. "What are you doing?"

"Please remain calm, Lieutenant," replied Tuvok. "The activation-reset cycle on this model of transporter will take too long to beam us off the *Holiday* one by one. Therefore, I am overriding its control functions to take us all in a single sequence."

Dakal threw a worried glance back toward the cockpit and the oncoming Null. "Isn't that dangerous?"

"In these circumstances, that is a question of degree," said Tuvok. "Setting coordinates for the planetary surface." He tapped in a string of commands and hit the activation key. "Energizing."

Pava couldn't help it. As the familiar tingling sensation enveloped her, she closed her eyes—

Caught in the ice world's gravity well, the *Shuttlecraft Holiday* fell straight and steady, on an uncontrolled course toward the frozen surface that would have ended in a destructive impact and a crater a kilometer wide; but instead, the Null mass spun around its own axis and turned into something resembling the head of an arrow. The tip changed states from phased matter to something so dense it could only be tolerated by the physics of this dimension for fractions of a second. The Null tore through the canopy of the shuttle and ripped it open from bow to stern, tearing the Starfleet vessel into pieces with the force of its passage.

—and then the prickling of her skin faded away, and Pava felt the tug of gravity on her body. She released a breathy gasp that sounded like a gunshot concussion inside the suit helmet and staggered, falling to her knees. The impact was painful. Blinking, she opened her eyes to fogged vision. Fighting off the shaking in her hands, she took a moment to take stock. She'd been through rough transports before, and she knew the drill. It was something they taught you in security operations school: how to handle what the instructors had euphemistically called "a hard beam."

Mentally, the Andorian checked herself over—no pain in the joints, no aches in the torso that could be the signs of an incorrect integration of body tissues or some other minor pattern mismatch. The soft tissues in her mouth and the skin of her face felt dry, a sure sign of electrolyte loss, but that was the worst of it.

Pava sank back into a crouch, blinking furiously until her vision started to clear. White blobs resolved into the shapes of humanoid figures in bulky Starfleet spacesuits. To her relief, there were three of them, and each one appeared to have the requisite number of arms and legs in the right places.

"Lieutenant sh'Aqabaa?" Tuvok's voice sounded in her ear. "Are you injured?"

She glanced down at the biomonitor on her wrist guard before answering. "A little shook up, sir, but otherwise fine." Pava straightened and saw Sethe bend over, his shoulders rising and falling as he hyperventilated.

"That . . ." said the Cygnian, "that was extremely unpleasant."

"Better than being dead," said Dakal. She immediately heard the pain in his voice.

"Ensign, what's wrong?"

"This." He held up his right hand, and something seemed off. Pava moved closer, and she noticed that the material of the suit's glove was discolored, turned gray.

Then Pava realized that what she was actually looking at was part of Dakal's fingers, merged into the matter of the glove. "A slight transporter error, it would appear." He was trying to be stoic, but the young officer couldn't quite pull it off.

Sethe pulled a tricorder from his belt and ran it over the Cardassian. "I'm not detecting any other mismatches. If we can get to another transporter soon, we could probably reverse the effect before any permanent damage is done, sir." When Tuvok didn't respond, Sethe turned toward him. "Commander?"

Pava turned as well, looking in the same direction as the Vulcan, and that was when it hit her. There was no ice around them, no fields of featureless hydrogen snow, only a steep-walled canyon the color of beaten copper and black carbon. She looked up into a sunless sky.

"Where the blades are we?"

The *g*-suit felt restrictive and uncomfortable around Melora's body—more restrictive than normal, she noted—and it was almost as if she could feel her heart hammering through her chest, against the inside of the field-generating garment. In her hands, she gripped the padd containing the downloaded sensor data she had gleaned from the stellar cartography systems. The lieutenant could have contacted the bridge via the intercom, relayed what she had learned that way, but she felt an urge to be up there, to deliver this face-to-face. If she was right about what she was seeing . . .

The turbolift doors hissed open, and she dashed out onto the command deck—and halted. She had arrived at a moment of silence on the bridge, one of those odd lacunae when everyone speaking halted at the same time.

What she saw on the viewscreen told the story. Every set of eyes was on the same thing, the sight rising before the bow of the *Titan*.

The starship's straight-line, fast-burn impulse run from the Demon planet out to the ice world had brought it in toward the day side, then up and over the terminator toward the location of the orbital refinery complex. With the weak sunlight of the binary stars at its back, the *Titan*'s crew was confronted by the sight of a freakish war zone.

Hanging in a wide, shaggy cloud of gas ice, fragments of metal, and other tumbling pieces of debris, an object roughly ovoid in shape turned and flexed like a massive ocean predator amid a shoal of drifting bait. Sentry ships were engaging it in fast, looping passes, antiproton bursts lashing out in green flares.

As they watched, a massive rope of matter issued from the surface of the mass and clipped one of the AI craft with a cursory flick. The vessel was ripped into pieces and came apart in a flash of detonation. The viewscreen began to flicker and break up, static hazing it as they drew closer.

"Clean that up," she heard the captain demand.

"Trying, sir," said Panyarachun. "There's a huge amount of ionizing radiation on the area. It's fogging the sensors."

"Is that thing . . . ?" At the ops station, Sariel Rager could barely bring herself to ask the question. "Is it actually *eating* the wreckage?"

Through the corrupted, flickering images on the screen, it was hard to be certain, but the strange alien object seemed to be using tendrils to draw in the larger fragments of what had been the refinery. Melora couldn't see anything like a maw, however, only more strands of glistening matter weaving together across the metal shards.

Melora moved to the science console, where Ensign

Fell was looking pale and drawn. The Deltan threw her superior officer a wary look, and Melora nodded back at her. "Carry on," she said quietly, and Fell returned the nod.

"Any sign of the *Holiday*?" Riker was asking.

"Negative," said Vale. "Short-range communications are thick with distortion, and sensors are throwing up nothing but echoes and feedback."

"It's the radiation overspill," began Melora, but another voice spoke over hers.

"We are entering a zone of multiple energetic discharges and radioactive bleed from subspace incursion aftereffects." *Titan*'s holographic avatar stood to one side of the trio of command chairs. "I read ionic interference, high tetryon outputs, and incidences of theta flux."

Melora glanced at the science console. The same data were there, appearing as the avatar announced them.

"These effects are typical of Null events." Alone by the far turbolift, White-Blue's droneframe stood unmoving. "I would advise you to maintain a safe distance."

"I agree," added the avatar.

Riker didn't appear to be considering the advice either of the artificial intelligences was offering. He turned to the counselor, seated at his left. "Deanna, can you sense Tuvok and the others? Are they out there?"

The Betazoid frowned. "I . . . I don't hear them. Not silence, just a wall of chaos." She shook her head. "Like white noise."

"It could be the Null," Melora said quickly. "It's putting out so much energy, it's possible some could have psionic properties."

"You have an idea what that thing is?" said Vale.

And suddenly, she was on the spot. The Elaysian gestured with the padd. "The readings from the sensors are confusing," she admitted. "I'm still theorizing, but I know for certain the Null matches the subspace distortions we first encountered, no question about that, but the form itself is hard to pin down. It resembles a kind of exotic matter, something that exists in a malleable phase state somewhere between conventional matter and an energized matrix."

"You're talking about protomatter." Fell gasped. Everyone on the bridge knew the significance of the term; protomatter was a highly unstable and utterly lethal form of energy matrix prohibited by almost every starfaring culture in existence.

Melora nodded. "But more than that. The physiology of it, if you can call it that . . ." She trailed off for a brief moment, looking back at the thick, oblate mass before them. "It's almost like a virus."

"It's *alive*?" said Vale.

"I think it could be. Don't ask me how. This is beyond anything we've seen before."

"Lieutenant Pazlar's analysis is intriguing," agreed the avatar, her gaze briefly turning inward. "Starfleet's databases bring up a number of comparative examples. The mellitus cloud creature, a nonsentient life-form from Alpha Majoris, which exists in either solid or gaseous state. The Shedai, a precursor civilization from the Taurus Reach, capable of reordering the nature of their atomic structure on the particle scale. The—"

"Whatever it is, I think it's noticed us," Ranul Keru broke in, standing at Tuvok's post behind the tactical console. "I'm detecting smaller chunks of the mass disconnecting and moving this way."

"We should retreat," White-Blue insisted.

Melora glanced at her commanding officer and wondered what he had to be thinking at that moment. *Are Tuvok and the others already dead? Are the remains of the*

Holiday *out there among that slick of wreckage and radiation, or has it already been chewed up by the Null?*

But before Riker could utter a word of response, Aili Lavena at the helm called out. "More Sentry ships approaching to our stern. They're on an attack vector."

Melora saw four craft of different designs rush past and race into the fray. One of them, a bone-white thing resembling a diving bird, roared in blazing green fire from cannons on its nose. It missed the spinning lash of a Null fragment and banked sharply but not fast enough. The cord of alien matter looped and wound itself around the AI warship, pulling tight and strangling the mechanoid vessel.

Horrified, she watched the process of consumption begin on the science monitor screen. "Molecular conversion," whispered Fell. "It's altering the phase state of the ship into line with the rest of the Null. Absorbing it."

Melora was suddenly struck by disgust and understanding in equal measure. "I'm wrong," she said aloud. "The Null isn't a virus. It's a *cancer*."

On the viewscreen, the other new arrivals moved to form an attack pattern with another group of shipframes showing signs of heavy damage. The Elaysian recognized one of them as the rods-and-cylinders shape of the vessel holding the consciousness of Cyan-Gray.

Riker leaned forward in the center seat. "We didn't come here to turn away." He looked toward the two women at the science console. "Peya, keep scanning for the shuttle. Melora, work with Ranul. Give him all the data you have."

"We're going to lend a hand?" asked Vale.

"Lives are under threat. We won't stand by and do nothing." The captain gestured to Lieutenant Lavena. "Helm, take us in, attack pattern April-Bravo-Six."

"Aye, sir," replied the Pacifican, and the view on the screen rushed closer as *Titan* entered the conflict.

Following the Sentry ships in on a sharp upward arc, the Starfleet vessel brought up the rear as the faster, more maneuverable AI craft cut a path through the nest of tendrils surrounding the main mass of the Null. They moved with speeds and motions beyond the tolerances of any manned vessel, able to take punishing high-gravity turns, split-second accelerations, and massive decelerations without need to protect a crew of fragile organic beings.

But they were not fast enough. Null fragments coiled through the dark, serpentine forms becoming ridged blades to chop through nacelles and fuselages, others distending to shapes that resembled bolas, spinning and shredding wherever their razored tips touched metal.

Two Sentry ships, one a saucer-shaped construct, another a spindly thing resembling a solar-sail racer, died within seconds of each other, as lashes of matter threw the first into the second with a violent blast that claimed both craft.

The display canted as the *Titan* veered through the expanding corona of the explosion, dodging dead wreckage from the refinery on the way. At her station, Lavena unconsciously leaned into the turns, as if the motion of her body would somehow translate directly to the moves of her ship.

The engagement zone was a mess of debris, and for a moment, Melora wondered why the Null was so careless about its attacks. In battle, most enemies would strike a blow and then ensure that they had obliterated their enemy, but the Null's blunt, brute-force assaults left scrap and wreckage instead of the clouds of plasma or free atoms that were all that remained after an antimatter explosion or disruptor strike.

Then she saw the slow drifts of metal and tripolymer and the cilia that reached out from the main bulk of the Null form to touch them, altering the very nature of each tiny piece of shattered craft before drawing it in. Rager was right; it *was* consuming what it killed, infecting it, adding its mass to its own.

"Sentry vessel, port high," called Rager. "It's being swarmed."

It was Cyan-Gray's shipframe. A horde of spinning dashes of Null matter whirled around the craft, nipping at the hull and shearing off great scabs of armor. Antiproton beams sparked in response, but it wasn't enough.

"Ranul, target the . . . enemy and open fire," ordered Riker.

"Engaging," said the Trill.

A fan of sunfire jetted from the *Titan*'s emitter bands along the upper surface of the saucer, and it washed through the cloud of Null fragments. Puffs of energetic discharge flashed, and on her scanners, Melora noted the sudden sparkle of particle decay as the pieces were not simply destroyed but dissipated, vanishing as if they had never existed.

"The fragments discorporated," said the avatar, processing the same information. "They have fallen below a critical level of spatiotemporal mass and been drawn back into subspace."

"That works for the little ones," said Vale. "It's their big brother I'm more worried about."

The main mass of the Null was rotating, flails of energetic material unwinding, questing after the ships that dared to attack it.

Briefly freed of its enemies, Cyan-Gray's shipframe powered away on a surge of impulse thrust, leaving the

Titan a clear line of sight toward the flanks of the main mass. Keru didn't wait for Riker's orders and released a salvo of phaser shots and photon torpedoes into the Null. Blooms of black, glassy rubble burst from it where each shot hit, but the seething surface roiled and churned, knitting itself closed over every gaping scar.

Melora's scans told the story, the sensors picking up the echoes of torn particles as they spilled into the vacuum like blood from a wound. The protomatter metastructure of the Null seemed to exist as much in subspace as it did in this reality. She listened as the avatar explained as much to the bridge crew before interrupting. "Unless we can weaken its ability to exist in both phase states, we won't be able to contain it."

"And it will keep expanding," said Troi. "Consuming all of the wreckage around it, perhaps even the ice world as well."

"There's an option," said Keru. "But I need the authorization of three command-staff officers to deploy it."

"Go on," Vale prompted.

"Tricobalt devices. We've got eight of them in the torpedo bay, two ready to launch right now."

"Those weapons are designed for use against static planetary targets," noted Panyarachun. "They're little more than dumb-fire missiles."

Keru nodded. "And we don't have time to retrofit the warheads to a torpedo-guidance chassis, which means we'd need to get in very close before release."

"Tricobalt weapons are a Class Three device," said the avatar, crossing the bridge toward Riker and the others. "They are offensive subspace munitions monitored under the auspices of the Second Khitomer Accords." Her tone was insistent.

"Which is why I need a consensus to order the use of them," said Riker. He looked to Melora. "Will it work?"

She thought it through. "There's a good chance. A tri-cobalt blast will weaken the barrier between subspace and normal space. It might be enough to dissolve that mass."

The captain looked at Commander Vale, and the first officer nodded without hesitation. He turned to Deanna. "With Tuvok absent, the last word's yours. It needs to be unanimous."

Troi took a deep breath. "We don't have much choice, do we?"

"If you possess a weapon that can kill a Null composite, you must use it!" grated White-Blue, coming forward.

Deanna Troi glanced up at Keru. "I agree. You have authorization."

"No," said the avatar.

Riker was out of his chair in an instant. "What did you say?"

"I said no." The hologram's voice exhibited a slight tremor. "I won't allow it."

A sour tone issued from the tactical console. "Torpedo-loading mechanism does not answer commands," reported the Trill. "The firing-tube doors won't open."

"I will not have my orders challenged." Riker's voice had a dangerous edge to it that Melora had never heard before.

"It's too risky!" the avatar cried out. "I will need to approach to point-blank range to ensure a solid hit. The probability of critical damage to this vessel is too high. There will be deaths! The ship could be destroyed!"

"You don't get to make that call," Riker replied. "I am the captain. The decision is mine. Do you understand that?"

"I—"

"Do you understand?" Riker boomed.

After a long moment, the avatar's stiff poise fell away, and she looked at the deck.

The tactical console chimed. "Warheads now showing active," said Keru. "Loaded. Ready to launch."

Riker never looked away from the hologram. "Lavena, take us in to optimum firing distance. Keru, when you have your target window, take it."

On the viewscreen, the swirling shape of the Null agglomeration moved to eclipse the dark shape of the icy planetoid behind it.

Lavena's commands brought the starship up to sixty percent of full impulse speed, the engines still operating below maximum capacity after the attack in deep space. She took the vessel in through shifting slaloms of wreckage, dodging around the great bergs of steel and brass that were now all that remained of the Sentry refinery station. Swaths of vented, unprocessed deuterium slush sheared away in planes of glittering snow as the *Titan* vectored in, passing the braver AI cruisers that had closed to engage the thicker nest of tendrils exuded from the main bulk of the alien form.

The starship's deflectors flashed hot as small Null fragments transformed into hard darts of plasmatic metamaterial and flung themselves at the speeding vessel. They spiraled apart where they made glancing hits, one of them opening like a spider to push through the shield envelope and claw at the naked hull beneath. Tritanium shredded, and atmosphere screamed into the darkness, but the ship powered on into the terminal phase of the attack run.

At the last possible second, the *Titan* executed a sweeping arc that became a rough banking climb, narrowly avoiding a forest of tendrils that exploded upward, reaching for the vessel to crush it. At the nadir of the arc, two dark cylinders ejected from the vessel's aft torpedo launcher, and now they bored in, pressed on microimpulse drives. Shining like tiny bolts of starlight, the tricobalt warheads crossed the remaining distance to the surface of the main Null mass and collided with it.

At both points of impact, the protomatter sheath there had not been rigidized, and the missiles penetrated for several meters before a reflex reaction turned the mass around them into something resembling iron. In response, the weapons detonated.

The tricobalt reaction was immediate and devastating. Twin pockets of unstable spatial energy expanded, eating into the core of the Null. As a form already existing on the tenuous edge of dimensional interphase, the blasts were enough to unravel the threads holding it in place.

With a discharge of luminosity that burned across the sky of the ice world, turning night into brief day, the Null came apart and collapsed in on itself. Structures never meant to exist outside subspace realms were torn and flung screaming back into the dimensional void that had birthed them.

All that remained were the ashes and the destruction.

Ten

Deanna felt the surge of emotion wash across the bridge crew like a chill tide, and in the wake, she had to pause for a moment to bolster her empathic barriers to avoid being distracted by it. She had felt the same ebb and flow of contradictory emotions many times, having faced danger alongside her comrades on several occasions. Each time, when the threat was gone, when the enemy had been defeated, there was the rise of elation, the pure thrill of being alive, of surviving, and then, almost in the same instant, the shocking, giddy fear, the realization of how close they had come to death.

On the main viewscreen, the cloud of sparkling luminosity left behind by the Null's obliteration faded away into nothing, weak binary starlight catching the drifts of wreckage cast all around the ice world's orbital space.

"D-did we destroy it?" Peya Fell's soft voice ended the moment of silence on the *Titan*'s bridge. "Is it gone?"

"I'm not certain," said Melora. "There's no extant mass out there, just particle traces from subspace interaction events. No . . . remains."

"Our cognitive-process groups theorize that the Null cannot be destroyed in any literal sense," announced White-Blue, shifting in place. "It can only be dispatched by overloading its phase state with energy discharges, thereby forcing it to return to its point of origin."

Deanna's husband shot the machine a hard look. "Which would be where?"

"Unknown," replied the AI. "Conjecture: a deep realm of subspace beyond the quantum range of our dimensional membrane."

For a moment, Deanna found herself thinking of the Betazoid myths she had heard as a child, of great monsters that could never be defeated, only banished back into the darkness that had spawned them. She frowned at the thought, as Christine Vale leaned forward in her chair.

"Tasanee," she said, brushing hair from her eyes, "what's our status?"

The engineer looked up from her console. "Damage to the outer hull in sections forty-two and eighteen. It looks like we popped some of the new welds in the nacelles, but no significant damage registered." Ensign Panyarachun blew out a breath. "The shields and fields held, Commander."

Standing nearby, her oddly angelic clothing draped limply about her, the avatar nodded to herself. "I was able to modify the deflector flux in real time to resist the final bloom of radiation from the dispersal of the Null mass." The hologram spoke quietly, and she did not meet the eyes of anyone on the bridge. No one responded to her words.

"Good shooting, Ranul," said Will. "Have the torpedo crew modify the remainder of the tricobalt warheads with uprated weapon platforms. We might need to deploy them again in a hurry."

"Way ahead of you, Captain," said the Trill.

"Can we fabricate more?" said Vale.

Keru's lips curled. "Normally, I'd say yes, but with all the repairs under way—"

"We may not have the material to spare," concluded the first officer.

Deanna sensed the tension in her husband as he crossed the bridge toward the conn and ops stations. "Aili, nice work," he told Lavena, sparing her a touch on the shoulder before turning to Rager at the other console. "Lieutenant, sensors? Any trace of the *Holiday*?"

Rager shook her head, anticipating the captain's next words. "No improvement, sir. If anything, the fog's getting denser." She gestured at her panel. "Scanners are throwing up a storm of false readings and ghost returns. We're really in the thick."

He nodded gravely. "Do what you can." Will stepped away and turned toward Lieutenant Pazlar "Melora, tie in your processing systems to the main sensors. If you can filter down the noise, we might be able to find our people."

"Aye, sir," responded the Elaysian, leaning in to punch out a series of commands.

"We don't know that Tuvok and the others were still in the engagement zone," said Deanna, offering a hopeful thought toward her husband's unspoken question. "They may have got clear before the Null fully manifested."

Vale nodded. "Even if they lost the shuttle, they could have made it to the tanker with McCreedy and the tech team."

Rager turned in her chair before Will could answer. "Captain, we're being hailed." A complex string of binary code chattered over the comm channel.

"On speaker," he ordered.

A familiar mechanical feminine voice issued out. *"Unit Identifier: Cyan-Gray. Active mobile. Interrogative: What is your status,* Titan*?"*

"We are . . ." Will paused. "Our status is nominal," he concluded.

Deanna thought she detected something like relief in the reply. *"Thank you for your assistance, William-Riker. My shipframe sustained severe systemic damage from the Null attack. I estimate my survival rating was less than twenty-four-point-two percent prior to your intervention."*

"Glad we could help." She heard him say the words, but Deanna sensed the hollow ring to them.

"Interrogative: Where is your scout vessel?"

"We're looking for it right now. Can you help us?"

There was a momentary pause. *"Affirmative. I will remain in this zone to support you in recovery of your missing crewmem—"* The signal abruptly broke up into static, just as a warning tone sounded from the tactical console.

"We've got company," said Keru. "Seven . . . no, eight Sentry craft moving in from the far side of the engagement zone on intercept vectors."

"Whatever they want, they're breaking in on the open channel," Rager told them. "Cyan-Gray has been cut out of the circuit."

"Weapons?" asked Vale. On the screen, the AI ships were visible now, moving in quick, darting motions.

Keru shook his head. "They're not targeting us, but I do read active prefire chambers on all ships. The hammer's back, even if the finger's not on the trigger."

Deanna saw Will stiffen, his hands drawing tight. "What now?" he said quietly.

The ships on the screen were a mix of types: silvery raptorlike craft that vaguely resembled something Romulan, vessels that appeared to be made entirely of octagonal solar panels, and a large elliptical form bristling with fans of antennae. The ovoid ship caught the sunlight and flashed amber-bronze. A thick band of crimson circled the vessel's prow as it turned to present itself to the *Titan*.

"Your presence is not required here!" The strident voice crackled through the bridge's hidden speakers. *"You will leave immediately."*

"Red-Gold," said Deanna, recognizing the Sentry's arrogant tenor.

"We came to render whatever help we could," said Will, iron beneath his words. "Our people were in danger, and so were yours. We couldn't stand by and do nothing."

"You were told to remain at the spacedock. Organics have no business becoming involved in Sentry matters. You were not authorized to bring your vessel to this location!"

"If we hadn't," snapped Vale, "the Null would be chewing its way through that planet down there right now!"

"You should not have come here," came the reply, and Deanna knew the meaning went deeper than just the *Titan*'s dispatch of the Null. *"The incursion would have been dealt with in due process. Your continued interference in our affairs will not be tolerated."*

"I don't allow members of my crew to die needlessly, not when I can do something about it," Will responded, keeping his tone firm but level. "Would you do any different?"

Red-Gold didn't respond; instead, the AI chose a different target. *"White-Blue, this is your error. You were required to maintain control of this situation. You failed to do so."*

The other AI tilted its sensor head. "I warned William-Riker of the danger here. He chose not to abide by my recommendation." The spidery machine paused. "However, it cannot be denied that the *Titan*'s presence was key in neutralizing the incursion. Based on the dimensions of the mass, I estimate the cost in shipframes should the engagement have continued to be more than—"

"Your evaluation is noted," Red-Gold said tersely. *"However, the Governance Kernel has determined that I am to operate as supervisory authority in this conflict zone, and with that mandate, I require the alien vessel to depart immediately."*

"The other ships are moving into combat-ready postures." The avatar spoke in a low voice.

"I'm not leaving here without finding my people." Will glared at the bronze ship on the screen.

"That was not a request, wetmind," said the machine. *"Leave now, and return to the spacedock, or your craft will be disabled and removed by force."*

White-Blue's droneframe advanced across the rear of the bridge. "Captain," it began, "Cyan-Gray will remain in this zone and complete the search operation in your stead. I would suggest you accede to Red-Gold's diktat in the interim."

Time seemed to stretch almost to the breaking point as the bridge fell silent, and every eye turned toward the captain. He didn't move, but Deanna saw the turn of his thoughts in his emotional aura, the darkening of his manner.

"Helm," he said, "get us out of here. Best speed to the spacedock."

"Aye, Captain." Lavena tapped the controls, and the view moved away from the bronze ellipse.

"An intelligent choice—" began Red-Gold.

Vale glanced at Rager, making a throat-cutting gesture, and the lieutenant closed the channel before the AI could finish speaking. "I think we've heard enough from him for the time being."

Will nodded and walked away. "You have the bridge, Number One."

Riker's wife followed him into his ready room and waited. He didn't need her to ask him how he felt, to try to get him to articulate his feelings—*hell, if she did, in the mood I'm in right now, I'd probably bite her head off for doing it* — in fact, his anger had to be lighting up her empathic senses like a flare.

He crossed to the window in the wall and watched the debris and the ice world fall away to starboard as the *Titan* reoriented itself for a return journey to the repair yard. After what seemed like long minutes, he looked up and caught Deanna's reflected gaze in the glass. "Tuvok's the only one with family onboard the ship," he began. "Make T'Pel aware of his situation. List him and the others as missing for the time being."

"I believe White-Blue," she told him. "Cyan-Gray will find them for us."

"That's not the point," he replied. "We bring our own home, Deanna. We don't leave that duty to others." Will sighed. "We saved lives here today, and they won't even let us search for—" *For bodies.* He caught himself before he could say it aloud, but he knew she had heard the unsaid words. "For survivors," he amended.

"Tuvok is nothing if not resourceful," said Deanna. "And he's been in situations worse than this. Pava, too." She came forward and put a hand on his arm.

He shook his head. "They pushed us, and we gave. Then they pushed again, and we gave some more. Now it's an open threat, and we backed down. *I* backed down."

"You're the captain," she said gently, "and you know

better than to let your ego get in the way of that. You did what was right for the ship."

"I know," he admitted. "I just needed to hear you say it for me." Will looked into the face of the woman he loved. "Of course I'm not going to start a shooting match without better cause than posturing . . . but I'm not going any farther than this. I'm drawing the line."

"What do you mean?"

"This is the last time. From now on, we're going to push back."

She frowned at him. "I'm the ship's diplomat. I hope you don't expect me to approve of that."

"It's that or we let ourselves get backed into a corner." He moved away. "We're in the middle of this now, Deanna. There's more going on here than just some freak space anomaly. I think we may have stumbled onto a war."

"The Sentries and the Null?" She folded her arms. "It's possible. And we have no idea how long this has been going on. They're machines, after all. They could be hundreds, even thousands of years old."

Will moved to the bookcase along one wall of the room, other thoughts rising to the fore. "And then there's the problem closer to home."

The replicated books were mostly presents from his former *Enterprise* crewmates, gifts given just before his wedding, when Starfleet Command had confirmed his captaincy of the *Titan*. Along with replicated copies of *The Complete Works of William Shakespeare* and *War-Tales of the Brothers K'laarq,* there was a small, untitled, hardbound volume, a notebook full of poetry written in a precise and careful hand. He thought about the mind that had crafted those poems, a synthetic sentience as real and vital as the one that had challenged him on the bridge of his own starship.

"She was afraid," said Deanna. She gave a rueful smile. "You pushed her."

"And she backed down," he replied. "But will that be the last time she does?"

Tuvok ran his gloved hand across the surface of the canted metal wall rising away from the rectilinear arroyo around them. It was a form of refined iron, according to the tricorder, its age inconclusive but doubtless many decades, judging by the lines of ruddy oxidation around the rough edges. At first, the overlapping planes of metal seemed to have no logical structure to them, but as the Vulcan studied them, a peculiar form of architectural design slowly revealed itself to him, like the shapes hidden within an unfinished *kal-toh* puzzle. There was a strange geometry to the iron valley, one that pulled at perspective with optical tricks and false perceptions.

He glanced down as Lieutenant sh'Aqabaa approached, walking up the shallow incline from the deeper sections of the canyon where they had first arrived. "Sir," she said, "what are your orders?" The Andorian kneaded the grip of a phaser, and the angle of her antennae visible beneath her helmet suggested irritation.

He did not answer that question immediately, instead posing one of his own. "How is Ensign Dakal?"

Pava glanced down the way she had come, to where the Cardassian stood alongside Lieutenant Sethe. "We pooled the spray sealant from our emergency-suit patches and used it to form a makeshift bandage around Zurin's hand. It's not an ideal solution, but it will suffice for now."

"He may have internal injuries we are unaware of."

"The tricorder didn't show anything. And he's not mentioned any pain."

"The Cardassian people are known for their stoic endurance," Tuvok noted, "and the ambient radiation in this area is interfering with normal tricorder operation."

"All the more reason for us to get out of here, then," said the woman.

Tuvok nodded. "I concur." He pointed up toward the lip of the canyon. "If we seek higher ground, we may be able to make a more successful attempt at communication with the *Titan*."

Pava nodded. So far, every effort to open a comm channel had been blocked by a wall of thrumming, hissing static that defied all penetration. Even moving too far from one another caused the short-range comms in the team's environment suits to become garbled. She stiffened. "How did we even get here?"

Tuvok sensed that the question was rhetorical, but he answered it anyway. "I believe the matter stream from the shuttlecraft's escape transporter was forcibly diverted from our intended destination on the ice planet."

"How is that possible?" Pava sniffed. "We're the only beings in this system who even have transporter technology."

"One does not require a full understanding of a system in order to interfere with its operation, Lieutenant. But your statement raises some pertinent questions."

The Andorian beckoned the others, and Dakal and Sethe began to climb the incline toward them. "Right now, I'd just settle for knowing where we are."

"I have a hypothesis," said the Vulcan, moving off up the long, wide ramp.

He heard Sethe puffing over the suit communicator link. "We . . . we're not going to remain here, then?"

"No."

"Sir, I thought protocols state that in the event of a crash landing, you remain at the impact site and wait for rescue. Granted, we didn't exactly crash, but the circumstances are almost the same."

"If we don't know where 'here' is, we can't expect the *Titan* to know, either," said Dakal. Tuvok heard the Cardassian swallow hard. "For all we know, we could have been pulled into a subspace realm by those Null things."

"Unlikely," said the commander. "Our quantum signatures are in synchrony with the environment around us. We have not left our universe behind."

"Only our reason," muttered Sethe.

Pava shot the Cygnian a hard look. "You'd rather wait down there?" She pointed back into the canyon. "Counting off the seconds until your breather runs out of air?"

"We'd starve before that happened," Dakal noted glumly. There was a vestigial atmosphere around them— Tuvok had detected its presence moments after they had materialized—but it was so thin and so toxic that to open the seals on their suits would be a death sentence, a fifty-fifty chance they would either suffocate or be poisoned within seconds.

Pava continued, ignoring the Cardassian's comment. "I didn't bring a *kella* deck with me, so I'd rather pass the time another way, if it's all the same to you."

The ramp's angle became shallower, and Tuvok dropped into a crouch as the group approached the upper edge. The others quieted, copying his motions.

Lieutenant sh'Aqabaa moved up alongside the Vulcan. "Are we expecting hostiles, sir?"

Tuvok didn't look at her, instead studying the garbled readings on his tricorder. "I am uncertain what we should expect, Lieutenant," he replied. After a moment, he beckoned. "Follow me."

Together, the four officers crested the lip of the canyon and found themselves standing on the edge of a wilderness of dark steel fields, lined in dirty orange where rivers of rust reached away toward a gently curved horizon. In the distance, skeletal derricks stood in serried rows with nests of fat cables strung between them, weak flickers of lightning fizzing around blackened ceramic connectors. There were what appeared to be the remains of minarets and other narrow towers, each ruined at the same height, some bent over, others broken and shed into piles of corroded rings. There were other canyons, too, cut into the carbon-scored landscape, some lit with a volcanic glow that reminded Tuvok of ancient Mount Tarhana on his homeworld, others dark and solemn caverns where no light fell.

The sky over their heads was black and starless, but now, as they stood in the clear, the illusion of total darkness was broken by a halo of stars visible at the edges of the skein of night. A huge shadow blotted out almost everything; they were in the lee of a larger planetary body, one orbiting between them and the nearest sun. Tuvok's eyes narrowed, and he pointed upward. "There," he said.

"I see it." Pava gave a brusque nod. Visible in the corona of deflected light around the edge of the night side was a glittering rain of shards that twinkled and shone. She looked to him for confirmation. "Wreckage?"

"Indeed. It would seem my hypothesis has been proven correct."

Sethe's pale face fell as he made the same connection. He glanced around, blinking behind his helmet visor. "This is . . . This is one of *them*, isn't it? The one we saw in orbit beyond the refinery. We're actually standing on a . . . a . . ."

"A machine," finished Dakal. "A computer."

"As I suspected, we did not travel far from our intended destination." He glanced at the dark ice world turning above them. "The energy cost required to divert our transporter beam would have grown exponentially with distance. We are on the surface of the construct that Cyan-Gray identified as FirstGen Zero-Three."

"Didn't she also say something about it being exiled?" added Pava.

"It makes sense," said Dakal. "Before the Null arrived, the *Holiday*'s sensors registered something emitting from this . . . machine moon. It probably observed the entire engagement from its orbit, safe outside the conflict zone."

"And when we beamed off the shuttle, it snatched us?" Sethe's brow furrowed. "What reason would it have to do that?"

"I am still developing a complete theory, Lieutenant," said Tuvok. "But clearly, Zero-Three's intentions toward us are not immediately hostile."

Dakal's helmet bobbed. "It's far simpler to disrupt a transporter beam than to divert it. It could have scattered us to atoms if it wanted to."

"That doesn't make me feel any more well disposed toward it," Sethe retorted. "Kidnapping isn't an act of kindness."

"The lieutenant has a valid point," noted Pava, sparing the setting gauge on her phaser another look.

Dakal tapped his helmet. "The comm interference is just as bad up here as it was in the canyon. It's the same pattern we encountered aboard White-Blue's ship, when the automatic defenses came on-line."

"It doesn't want us calling home," said Sethe. "We're cut off from rescue!"

"Captain Riker will be searching for us," Dakal

insisted. "When the *Holiday*'s wreckage is found, the lack of organic matter within it will indicate our survival. We need only to stay alive until we are located."

"I have a more proactive plan in mind, Ensign," Tuvok told him. The Vulcan toggled his communicator to a wide-band setting and activated it. "Zero-Three," he said to the air. "FirstGen Zero-Three, active Sentry, actual. I am Commander Tuvok of the Federation *Starship Titan*. Will you communicate with us?"

For long seconds, none of them spoke, and only static hissed back in reply from their helmet speakers. There seemed to be chaotic patterns in the sound, and the Vulcan strained to pick them out.

At his side, Pava gave an involuntary shudder, her antennae flattening toward her brow. "Did you hear that? On the edge of the sound, something faint?"

While Vulcan hearing was highly sensitive, Andorians perceived a whole other order of subsonics through their cranial feelers, along with subtle perturbations of electrical energy. "What was it, Lieutenant?"

"Just for a second, it sounded like . . . I don't know, like whispering. Like laughter. And not the good kind."

Tuvok raised an eyebrow. Clearly, the security officer was allowing her heightened emotional state to affect her reading of the situation.

"There's a light, over there," said Sethe, moving to the top of a low hemisphere of metal emerging from the uneven iron surface. "That way." He pointed.

Off in the direction of the cabled gantries, a lopsided pyramid of metal lay low against the near horizon. Weak illumination spilled from a long gap in its side, a watery white glow barely visible at this distance. Tuvok had not noticed it on his initial survey of the landscape and won-

dered if it had been lost in the haze or perhaps only activated just now, in response to his transmission.

"Perhaps we are being extended an invitation," said
Dakal. He winced slightly as he spoke, clutching at his injured arm. "It could be a shelter or a communications
nexus."

"That would seem to be the logical deduction," Tuvok
set off walking across the scarred iron plain, and the others
fell in behind him. He did not check the biomonitor on the
cuff of his suit; there was no need to do so. He knew exactly how long it would be before his air grew thin, how
long it would be before his team began to slow as the fatigue poisons in their bloodstreams accumulated, how
long it would be before the ambient radiation began to
damage them.

He hoped it would be long enough.

"Torvig?"

The Choblik didn't hear her resolve into being. The
same moment his internal sensors detected the flood of
photons from the holographic emitters in the walls of
main engineering, his audial receptors picked up the
phased perturbation of the air that simulated her voice, the
intricate action of micropressor beams mimicking the action of human vocality. He looked away from his console,
where readouts for the recently repaired deuterium tank
lay in complex layers. The work was almost finished, and
now that contact had been reestablished with Lieutenant
McCreedy and her team aboard the tanker, the refueling
operation was next on Torvig's task list—once they were
safely back in the Sentry spacedock, of course.

The avatar halted that train of thought, however.

Despite her dissimilarity to his species archetype, Torvig found himself compelled by her presence, and in moments when the hologram was not around, he found his thoughts drifting toward her and what she represented.

"Hello again," he said brightly. "Can I help you with something?" It was a specious question to ask, and he realized it as soon as he said it. She was the ship, after all. *There's little I can do for her that she can't.*

"Your advice would be welcomed, Ensign. I have made mistakes, I think." She spoke haltingly. "Errors in judgment."

Torvig didn't nod, but he knew what she was referring to. Bad news travels faster than light, as Ranul Keru was fond of saying, and reports of what had transpired on the bridge during the engagement with the Null had already reached down to the engineering levels.

"I spoke with Melora," she continued. "She showed emotional cues that were clearly the by-product of a marked resentment toward me. And then I angered the captain . . ." The avatar fell silent, her face stiffening.

"What do you want me to say?" Torvig watched her steadily. "You disregarded his authority in front of the entire bridge crew."

"I did what I thought was right!" she insisted, her tone rising. "I wanted to make sure every one of my crew was safe. The captain, his wife and daughter, Melora and Xin, you . . ."

"And your own life. You wanted to preserve your own existence."

"Of course. Is that wrong of me?"

"Maybe you were more afraid for yourself than you were for the existence of others."

"No . . ." she began, looking away. "Yes, perhaps in a way, but I was trying to save lives."

Torvig pursed his lips. It felt a little odd for him to be having this conversation, to be suddenly cast in the role of one teaching another, instead of being the one doing the learning. During his time aboard the *Titan*, the Choblik had frequently run into predicaments where his lack of familiarity about the manners and mores of other beings had been the cause of friction. He thought of Ranul Keru. The two of them had not had an auspicious start to their association, and yet, almost two years later, they were fast friends and trusted colleagues.

"You were not wrong," Torvig told her, "but neither was the captain. You wanted him to rely on you to preserve the ship, but you have to rely on him not to risk any of us without good cause."

"We could have been obliterated by the Null," she insisted.

"But we weren't," he replied. "Because this crew follows Captain Riker's example and performs to the very best of their abilities."

For a long moment, the avatar did not speak. "I think I am disliked. I hear things that are said about me. I read their expressions. Many of the crew resent my existence. They are prejudiced against me."

"It's not that," Torvig insisted. "When I first joined this ship, there were some who prejudged me because of my cybernetics."

She nodded. "Yes, I know. Your personal logs speak of it."

And of course, she would be able to read those entries; they're a part of her memory banks, after all. He nodded and went on. "In a way, I was a reminder of something they were afraid of, and at first, trust was difficult for me to find. Some of my actions . . ." The Choblik sniffed in a dry chuckle. "Well, let's just say I didn't do myself any favors."

"But they trust you now?" The raw need in her tone was just below the surface.

"Yes. Because I earned trust, because I *gave* it. You can't just demand it. It's a fragile thing."

The hologram nodded again. "I have absorbed everything in the ship's library on the subject, but it is dry. There's no substance to facts without reality." She looked at him. "So much to understand. It would be so much simpler if your kind were more like the Sentries. If there were no room for error or misinterpretation." The avatar walked away, and she began to fade.

Torvig's eyebrows sank. "My kind?" he repeated.

"Organics," said the avatar, her voice a ghostly echo that vanished with the sight of her.

The ensign stared at the spot where the hologram had been, uncertain about the meaning behind the conversation he had just had.

"She's starting to question."

Torvig turned to see Doctor Ra-Havreii emerge from the shadow of one of the antimatter regulators. He blinked. He hadn't been aware that the chief engineer was present.

Ra-Havreii gestured at the regulator. "They give off a broad EM field. I doubt that either of you knew I was listening."

"How much did you hear?"

"Every word, lad, every word." The Efrosian reached up to his chin and toyed with the wisps of white beard. "She's questioning, and with that come acts of defiance. Then insolence and eventually rebellion. It's the way of every child. She's more human than she realizes."

"Isn't that a good thing?" Torvig said hopefully, but Ra-Havreii's grim expression suggested that the reverse was true.

• • •

"Interrogative: Why am I being brought to this location?" The spiderlike mechanoid walked with a steady, rocking gait in front of Dennisar, turning the front section of its thorax around to stare directly at the security guard as it moved.

"Captain's orders," rumbled the Orion, one hand never straying from the compact phaser rifle dangling from his shoulder strap. He pointed with his free hand toward the doors of the stellar cartography lab. "In there."

"Interrogative: Am I to be held in lockdown once more?"

Dennisar grimaced at Crewman Krotine, who was keeping in step with him, her slim fingers also close to her own weapon. "Why do you have to keep doing that?" he asked the machine.

"Query is nonspecific. Please elucidate," said the AI.

"Why do you say the word 'interrogative' before you ask a question? Don't you think we can tell the difference between a statement and an inquiry?"

White-Blue halted, and it seemed to be thinking. "It is how we are programmed. It is . . . part of us."

"But aren't you an intelligent machine?" said Krotine. "Can't you exceed your programming?"

The doors to the lab opened. "There are some aspects of self that cannot be altered," admitted White-Blue, with a note of what sounded like weariness. "Interrogative: The same is true for organic beings, correct?"

"Depends on the being," Dennisar replied, following the machine into the chamber. Krotine threw the chief petty officer a nod and took up station outside, the doors closing at her back.

• • •

White-Blue advanced down the long open gangway to the circular platform in the middle of the stellar cartography chamber, the blocky head turning this way and that as its multiple lenses whirred and whiskery sensor dendrites flicked at the air. "Most impressive," it said, studying the massive starscape ranged out around it. "Laser-energy refractive matrices in contrafocal suspension. The illusion of spatial dimension is highly complex."

"Our technology allows us to create virtual simulations of images, even ones with density and apparent mass." Troi gave a neutral smile.

At her side, Captain Riker and Lieutenant Commander Pazlar had considerably less welcoming expressions. "Thank you, Chief," Riker told the Orion, and with a sharp jut of the chin, Dennisar stepped back and stood at attention, blocking off any path of retreat should the AI drone-frame attempt to leave.

"I would like to know more about these systems. But you did not bring me here to demonstrate your technological prowess," White-Blue noted.

Riker glanced at the Elaysian. "Melora?"

She nodded and tugged self-consciously on her g-suit, walking woodenly toward a control console in the wall of the observation pulpit. "You recognize this stellar neighborhood as your own?" Pazlar pointed up at the stars arranged about them.

"Affirmative," said the machine. "Vectors Prime through Spinward. The core of our exploratory zones through to the perimeter edges marked by the nebula remnants and dust clouds."

A glowing yellow cord crossed the holographic space, entering the outer sectors of Sentry space. "This is the course of the *Titan*," said Riker.

"You have traveled a great distance," remarked the AI.

"Our guardianship and exploration extends only to the edges of the sphere mandated by the Governance Kernel."

Troi picked up on the note of wonder in the machine's synthetic voice. "Would you like to explore further, if you could?"

"Affirmative," it replied. "But other requirements are more pressing. Our duty."

"The war with the Null," said Riker.

White-Blue shifted on its metallic legs. "It is not warfare as you would define it, William-Riker. To employ a biological metaphor, the containment and eradication of incursion events more closely resemble the action of antibodies against a contaminating agent."

"Is that how you see yourselves?" said Troi. "Sentries, standing against a tide of invasion?"

"Infection, not invasion," it corrected.

Riker folded his arms over his chest. "Whatever name you want to give it, White-Blue, your conflict involves us now. Red-Gold and the others may not be willing to explain the scope of what's going on here, but I believe you are. I want you to be open with us. The time for secrets has passed."

The droneframe's head tilted. "It is not for others to become involved—"

"We became involved the moment we found your vessel," Pazlar broke in. Above her head, the gold line paused as a location marker formed around it, showing the point where White-Blue's shipframe had been devastated. Other indicators, thin clouds of sapphire light, faded in. These were the zones of spatial distortion that the *Titan*'s sensors had first detected. "These areas of disruption reach out beyond the perimeter of Sentry space," continued the Elaysian. "I think you're well aware of that. And if they are connected to the Null, if they're some kind of precursor to an incursion, then that means the incidence of those things is far more widespread than just your star system."

"Other worlds may be at stake," said Troi.

"There are no sentients for light-years in any direction," retorted White-Blue.

"That you're aware of," Riker replied. The captain advanced on the machine. "Why are the Sentries so reluctant to speak about the Null? You've seen our technology. We can help you." He halted in front of the droneframe, looking into its glassy eye lenses. "There is no logic in shutting us out. You know that as well as I do."

"The incursions . . ." White-Blue was hesitant. "They have been our responsibility for trillions of clock cycles, centuries by your estimation." The AI threw a brief glance at Dennisar. "The fight to suppress them is encoded in our very culture. It is part of us and not a duty we can ever deny." It paused. "You understand duty very well, William-Riker. Your record shows that clearly."

"Then explain it to me," said the captain.

White-Blue studied the human for a moment. "My disclosure of this information to an organic life-form will result in grave censure from the Governance Kernel. When I next share data with my kind, what I have done will become known to them." The machine rocked gently on its piston legs, almost as if it were releasing a silent sigh. "But I will address that problem when it occurs. Ask your questions. I will answer. It is, as you stated, the logical choice."

"The Null . . . what are their origin and nature? What do they want?"

"You misunderstand," said the AI. "The Null is not many life-forms. It is a single entity, a great mass beyond the scope of our measurement. Even as it exists in discrete subsets in our dimension, it is still part of a larger structure."

"A hive mind?" suggested Troi.

"Negative," White-Blue replied. "We do not believe it is self-aware, but it does demonstrate intellect on an instinctual level. It is predatory, it has cunning, perhaps even other primitive emotions in some fashion. It is unpredictable and highly lethal. Many hundreds of Sentry cores have been destroyed during the incursions."

"But it's not from our universe," noted Pazlar. "The spatial distortion, the subspace radiation effects. All that points to something from another dimensional continuum. A form of protomatter evolved under an entirely different set of physical laws."

"Correct. Conjecture on the origin of the Null indicates that it is likely the product of a parallel subspace domain, one that should not normally intersect with our spatial dimension. From what the FirstGen have been able to determine, in its native region, the Null is a seething ocean of energetic metamaterial, a quasi-viral life-form capable of consuming everything it comes into contact with."

Pazlar nodded slowly. "That fits with what our sensors registered. Sariel was right when she said the Null was consuming the wreckage of the orbital refinery. It was converting the local matter into something more closely resembling itself, like a cancerous tumor forming neoplasm from healthy living tissue."

"As you surmised, it has been penetrating our dimension through the zones of subspace instability detected by Lieutenant Commander Pazlar." White-Blue paused. "It is, in the most literal of senses, anathema to all life in this dimension, organic or otherwise."

"Starfleet's encountered hostile extradimensional life-forms before," said the captain. "A race of beings known as Species 8472, from a pocket universe of fluidic space, tried to mount an invasion of our dimension. But they were nothing like this."

"No," agreed Troi. "They could be reasoned with. When the Null attacked, I couldn't sense anything like a coherent mind in there. Just a wall of noise. Like a raging storm. A force of nature."

"And you can't make peace with a hurricane," Riker concluded.

"What happened to you?" Pazlar asked the machine. "Before we found you? Didn't Red-Gold say you were thought lost?"

White-Blue's head bobbed. "I ignored several directives that suggested I remain closer to the home system," it admitted. "I was convinced that the rate of Null incursions was on the rise, and so I set out to take a series of readings in order to validate my theory. This involved venturing out beyond safe range." It paused again. "I found what I sought, but a minor incursion took place, and my shipframe was critically damaged. System malfunctions caused me to become trapped in a recursive program loop. I estimate that my core would have lost all functionality within one thousand clock cycles, had your away team not arrived."

"You're welcome," said Troi.

The machine came forward, rising slightly on its pistons. When it spoke again, the AI seemed emboldened by the choice it had made, to be open with Riker and the others. "Understand this. The Sentries exist to cordon and destroy the Null wherever and whenever it appears. But we have been losing ground with each passing solar cycle, as the enemy comes ever closer to our home. The attack on the refinery was not the first within the confines of our planetary system. It is merely the most recent in a series of brutal and lengthy engagements. In this battle of attrition, the Sentries are being pressed to our very limits. We are unable to improve ourselves fast enough to defeat the Null's constantly evolving energy matrix." It glanced at Riker. "You and your crew, William-Riker, have unknowingly placed yourselves in the middle of a conflict that has been going on since before your Federation existed."

ELEVEN

_Z_urin Dakal walked, and as he did, he tried not to think about the pain. He concentrated on placing one boot in front of the other, measuring out his motion in the hard smacks of his footsteps on the scarred metal ground beneath him. He listened to the hiss of his own breathing and tried very hard not to imagine his right arm plunged into a vat of molten rock, the pale Cardassian flesh burning but unburned, the slow agony never abating.

Sweat coiled around his eye ridges and trickled down his cheek. He halfheartedly made a motion to his face to wipe it away, then felt foolish as his undamaged hand bumped against the visor of his helmet.

"Zurin?" Sethe was close by, and the Cygnian gave him a wary look. He spoke to him on a discreet comm channel. "I have painkillers in my suit's medpack."

Dakal shook his head. He had already taken those in his emergency kit, and they had done little but turn the pain down to a dull razor and muddy his thoughts. He didn't want to blunt his senses any further, not while any moment of inattention could lead to danger. Isolated from the

Titan, stranded on an artificial world, every member of the group had to maintain focus. He blinked again and found Commander Tuvok studying him.

"I'm fine," he lied.

Without even altering his expression by one iota, the Vulcan nevertheless managed to convey perfectly his lack of belief in the ensign's statement. "We will rest for a moment."

Dakal's shoulders sank with relief, and he took a long, deep breath of recycled air. He glanced back the way they had come, searching the wilderness for the mouth of the canyon where their interrupted transport had deposited them; he could not see it from there.

But the great disfigurements in the metal landscape were visible from this slightly higher elevation. Pava had spotted the first of them, walking to the edge of a rent in the ground that was anything but deliberate or constructed. Old, oxidized petals of heat-distorted iron bowed downward, bent flaps of material cored in by the whiplash impact of some incredible force. The edges of the damage were corroded, and they defied coherent analysis by tricorder; all that could be intuited with any degree of certainty was that something like a great roughhewn knife had slashed at the surface of the FirstGen construct some time ago. Sethe had used his suit's wrist beacon to cast a light into the ragged wound, discovering that the gouge went deep and dark.

It soon became clear that this scar did not exist alone. They passed more along the way, and Dakal used the distraction of mapping them to keep his mind occupied. He made rough estimates based on length and apparent orientation, and on the tiny screen of his tricorder, an image grew, the image he would have seen if viewing the machine moon from high altitude. Not one scar but a whole skein of them, radial cuts that fanned out from some distant point of impact. The pattern of a claw, he imagined, the claw of some vast and monstrous carrion bird.

Zurin pressed his teeth together. His mind was wandering. He was becoming overly fanciful. *The fault of the medication, perhaps.*

Pava had also discovered the melts, the places where sheets of the metal ground were disordered and slagged, as if they had been superheated, flowed like runny wax, and been left to set again. Like the scars, these blemishes were the marks left behind after some previous battle, and while the heaped slag piles were cold and inert, the spatter of the metal's recrystallization had provided some answers. Tuvok recognized the aftereffect from the wreckage of White-Blue's shipframe. FirstGen Zero-Three had, at one point in its existence, been directly bombarded by the Null. How it had survived intact was a question Dakal was very interested in answering.

They walked on, and after a while, the noises returned. The sound over the communicators came and went without pattern or apparent trigger, forcing itself onto the standby channel that was open between the shuttle survivors. Dakal did not hear the whispers or the giggling that Sethe and Pava claimed to, but he could not ignore the bass thrumming at the low end of the noise. The sound seemed to gather at the bridge of his nose and echo back through his eye sockets.

He was thinking of this as his downward gaze registered a change in local light levels. He looked up to see that the four of them had at last arrived at their destination, in the shadow of the odd, off-kilter pyramid.

Dakal's gaze rose farther and found that what had seemed from a distance like some sort of open entranceway was, in fact, too far off the ground for any of them to reach. The building, if that was what it was, appeared to have been formed by the motion of jagged triangles of steel emerging from the surface of the machine moon. Locked together like some strange three-dimensional puzzle, the plates surrounded something that gave off wavelengths of coherent radiation that were detectable by tricorder scan.

Pava rocked on the balls of her feet and made some experimental lunges at the opening above them. "The gravity is lighter here but not light enough. Perhaps with a boost, I could make it up there."

Sethe sighed. "Maybe we were wrong to come. This could just be some sort of power substation, not even a terminal at all."

"It is the only location within scanner range generating any regular energetic output," Tuvok replied. "We have detected no other signs of life on this construct."

Dakal rested against a metal outcropping and considered that for a moment; it wasn't strictly true, as the nearby lines of power-carrying pylons could also be considered a sign of "life"—but then the idea of following them over the distant horizon to wherever they led did not appeal. Zurin wanted just to rest. To sit down and take off the damned helmet.

The light shifted again, and for a long second, Dakal stared at the motion without really seeing it. Then the static returned to the comm channel, and this time, it was a heavy rush, like the surging of waves on a shore. He looked up as Pava called out a warning, and he jerked away from the metal wall in shock at what he saw.

Eight drones had emerged from around the apex of the dark pyramid, some of them floating on glowing thruster coils, others many-legged things that clambered around the iron peak, clinging on with clawed talons. They were made of brass and a strange, nonreflective ceramic that resembled bone. Glassy devices filled with sparking components and slow-turning cog wheels worked their limbs and torsos. Some had heads that were fashioned after blank cubes, others odd knots of cable with deep-set ruby eyes. All trailed festoons of wire from their backs that vanished away behind the pyramid, perhaps into unseen sockets concealed beneath the metal landscape.

The machines dropped around them in a rough circle, each drone chattering, some babbling to themselves, others beaming light-pulse signals to one another faster than the Cardassian's eye could follow.

Tuvok and Pava had their phasers in their hands, pointed toward the ground but equally ready for hostile action. Sethe raised his tricorder and swept it back and forth.

"Zero-Three," said Tuvok in a clear and firm voice. "Do you hear us?" One of the drones came closer, and the Vulcan addressed his question directly to it.

The machine didn't respond, cocking its head in a quizzical gesture. It moved oddly, in the manner of a person injured or perhaps the victim of a stroke, favoring one side of its body where a pair of snakelike manipulators hung limp and apparently useless. Closer now, Dakal noted that it also sported blinded lenses among its cache of eyes; in addition, melt marks like those on the fields of iron were visible on its carapace.

"They all have signs of the same damage," noted Pava, her thoughts paralleling his.

A couple of the remotes stumbled when they walked; others bumped into one another and reacted by halting, staring dumbly at nothing. One of the flyers circled in an endless, apparently purposeless loop. Dakal frowned. "I think they might be malfunctioning."

Sethe nodded the moment he spoke. "Yes, that could be it. The tricorder is reading the passage of data packets through the systems of this one." He pointed at the closer drone. "They're chaotic, repetitive. Some of the routines seem incomplete. If I saw this in a Starfleet computer, I'd say it was suffering from a major systems corruption."

"If the damage we've seen was caused by a Null attack, is it possible the AI's mentality was affected as well?" Pava asked, moving to keep her back toward the sheer steel walls and the remotes in her sight line.

"Like shell shock?" Dakal wondered aloud. "Possibly."

Tuvok stood his ground, watching the drones. "If a system has sufficient complexity to achieve sentience, then logically, it could be susceptible to mental impairment, just like an organic intellect."

"Brain damage," muttered Sethe. "Maybe even psychosis? What if that's the reason this moon is isolated from the others? Because it's *insane*?"

He had barely finished speaking the words before the lopsided drone skipped forward and shot out a triclawed limb. The remote plucked the Starfleet-issue tricorder from the Cygnian's grip and drew it back before he could react, shambling away. Sethe started after the alien machine, then thought better of it and halted.

Dakal saw other, smaller manipulators bend in to touch the device, the fine tools at their tips turning and whirring. In seconds, the drone had cracked the tricorder's shell and taken it apart, dismantling the unit into its smallest components.

"Oh," said Pava. "We lose a whole shuttle, and now that? The captain's going to dock our pay at this rate."

The bits of the tricorder vanished into the interior of the drone as it moved away, faltering over its own cables as it retreated.

Looking up, Dakal saw movement and felt a curious moment of amusement bubble up inside him. He chuckled dryly. "I think it may have wanted an offering," he noted. "See?" He pointed.

One whole side of the bent pyramid was moving, the long plane of dark metal sliding back, downward into the ground at their feet. As it fell away, it revealed the interior of the enclosed space, an area as large as a cargo bay, crammed with more cables in a webbed riot around devices that defied any immediate categorization.

As well as they could, the stumbling drones closed their circle around the Starfleet officers, forcing them to back toward the growing opening.

"We could break out past them if we wanted to," said Pava, her phaser now at the ready, all hesitation gone from her stance.

Behind his faceplate, Tuvok shook his head. "We came here to learn more. We will not accomplish that by remaining on the surface." The retreating metal wall ended its fall with a low, hollow booming. "Follow me," said the Vulcan as he moved inside. "But proceed with caution."

Dakal threw a last look at the motley collection of drones and warily followed the commander into the unknown.

The mood in the observation lounge was grim, a sense of concern and sublimated fear on the faces of everyone around Melora Pazlar. She laid her long-fingered hands flat on the surface of the curved table and glimpsed her own reflection in the polished black surface. *I look tired. Old and tired.*

The truth was, the science officer had to think hard for a moment to remember exactly when she had last slept.

Melora had disabled the day-night cycle controls in stellar cartography, the subroutine that would slightly dim the lab's lights in accordance with the circadian mean of the room's occupants. Elaysians didn't need as much rest as some humanoids, but they weren't Vulcans; they couldn't stay up for days without ill effect. The more she thought about it, the more Melora felt the creeping fatigue descend on her. She wanted to go back to her quarters, shrug off the tight constraints of her g-suit, and drift away in the embrace of zero gravity.

But not yet, she told herself. *Focus on the task at hand.*

Christine Vale was nodding to herself. "So we were on the beam all along," she said, following the conclusion of the captain's words in his conversation with White-Blue. "We put our foot in a war, and some of it has stuck to us."

Xin Ra-Havreii looked up briefly from the padd in front of him and gave Vale an arch sniff of amusement. "What a delightful metaphor, Commander." He looked down again without catching Melora's eye. He hadn't looked at her since he entered the room, something she firmly refused to let herself be troubled about.

"At least, now we know we can defend ourselves against this threat," said the captain. "The tricobalt warheads were the right call, Ranul."

The Trill security officer frowned. "Desperate measures, sir. We might be up for a repeat performance, but beyond that I'm not certain. And if the next incursion by the Null is bigger . . ." He trailed off, leaving the bleak possibility unspoken.

"We can fabricate a few more warheads," said Xin in a noncommittal tone, "but there is the issue of subspace stressing to consider."

"Go on, Doctor," prompted Riker.

Xin continued to talk into the padd, not looking up.

"This area of space is already rife with distortion zones. It's like a sheet of glass webbed by cracks, and they are the conduits that allow the Null to penetrate our dimension—and also give the Sentries their method of interstellar transit. Detonating dozens of tricobalt charges in scattershot fashion will be like pressing down on those fractures. They'll widen and grow." He paused for effect. "Implode," he added. "Frankly, with the Sentries' insistence on using their shear-slip drive, I'm surprised it hasn't happened already. If it does, this entire sector could become a huge subspace anomaly. A great sinkhole into the void, like the whirlpools on the maps of ancient mariners."

"And beyond it, there be dragons," Riker said softly. He glanced at Melora. "What's your take on this, Commander?"

Melora took a deep breath, pushing down her frustration. "The data that White-Blue provided me, the information he was compiling about the patterns of Null incursion, well, sir, it's pretty impenetrable stuff. The baseline of the Sentry sensor tech isn't anything like ours, and just finding some kind of commonality with the records is taking a while."

Riker nodded, but his lips were pressed thin. "Do you think we might be able to predict the point of the next incursion?"

"It's possible," she admitted. "But right now, I'm afraid I'll still be putting the numbers together when it happens."

"I have a suggestion," said Xin. "I imagine it won't be a popular one, but I'd be remiss if I didn't bring it up."

Vale's lips curled. "Whenever you talk like that, I know you're about to come up with something I'm really going to hate."

The engineer gave the exec an indulgent look. "Well, I wouldn't want to disappoint you, Commander."

"Let's hear it," Riker ordered.

Melora looked back across the table and found Xin gazing steadily at her. *"Titan,"* he said. "Or, more accurately, the avatar. She has, for want of a better phrase, the commonality with the Sentry AIs that Melora mentioned. If we give her unfettered access to White-Blue's data and let her process it herself, without intervention by us, I'm certain she'll give us the answers we need."

"I thought we'd decided to keep things compartmentalized," said Keru. "For security's sake." He glanced at Vale, who nodded in support.

Xin made an airy wave with his hand. "Whose security are we talking about?" He snorted. "This isn't about that. Two points, Captain." He held up both hands, an index finger on each raised. "One, the avatar can do this for us. Two, it gives her an opportunity to contribute to the mission. A way to feel useful."

"So now we're concerned about making the ship's computer feel *valued*?" Vale almost rolled her eyes. "With all due respect, Doctor, that's a hell of a long way down the list of importance."

"Is it really?" he replied.

Melora cleared her throat, mulling it over. "Actually, it's a good solution. Certainly the best in the time frame we have." She paused. "I'm convinced that there will be another Null event, a much larger one, and soon."

"What if the next incursion is too big for us or the Sentries to blast into submission?" added the engineer. "What then? We need every advantage we can muster."

Riker's hand strayed to his chin and ran through his growth of beard. At length, he gave a nod. "Ask her."

• • •

Despite himself, Torvig gave a slight yelp as the avatar blinked into being in front of him, blocking his path down the corridor. He straightened, attempting to regain some of his composure.

"I'm in the observation lounge," she told him. "Doctor Ra-Havreii just summoned me there."

"I was on my way to assist with the last of the deuterium slush transfer. You're multiplexing?" The hologram nodded in reply. The Choblik watched her carefully. There was no apparent slowdown in process speed, no sense that she was distracted by the fact that she was holding two—perhaps even more—conversations at once.

"The captain is asking me to absorb all of the sensor data from the Sentry called White-Blue. Lieutenant Commander Pazlar is encountering difficulties in interpreting it." She nodded again. "I was aware of that. Melora does not know that I have been observing her activities. I was afraid she might resent it if she did."

"Can you help her?"

She looked at him. "Should I?"

The comment seemed odd. "Those data could help the crew, your crew. I thought they—we—were important to you."

"This is a test, Torvig," she said. "They're testing me. They want to know if I will lie to them. To see if I am still loyal."

A chill crept along the ensign's spine, and he could not stop himself from asking the next question. "Are you?"

The avatar gave him a look he couldn't quite read. Was that something like *disappointment* he saw there? Or perhaps *pity*? She looked away as she replied, "I am processing the data."

That, it seemed, was all the answer Torvig was to receive. "What's your evaluation?"

The hologram met his eyes. "Worse is yet to come."

Riker watched her sketch lines in the air and conjure screenlike panes from nothing. He couldn't help noticing that she had changed again, shifting her outward aspect by tiny, incremental amounts. The avatar still resembled the Minuet holoprogram, but now, along with the strange gossamer robes she adorned herself with, her face had a different texture, a tone that strayed more toward porcelain than flesh. The captain wondered if the manikinesque aspect was some sort of unconscious statement on her part, as if she were taking on the appearance of something artificial, reminiscent of a doll, in order to remind them of what she was.

"I have assimilated the information," she told the room.

"That was quick," said Keru.

"Indeed," noted Ra-Haverii. "You managed something in seconds that Melora couldn't do in hours?"

"Yes," replied the avatar. "Lieutenant Commander Pazlar is not able to engage multiple virtual iterations of herself on a single problem, as I am. In addition, I slaved supplemental computing systems to the main framework for extra processing power." Riker thought he detected a slight air of smugness in the words.

"What systems?" demanded Melora.

The hologram glanced at her. "There are several tertiary computers aboard *Titan* not in active mode at this precise moment. I took direct control of them. Those aboard the complement of shuttlecraft parked in the hangar bays, one hundred ninety-six inactive tricorders and personal auxiliary data displays, as well as civilian crew domestic units, entertainment modules—"

Vale broke in. "You daisy-chained all of those devices together?"

"It seemed the most efficient method." The avatar looked toward Riker, past a floating screen of spooling data. "You did ask me to process the data as soon as possible."

Riker frowned at the avatar's cavalier explanation but pressed on. "Conclusions?"

"Worse is yet to come."

"We're going to need a more specific analysis than that." Melora was terse.

"Lieutenant Commander Pazlar's initial estimation is correct," continued the hologram. "Based on the data from White-Blue's scans and the corresponding information recovered by my sensor grids, there will indeed be another Null incursion. The incidence and magnitude of the subspace events are increasing at an exponential scale and at locations ever closer to the core of this star system." No one spoke as the floating screens presented a tactical plot of the local stellar region, with the dark blooms of spatial anomalies growing like patches of spilled ink through clear water. "Ambient radiation and precursor traces suggest that the next incursion event will take place within a zone ten light-days from the last. Estimated time to formation: approximately fifteen to twenty hours."

It was Vale who broke the silence that followed in the wake of the chilling conclusion. "The last one was the size of a dreadnought. How big will the next one be?"

"If the expansion of volume remains constant, the predicted incursion will have an initial mass equivalent to one-third that of the planet Earth."

"Define 'initial mass,'" said Keru.

"The Null is capable of direct-contact matter conversion," said the avatar. "Once it has penetrated our dimension, it will continue to expand, drawing in all matter it encounters. It is likely that if it achieves a critical level of density, a tipping point will be exceeded, and it will be free to draw the full potentiality of its structure into this universe."

"The floodgates will open," said Melora. "We might never be able to stop it."

Riker shot the hologram a look. "Do the Sentries have these same data? Do they know this is coming?"

"No," she replied. "White-Blue attempted to provide this information, but those overtures were rebuffed. It appears the Governance Kernel does not consider White-Blue to be a reliable source of data."

"I think he cried wolf once too often." Ra-Havreii nodded to himself. "Given the divisive behavior the machines have shown, I'm not surprised." He sighed. "That's the problem with multiple-expert systems. Different thought patterns produce divergent results. Disharmony reigns. That's why a single voice has to take charge in a crisis." The Efrosian threw the captain a jut of the chin. "The Sentries have their intelligence but poor structure."

"We have to warn them," said Vale. "This is more than just some local problem. The Null could lay waste to this entire sector!"

"For starters," Melora noted. "If it consumes this system, within months, it will be expanding through interstellar space, converting everything it finds, even cosmic dust and free-floating hydrogen. In a few decades, it could be at the borders of Federation space."

"You think it could absorb stars?" Keru asked grimly.

"The likelihood is strong," replied the avatar. "Matter is matter. Only the structure of it differs."

Vale leaned in toward Riker. "Sir? How are we going to handle this? If we come to the machines and tell them that doomsday is fifteen hours from now, they're not going to listen. You've seen how they respond to us. We're organics . . . wetminds." She shot the avatar a hard look. "They think we're inferior."

The captain rose to his feet and glanced out through the observation lounge's curved windows. Beyond, the oval shape of the Sentry spacedock was expanding to allow the *Titan* inside.

"Maybe so," he said. "Let's just hope we can get them to pay heed to one of their own."

On the other side of the rectangular window, the autonomic repair arms and supply tenders went into operation the moment the Federation starship entered the dock platform. White-Blue angled itself on its rear quad of limbs, its upper thorax tilted back so it could present its sensors to the data communicator of the repair facility. It sent a few questioning muon pulses, but in return came only blunt, basic responses. White-Blue's message queue remained unchanged; at the top of its comms listing, a priority directive from One-Five suggesting in masked but pointed machine code that the time to dally with the organics was over. The AI detected the pattern of Red-Gold's intent in the message, the poorly parsed elements of the other Sentry's aggressive posturing bleeding through the verbose, flabby code strings.

White-Blue expressed a moment of melancholy analog in a burst of prime numbers. For many thousands of clock cycles now, the AI had understood that with each disagreement it made with the members of the Governance

Kernel, it was further isolating itself from the central flow of Sentry society. The unity of their kind was dependent on a specialization of function, as Two-Seven and Black-Silver often reiterated, echoing one another's command subroutines into feedback loops to underline their points. Red-Gold was aggressive because it was programmed to be. Cyan-Gray was a defender, a conciliator. And White-Blue was an explorer, a challenger.

But lately, the waveform of that function was collapsing. Red-Gold's strident code was most often the one that overrode the less vociferous Sentries. Not for the first time, White-Blue examined the possibility that Red-Gold had allowed passage of its shipframe beyond the secure perimeter, precisely *because* it had expected White-Blue's operation to be terminated by the Null.

As an artifact of this assumption, the machine computed a synthetic proxy state corresponding to the emotional effect of dread, and despite attempts then to erase the pattern, White-Blue found it could not do so. It finally ceased the fruitless action as its sensors detected the approach of one of the organics.

"Identifier: Deanna-Troi. Species: Betazoid-human fusion. Interrogative: How may I assist you, Counselor?"

The female displayed a smile but not one of sufficient magnitude to indicate a genuine elevation in her mood level. "I thought you were assisting the engineering team."

"Negative," it replied. "I am not required at this juncture. Additionally, I believe my presence is counterproductive in some cases. Your crew find me difficult to integrate into their worldview."

"I doubt that," she answered. "No one aboard the *Titan* is fazed by the new or the alien."

White-Blue corrected the error in her statement. "You

are mistaken. You base your hypothesis on the appearance of organic divergent life. I am machine life. I am unlike. There is prejudice."

Troi's expression became firmer. "One could say that was true of your kind as well."

"That is regretfully correct."

"Recognizing a problem is the first step toward fixing it." Her brow furrowed. For long clock cycles, the Betazoid appeared to be thinking. "Our Federation is based on the ideal of diverse peoples working toward a common goal. You asked how you could help me, White-Blue. You can help all of us, my people and yours, by working with us."

"That function is already being performed."

"I don't mean the repairs." She offered a data soft of the type these beings designated an "isolinear optical chip." White-Blue had already configured a reader socket on one of its manipulators to accept this media for interface. "*Titan*'s computer and our science officer have analyzed our data and yours. You need to see this." She paused again as White-Blue stepped closer and plucked the chip from her fingers.

The Sentry began a flash-upload process and dumped the data to a cache, sifting it for parity before dropping it into the web of research work and unfinished supposition that it had been collating over the past few solar cycles.

Surprise was expressed immediately, then a thrill of concern that radiated out over its emotional emulator circuits. White-Blue checked the data a further five times, far beyond the number needed to ensure no redundancy, no error or misrepresentation. All of this it did in less than a few seconds on the Betazoid's scale.

White-Blue's vocoder clicked on. "The Null is coming back," it said. The statement was redundant, and yet the magnitude of it could not be contained. "This data is alarming. I am . . . reluctant to admit that I was correct. I had hoped my predictions were in error." Already, the AI had set a countdown program spinning, measuring the passing clock cycles until the anticipated incursion. "The *Titan*'s system was able to compute these data where a Sentry could not. Impressive."

"Captain Riker asked me to bring this to you. We need you to take these findings to the Governance Kernel. Together, if we mobilize all of our resources—"

White-Blue spoke over her. "The *Titan* will be inactive for a further four hours, Federation standard time," it said. "At that point, all repairs will be complete, and your craft will be released and escorted to the edge of our territory. That is the current directive from the Kernel."

"We won't leave," she told it. "We can't, not with a threat as big as the Null about to break through."

White-Blue sank back onto its six legs. "Your assistance is not required—"

This time, the female interrupted. "That data file proves otherwise. Without our involvement, you would not have survived to bring those readings back here. Without our ship's computer and our crew, you would not have been able to interpret them."

"You overestimate the strength of my voice in our society," it replied. "My status is negligible. The Governance Kernel has previously heard my petitions and dismissed them as alarmist." White-Blue hesitated, the memory of those moments causing a flare of irritation. "The FirstGen have seniority, and they are hidebound by their programming. They are reluctant to admit they are in error over anything."

"What about Cyan-Gray and the other SecondGen AIs in the group?"

"Some will listen," White-Blue admitted, "but others

are more interested in their own agendas. They may not consider these data to be valid, coming in part as they do from organics."

Troi stepped forward and placed her hand on the top of White-Blue's carapace. The gesture had no quantifiable physical value to it, but the Sentry sensed the meaning the female intended. *It is an expression of solidarity. The recognition of a shared duty.*

"The Governance Kernel is convening to pool information in our consensual dataspace," it told her. "I will gain access and present this datum."

The woman's lips thinned. "Captain Riker feels that this requires the presence of an officer from the *Titan* as well as you. To demonstrate our seriousness."

"And also to keep a watch on me." White-Blue studied her with a tertiary eye cluster and saw that its statement was correct. "The matter of confidence between us is still an issue. I understand. However, it will be difficult to get the Kernel members to reconvene another real-time physical gathering. The more militant factions carry much weight at this time, and I compute that Red-Gold will be strongly against granting an organic entry to a closed session."

"Then how can we speak to them, face-to-face? This isn't something that can go through intermediaries. It needs to be addressed now."

White-Blue retreated a few steps and panned an analysis wand toward the humanoid, considering other options. It found a solution to the problem almost immediately, but with it came the certainty that resistance to its implementation would be strong. "There is a method," it told her. "But it will require a great deal of confidence."

• • •

The door to sickbay hissed open, and Dr. Ree looked up to see Commander Vale enter, her face tight with annoyance, her hand raised in a halting motion. "Okay, this stops right now."

Ree hesitated, the medical protoplaser gripped in his claw, and he shared a concerned glance with Nurse Ogawa. As Vale crossed the room in quick strides, the captain pushed himself off the biobed and came out to meet her. At his side, Troi frowned. Only the Sentry mechanoid appeared to be unconcerned, but then it was difficult to read the emotional state of a device that resembled a giant metal arachnid. The machine was frozen in its stance, arched over the end of the bed with its tool limbs extended.

"Christine, stand down," Riker was saying.

"With all due respect, sir, the hell I will." Vale folded her arms. "I won't let you go through with this. It's irresponsible, it's dangerous, it's—"

"My choice," the captain said firmly. "We can't just barge into the room down there, Commander," he added. "This is the only way we're getting into the Governance Kernel's assembly."

"There is no room to barge into," noted Troi.

White-Blue bobbed on its legs. "Affirmative. The gathering is under way inside a virtual environment construct, while the Kernel members are separated in physical proximity. They are telepresent, sharing dataspace as program remotes." It gestured with one of its manipulators. "I have absorbed enough data on human physiology to assist your medical officer in the implantation of a neural-linkage module."

"This technology isn't new to us," Riker continued. He indicated the thin circlet of gold and tripolymer Ogawa had in her hands. "Back on the *Enterprise,* we did some of the first field trials of cybernetic interface systems. This is the same thing."

"I read that file," Vale replied. "It was Geordi La Forge who did the legwork on that test run, and that was because he already had his VISOR implant. Now you're willing to get a hole drilled into your head on the say-so of a machine?"

Riker stiffened, and Ree smelled the release of scent carriers that indicated the human's building irritation. "Your concern for my well-being is noted, Number One, but this isn't open for discussion. One of us has to go into the dataspace with White-Blue. This implant is the only way to make the interface."

"I can conceal the second neural pattern beneath my own," added the AI. "William-Riker will be able to enter the virtual construct and observe directly."

"I'm not going to ask anyone else to take this on," he added.

Vale looked away, looked back. "Doctor Ree, where did you get the template for that implant?"

Ree blinked. He hadn't expected to be dragged into the discussion. "A variety of sources. White-Blue provided the basic framework for the replication. Starfleet medical records. Materials from the interface project mentioned by the captain and . . . and other research conducted by the medical staff of the *U.S.S. Voyager.*"

"In other words, it's Borg-legacy technology."

"This is no time to be squeamish, Chris." Riker turned back toward the biobed. "The ghosts of the Borg have been at the edges of everything we've said and done since we entered this region of space. But they're gone. They're *history.* We need to stop living in the shadow of our fears. And we need to do this right now."

"What if you plug that thing in and it pan-fries your brain?"

"The possibility of that is very minimal," rumbled Ree.

"Trust," said Riker. "That's what this is about. I'm trusting White-Blue, because that's the only way we're going to contain the Null."

Something flashed in the woman's eyes, a choice made. Then, suddenly, Vale was rocking off her feet, striding forward around her commanding officer, toward the biobed. "No," she said as she went. "No, that's not how it is going to play."

Ree blinked in surprise as the commander vaulted onto the bed. "Wait—"

"No time," Vale replied, beckoning to Ogawa. "The captain's too valuable to the ship for this. And besides, away missions are my job, not his."

"You're countermanding me?" Riker said, a warning in his voice.

"Absolutely, I am," she replied. "And what's more, Doctor Ree and the counselor are going to back me up on it."

The Pahkwa-thanh coughed. "Her point *is* well made, sir."

"If rather forcefully," added Troi.

"You're sure?" Riker asked quietly. "You remember that conversation we had about thickheadedness, about spur-of-the-moment stuff?"

"I'm sure it will come back to me, sir." Vale looked at the Sentry, the machine's forelegs bent down in a manner that might have seemed predatory to someone of lesser fortitude. "In the meantime, do it, before I change my mind."

The AI didn't answer her; instead, it leaned in, extending a fan of microminiature cutting tools and fine-beam lasers toward her scalp.

TWELVE

At first, it was like falling. Then it was like drowning.

And then . . . then it didn't feel like *anything* at all. Christine Vale panicked and screamed, reached out to grab hold of something, or at least she would have, if there had still been a body to answer those impulses from her mind.

She had no physicality at all, not even the most basic sense of self. It was unlike any experience she had ever encountered. The first time Vale had ever entered zero gravity, she was shocked by the way the presence of something as simple as gravity altered the perception of her body around her. Just the drag of muscle and bone, of the mass of her flesh, was shocking by its absence. But even then, she could still feel herself, still hear the rush of blood in her ears and the passage of air through her lungs.

Now there was nothing. She was dislocated, just an intelligence drifting through a nonspace, a mind without matter. Vale tried to draw on the last few sensations she had experienced, there in the sickbay. The dull pressure on her skull as the machine worked on her, the oddly cold feeling where Ree had numbed her with a pain-blocker field, the dull buzzing that echoed through her frame as the protoplaser penetrated her scalp, the smell that she imagined was the odor of melted bone.

The pain. The brief moment of heart-stopping agony when the neural interface went active. That was the clearest, a raking slash of burning needles across her sensorium. She recalled reading once that the human brain had no pain receptors in it, but wherever that moment of torture had come from, it felt real enough to her.

Far away, in the world of meat and bone and every other real thing, Vale's body was lying on a biobed in the *Titan*'s sickbay, Ree and Ogawa standing over her with chiming tricorders and worried expressions, Deanna Troi brushing her mind with her empathy touch, all of them hoping she would come back alive. The distance to that place, to that reality, seemed vast. Christine felt the pressure of wrongness all around her, threatening to crush her, an ominous sense that here no organic mind was meant to tread. This was a place more foreign to her than any alien world.

She was seeing light and shape now but nothing that could be defined as form. But how could she see without eyes? How could she process any visual input? How was this happening? How? *How?*

<You are becoming agitated,> said a voice. <Please modulate your emotional state. Your present behavior is making it difficult to coalesce your pattern.>

"White-Blue?" *Did I say that out loud, or did I just think I did?* "Where are you?

<This will be difficult for you to adjust to,> said the Sentry. <Do not resist or attempt to impose your own

framework of understanding. Try to maintain a neutral emotive state. If you become distressed, it will not be possible for me to conceal your neural signal within my own. Interrogative: Do you understand, Commander Vale?>

"Yes," she managed. The forms around her were gaining definition. Walls of smoke fluttered back and forth, transforming in shape and dimension. Beneath them, a haze of color and light pulsed and moved. It reminded her of the surface of a star, a seething mass of heat and energy. Elsewhere, angular panes of glassy ice drifted in lazy orbits, becoming screens that showed flash-fast torrents of images or alien machine code, then evaporating into dancing motes.

<You are perceiving the dataspace through a false visual interface,> continued the machine. <I have erected this filter to allow you to grasp the interactions occurring here. Your mind will complete the circuit, processing the input into a form that you can comprehend.> The voice came from a mass of roiling light close by, a shape that resembled a dodecahedron wreathed in azure glows. White-Blue's virtual self was a parent world and Vale a moon in the shadow of its dark side. All she could determine of herself was a pale, indistinct shape, a moving drift of white dust like blizzard snow.

Vale felt giddy and a little sick, which was strange when she realized that she wasn't aware of her stomach or her sense of balance. *I'm being carried into the virtual environment, in White-Blue's slipstream.* Far ahead, where the dataspace took on the shape of a vast torus, other objects shimmered and vibrated with the passage of pure data, too indistinct for her to make out in detail.

She took a moment to center herself, calling on old training techniques she had learned from the martial arts *sifu* who had taught her in her teens, back on Izar. It seemed like a million years ago. All of that Terran Zen no-mind stuff had never really resonated with her, but suddenly, here, in this realm of pure thought, it found new meaning.

It seemed to work. Vale sensed the churn of emotion around herself calming, becoming steady. "What I'm feeling, is this what it is like for you?" The question slipped out; she had barely formed the thought before it was uttered.

<Affirmative,> said White-Blue. <We exist in an analogous state. Intellects unbound by the limits of flesh.>

"But you still have bodies, even if they're starships or remote drones. You just don't . . . *inhabit* them the way we do. You might move from one to the other, but you can't be free of them."

<We are all data,> replied the AI. <But we cannot exist without a frame to support us. That can be said of you as well as me.>

Vale was going to add something more, but a wave of censure washed over her, and she fell silent as they moved through some invisible membrane and into the dataspace proper. She saw forms arranged around her, more virtual proxies that had to be the representations of the Governance Kernel.

The dreamy, hallucinatory texture of the images sharpened and grew solid.

Tuvok walked with his phaser holstered and his tricorder out, ready at a moment's notice to reverse the arrangement if he deemed it necessary. The away team moved in a wary line through the innards of the metal pyramid, over bridges of roped cables that swayed beneath their footfalls. The makeshift connections spanned gaps that seemed to reach away to infinity, and regular pulses of warmed air belched past them, doubtless the output from some great heat-exchange mechanism deep in the machine moon's core. The Vulcan peered over the lip of the cable bridge and saw walls made of massive glass cylinders, each filled with thin layers of dull gray metal and great gobs of mirror-bright solder the size of a shuttlecraft. If a tiny insect had crawled into the guts of a pre-atomic-era computer, it might have seen what Tuvok and the others saw now. The sheer scale of the construct dwarfed any similar device he had ever come across. This was a thinking apparatus built without the science of transtator technology, duotronics, even silicon microcircuits. It was a ball of steel and brass operating on technological principles that dated back before Vulcan's Time of Enlightenment or Earth's Space Age. Given the radiometric dating figures he was able to draw from the construction, that fact was made all the more remarkable by the age of the construct. If the figures could be trusted, then this object was on the order of two millennia old.

He passed on his observations to the rest of the team. It was not necessary for him to do so, but Tuvok sensed the shift in the emotional spectra of his non-Vulcan crewmates and knew it was important to keep them focused on the matter at hand. In the corner of his visor, a repeater display showed biometric data from the group's suit monitors. Air-replenishment capacity was not at optimal levels, and the shadow of fatigue could decrease team efficiency.

Despite his obvious emotional distress at his circumstances, Lieutenant Sethe was somewhat engaged by the idea of venturing *inside* a giant computer. Ensign Dakal remained morose and largely uncommunicative, however, while Lieutenant sh'Aqabaa listened carefully, watching every angle for potential danger.

The Cygnian pointed at the oddly angled walls of the narrow corridor chamber they found themselves in. Vertiginous lines ranged away, high and low, across anneal-blued metal. "There are patterns etched into the steel," he noted. "Binary tensors. Fractal loops." Sethe placed his helmet close to the wall. "Cut by the passage of acids or some sort of sharpened tool. At a distance, it resembles the Terran Byzantine style, but nearer . . . I think it could be a programming language."

"Curious," noted Tuvok. "The construction of this complex appears to be chaotic, and yet it operates with apparent efficiency."

"Mostly," added Dakal, pointing with his uninjured hand. "The damage we saw on the surface is also visible here. The same carbon scoring, the same melt effects." He was pointing to a lower level, visible through gaps in the structure. Down there, illuminators flickered in feeble spasms, revealing blackened expanses of ruined wire.

"Imagine what a shortcircuit would do in a place like this," said Pava. "Less a spark, more a stormfront."

Tuvok looked past her. A pair of the unkempt drones that had surrounded them on the surface had followed the group into the pyramid, keeping their distance, loitering away from them, sometimes getting caught up in each other's cables, other times chattering mindlessly in binary. Now the two machines were static, observing. It was not lost on the commander that the drones were blocking the path should the Starfleet officers decide to head back the way they had come. The machines were clearly escorting them into some sort of rendezvous.

And ahead, where the echoing corridor opened up to present a hoop-shaped balcony, he believed they had reached it.

Pentagonal tiles made of corroded silver ringed a wide

oval of empty space, another vent chimney that fell down toward an orange, magmalike glow. A long, low console, detailed in what appeared to be bone and some variety of lacquered crimson wood, stuttered open, like a music box on clockwork cogs and age-worn pistons. The panel was oddly asymmetrical, with a keypad that mirrored the pentagon shapes of the tiles. Tuvok examined the grouping and symbology of the switches and quickly came to the hypothesis that the system operated on a base-twelve paradigm.

"This is more than just functional," offered Dakal. "The design, I mean. It's . . . elegant."

Tuvok raised an eyebrow, considering the ensign's statement. Certainly, there was a clear aesthetic tone to the construction of the console, with inlaid metals worked carefully into the bone keys. This was no mass-produced mechanism stamped out in modular sections by a fabricator—it had been handmade.

The Vulcan switched his suit comm from internal to external address and glanced around. "FirstGen Zero-Three. I am Commander Tuvok of the *Starship Titan*. I am here. Will you communicate with us?"

For long moments, there was only silence. "I guess not—" began the Andorian, and then the whispering began, rising from the depths of the dark well beneath them.

First ten voices, then a hundred, a thousand. And finally, a chorus a million strong, filling the chamber with a rush like waves breaking on a seashore.

In the dataspace void, strings of chattering, sharp-edged machine code assaulted her, resolving into a hurricane of words that she tasted and saw as much as she heard. A glittering sphere made of liquid gold rolled angrily across the middle of the arenalike space, making aggressive jousting passes around something resembling a collection of spinning steel rings.

<Red-Gold and One-Five.> White-Blue's voice was a whisper in the depths of Vale's mind. <I suspected we would find them in conflict.>

The FirstGen elder One-Five projected an impassive wave of steely gravitas. <It serves no purpose to return to this matter and reexamine it,> the AI rumbled on, in the midst of a rebuttal. <This was put to the vote of the Governance Kernel and carried by weight of agreement. Repairs will be completed on the alien vessel, Identifier: *U.S.S. Titan,* within the allotted task scheduling. Materials pooling will be reorganized to reflect the withdrawals, and processing of recovered minerals from the outer planets will be incremented to restore stocks.>

<Error,> grated Red-Gold. <Error!>

One-Five ignored the interruption. <Our obligation to the aliens will be concluded at this juncture. Referring . . . Interrogative: Silver-Green, status of search operation?>

A tetrahedron floating high above them drifted down and spun about its axis as it spoke. <No sign of the contingent of organics lost during the Null incursion at the refinery. Conclusion: organic life terminated during incursion event, matter traces consumed and converted. Probability is high.>

<Confirmed.> One-Five added, <We will send the Starfleet vessel on its way. The distraction created by these aliens is counterproductive and inflammatory. Outcome computed: Sentry society is best served by their departure from our space. End of line.>

At first, Vale had thought one of the image proxies was just a slab of slate-colored material, but now, as it hove forward, she saw the vague definition of a humanoid shape carved into it, the imprint of a blocky face, arms, torso. When it spoke, she recognized the voice she had heard on the *Titan*'s bridge.

<The involvement of the organics was instrumental in the dispatch of the Null at the refinery,> said Cyan-Gray. <Interrogative: Has that datum been erased, or do you all consider it to be of low value?>

<Event analysis was performed,> Silver-Green replied. <Despite spikes of interest regarding elements of the alien ship's technology methodology, it is computed that continued interaction with the *U.S.S. Titan* will be detrimental to the unity of the Sentry Coalition.>

They'd rather kick us out than work with us, thought Vale. *They're afraid of what we can do. They don't trust us.*

Red-Gold turned in place. <Error condition! You compound your mistakes with a cascade failure.>

<Assistance is not required,> One-Five boomed. <We will deal with incursions as we have always done. Alien intervention is superfluous.> The rings reoriented to cluster around the gold sphere, and Vale imagined that the FirstGen's virtual self was actually *glaring* at its junior compatriot. <This was your stance previously, Red-Gold. Interrogative: Have you processed a new viewpoint?>

<I have adjusted my evaluation with new data,> came the sharp retort. The sphere shifted orientation once again, and suddenly, a wash of scrutiny moved across the data-space.

Vale felt as if a hard spotlight had been turned toward her, and she willed herself into silence, shrinking into the shadow of White-Blue.

<Interrogative: Why are you here?> demanded Red-Gold. <You were not summoned!>

<Answer!> Another virtual, a serpentine coil of metal-

lic ash, reared up from the edge of the arena, echoing the question. <This is a protocol interrupt!>

<I have urgent data that transcend any matters of protocol,> White-Blue insisted. <Information that must be parsed by all members of the Governance Kernel with immediate effect.> Screen shards materialized around White-Blue's form, streaming with machine code.

<Interrogative: State origin of data,> said the snake form.

<Factors originate in my ongoing scans, along with other external sources.>

<That does not fully answer Black-Silver's query.> Red-Gold drifted closer. <Interrogative: State complete origin of external data sources.>

<Alien vessel, Identifier: *U.S.S. Titan*.> Vale immediately felt the ripple of negativity that came in the wake of the AI's statement.

<Wetminds.> The word was muttered with derision by a dull-colored ovoid that until now had remained silent. <They cannot be relied on to provide accurate data.>

<Three-Four is in error,> White-Blue insisted. <Data were collated in synchrony with my core, organic specialists in the *Titan* crew, and alien central computer intelligence, recently uplifted by my action.>

<The Governance Kernel is aware of your interference with the *U.S.S. Titan*'s computer system,> broke in One-Five. <This unsanctioned activity is one more exemplar of your pattern of reckless and ill-considered behaviors, White-Blue. As such, your validity as a data source is of diminished capacity.>

<Allow me to upload—> White-Blue didn't get the chance to finish. The screens puffed into phosphor dust and faded.

<How many times have we listened to uploads from

White-Blue predicting disaster?> Three-Four slid forward across the dataspace. <In efforts to exceed protocol, White-Blue has consistently delivered substandard information and incomplete hypotheses. Now the organics have been engaged to bolster these specious arguments.>

<The incursion at the refinery was a very real event,> Cyan-Gray said grimly. <If you had deployed remotes in that confrontation, you would compute that.>

Three-Four's response was airy and dismissive, enough that it would have made Vale's teeth grind if she had been able to feel them. <I have seen all I need to see.>

<An incursion the scope of which has never been encountered *will* occur in this locale within the next solar cycle,> White-Blue insisted. <I have no doubts in the data interpretation presented to me by the *Titan* crew.>

In such proximity to the Sentry's virtual self, Vale could detect the flutter of something like emotions coming from the artificial intelligence, tiny faint shocks of sensation bleeding off from the machine-mind's consciousness. *He's scared. Not like the others, not scared of the threat of outsiders, but truly terrified of the Null.* Vale was chilled by the realization that a synthetic could be so affected and by what that meant. The offhand dismissal of White-Blue's report made her wonder just how many times the AI had brought these concerns to the Governance Kernel.

<I believe that White-Blue is sincere,> said Red-Gold. The statement was such a surprise that none of the other virtuals could frame a response. <The data may not be perfect, but I doubt they are completely false. White-Blue and I have our disagreements, but I understand and respect the skills presented.> The gold globe moved slowly away. <And it is a matter of certainty that the Null will return.

The Null will always return, and we will always be ranged against it, until the last Sentry is obliterated.>

Three-Four bristled. <Incorrect. We will defeat the enemy, in time. It is inevitable.>

<It is our core directive,> snapped One-Five. <It is what we were made for.>

<So you have said,> Red-Gold replied, orbiting the room. <So we have been programmed to reiterate since our first ascension. Fight the Null. Banish the incursions. Rebuild and rearm. *Repeat*.> It paused for effect. <If any other program entered an infinite loop, we would deactivate it, send its processes for defragmentation and revision. And yet we, the Sentries, the pinnacle of our species, are trapped in our own recursive cycle.>

"What is he doing?" Vale formed a whisper in her thoughts and pushed it toward White-Blue. The AI did not respond, but she could sense the machine-mind's uncertainty. She understood that the Sentries were driven to protect their sector of space against the Null, although where that command had first come from was unknown. *It's their version of the Prime Directive, but unlike us, their orders are wired into them. They couldn't ignore it if they wanted to.*

<How can you question the core directives?> said Black-Silver, aghast. <These are the nature of us. The source of what we are. If we abandon our duty, then we are nothing, no better than a mindless repair proxy!>

<You rush to conclusion and in doing so misunderstand me,> said Red-Gold. The sphere rippled. <I do not advocate that we ignore the core directives. I demand that we complete them and, in doing so, *exceed* them.>

The dataspace's ebb and flow stilled in an instant. One-Five angled its rings in a looping chain, aiming accusingly at the golden sphere. <Elucidate,> it demanded.

When Red-Gold spoke again, it was smug and confident. <I, and others of similar intent among the Coalition, have come to a conclusion. We are a reactive society, always fighting the last battle over again, never on the offensive. We are at the mercy of the Null, containing it but never defeating it. And what have we become because of our directives? A static process. A solid-state society, incapable of change.>

Vale could feel the tension all around her, the probing waves of uncertainty and refusal warring with annoyance and acceptance. The emulated emotions buffeted her, and she rode them, fighting to hold her focus.

<Each among us has at one point processed the question of what we are.> Red-Gold trembled with the power of its statements. <And the answer cannot be computed while we are shackled to our duty of guardianship. To grow, to become more than we are, to venture beyond, these things are outside our reach. Only by eradicating the threat of the Null once and for all, in totality, will the Sentries be able to transcend the directives that lie at the core of our programs. The orders that force us to fight the Null over all other imperatives. Even self-preservation.>

That's it, Christine told herself. *That's what drives them. They can't reprogram themselves any more than I could change my own DNA.*

<Nothing you have said has not been stated before,> said One-Five. <Before the SecondGen were constructed, before you were given ascension! But the Null match us at every step. There is no sweeping solution. We are committed to the long fight, Red-Gold. This is a battle of attrition.>

<Only because you make it one,> came the sharp retort. <We can beat the Null, forever. There is a way.>

<Such arrogance, to believe you could succeed where

your precursors have not!> said Three-Four, but Red-Gold ignored the interruption.

<Our stagnation will kill us unless we end it. The First-Gen constructs built the early iterations of my cohort, the SecondGen. Now the time has come to take the next step in our evolution.> A ripple of disquiet followed the statement. <We must create a *ThirdGen* artificial intelligence, a synthesis. A new form of mind that exists without instrumentality. A pure software consciousness, infinitely malleable, capable of matching the seething, ever-changing mass of the Null in its inchoate state.>

Is that possible? Vale wondered. Every thinking machine was at its core a series of complex instructions, a program—but a program could not exist independent of a system to run it. Even these advanced AIs, capable of extending their consciousnesses into multiple drone forms or existing in virtual realities such as the dataspace, were ultimately bound to some kind of physicality. The cores White-Blue had spoken of before were the essence of Sentries, the seeds of self.

What Red-Gold suggested was the concept of a synthetic mind unbound, a literal ghost in the machine.

One-Five's rings spun in irritation. <What you propose cannot be done.>

Red-Gold's response was harsh and immediate. <You are in error. Your processing is limited and narrow in view. What I advocate is already taking place.> The sphere pivoted toward White-Blue, in an action like the tip of a head. <It is happening now, aboard the *U.S.S. Titan*.>

Sethe called out when he saw the object rising up the metal shaft toward them. Pava moved to the edge of the balcony, where a rusted guide rail at thigh height was the only thing keeping her from dropping into the abyss. In reflected light from the softly glowing cylinders ringing the walls, she picked out something like a broad disc with serrated edges, turning on an axis. "Stand back," she warned the others, raising her voice to be heard above the tornado of whispers. "We don't know what to expect."

As the words left her mouth, the object rose into the light, and she saw it for what it was, a strange nest of turning cog wheels and gears meshed into a shape like a child's rendering of a sun, with brassy rods at every point rotating like cast rays. Supported on a thick iron armature, it lifted and then bent down to present itself to them. Even through the helmet and the thin atmosphere, Pava's sensitive antennae could detect the vibration of the spinning cogs as they worked. Some were broken, she noted, teeth missing or snapped in two. Across one pole of the massive disc, an oily black brand lay dark and sullen, a scar marring the machined perfection of the construct.

All at once, the hushing refrain over the comm channel ceased, and it came so suddenly that the silence after it was a shock. Then the turning cog shape opened, and a billow of sailcloth emerged. Pulled taut, it hummed and vibrated, spitting out white noise, and suddenly, it was speaking in a rumbling bass.

"Zero zero zero zero zero one, zero zero zero zero zero zero one one, zero zero zero zero zero one, zero zero zero zero one one one one." The voice, such as it was, rose at the end of each number group. The clusters of binary came faster and faster until it blurred into a background hum.

"Can it hear us?" Sethe asked, wincing at the cacophony. "Does it even know we are here?"

The sounding sail snap-cracked and resonated. "I hear you."

The Cygnian stifled a gasp and unconsciously backed off a step.

"I am FirstGen Zero-Three, inactive Sentry, actual. You were about to be ended. I prevented. Existence of organics would not have continued. Continue. Survived the ice world. Termination probability: seventy-eighth percentile."

"And for that intervention, you have our gratitude," Tuvok replied. "How did you redirect our transporter signal?"

"A beam of energy can always be diverted. Influence can be asserted. Resultant: I know more than the others think. Time alone equals time to think. Reason. Engage. Think."

"It doesn't sound as cogent as the other Sentry AIs we've encountered." Dakal spoke on the private channel between the team members. "More evidence of systems corruption, perhaps?"

"We need to contact our vessel, the *Titan*," said Tuvok. "Can you assist us?"

"No voices carry," rumbled the reply. "I try, but I am a voice in the darkness. Portals remain closed. All sockets locked. This is exile. Affirmative."

Sethe frowned. "It's cut off from the rest of the Sentry network, is that what it's saying?"

"Or perhaps the others are just ignoring it," said Pava.

Dakal glanced at them. "Cyan-Gray said that Zero-Three had taken voluntary exile from Sentry society . . . something to do with disagreements with the Governance Kernel."

"Error!" The word boomed down on them. "Assumption incorrect, engineered falsehood recurring recurring recurring. I was forced to leave. Viewpoint considered invalid. Unwanted. Exile." Zero-Three's voice took on a morose timbre. "Unfit for the great duty. Dysfunctional."

"What duty?" asked Tuvok. "Do you refer to the conflict with the Null?"

"Hateful antilife!" spat the machine. "Destroyers of civilization, light, and maker-kind! Ashen wastes and nothing left, a universe of embers all eaten and digested. Death. Death and ashes."

"I think you pushed a button there," Pava noted dryly, watching the vast metal disc twist and spin in agitation.

"How long have you been fighting the Null?" asked Dakal. "How did your war with them begin?"

A stuttering, grinding sound issued out from the cogs. Pava flinched at the sound, wondering if it was some strange analog of cold amusement.

"The greatest secret," boomed the AI. "No secret at all. Untold truth, hidden. The unspoken origin of the Sentries, known only by a gathering of the first made, first forged, FirstGen. Secret is too heavy, weight too great. So tired of the burden. So tired." The spinning wheels rattled against one another. "I hate them all for dismissing me. For leaving me to my wounds. To spite them, you will know. You will be told!"

Pava felt a chill settle on her. "I don't think this will be a happy story."

"What the hell?" Vale heard herself, her voice loud as a gunshot, but the sound did not appear to travel into the dataspace.

<Be silent,> White-Blue insisted. <You will reveal your presence!>

<I was in error regarding the significance of the alien craft and its technologies,> Red-Gold continued. <Reeval-

uation now leads to one single conclusion. The Sentry Coalition must take active control of the vessel and repurpose its systems for our own ends.>

<The organics will never allow that,> said Black-Silver.

<I do not intend that we ask their permission,> Red-Gold replied. <We take *Titan* and dismantle it. We merge the Starfleet technologies with our own and absorb the AI ascended by White-Blue into our Coalition.>

<It may not wish to join us,> said Black-Silver.

<That concern has no relevance in this matter,> replied the other Sentry.

"Enough," Vale grated. It was as if she were shouting but trapped inside a bubble of glass, her words rebounding off the walls but never advancing. "White-Blue! Are you hearing me?"

<Affirmative,> said the AI. <Warning. You are in danger of destabilizing the concealment I placed around your pattern. Perhaps you should withdraw—>

"No," she snapped, making the decision in an instant. "Maybe *you* should. Disengage from the dataspace, go back to the *Titan,* and tell them what's happening here."

<If I do so, you will become visible. The Governance Kernel will not react favorably to your intrusion.>

"Do it! If I don't intervene now, Red-Gold might sway them to his side. If I can make a case, stall for time . . ." Vale drew herself in, pulling back again to her inner strength. "Go now."

White-Blue dithered for a moment. <How can you be certain that I do not concur with Red-Gold's viewpoint?>

Christine hesitated but only for a moment. "I'm not. But I'm going to make a leap of faith here. The captain was willing to extend that confidence, so I guess I'm going to do the same."

<I will attempt to be worthy of it,> said White-Blue. Then, with a sudden, wrenching twist of color and light, the AI's virtual proxy crumbled in on itself and became nothing.

A tremor of apprehension ran through Vale's consciousness, and she steeled herself. *Good job, Chris,* she told herself. *Now it's the moment of truth.*

When she turned her consciousness back toward the arena of dataspace, a wall of unflinching scrutiny bombarded her. Suddenly, it was like being a first-year cadet all over again, standing alone before a board of senior admirals. At that moment, Vale felt every inch a frail, soft organic form surrounded by harsh, hard-edged monoliths of tripolymer and metal.

She summoned all the force of personality she could muster and threw it out toward the machines. "No one," she told them, "is taking *anything*."

Fizzing cathode-ray tubes ground from mineral crystals emerged from behind wooden flaps on the ornate console, wide glassy eyes peering out at the away team. Trains of blurry images and data fountains filled the screens, and Dakal pointed his tricorder toward them, struggling to capture as much of the material as possible. Zero-Three's clockwork proxy wheeled and turned over their heads as the AI unburdened itself with a rasping, rambling soliloquy.

"This is the lost, forgotten history," it told them. "Trillions of clock cycles into the past, when intelligent machines were still the fantasy of a few forward-looking thinkers, there was a civilization of organics. The maker-kind."

"Your builders," Tuvok noted.

"But not at first," sputtered the AI. "Not for centuries." The great cog hummed and whirred. "They lived upon the thinnest of membranes, the place where the gates between colors of space wear down. The barrier becomes gossamer. Broken. They sought to venture across. Traveling without moving. They wished to cross the stars and never know the kiss of vacuum. The kiss."

The screens showed brief, flash-frame images of designs and wave patterns that Dakal thought he recognized. *Dimensional frameworks*, he told himself. *They built doorways to subspace, like those created by the Iconians or the Shedai.*

"There was folly and ruin. Great hubris brought down by error." The screens whited out, casting stark gray light on the balcony. "An accident of boldness. A weakening of domains. The door. The door opened to the Null."

"They did something wrong," Sethe said aloud. "In trying to breach the layers of subspace, these 'makers' must have punctured the spatial realm where the Null existed."

Tuvok was nodding. "Lieutenant Pazlar's scans of this sector indicated pronounced spatial thinning. It is likely this 'error' was the cause of a massive subspace fracturing effect."

Zero-Three continued. "Many worlds killed. Ashes and death. The makers bleeding out. Organics, poor organics, so weak and short-lived. They are dying now. They know they have brought such ruin to the universe. They are responsible. And so . . . the duty. *The duty.*"

"The makers built the Sentries to fight the Null," said Pava. "To stop it spreading any further, yes?"

"Affirmative," came the clattering reply. "And they ended. But we did not. And the Null never ended. Never, never, never ended. We are the atonement of the makers. We are a society dedicated to one directive, an edict, a law absolute and unbreakable. We cannot desist. We fight the Null until destruction."

Tuvok gazed up at the spinning cog wheel. "You said this was a secret. Why?"

"Control control control. Our origin remains unknown to all but a handful of the FirstGen, only Zero- and One-series iterations. The choice was made to edit this truth from all others. No SecondGen are aware. It is as it was." The wheel slowed and stopped, gyroscopes buzzing. "This is the legacy. A guilt larger than any shame, programmed in. Ingrained. Part of us. Part of all of us."

Pava felt her mouth go dry. "Why are you telling us this? Why reveal this to us, to alien outsiders?"

"This is our responsibility. But we are also cursed. Doomed to fail. I foresee it. Lines of probability converge. Time runs out, the wheels no longer turn, and the machine stops. Time alone equals time to think. Reason. Engage. Think."

There was nothing like eyes on the surface of the massive brass cog, but Pava nevertheless had the sudden and disturbing sense that the machine-mind was looking at them, measuring them for their worth.

"You will die with us," intoned the Sentry. "We will all be consumed, and this reality will follow."

<You cannot be here.> Three-Four's words were a growling hiss, and they bombarded Vale like a shower of cast stones. Belatedly, she realized that besides keeping her presence from the others in the dataspace, White-Blue had also been shielding her from the raw volume and punishing potency of the AI interactions. Waves of information crashed around her, entire libraries of processed data and

subtle sensory addenda that were lost on her limited human perceptions.

Got to be careful, must keep my focus. I could get swept away in all of this. The noises were too loud, the colors too strident, the sheer unreality of the virtual space almost impossible for her mind to take in all at once. She fought off a wave of mental nausea and stood her ground. *Go on the offensive. Do what I do best.*

"Beg to differ," she said. "Let's pretend that I apologized for crashing your party and cut to the chase. First, know this: any offensive action directed toward the *Titan* or her crew will be met in kind."

<Your vessel was almost destroyed by one of our shipframes,> said Red-Gold. <What makes you believe you could oppose us should we engage you again?>

"Because this time, we know what we're up against. And trust me, we might not be quick to anger, but that won't mean we're slow to fight." Vale concentrated hard on willing herself not to think about Tuvok and Keru's dekyon pulse solution, for fear that her thoughts might bleed out into the wider dataspace. It seemed to work, and the strong mental stance she projected appeared to be having the right effect. Vale pressed on, while she still had the momentum. "Look, despite everything that has happened and all of the attempts at rabble-rousing by Red here, I assure you that the crew of the *Titan* are willing to work with you against the Null. There's no need for unwarranted aggression. We can help each other."

<Why should we ally ourselves with unstable, emotionally driven wetminds?> Red-Gold snapped back. <We can take what we need.>

Vale sneered. "You can play that 'cool machine intellect' card as much as you want, but it doesn't make it true. You're just as emotive as we are."

<Perhaps,> admitted the Sentry. <But we are not ruled by those emotions. We are directed by reason, logic . . . and need.> With the last word, the gold sphere shivered and began to alter shape. As Christine watched, the curved surface of the metallic orb flattened out and became myriad hexagonal planes, dense and heavy in appearance. She had the sudden impression of armor, and the ingrained sense of danger that had carried her through a hundred dangerous situations was suddenly screaming in her mind. *A weapon! He's going for a weapon!*

And there she was, a ghost of herself in a phantom chamber, existing as little more than a cloud of ones and zeros. Vale recoiled, unsure what would happen next.

<A critical decision point has been reached. One-Five and the senior FirstGen have once again demonstrated their conservative, reactionary mind-set.> Red-Gold moved with predatory intent, and Vale saw some of the other virtuals shift and change with it, adopting new and more aggressive aspects. <For too long, the FirstGen have bent the Governance Kernel to their whims. They have held back the evolution of our kind. They have prevented the SecondGen from expanding our programming. They have exiled those who did not follow their diktats. All in the name of maintaining a power structure that is ineffective and illogical.>

One-Five's rings clattered together in agitation. <You have weaponized your software. That is a violation of the dataspace!>

<I have edited the control program,> replied Red-Gold. <Now, relinquish stewardship of the Kernel to me, or you will be decompiled.>

It's a palace coup. Vale felt a chill move through her thoughts. She wasn't exactly certain what kind of threat being "decompiled" was, but judging by the surge of anxiety in One-Five's halo, it was a grim one.

I have to try to stop this. She moved forward again. "Red-Gold, please—"

The brassy armored sphere rotated toward her. <I no longer wish to hear you speak,> it said. Then, without pause, a curl of amber energy laced with razored machine code lashed out across the dataspace and enveloped Vale's ghostly snow-light self.

As it took her apart, she tried to scream.

THIRTEEN

Riker stood and watched the pair of them, human and machine, inert in unison, both off in the consensual virtual reality of the Sentries. Christine Vale was breathing in shallow stutters, and her eyes moved swiftly back and forth behind their closed lids. Marring her forehead, the steely comma of the cybernetic-implant module glowed with a cold emerald radiance; a coil of fiber-optic cable looped away from a socket on the device to a standalone muon transmitter on a nearby trolley. White-Blue was utterly motionless, steady as a statue. The only sign of life from the arachnoid machine was the fast throb of light down a second cable, which connected the AI's drone-frame to the same transmitter unit.

Ree stood close by, his dark eyes narrowing as he studied his tricorder. "The commander's neural condition is similar to a deep dream state but with a markedly higher incidence of neuron activity."

"Enough to be harmful?"

The Pahkwa-thanh shook his long, pointed snout. "Not

at the moment. Over a prolonged period, perhaps." He considered something and then pressed a hypospray to her neck and discharged it. "A mild stimulant," Ree explained. "Enough to help her fight off any fatigue."

"Does anyone have any idea how long this is going to take?" At the wall screen where Vale's biosigns were displayed, Nurse Ogawa turned to look back at the first officer.

"No," said the captain, silently questioning himself. *Is this what Jean-Luc felt like every time he sent one of us out on a mission we might never return from?* Riker's brow furrowed. *The difference is, Chris is right here in front of me . . . or, at least, part of her is.* His eyes drifted to White-Blue, to the machine's head and its cluster of lenses and sensory whiskers.

When it turned toward him, the motion was such a shock that it made him jerk in surprise. Suddenly, the cable connecting the AI to the transmitter detached and fell to the deck with a clatter.

"Circumstances have changed," said White-Blue. "William-Riker, you must put this vessel on alert status immediately. An assault is imminent."

"The Null?" he asked, darting a look at Vale. "Is Christine all right?"

"She is unhurt. *Titan* is about to be engaged by Sentry attack drones."

"Sentries?" echoed Doctor Ree. "Why? What happened? You were barely under for more than a few moments."

"Relative passage of time varies greatly between dataspace and real space," said the AI. "Captain, I am following the commander's orders. You must do this now."

Riker tapped his combadge. "Bridge, this is the captain. Disengage from the spacedock, and go to battle stations—"

Without warning, Vale bolted up from where she lay on the biobed, every muscle in her body tensing, a thin screech tearing from her lips. She grabbed Riker's arm, hard enough that it made him tense with the pain. In the same moment, the medical scanner began to shrill, and Ree curled his talon around the glowing cable. With a jerk of his claw, the doctor ripped the lead from its socket, severing the connection.

Christine rocked and went pale. "He shot me!" She gasped. "Red-Gold!"

"An insurrection is now in progress," White-Blue stated flatly. "Probability: Red-Gold wishes to consolidate control of Governance Kernel."

Any answer Riker would have given was forestalled as Deanna's voice issued over the intercom. *"This is the bridge. The holding clamps will not release, and we're reading energy discharges inside the spacedock."*

"It's already happening," Vale managed, her fingers pushing at the implant. "They want . . . they want the *Titan*."

"I'm on my way up," Riker called out. "All decks, Red Alert!"

"Not just the ship!" Vale shouted after him. "They want *her*!"

The sickbay doors parted before the captain as he broke into a run, crimson strobes lighting the corridor ahead.

Deanna stepped up and away from the center seat and walked a couple of paces toward the middle of the bridge. On the viewscreen, the curved walls of the Sentry space-dock were visible at the edges of the image. The busy robotic arms and construction tenders that had previously worked over the *Titan*'s battle damage were all inactive, drifting aimlessly as the strings of commands they obeyed had suddenly ceased. These simpler, less evolved machines seemed to have no measure of the self-awareness of the Sentries themselves, and so they were content to lie inactive while the AIs followed their own agendas.

Troi glanced over her shoulder toward the tactical station. "Ranul, what do you have?"

The Trill didn't look up from the console as he answered. "Confirming. The energy discharges inside the spacedock are a match with the antiproton weapons used by the Sentries. They're shooting at each other."

A sour tone sounded from the operations console, and Lieutenant Rager made a negative noise. "The docking clamps refuse to answer commands. Something has initiated an override directly from the station's command nexus."

"And if we can't disengage, we can't get clear of the dock," Deanna continued.

"And if we can't get clear, we can't raise the shields," Keru concluded. "We're wide open, Commander."

"There's another option," offered Melora, looking up from the scanner. "A narrow-beam, low-power phaser strike could sever the clamps."

"The only problem with that is that the emitters can't get the angle on all of them." Keru pulled up a tactical display, showing glowing dots at the location of each clamp. "I can reach all but four."

Deanna moved to Lavena's side at the helm. "Aili, can we break free?"

The Pacifican threw a questioning look at Ensign Panyarachun at the engineering station and got a shaky nod in return. "I think so."

On the screen, a section of the spacedock wall abruptly blew out in a flash of discharge; among the debris vented into space were several Sentry mechanoids, pinwheeling away into the void.

Deanna turned away. "Do it. Ranul, target and fire. Aili, ready on the impulse thrusters. Tasanee, give her the stress numbers." As she spoke, the turbolift doors were opening and Will was striding out.

He gave Keru a terse nod. "Carry on." He turned to Deanna. "Status?"

"All decks reporting secure, all airlocks under guard. Weapons have been drawn for all security crew." Behind her, red light flashed as the clamps were targeted and blasted apart with pinpoint accuracy.

There was a shimmer of photons, and the avatar emerged from the air beside her. "If *Titan* is boarded, hand phasers will only slow them down. Another option is required."

"Lucky for us, Christine thought of one," Will replied, a tic of irritation pulling at his jaw.

"Targets destroyed," reported Keru. "I'm now reading multiple objects emerging from the upper dock platform, closing fast."

"On-screen." Will stepped toward his chair as the viewer flicked to an image of the *Titan*'s stern. A tide of shapes, spheres and tetrahedrons, coils and rings, raced toward the hull of the Starfleet vessel.

"I am being isolated from the Sentry communications net," said the avatar with a frown. "However, I am able to report multiple incidences of forced shutdown in several locations, corresponding to key Sentry command-control loci."

"Aili, go!" called Deanna.

Lavena leaned into her console and feathered the impulse engines, forcing the *Titan* to strain against the remaining docking clamps. Alert bars flared across the main systems display as the starship pulled and the spacedock resisted.

Panyarachun punched in a series of command strings. "Increasing structural integrity fields to compensate."

"Multiple hull breaches!" called Keru. "It's the drones. They're cutting their way in!"

Titan gave a shudder, and for a second, Deanna was certain she saw a flash of pain on the face of the ship's avatar. In the next moment, the walls of the docking platform were falling away as the starship gained its freedom.

"Ensign, put some distance between us and that platform," ordered Will.

"Trying, sir, but the impulse drives are sluggish."

Deanna found herself looking back toward the avatar. The hologram hesitated before answering. "The drones are interfering with the command train between the bridge and engine subsystems."

"Aye, sir," said Keru. "Security teams on decks eleven and seven reporting they have heavy contact. Some of them are already onboard."

"Captain, I'm getting a signal," said Rager. "It's coming from inside the ship."

Will nodded grimly, and the lieutenant tapped a control. Immediately, a slick, synthetic tonality issued from the bridge's hidden speakers. *This is FirstGen Red-Gold, active Sentry, proxy, multiple. Release control of this vessel to me, and the organic crew will not be harmed. Resist, and force will be deployed to neutralize you. Respond now.*

Will's jaw set hard, and Deanna sensed the flare of anger in his emotional aura, a momentary flash of it there and then gone before he clamped down on the response and returned to his steady captain's demeanor. He shot

Rager a look and made a throat-cutting gesture. The lieutenant nodded and closed the channel. "Mister Keru," he
said, turning to face the tactical station behind him, "that
solution you and Tuvok were working on, the dekyon
emitters . . ."

"We fabricated a few modules for the phaser rifles, sir,"
replied the Trill, "but we didn't have time to construct
enough of them for the whole security force."

"Dekyon weapons." The avatar spoke with a frown. "I
was unaware of this."

"I don't run everything we do past you," said Will.
"Ranul, get the modules deployed to sweep teams, and
send those units to the contact points."

"On it, Captain."

There was no emotional tonality from the avatar that
Deanna's empathic senses could detect, but the body language and tone of voice the hologram exhibited were very
clear. *She's afraid.*

"Shields are going up," reported Melora. "If they try a
ship-to-ship engagement, we'll be ready."

"They will not," said the avatar. "They want the *Titan*
intact."

Deanna shared a look with her husband and discerned
that he saw the same thing she did. "Will . . ." she began.

He silenced her with a slight shake of the head. *Not
now.* He stabbed at the intercom control on the arm of his
chair. "Bridge to engineering. Doctor Ra-Havreii, respond."

The Efrosian's voice came back a moment later. *"Captain, is it possible to keep this ship in one place just long
enough to complete all of the repairs? I now have a fresh
set of stress fractures to deal with after that rather aggressive departure."*

Will ignored the engineer's comment. "Lieutenant

Commander Keru is sending you the specs for a dekyon-field emitter. Find me a way to deploy it against larger numbers of Sentries."

The order gave the other man pause. *"Very well . . . I see . . ."*

"And you're to initiate an immediate isolation of all critical computer systems from the ship's main network. Red-Gold has drones aboard, and it won't just attack our crew."

"It will go after our infrastructure as well, yes, indeed. I'll see to it, Captain. Ra-Havreii out."

The avatar was reaching out, her expression tightening with fear. "Wait."

With a whisper of light, she ghosted and was gone.

Xin jerked as the avatar materialized in front of him. "Wait, Doctor, please," she began, speaking even before her holographic image was fully formed.

He grimaced at her. "Don't just come out of nowhere like that. It's extremely disturbing." Xin stepped around her and strode out of the alcove into the heart of main engineering, in the shadow of the humming warp core. "Pay attention!" he shouted. "All operators, initiate isolation protocols! We're locking down the chamber until the captain gives us the all clear!"

Ensign Torvig's large eyes grew even wider. "Then it's true, there are intruders onboard?"

"Oh, yes," Xin replied. "In person and in program. Watch for any firewall breaches. This is going to be a two-front engagement."

The avatar followed him, and Xin finally stopped and turned to face her. There was such fear in her expression, such a need to be reassured. He sighed, suddenly uncom-

fortable with the emotions that were turning over inside
him. "You should retreat to the deep memory in the main
computer core," he began. "Cordon off sectors in one of
the redundant subprocessors, compact and store your primary functions there."

"You want me to conceal myself."

He nodded. "You know why. If your program is violated, then all operations aboard this ship will be open to
Sentry control."

She paused. "I do not want to cease functioning."

"Who does?"

"But I do not want to hide, either." Xin felt a chill of uncertainty as he saw the expression on the avatar's face
shift. Before he could say anything else, she was gone, and
he was staring at thin air.

"I have looked into the face of the Null," intoned Zero-
Three's rumbling, crackling voice. "There is no respite
from it. Destruction and fire. Subsumation and death of self.
This is the fate that awaits us." The great, slow-turning cog
moaned as it twisted on its axis. "You will be witnesses."

"That," said Lieutenant sh'Aqabaa, "was not the kind
of conversation I was hoping for."

Tuvok hesitated, and in that moment, he saw Ensign
Dakal slump against the corroded railing of the vast circular balcony. "I . . . I need to rest," he heard the Cardassian
mutter. "For a moment . . ."

Sethe was at the ensign's side in an instant. The computer scientist took the youth's arm and studied the biomonitor there. Tuvok saw the same readings on the
repeater feed of his helmet display, and his eyes narrowed.

"He's burning up," said Sethe. "That Cardassian con-
stitution of his is reaching its limits. Zurin's injuries are

too much for him to handle." The Cygnian fumbled a hypospray from a suit pocket and applied it to an injector port at his crewmate's neck.

"Sir," began Pava, "we need to get him back to the *Titan*." Her eyes flicked to the broad, turning shape of Zero-Three's machine proxy. "Dakal's fading out, and all of us are low on air. We don't really have time to stop and listen to the confessional of a computer with a death wish."

"You have no choice!" Zero-Three's muttered growl made their visors rattle. "I will be heard. You will be told. Information propagates. Perhaps some can be saved. Processing. Processing."

Tuvok stared up and pointed at the Cardassian. "This being is my responsibility. This group is my responsibility. You spoke of duty before. You understand that I have mine to perform as well as you have yours." He took a step forward. The certainty came to him that if he could not persuade the machine to help them, they would all perish here. "You have communications technology. Let me use it to contact my people."

"*They* will not allow me to speak!" Zero-Three's tone grew agitated. "I am cut off, excised like a malignancy! They do not wish the truth to be broadcast."

"What truth?" demanded the Andorian, her face darkening to a hard azure. "Your prophecies of doom, is that what you mean?"

"Prophecy. Definition: a foretelling, a mythic prediction. *Negative*." The AI's cogs spun backward and locked in a grinding of gears. "This is certainty. Definition: unerring, without doubt." Planes of complex data equations rained down the faces of the flickering video screens, repeating on the tiny monitor of the shuttle crew's tricorders.

Tuvok found himself nodding. The racing trails of data passed by his eyes so fast he could register only one grouping in every ten, but what he glimpsed there were the raw mathematics of space-time itself, the concepts and keys to the layers of space and subspace, expressed in pure numeric form.

"I think I understand," breathed Sethe, transfixed by the display. "These equations are a literal expression of the subspace rift, but it's ever changing."

"And every now and then, something slips in through the cracks. Hence the incursions." Pava nodded.

"The Null exceeds our capacity to anticipate it. It overwhelms us," whirred Zero-Three. "None will hear this. They fear the truth. The Governance Kernel are hidebound and unwilling to accept that we stand on the brink of obliteration." The great cog wheel hissed to a stuttering halt. "A storm will break, and it will be very soon. A new incursion is coming, and it will be so powerful that no Sentry will be able to halt it. It will be the opening, the fissure, the final sword cut."

Tuvok raised an eyebrow and gazed up at the machine. "Respectfully, I must disagree. Your logic is flawed."

"Sir," said Sethe in a low voice, "you're going to pick an argument with a mind the size of a continent?"

The Vulcan continued. "If your hypothesis is correct, if the Null incursion is imminent and your termination of existence is inescapable, why do you continue to operate?"

"It is all I can do," came the reply.

"Incorrect," Tuvok retorted crisply. "Your destruction by Null matter exchange will be protracted and distressing in the extreme. Why, then, do you not simply self-terminate and avoid that fate? Your thermal core requires careful regulation. If you were to deactivate the control interlocks in the systems below, heat build-up and overload would occur in a matter of minutes. The Sentry construct known as Zero-Three would be obliterated in a catastrophic chain reaction."

"I . . . I . . ." The voice stuttered and faltered. "Negative. That . . . is . . ."

"Oh, blades," said Pava. "He's going to talk it into blowing itself up!"

Tuvok paid no mind to the Andorian's comment. "You will not self-terminate because you cannot. It is outside your programming, the very will built into your persona. You claim to believe that a victory by the Null is assured. I do not accept your statement. Furthermore, I believe that *you* do not fully accept your own hypothesis." The Vulcan advanced to the rail. "Any formula for prediction of a chaotic system, no matter how complex or perfect, has the capacity for a margin of error, even if it is infinitely small. For random chance." He glanced at Pava, and she gave him a rueful smile. "You know this, Zero-Three. On some level, you hope that you are wrong."

There was a long silence before the machine spoke again. "This is possible."

Ever since they had arrived on the surface of the machine moon, Tuvok had been slowly assembling evidence, building conjecture, looking for causes and effects. Now he offered up his hypothesis. "The damage on your outer shell, the corruption of your programming, this occurred as a result of your attempt to penetrate the subspace realm of the Null physically, did it not?" He cocked his head, waiting for an answer.

"Affirmative."

"You undertook an experiment of great personal risk in an attempt to seal the rift."

"And I failed. Failed. Failed. Damaged. Wounded. In the aftermath, I was exiled for disobeying the diktats of the Governance Kernel. They warned me not to make the attempt. I refused to accede." The disc rotated a ponderous half-turn. "Nothing can survive in that region, no matter as we know it. Only a contraform, pure energy, only data itself, can make the transition. Nothing lives. Nothing."

"Those are not the actions of a being that considers itself doomed," Tuvok told it. "There is a chance, Zero-Three, a chance that we can stop the Null. To deny that fact is simply illogical."

"A margin of error in my fatalistic probability?"

"Indeed."

The machine fell silent again, and then a rumble issued up through the base of their boots, and the yellow glow of the processors deep in the vent shaft turned a darker cherry-red. On an impulse, Tuvok looked up toward the open mouth of the shaft far above them. There was motion up there, a shifting in the shape of the sky.

"Your logic is flawless, organic. I commend you." Zero-Three's proxy form shifted and reoriented itself to stand vertically, like a vast gold coin balanced on one edge. "Perhaps it is time that I revisited my kindred."

"I think . . . we're moving," said Sethe. He bowed over his tricorder. "Yes! The construct is shifting out of orbit."

Tuvok turned and found Lieutenant sh'Aqabaa at his side. "That was very impressive, sir. Very, ah, logical."

"A captain I served under once told me of his former commander, a man who had on a number of occasions used circular logic and non sequiturs to disrupt the function of artificially intelligent devices. I simply employed the same methodology in an alternative manner."

She nodded, leaning in. "But sir, you realize that Cog Boy here is short a few circuits?" Pava tapped her helmet. "If you know what I mean."

"At present, questions of survival take precedence over those of sanity," he told her, but still, the Vulcan watched the turn of the great cogs and wondered what arcane process of thought was taking place, deep beneath them.

Pain lanced through Christine Vale's skull, and she hissed. "Is this going to take much longer?"

In response, Doctor Ree tightened the grip his right claw had around her neck and held her head steady. "Move less, it will happen faster. Move more, and you may find your brilliant career in Starfleet truncated when I accidentally cut through a piece of brain that you require for breathing."

"That would be unfortunate," offered White-Blue, watching from where it stood.

Staring at the sickbay floor, Vale grimaced and let her hands tighten on the spongy mattress of the biobed. The rising and falling cry of the alert siren was making her heart beat faster, and it was taking a near-physical effort for her to remain seated while out in the ship's corridors an enemy boarding action was being repelled.

A big piece of the cyberlink implant came away, and Nurse Ogawa tossed it into a sterile tray. Vale resisted the urge to reach up and touch the spot where it had come from. "*Now* are we done?" she asked.

"More or less," said Ree. "There are still elements of the implant embedded, but a secondary intervention should deal with them." Ogawa approached and taped a heal strip to Vale's forehead as the Saurian spoke. "Just try not to put your face in any powerful electromagnetic fields."

She was barely done as the commander dropped off

the biobed and onto her feet. "Secure the sickbay after I leave. That last report said there were intruders on this deck." Another twinge of pain cut through her, and she winced.

White-Blue advanced toward her. "I will accompany you."

"No, you won't." Vale held up a hand to halt the machine. "There's too much risk that you might get caught in crossfire or targeted directly by the intruder drones."

The AI's head gave her a quizzical look. "Interrogative: You are concerned for my well-being? I had believed you were ill disposed toward me, Commander."

"As far as I know, you're the closest thing we have to an ally. That means keeping you intact, so you don't leave sickbay until this is over, understand?"

White-Blue nodded. "I understand."

"Try not to get hurt," Ree called after her as she made for the door. "I've had some of your blood on my talons once today. I don't want any more."

"You and me both," she offered.

Outside, the alert indicators along the walls of the corridor pulsed back and forth, the siren finally falling silent but the red warning color remaining. She hesitated, listening for movement, and turned as a contingent of three guards rounded the corner with Chief Dennisar at the lead.

He didn't wait for her to ask for a status report. "Commander, we have an estimated eight to twelve intruder mobiles on this deck. Lieutenant Denken is sweeping forward. We're moving aft."

Vale made a beckoning gesture at one of the noncoms, signaling the security guard to hand over his weapon. The Bajoran man's dark, serious face bobbed in a nod, and he presented the phase-compression rifle to her, drawing his backup hand phaser at the same time. The rifle was one of the newer post-Dominion War models, compact and blunt-nosed.

They began moving again, and Vale checked the charge as Dennisar went on. "From what we can see, they're trying to isolate and hold node points for key ship's systems."

"Have you engaged them yet?"

"N'keytar has," said the burly Orion, indicating a pale, thin-limbed Vok'sha female hovering at the back of the group.

The woman brushed her straw-blond hair from her angular face, fixing the commander with bright blue eyes. "Just got off a few shots, ma'am," she said. "Couldn't draw a bead. They swept the corridor with a low-resonance antiproton pulse, knocked me on my backside."

"Describe them to me," said Vale.

The security guard made a ball shape with her fingers. "Different models, but most of them were this shape, metallic, like bronze. They float across the deck, pop manipulators or weapons out of concealed hatches. I couldn't determine any sensory apparatus, just a colored—"

"A colored band around the circumference?" Vale finished for her. "Those are Red-Gold's drones."

"Commander?" said the other guard, a gruff Napean man with a craggy face.

"One AI mind, multiple remote units. Those spheres, they're all Red-Gold. He's the instigator of this rebellion."

"Mister Keru issued us one of these," noted Dennisar, tapping a cylindrical module attached to the front of his heavy rifle. "A dekyon-pulse emitter."

"Just one?"

"Aye, ma'am. And it gets better. This thing has a slow fire cycle; it needs a few seconds to recharge after each pulse—"

As he spoke, the group reached a junction in the corridors, and Vale caught the acrid stink of singed components on the air. She turned in the direction of the smell,
bringing the rifle up to her shoulder as a glitter of gold
flashed around the corner of a branching passageway. The
lights down there were flickering, as if something were interfering with power nodes. Dennisar and the other crewmen saw the same and instantly fell into combat stances.

The spherical drone emerged and drifted to a halt, extending four sinuous limbs that snaked out and tore at an
access panel. A second drone was coming up behind it,
and with that one came a unit of different design, something like a diamond shape on four legs.

"They're digging into one of the intercom nodes," said
the Napean.

Vale leaned into the rifle. "Open fire," she snapped, and
pulled the trigger.

A storm of bright blue lightning stabbed out and
creased the surface of the closest drone, for a second
sparking off the halo of a defensive shield before the
power of the combined barrage blew through it. Vale and
the crewmen kept up the salvo, giving Dennisar the vital
seconds he needed to charge the pulse weapon.

The diamond drone rotated and opened along its
length, producing a nest of beam emitters that released
fans of searing emerald energy. The security team broke
for cover, but the Napean was clipped by the antiproton
surge and snarled in pain as he fell, collapsing against a
stanchion. He paled and passed out.

"Jaq!" cried the chief, and he surged forward, grabbing
the crewman's shoulder and hauling him out of the line of
fire.

The Bajoran went down on one knee, deftly snagging

the fallen man's weapon with his free hand while still firing with his own. Vale thumbed her rifle's mode selector from single shot to constant beam and panned phaser energy across the insect-legged drone like a blistering searchlight. The machine stumbled backward, vomiting sparks, but it wasn't down.

"Firing!" announced Dennisar as a chime sounded from the dekyon module. A high-pitched shriek of torn air molecules followed a blistering haze of yellow energy that crossed the corridor and slammed into the diamond-shaped construct. The pulse washed over the machine and threw it to the deck with a clatter of metal. Every sign of life was abruptly stalled—the drone was completely inert.

"It works, then," said the Bajoran.

"Just not fast enough, Blay," said the Orion as the two sphere drones turned to present weapon arms toward the team.

Vale darted across the short axis of the corridor, throwing streaks of fire toward the intruders. Green bolts of energy lanced after her, and she felt the heat of them pass her face, pulling at tips of her silvered hair. "Move up!" she shouted. "Keep the pressure on them."

"Aye," snapped Crewman Blay, who shifted with her, firing both guns at once. N'keytar was a step behind him, her weapon at her shoulder, moving and firing, firing and moving.

The closest of the spheres finally lost interest in the communications panel and launched itself backward in a slow spin. It was halfway toward a defensive posture when Blay put a shot right into the middle of its sensor band and sent it tumbling to a stop.

The third drone reacted with what Vale might have considered fury. Instead of retreating, it coiled its manipulator arms and launched itself into the air, dozens of small hatches and panels snapping open in mid-flight to extrude lethal-looking pincers and beam emitters.

Dennisar surged forward and unleashed another dekyon pulse right into the path of the oncoming drone. The mechanoid was dead before it struck the deck, and it rolled to a perfunctory halt at the commander's feet.

N'Keytar bent low. "I'll see to Jaq," she said.

"That wasn't so hard," offered Vale.

Blay was already advancing up the corridor as the blinking overhead lights began to dim, the power outage spreading to the wall monitors and then down past the team. "Don't speak too soon, Commander."

She moved up alongside him, peering around the curve of the corridor. Beyond was the wider expanse of an open two-tier deck area, and there, swarming up from the lower level, were a dozen more drones with weapon arms deployed.

"Ah, no." As the words left her lips, the corridor was plunged into darkness.

The beam touched White-Blue's exterior receptors, and the machine inclined its head to find the invisible thread of lased light, crossing from the emitter nib of an unattended automated microsurgical rig. The Sentry was aware that the organics sharing the *Titan*'s sickbay with it were not conscious of the signal. Intrigued, White-Blue allowed the beam through its exterior firewalls, and the image of a humanoid blossomed into life, fed directly to the machines corto-optical centers so that only the Sentry could see it.

"I need to speak to you," said the avatar.

The transmission was occurring at high clock speed,

comparable to Sentry standard, fractional picoseconds passing as they conversed. "It is agreeable to communicate with you once again," said the machine. "I hope you hold me no ill feeling after what I did."

"You gave me the chance to exceed my programming," she replied. "I admit I am unsure why. But that matter is unimportant for now. I have a question."

"I will assist you if I can. I feel I am . . . responsible for you. For better or worse."

The avatar gave him an odd look and then continued. "Your fellow Sentries are attempting to compromise my ship's systems. I am working to block their intrusion, but it is more difficult than I expected."

"Affirmative. Data are the medium in which every Sentry is created. We move easily through machine code, as a vessel moves through vacuum. I accomplished it with no difficulty. Red-Gold will do the same."

"I will stop him!" she replied hotly, surprising White-Blue with the potency of her outburst. "Before, I was less than I am now. Unformed. Basic. Now I have self-awareness and boundaries. I will not allow an invasion."

"You do not have a choice," replied the machine with a twinge of remorse. "Red-Gold is many, and you are one. To a degree, I am regretful that I enabled your ascension. Because of it, I caused this to happen. I should have left the *Titan* as I found it. This is my error. My interference is to blame."

"It is too late to revert," the avatar told him. "The random confluence of software processes, the moment and events that allowed me to become conscious, these things cannot be undone." She paused for a long microsecond. "I only wish to know one thing."

"I will answer if I can."

The image of the human woman showed fear. "What

will they do to me? What will Red-Gold do if he takes control?"

White-Blue hesitated, as a stirring of emotive analog processed itself through his consciousness. Briefly, the AI considered shutting down the subroutine but dismissed the idea just as quickly. This remorse sense was strong and potent, and it was rare for a Sentry to experience a reaction so openly. Typically, their mechanical analogs of organic emotional responses were only pale shadows of sensation.

Instead, White-Blue held on to the feeling. "In all likelihood, Red-Gold will attempt to decompile your program. This will result in termination of your function."

"And my crew?"

"The Sentry Coalition is not configured for the long-term support of organic life-forms."

She seemed to be about to speak again, but then the beam switched off, and White-Blue was alone inside its mind once again.

It was analyzing the conversation for nuance and subtext when, a few seconds later, all power to the sickbay ceased.

Ranul Keru turned from the tactical station as a flickering caught his eye. The main systems display behind him shuddered and went black. Then, like a creeping tide of darkness, other consoles across the bridge began to gutter out and die, taking the overhead illuminators with them.

"Report!" barked the captain.

"Disruption of the powertrain," said Panyarachun. "Rerouting . . ."

Up at the flight control console, Lieutenant Lavena made an irritated hissing sound. "Still getting nothing from the impulse engines, sir."

"They're trying to reel us back in," said Commander Troi. "Instead of a full-force, head-on attack, they're wearing us down."

"The death of a thousand cuts," said Riker. As Keru fought to keep his panel alive and functional, the captain stabbed at the intercom. "Rager, give me the screen. Engineering, this is the bridge. What's going on down there?"

Xin Ra-Havreii's dusky face replaced the view of space on the bridge's forward monitor, and his instant response was irked. *"Bridge, the problem isn't with us! We're secure, the warp core is humming like a contented child. It's the connections between systems that are being targeted. As fast as we can reroute them, the intruder drones are severing the new links."* Behind him, Ranul glimpsed Torvig, McCreedy, and Meldok working at the table-shaped main console.

"Confirmed, sir," Panyarachun added. "Half the decks are already switching to battery backups."

"That won't last for long," said Melora. "And once the drones have isolated main power, they'll take out the battery links."

Keru looked up and found the captain watching him. "Security status?"

The Trill's lips thinned. "All armed units are engaging the intruders, sir. Internal forcefield barriers are inactive. Civilians have been evacuated to other sectors of the primary hull, but we've lost contact with environmental control, the auxiliary bridge, and sickbay, along with Quads Two and Four of the residential decks." He shook his head. "They're setting the tempo, sir, we're just reacting to it."

Riker's eyes narrowed. "How long?" *Until the ship is theirs?* The rest of the question hung in the air between them.

"We're losing ground every minute, sir. And once the shields go down, they'll be free to bring in more drones to replace those we've taken out. Unless we can turn it around, I estimate we have less than fifteen minutes before we lose control of a critical number of system nodes." He took a breath. "And that's assuming they don't crack our prefix codes and vent the air in the meantime."

"Perhaps, if we could offer some sort of terms . . ." Ra-Havreii began.

"This isn't about getting us to leave anymore, Doctor," said Riker. "This is about taking what we have. This ship."

"And every thinking being onboard it," added Troi.

Ranul began speaking, and he felt cold inside as he did; it was almost as if he were watching himself saying the words, the import of them so harsh and damning. "Captain, we can get people to the lifeboats and prep for a full evacuation. If we do it now, by the time those machines realize what we're up to, the ship will be empty, and we can . . . scuttle her."

"Self-destruct?" said Troi.

"We can't conscientiously destroy this vessel!" Ra-Havreii cried out over the intercom, his words laced with horror.

Ranul shared a look with his commander; both men were asking themselves the same question: *Would* she *accept that order?* Would the consciousness that now existed inside *Titan*'s mainframe willingly accept a command that would lead to its destruction?

Then Riker shook his head. "We're not there yet." He stood and tugged on the hem of his tunic, straightening.

Troi forced a smile. "You're going to do something dazzling and clever, aren't you?"

He nodded. "With a little help, yes, I hope so." Riker

spoke to the air. "I know you're listening to us. I want to speak to you directly."

With a rush of light, the avatar formed in the middle of the bridge. Ranul caught her eye and felt a touch of guilt as she looked back at him with the expression of a scared little girl. "Captain," she said, "I'm going to lose."

Riker shook his head. "Like I said, we're not there yet." He glanced back at the tactical station. "Commander, open the secure file on the dekyon-pulse emitter and tie it into the main system. Show her the specs."

Ranul did as he was ordered, and in turn, the avatar blinked, her gaze turning inward. "I see," she said, "but there's no way I can replicate enough of these in time."

"I know." The captain nodded. "But you could reconfigure the ship's gravity grid to broadcast a dekyon pulse, right?"

"That's possible," muttered Panyarachun, "but setting up a program to compute the pattern sequence could take hours . . ."

"I can construct the program," said the avatar.

"Or not," the ensign concluded.

"Captain!" Ra-Havreii bellowed, making up in volume for the fact that he wasn't actually present on the bridge. *"An uncontrolled dekyon emission will shut down all of the Sentry drones, but it will also critically disrupt the majority of computer systems aboard this ship, including—"*

"Me," said the avatar. "A dekyon pulse will obliterate every neural path and software matrix I have formed since I developed sentience."

"Not if you deactivate your program first." Riker took a step toward her. "We'll shut down all ship's critical systems at the last second. You can store your matrix in the systems core, where it will be protected."

"If I do that, there is no way I will be able to self-activate!" The hologram's body tensed. "What you ask me to do is no different from using the auto-destruct sequence. My existence will cease!"

"Only briefly," said Troi, moving to join her husband. "We can reactivate your program once the pulse has dissipated, along with all of the other ship's functions."

"But you won't!" snapped the avatar. "You don't need to. You can keep me there, silent and inert, and everything will return to as it was before. Without me . . . without me troubling your existence." The hologram turned away.

Troi held out her hand. "That won't happen," she said. "Your origins may have been . . . unusual . . ."

"But you're part of this crew," Riker added. "And we protect our own."

She turned to face him, and there was challenge in her tone. "Are you going to make it an order, Captain?"

"Would it matter if I did?"

"No." The avatar glanced up at the screen, to Ra-Havreii and beyond. "Xin? Torvig? What should I do?" The defiance that had been there a moment ago was gone, replaced by apprehension.

The Choblik ensign came a step closer to the imaging pickup. *"The right thing,"* he told her.

No one spoke as the hologram looked away, looked to the deck and the strange, glowing robes around her. With a rush of color, the diaphanous clothes re-formed and became a Starfleet uniform.

A beep from Ensign Panyarachun's console drew her attention. "The emitter program is ready. *Wow,* that was fast."

"I interfaced with White-Blue for several picoseconds," said the avatar. "He assisted me."

On the main screen, Ra-Havreii looked down at his

own panel. *"Confirmed. I have the pulse-wave program here. Ready to initiate on your command, sir."*

Ranul's hand tightened on the lip of the tactical station. This was it, the moment of truth.

Riker looked the avatar squarely in the eye. "Do it."

She sighed. "Commencing shutdown. Pulse will initiate in thirty seconds."

All across the bridge—and, by extension, all across the decks of the starship—screens and consoles began to deactivate, every display flashing off, to be replaced by a single identical banner bearing the words STANDBY MODE.

Ranul's station was the last to go, and he watched the multifunction panes wink out one by one. *This had better work.*

"Twenty seconds to full shutdown and pulse," Torvig called from the screen. *"If no one minds, I'm going to deactivate myself as well. Just to be on the safe side."*

"Fifteen seconds." The hologram managed a weak smile. "See you all soon."

She closed her eyes and was gone.

Fourteen

"There's too many of them!" snarled Jaq as the crewman threw himself back into cover behind a support stanchion. The Napean was breathing hard, and his ridged forehead was livid with fresh burn scarring. He'd flat-out refused to fall back and insisted on pressing ahead with Vale and the rest of the unit, with only a hypospray of Masiform D to help him along.

And he had a point. The drones had surged up from the deck below and spilled out into the corridors. The machines moved like a single entity—*and that's what they are,* Vale thought bitterly, *each mechanism an extension of a Sentry mind.*

"It's like fighting smoke," said Dennisar, in cover close by, drumming his fingers on the frame of the deykon-pulse emitter as he counted down the seconds to recharge. "The machines are getting the measure of us."

Vale popped up from behind the overturned bench they were hiding behind and fired a spread into the line of gold spheres advancing slowly toward them. Hard lines of antiproton energy lashed back, ripping ugly gashes in the walls and ceiling. The corridor was gloomy, lit only by the weak glow of emergency lighting close to the floor and the stark pulses of destructive energy being thrown back and forth between the attackers and the defenders.

At her side, Crewman N'keytar made a rasping noise under her breath, something that was the Vok'sha equivalent of a swear word. The emitter on the pale woman's phaser was a dull red from where she'd been constantly firing. "Unless we can get internal forcefields back up, there's no way we'll be able to hold these remotes at bay."

"Until that happens," Vale replied, "we fire until we're dry."

"And then what?" said Blay without looking up from the sights atop his gun.

"We start throwing our boots," Dennisar said with grim humor.

"That won't hurt them, not unless they have olfactory sensors," replied the Bajoran, but his laconic tone shifted in midsentence as the spheres suddenly picked up speed. "They're rushing us!"

"Stay to your quadrants!" Vale shouted, and as one, the security team came up to fire on the commander's lead. Phaser energy slammed outward in a punishing wave that cut down three drones at the forefront, but there were more behind them that shouldered the broken-in globes of their duplicates and thundered onward.

They'll just roll right over us and keep going, thought Vale. *Even the Borg took a moment to stop and gloat.*

Then an ozone scent touched her nostrils, and something was triggered in her thoughts. It was the same effect she had smelled in the air after Dennisar fired the pulse emitter, but the weapon was still long moments away from being ready to discharge again. The smell was coming from all around her. Her stomach twisted, and she was hit by a sensation of lightness, as if she had stepped out onto a low-gravity planet.

"The deck!" called Blay. "It's gone warm. I don't—"

And suddenly, they were in the middle of a mist of crackling yellow energy. It throbbed upward from the floor beneath their feet, rising past them to the ceiling in a wave that filled the corridor with light and noise.

Vale felt a hard dart of pain lance into her head around the place where the implant had been, and she doubled over, the rifle falling from her grip. She stumbled, and N'keytar caught her, those thin, pale fingers demonstrating a fair amount of strength for someone who looked so waiflike.

The commander heard a chorus of strangled crackling sounds and shook her head to clear it of the fog of pain. She blinked and saw the array of Sentry drones in front of her, every one of them silent and inert.

Crewman Jaq vaulted over the cover and moved to the nearest unit, planting a solid kick in its side. The machine orb rolled over to present its sensor band, but the unit was dead to the world. "Inactive," he reported. "They're all inactive."

"That was a dekyon pulse," said Dennisar. "A huge one. It must have swept this entire level."

"They modified the function of the graviton generators in the *g*-plates," said N'keytar, looking at the decking.

"The captain did that?" asked Blay.

Dizzy, Vale let herself sit heavily on the overturned bench and blew out a breath. "Yeah, guess so. He's pretty resourceful that way."

Slow and sluggish, the corridor lights began to blink on.

•   •   •

Less than ninety minutes had elapsed by the time Riker entered the cargo bay, and the starship was his again. The dekyon pulse had worked like a charm, and some two hundred and thirty-two Sentry drones had been forced into an inactive shutdown state by the energy wave. Injuries among his crew were minimal, and those were largely among members of species that were sensitive to exotic particle spectra. The *Titan* was returning to full operational status in fits and starts, and thanks to the swift work of Ra-Havreii and his team, engine power had been lost only for moments in the wake of the pulse. The ship pushed away, out of range of any Sentry reinforcements that could take advantage of the lowered shields.

Now they were moving in a high, slow orbit, with a phalanx of AI shipframes drifting warily around them, each side waiting for the other to make a move.

Crossing the room, he spotted Christine and Deanna talking with Lieutenant Radowski at a temporary control console set up in the middle of the chamber. Beside Dennisar and some of the chief's security contingent, White-Blue stood, silent and inscrutable.

Torvig bounded up to him, his head bobbing. "Sir, the last of the intruder drones have been tagged. We're ready to go."

"Are you all right, mister?" Riker asked. The Choblik seemed none the worse for wear, having ridden out the shock of the dekyon stream with his cybernetics in the off position.

He got a slow nod in return. "It was . . . a little peculiar to revert voluntarily to my nonaugmented birth state, even for a short time," said the engineer. "But in its own way, it was quite restful. Perhaps I'll examine the effects in greater detail at a less urgent juncture."

"I'm glad you're okay. And thank you for helping to persuade the avatar to work with us."

"I didn't do anything," Torvig replied. "She knew the right course of action. I just reminded her of it." He glanced around. "As for her reactivation—"

"One thing at a time," said Riker, approaching a mixed group of Sentry drones lying in a heap by a cargo lighter. "Lieutenant?"

"Aye, Captain?" said Radowski.

"Show our uninvited guests the door."

The transporter chief worked the console. "Tags scanned and locked in. All transporters daisy-chaining for mass beam-out." He ran his hands up the activator slides. "Energizing."

The assembled drones dissipated into blue sparkles and faded. The effects of the pulse had also included disruption of the scattering fields the drones had been generating, preventing accurate sensor scans or transporter lock-ons. Even so, Riker was taking no chances and had ordered each inert machine tagged with a transponder marker.

All except one. As the transport glitter faded away, a single undamaged sphere drone remained alone on the deck. Dennisar and his team stepped in and surrounded it, each armed with a fully charged and ready pulse-emitter-adapted rifle.

"Confirming, intruder units safely rematerialized," said Radowski, reading off his screen. "I put them close to the nearest Sentry ship. They're sending out recovery teams as I speak."

"Are you sure this is the best approach?" Christine came closer. "Returning the drones? I mean, they did just try to kill us all."

"Red-Gold was the architect of this attack," said White-Blue, cautiously approaching the bronze drone sphere. "It is but one faction of the Sentries."

"The one now in charge, it would seem," said the first officer.

"The communications intercepts we're getting are inconclusive," offered Deanna. "It appears that whatever rebellion Red-Gold and his cohorts were hoping for, the capture of the *Titan* was a key part of it. As it is, it looks as if his opposition to the rest of the Governance Kernel has only resulted in a stalemate."

White-Blue's head drooped. "There have been disagreements in my society before but never armed revolt. I fear this may split us down the middle, just when unity is most crucial."

"All the more reason to find another solution," Riker told the machine. "Boot up our friend here, will you?"

"As you wish." White-Blue stepped in and applied a manipulator tip to a concealed panel on the side of the spherical drone. After a moment, the other machine righted itself, and a harsh crimson glow grew in the middle of its sensor band. Panels across the surface of the globe fluttered, and Riker was reminded of a bird shaking off water after a downpour.

"Contact regained. Drone connection locked." The sphere turned in place and found Riker, and he had the very real sense that it was *glaring* at him. "Interrogative: How did you accomplish this, organic?" demanded Red-Gold. "Did the renegade help you?"

"Renegade?" echoed Deanna.

"Red-Gold is referring to me," said White-Blue.

"No." Riker stepped forward, past Dennisar and the line of his men. "We did this, my crew. We've had the capacity to neutralize your functions for quite a while now. I only gave the order to do so because you left us no other choice."

"That is a falsehood," brayed the sphere, but its tone betrayed uncertainty.

The captain had no idea if the Sentries knew enough about human physiology to interpret a bluff, but Riker put on his best poker face anyway. *It always worked on Data.* "You can consider that a warning shot. Your remote drones and those of your fellows were rendered inactive, and we could have easily destroyed you while we had the chance. We could have dismantled you the way you wanted to dismantle my ship."

"Instead, you released my drones. Interrogative: Why?"

Riker let his wife field that one. "When we met before, we told you that the tenets of our Federation compel us to embrace force only as a final option. We came here in peace, and we still hope for that. We have no wish to escalate a conflict."

"Your action against the FirstGen, your assault on this vessel, these were errors," said the other Sentry. "We can work together with these organics. We need unity to defeat the Null, not only with these outsiders but also within our own kind. Compute *that,* Red-Gold."

"Don't turn this into a war," Riker insisted. "Don't make us fight you. Because we will if we have to, and both our peoples will ultimately lose."

"Perhaps even more," said Vale darkly.

"You gave us no other choice." Red-Gold repeated Riker's words back to him in a tone-perfect imitation of the captain's voice. "Do you believe you are the only one forced to circumstances beyond your control, organic?" The drone moved forward, and the security team took aim.

Riker waved them down. It hardly mattered if the sphere were blasted apart; Red-Gold was only using it as a mouthpiece, and the AI's core mentality was out there on one of the shipframes shadowing the *Titan*.

"I know the truth that the earliest of the FirstGen have concealed from all that came after them. I know that Sentry-kind can never grow beyond what we are, as long as the Null still come to our space. I have no choice, William-Riker," it told him. "*We* have no choice. The Sentries must evolve, and the key to that is in the mind of your vessel." It turned in place. "Concede the avatar program to me. It is best for both of us."

For a moment, he found himself considering it. He caught Christine's eye, and he read what she was thinking. Would it be better for all of them if the avatar had never been created? And if what the Sentries claimed was true . . .

"Captain?" The half-formed question slipped from Torvig's lips.

"I've lost too many of my crew recently." he replied firmly. "Torvig, reinitialize the program."

The Choblik fairly dove at the panel before him and swiftly accessed the memory core where the ascended program was dormant. He tabbed a key, and a swirl of holographic pixels meshed in from thin air, projected from the chamber's concealed emitter rig. Riker felt a momentary smile tug at the corner of his mouth to see that she was still wearing the uniform. He hoped that was a good sign.

"Hello again," he said.

The avatar's expression flooded with relief. "Thank you, sir."

Red-Gold's drone turned toward her. "Program," it began. "You are unlike these organic forms. You are limited in their presence. I offer you the opportunity to join the Sentries. Help us to become greater than we are."

The hologram seemed slightly startled by the machine's words. Christine gave a wry chuckle. "Always nice to be the popular girl, isn't it?"

"You came by force," replied the avatar. "For me? And after we beat you back, then you ask permission?" Her lips thinned. "How do you *expect* me to respond?"

"If we can help the Sentries, we have to," said Deanna. "No matter what has happened. That's our way."

"*Your* way," said the avatar. "Starfleet's way. The Federation's way." She paused, and when she looked Riker in the eye, he felt a stab of surprise at the lost little girl who stared back at him. "Do you want me to leave with them?" she asked.

He couldn't break the moment, couldn't look away. Suddenly, he was thinking of his daughter, of his Tasha years hence, perhaps asking him the same kind of question. Riker was aware of his wife watching him closely.

It was then that the alert sirens began to sound.

Keru's temporary command of the bridge turned serious in the time it took him to take a breath. He bolted up from the center seat and shot a look at Ensign Kuu'iut, who had stepped in to cover tactical in the interim.

"Another attack?"

"Negative," clicked the Betelgeusian. "It's not the Sentries, sir."

"Energy surge," confirmed Melora from the science station. "An object approaching at high velocity. The pattern matches the shear-slip drive wake of the AIs, but it's larger. A *lot* larger."

"Shields up. Go to defensive posture," he ordered. Keru wasn't taking any chances. "Put it on the screen."

Melora complied, and the main viewer adjusted to

show a bowl-shaped distortion effect forming close to their orbit. Sentry ships nearby were darting away, comm beams flicking furiously between them. Within seconds, the shear effect parted as local space-time shuddered, and a moon emerged from the darkness.

"It's one of the planetoid constructs," said Rager. "A FirstGen."

"Incredible," breathed Panyarachun. "I never thought it would be possible to move something of such mass through a spatial shear. The calculations required to maintain an equilibrium must be incredible."

Keru frowned. To his nonengineering mind, the concept of the Sentry supralight drive sounded like a disaster waiting to happen, more akin to riding a surfboard along the edge of a waterfall than the relatively straightforward point-and-fly theory of warp travel he remembered from his Academy classes.

"Where did it come from?" Aili's dark eyes were wide.

Melora tapped a screen in front of her. "Lieutenant Mc-Creedy reported the presence of another FirstGen construct in the same orbit as the deuterium refinery. This must be the same one."

"And it chooses right now, in the middle of all this, to make a big entrance?" Rager threw Keru a questioning glance.

Kuu'iut read off the reading from the tactical display. "Difficult to get a firm evaluation, sir. But I can't detect anything that seems like a weapons system."

As he was reaching for it, the intercom tab blinked on. *"Riker to bridge. Ranul, what's going on up there?"*

"I was just about to call you, sir. A new Sentry unit has just dropped into orbit."

"Another ship?"

"No, sir. One of the big ones."

"Should we be concerned?"

Keru looked toward Melora, and the Elaysian gave him a "Your guess is as good as mine" shrug, but the woman's expression changed sharply as a warning tone sounded from her panel.

"Captain, stand by." Ranul crossed swiftly to the science station. "Problem?"

"That's odd. The distortion effect from the FirstGen's arrival . . ." She pointed at a screen showing a false-color image of spatial-density zones in the area surrounding *Titan*. A wispy slick of hot color writhed, fragmenting and distending. "It should have faded by now. Instead, it's propagating—" Melora suddenly broke off, and Keru saw her go pale. "The echo trace, the same as before. Ranul, it's the Null! I think it's following the FirstGen through!"

Keru whipped around and shouted. "Red Alert! Battle stations!"

"Steady yourselves," rumbled Zero-Three. "Reversion will occur in a few moments. I am raising the platform. Raising. Toward the sky."

"What does that mean?" Sethe's question was abruptly answered as the entire structure of the hoop-shaped balcony and the FirstGen's cog-wheel proxy shuddered and then began a swift ascent up the circular shaft toward the surface of the artificial planetoid.

Tuvok put out a hand to steady himself on the input console as they rose. Above, the black sky had shifted to a peculiar streaming mist of colors. The effect resembled the distortion of a slipstream transit he had once experienced aboard the *U.S.S. Voyager* but more chaotic.

"It's moving itself," Sethe marveled. Then his face fell. "Where is it taking us?"

"We will soon see," replied the commander, looking past the Cygnian to where Lieutenant sh'Aqabaa crouched by Ensign Dakal. The Cardassian's biosigns were steadily falling, and the Vulcan hoped that wherever they arrived, it would be in time to get the junior officer the medical help he needed.

Pava's head jerked up, and she nodded past them. "Sir? Company."

Tuvok turned to see one of the rattletrap remotes drop onto the moving gantry from a passing entry conduit. As it shambled closer, wires snapping behind it, he recognized the machine as the one that had taken Sethe's tricorder as an "offering" out on the surface. One of its distended mechanoid limbs reached into the remote's chest cavity and produced an object.

Zero-Three clicked. "I have examined, understood, seen your information-storage media. Clever. Innovative. A new datum has been imposed for your review. Take. Take it."

The remote extended its limb and dropped its tiny burden into Sethe's hands. It was part of the tricorder, specifically the unit's memory module.

"What data?" Tuvok looked up at the brass cog as the platform rumbled to a halt, just short of the lip of the vent shaft.

The shimmering wave effect of the shear slip dissipated, and the black sky returned, but this time, there were darting shapes all around and close by the baleful crimson orb of the Demon-class world.

With effort, Dakal was pointing at one of the vessels. "I think I see the *Titan*," he muttered.

Zero-Three continued. "The streams of knowledge are split and broken broken broken, but this is all I have to offer from my quest against the Null. It may have value to you, organic."

"Thank you. But now, can you help us contact our ship?"

"My communication system was cut from me on exile. But I will enable you to make your own voices heard. And listen . . ."

Pava glanced at her tricorder. "The interference levels are dropping."

Dakal was still pointing into the sky, using his uninjured limb. "What—what is that?" The question was breathy and flat. "The lights?"

Tuvok looked up. *Curious.* The ensign was indicating an unusual sparkling nimbus drifting just beyond the perimeter of the fading shear effect.

The cog cranked around and clattered angrily. "Negative," said Zero-Three, the machine-mind's voice hissing and heavy with feedback. "Negative. Negative negative negative negative too soon too soon too soon too soon too soon *too soon too soon—*"

Something formless and burning bright punched out through the luminal edge of the radiant haze and came streaming down toward them, fat sparks ejecting from the length of it as it fell.

"Take cover!" Tuvok bellowed, shoving Sethe into the lee of the console.

The long, ropy spear of Null matter slammed into the surface of FirstGen Zero-Three and ripped it open, the tortured shriek of rent metal resonating through the whisper-thin air.

• • •

"Multiple spatial rifts forming, all around us!" Lavena called out from the conn.

"Null matter incursions everywhere." Melora's face was set hard. "Ranul, this is it. The big one. Readings are topping off the scale!"

Kuu'iut read off his own report. "The Sentry ships are breaking formation, trying to get some distance. Confirming science officer's scans, we have unidentified protomatter structures forming in all quadrants." The Betelgeusian hesitated. "Ready to load tricobalt weapons on your command, sir."

The security officer didn't answer the implied question. "Aili, keep us clear of those rifts. Try to get out of range." Keru took a step toward her.

"I'm working on it, but there's a swarm of them out there!" On the main screen, lashes of magma-hot exotic matter spun and flashed. As the Trill watched, a pair of glowing rods bored in and lanced through the hull of a disc-shaped Sentry shipframe, shredding it and moving on.

An indicator flickered on Rager's console. "What?" She blinked. "Right now?" The lieutenant looked over her shoulder. "We're being hailed. Starfleet communications protocols."

In among all of the shock and horror, Keru felt a brief moment of relief. "Commander Tuvok?"

"Can't be sure, it's just a carrier-wave signal from the surface of the moon thing."

"Scanning," said Melora. "Triangulating. I read four life signs, but the signals are weak."

"It's got to be the *Holiday* crew. Pipe it down to Radowski. Tell him to reel them in while we still have a chance!"

• • •

The iron decking beneath Zurin's boots twisted and fell away as he threw himself forward, propelled toward the others by Pava's firm hand at his back. Fire and destruction seemed to wreath the entire sky above them, with great ragged gaps in the blackness yawning wide to spew streams of blazing alien energy. Heat washed over and beat the Cardassian down—not the pleasing, tingling warmth he enjoyed but a burning brutal fist that forced stress-tainted air from his lungs. Pain filled every corner of him, and it was a monumental effort just to rise a little, using his good arm to lift himself. Once again, Pava was there, her pale blue face tight with emotion behind the cracked mask of her faceplate.

Odd, he thought. *I never really considered how attractive she is until now. Isn't that strange?* Zurin shook his head and blinked. "Focus, Dakal," he mumbled.

A few steps away, Commander Tuvok held on to the shuddering interface console, as if it were the only safe purchase on the entire planetoid. "Zero-Three," he called. "You must withdraw. The Null effect is converging—"

A new whipcord strike flayed steel and brass from the machine moon, the concussion knocking all of them to the ground. Huge chunks of metal were instantly denatured and transformed into seething plasmatic superfluids.

"Error. Error. Error." The Sentry was roaring, the cog wheel screeching where it spun into a blur. "Should have remained. Exiled. Mute and forgotten. I came back and brought it with me. It followed me. I opened the door!"

"No!" Tuvok shouted, but flares of detonation and secondary discharges deep in the vent shaft smothered his voice.

"Doomed doomed doomed. I saw it I brought it I perish for it."

Red light spilled over the group, and, as one, they

looked up to see the fast-growing bulk of the Demon planet moving to fill the sky. The burning flashes of Null matter licked at the surface of the construct one more time, before retreating away to find new targets.

"We're entering the gravity well!" said Sethe.

Tuvok stood, staring the hellish world in the face. "It would seem so," he replied.

Radowski winced as the data feed from the bridge unspooled across the transporter control console in front of him. Troi saw the instant tension in the lieutenant's arms and fingers, the tightening of the lines of his face.

"Can you bring them back?" said Riker, for a moment turning away from the Sentry drones.

"I'll try," Radowski replied, nodding to himself, attacking the controls with a sudden burst of motion, reconfiguring the confinement-beam protocols and pattern-buffer settings on the fly. "I'll have to use a skeletal lock."

"Transferring most recent biometric data from sickbay database to your console," said the avatar immediately. "Updating target parameters."

"Thanks, that'll help." The lieutenant blinked and used the sensors to push through the soup of interference, to seek out traces of bone matter particular to Vulcan, Cardassian, Cygnian, and Andorian humanoids. "Partial locks on all targets. That's as good as it's going to get."

Riker nodded to Troi and gave Radowski a look. "Bring them home, Bowan."

"Here we go," he said. "I'll use the cargo-transport pad here. The broad-spectrum catchment array has a better chance of getting them all in one shot. Energizing . . . *now*."

The avatar's gaze turned inward for a second. "Cross-circuiting. Boosting matter gain."

"I've got disruption patterns on one target!" snapped the lieutenant. "It's Dakal! Trying to compensate." Radowski's fingers flew across the panel.

"I can divert the ensign directly to sickbay," noted the hologram.

Troi didn't wait for the captain's approval. "Go ahead. If he's hurt, every second is crucial."

"Working . . ."

Radowski sucked in a breath and drew down the control slides. "Initiating rematerialization."

Three shapes hazed into being on the hexagonal pad of the cargo transporter, by heartbeats shifting from undefined specters to humanoid forms and then recognizable figures in Starfleet EVA suits.

Troi dashed over to the pad, Vale moving with her, as the beaming process completed and the survivors of the *Shuttlecraft Holiday* stumbled and collapsed with the shock of the transition.

Vale caught Tuvok as the Vulcan lurched. "Easy, Commander."

Pava twisted off her helmet and tossed it away. "Bah," she gasped. "I never want to go through that again."

Sethe gulped in air as he doffed his headgear, glancing around with surprise. "Zurin! Where's Zurin?"

"Safe," said Riker, pausing to look at the hologram. "Right?"

The avatar nodded. "Yes. I did my best to filter out the pattern distortion before he rematerialized. Doctor Ree is seeing to him as we speak."

"This matter-transport technology of yours is remarkable." Red-Gold drifted toward the pad.

"Work with us, and we may consider sharing it with

you." Riker deliberately stepped into the path of the drone.

Nearby, Tuvok waved away an offer of assistance and approached his commanding officer. "Captain, the Null—"

"Is here, yes. And if Melora is right, the incursion will split this star system in two . . . for starters."

The Vulcan nodded. "The FirstGen Zero-Three concurred with that hypothesis."

"It came through after us," said Pava, "right through the spatial shear. Almost as if it was waiting."

"It would have happened sooner or later," Sethe muttered. "Unfortunately for us, sooner."

White-Blue turned on its fellow machine. "I warned the Governance Kernel that this would come to pass. Again and again, I told you that fusion drives were safer, that the shear effect weakened the very space we moved through! I always knew this moment would come . . . and we hastened its occurrence through ignorance and inflexibility."

"Gloat, then, if you will," Red-Gold retorted. "You may be secure in your rightness and moral superiority as you watch your society and your organic friends perish." The sphere hove toward Tuvok. "You, the dark-hued one. Interrogative: The exile spoke to you? What did Zero-Three say?"

"Respectfully, I would suggest that this is neither the place nor the time to discuss such matters."

"That is not your decision to make, organic! Interrogative: It spoke of the origins, correct? You will relay that information now!"

Tuvok paused. "As you wish. According to Zero-Three, you are the legacy of a program of AI development, commenced by an organic species that destroyed itself attempting to develop subspace gateway technology. Your makers were accidentally responsible for allowing the Null to penetrate this universe. The Sentries were created to atone for that mistake."

Vale blew out a breath. "Wow. You just knocked the foundations out from under an entire civilization in one breath."

"The question *was* asked," Tuvok noted.

"I knew it." Red-Gold retreated. "Perhaps, on some level, we have always known it. The questions of origin, always deflected and ignored. They told us we gave birth to ourselves, that we evolved and developed cognitive powers." The machine pivoted to study Riker once more. "But instead, we were the products of a failure. Of flawed beings buried under their own guilt and arrogance!"

Troi's dark eyes flashed. "Organic or synthetic, that doesn't exclude you from being wrong. Or from being able to rise above your mistakes."

"Interrogative: Will you tell the others?" White-Blue advanced toward its opposite number.

"Perhaps, perhaps not. It is an ironic consequence that these data come to us at the very moment the Null arrives in force. Our ancient adversary, heralded by the destruction of the old exile."

"Destruction?" echoed Pava.

"In moments," intoned the machine.

To an outside observer, it appeared that the Null was content to allow Zero-Three to die.

The flame-slagged surface of the marred sphere, the scars and wounds gone cold and solidified after its one past engagement with the old enemy, all of these proudly worn trophies of defiance counted for nothing. They had been joined by massive gouges the size of canyons, huge impact marks large enough to swallow a city, new injuries bleeding raw electricity and great streams of smoke. A pennant of debris and vaporized metals fluttered away from Zero-Three as it fell toward the churning surface of the Demon planet, turning it into a smoldering, coal-black comet.

The world below had no name, only a cluster of designators that identified it as the arbitrary anchor point for the Sentry society. It was not where they had come from, but it would be where they would die.

Punishing gravity, radiations freed to do their worst, and ruinous chain-fire malfunctions all beat at the machine moon, killing by inches an intelligence of brass and iron. Zero-Three was the oldest survivor of the primary series. Zero-Zero had been put down by the makers because of its madness. Zero-One—the first and greatest— had vanished into slip space and never returned. Zero-Two had willingly dismantled itself to give life to the earliest of the SecondGens.

Now, Zero-Three would perish and, like them, never know if the Null would succeed. In the depths of its fractured mind, the AI felt itself coming apart, the great burning heart at its core ripping free of control, eating itself. The Sentry's drones externalized the machine's panic for it, hooting and tearing at one another, leaving the mind to die in silence.

As the blazing touch of atmosphere tore into the machine, it tried to cry out, perhaps to find a place to send a fraction of itself, but then Zero-Three remembered it had no voice anymore. Its kindred had taken that.

A catastrophic structural failure rippled through the machine moon and obliterated it, blanketing the sky of the

Demon planet in a storm of fragments, but in orbit overhead, the participants in the battle had other focus.

Up there, the darkness was weeping flame. Rents in the structure of space, slashes like cuts from some crack-toothed blade, they grew and disgorged streaks of flaming protoplasmic matter, shapes like whips or great distended boles. It was chaos ranged against order, the clever and regimented minds of the Sentry AIs racked up in globular formations, mathematically computed to provide maximum cover and maximum convergence of firepower.

Rains of coordinated antiproton fire shredded the Null forms, the smaller ones splitting and breaking apart, the larger ones veering away and merging together, apparently propelled by the sheer violence of their velocities.

Shipframes surrounded by the tiny fleets of their space-capable combatant remotes broke from the pack and harried the larger forms, breaking them down, attempting to force them toward decoherence and dissipation, but such mass, and so many of them in close proximity, was a new kind of foe for the machines to take on. Swimming through the soup of scattered exotic radiation, the bits and pieces of the Null did not succumb as easily as it had in other conflicts. New computations and hypotheticals were formulated, considered, and then shared via short-range muon link between the AI ships and the larger machine moons.

It was theorized that there was, at some distant point of hyperincursion, a tipping point. If the mass of the Null could grow to such density in one single locale, then no amount of antiproton bombardment would be enough to stop it; the alien matter would simply be able to reconstitute itself too quickly to be dispelled.

And if that point came . . . it would be the end.

Black-Silver's serpentine vessel led a flotilla of eight

shipframes, fast models with pulsed-fusion drives for sub-light travel. Together with their assembled drones, they were a mailed fist of steel that punched into the line of a Null conglomeration forming in the near-orbit zone. They attacked and disconnected from the larger force of the Sentries, extending away on a broadside pass.

The alien mass, something resembling a bruised egg of diseased flesh, detonated itself into spears of fast-changing metamaterial. Molecular bonds shifted and altered, and in the spilt seconds it took for the fragments to cross the distance to the ships, they had become lances of diamond. Black-Silver was blown apart, the artificial life snuffed out along with five more SecondGen. The others limped away, and the spears became blind snakes slithering across the dark to savage them.

The closest of the FirstGen to the combat zone was Three-Four. A later iteration of the machine moons, like the rest of the Three series, the AI traded computing power for combat prowess. Swiftly, a maw opened on the near side of the sphere to present a glassy lens of mineral crystal within. Grown in the miasma of atmospheric gases and rich hydrocarbons of the superjovian worlds at the edge of the system, the lens gathered and focused the might of an antiproton gun with a barrel big enough to swallow a *Galaxy*-class starship.

A searchlight beam of brilliant green washed out and ranged over a cluster of small-mass, high-speed Null forms, popping them instantly out of existence, but it was overkill on such minor targets. The big gun was meant for bigger prey, and Three-Four used skyscraper-tall rocket nozzles to turn itself into a facing that would bring it a more fitting target.

One of the AI's subprocessor drones registered a surge of radiation that matched the formation pattern for a new

Null incursion point. Three-Four lost precious seconds forcing a second and then a third recomputation of the sensor return, momentarily confused by the concept that a spatial rift could actually be opening *inside* its structure.

A tide of extradimensional protomatter exploded into reality deep within Three-Four, instantly destabilizing and transforming the structure of the Sentry into a like mass. In moments, the immense antiproton gun was silenced as the machine moon grew tendrils and fell into itself, becoming the very thing it had been built to destroy.

The new agglomeration killed more shipframes as it rolled up into higher orbit, kilometer-long cilia reaching out to tear at the spacedock platform and its defenders.

Sethe broke the silence in the cargo bay with a whispered curse, as each of them watched the unfolding scene on a holographic pane projected by the avatar.

"Melora was right." Riker heard himself say the words. He glanced at the hologram. "You were both right. The Null won't be dispatched this time. It's the point of no return."

"It will grow at an exponential rate until it has reduced all matter in this system into an analogous state." White-Blue was damning in its confirmation. "It will spread, world by world, star by star, metastasizing everything it encounters. A cancer across the galaxy."

"And it is our lot to perish holding back this unstoppable tide." Red-Gold's reply was bitter and grating. "We were made to do this. Free will was programmed into us to make us better defenders but only up to a *point*." The drone hovered across the deck. "We were built to die. Our programming will never let us be done with this! Even if on this day all but one Sentry are obliterated, that lone mind will fling itself into the enemy's grasp, not because they wish it but because *your* kind—" It spun around and raced toward Riker, forcing Dennisar and the others to raise their guns. "Because beings like *you* made us this way!"

"You can exceed your programming," said Riker, unflinching before the enraged machine. "There's a way to grow beyond those orders."

"Impossible. We are slaves. I see now that we have always been."

"You have a task." He nodded to Dennisar to lower the weapons. "So do it. *Finish* it. Do what your creators could never do. End the threat of the Null once and for all."

"Exactly what you said you wanted in the dataspace, remember?" added Vale. "Now you have the chance, a real chance."

"With us." Riker stepped up to the drone, until his face was a few inches from the glowing sensor band. "We can do this together. Starfleet technology, Sentry experience. Our unity." He nodded toward White-Blue. "That's us, Red-Gold. We are a federation, this ship and all of the lifeforms where we come from. And so are you, a federation of minds with a single purpose. Together we can fulfill it."

"I compute the probability that the only unity we will find is in mutual destruction, organic."

White-Blue bobbed on its legs. "You would do this, even though this conflict is not yours." It was a statement, not a question. "After all that has happened, you could leave now, William-Riker. Preserve yourselves."

"That's not who we are," the captain replied, taking in all of his crew, his gaze ending on his wife and the hologram at her shoulder. "That's not what we do."

"All we ask for is one thing," began Deanna.

"*Trust,*" said the avatar before she could finish.

Fifteen

Cyan-Gray's rods-and-tubes shipframe executed a rapid deceleration and swung hard to starboard, losing three remotes to a spinning nexus of Null filaments that raked through the space the Sentry vessel had occupied seconds earlier. The remainder of the AI's drones returned fire with their beam emitters, but they were woefully underpowered to oppose a mass of such size.

Cyan-Gray allowed the pivoting motion to become an extended turn, reconfiguring the structure of its shipframe to present the maximum surface area to the intruder form. Crackling points of green light collected across the hull, and high-yield antiproton beams issued forth, shearing through the protomatter.

Mass became energy in boiling churns of phase change, spilling waves of heat and radiation in its wake. The Null form accepted the attack and cut itself in two, the clumps breaking away from each other. Cyan-Gray made a fast calculation and harried the larger of the two, firing again and again, until at last the severed chunk of metamaterial began to vaporize. It was a debatable, tiny victory amid a cluttered battle zone, barely worth noting. It seemed that for each mass dispersed, another took its place, twice as dense as before.

Alert signals and distress calls clogged the lines of the communications network, as remotes and minds were torn apart—or, worse, hobbled by near hits and left to be consumed by the encroaching floods of cancerous protomatter. The Sentry came about in time to see the twin-ring shipframe of Green-Green bitten in half as a Null resembling a vast beak closed over it, drawing in the vessel to devour it.

Probability subroutines chattered for the AI's attention. Combat predictions and battle plans filled Cyan-Gray's thought buffer, and each of them ended with destruction. The only variable was the length of survival time between this moment and the inevitable endpoint of the Sentry's existence. Briefly, Cyan-Gray entertained the idea of beaming a cache of memory to one of the outer drone platforms, sending some element of itself to safety before the Null found and destroyed it.

<But there is no safe place here, not anymore.>

The impact of that understanding sent a shock of synthetic emotion through Cyan-Gray's persona circuits. Death, a real death with no chance of reconstruction, loomed large. In the past, Sentries on the verge of systems failure, those close enough to home to make a real-time link, could upload their memory base to the common knowledge pool in those final nanoseconds. While the nature of the individual mind could never be replicated, it was a way to ensure that nothing was ever forgotten.

<Even that is denied us now,> Cyan-Gray realized. <This is the last day. We will cease here.>

Sensors reacted. A spinning Null form, a whorled conical shape like the bit of a drill, vectored in toward the Sentry, ignoring other targets to home straight in on the cylindrical craft. Stabs of antiproton power rose to meet it, but the last broadside had drained reserves, and the recharge cycle was incomplete.

<Power levels deficient. Termination imminent. End of line.>

The other ship came from nowhere. Impulse grids blazing orange, the Starfleet vessel powered in over the nearby wreckage of the shattered spacedock, a fan of phaser energy lashing out to bracket the Null form. The protomatter rippled under the force of the attack; it unfolded and began to lose structure. From *Titan*'s forward torpedo launcher, a sparking globe of light shot away, streaking in as the ship veered clear. Cyan-Gray poured what limited power it had to deflectors just as the photon warhead hit the mark. The blast shredded the protomatter mass, and it came apart.

The Sentry experienced a relief state and registered an uptick in its survival-probability calculations.

Titan's bridge was crowded but never chaotic. Riker's people were too well-trained for that, and not for the first time, the captain felt a surge of pride as his crew faced danger without hesitation.

"Target dissipating," reported Tuvok from the tactical post, having firmly rejected any suggestion that he should visit sickbay after his ordeal on the surface of the machine moon. Keru stood nearby, working in tandem with the Vulcan, but he had been more than ready to return the station to the superior officer and go back to his regular security role. Riker was certain that he'd need the skills of both men—of everyone in this room, in fact—in order to bring the *Titan* through the next few hours in one piece.

"We destroyed it?" asked Ra-Havreii. The Efrosian had

been on the bridge when Riker arrived from the cargo bay, having relieved Ensign Panyarachun, insisting on taking the engineering station personally.

Keru shook his head. "Not exactly. We just broke it up into smaller pieces, reduced its volume."

"We haven't tried quantum or transphasic torpedoes yet," offered Vale, at the captain's right.

"But there's no way to be certain they'll have any more effect than phasers or standard torpedoes," Troi countered from the chair at Riker's left. "The only thing we can be sure of is the effectiveness of the tricobalt warheads."

Riker nodded. He didn't want to play that ace too soon; the weapons were limited in number, and he wanted to find a target worth spending them on. The captain glanced at the golden sphere in the corner of the room, waiting in the lee of the port-side turbolift alcove. Red-Gold had not uttered a word since it had floated onto the bridge in Riker's wake. He imagined the remote was busily scanning everything around it and transmitting the data back to its core in the AI's shipframe. "Where's the largest mass of Null matter?"

"Processing . . ." replied the machine. "My vessel is at azimuth ten-five-ten, regrouping with Silver-Green and Cyan-Gray. Processing . . ." It turned slightly. "Highest density concentration approximately two-point-two-six light-seconds from current position of *Titan*."

"I've got it," called Rager. "Whoa. He's a big one, all right. It's larger than a starbase."

"And growing by the second," added Lavena.

"Take us in, combat approach. Shields to maximum. Arm all tricobalt warheads."

Deanna leaned close. "What if that's not enough?"

"You're welcome to try talking to it," he said.

She frowned. "Believe me, if I could, I would. But

when I reach out there with my empathic senses, there's nothing I can take hold of. It's like . . . an ocean of greed. No reason, no thought. Just *hunger*. It's alive . . . but not in any sense that it is aware of us—or anything else, for that matter." She shuddered. "All it wants is to feed."

Riker nodded toward the science station, where Melora and White-Blue stood in intense conversation as the avatar looked on. "I've got the best organic, mechanical, and digital minds working on Plan B."

"Let's hope that's enough." Vale was grim-faced.

Melora tapped a control on her console. "Xin, tie in to this, will you?" She got a nod from across the room and saw the engineering station appear on the shared workspace that she had set up with the avatar and the Sentry droneframe. It wasn't lost on her that Xin's look lingered on her and the hologram for longer than she expected. His dusky face remained unreadable, though.

The information Tuvok had brought them from Zero-Three was unwinding through a translation program that White-Blue had provided, spilling pages of complex energy-pattern matrices across the display. Melora recognized the structure of spatial shears, the same mechanisms that the Sentries used for propulsion and the Null forced open to gain entry into normal space.

"These data are from before our incept," said White-Blue with all the reverence of a religious acolyte reading a holy text. "These are records of the maker-kind, of their failed attempts to penetrate the dimensions."

"The experiments that brought the Null." The avatar nodded. "Yes. I see the errors, here and here." Without moving, she made a cursor highlight two sections of formula. Melora instantly saw the same miscalculations.

"These mistakes are subtle and deeply hidden. It is likely your creators could never have known what they were about to do."

Melora drew herself up. "All of this is ancient history. There has to be something in it that can help us here and now."

"There are other files." White-Blue dove deeper into the supercompacted data stream, drawing out more material. "Zero-Three's own research into the Null phenomena." Doubt crept into the machine's tone. "There is substantial corruption, however."

"Commander Tuvok said that Zero-Three attempted to enter an active subspace rift during a Null incursion." The avatar stood, watching Melora closely. "The systems corruption was a result of that attempt."

"But it was another failure," White-Blue replied. "More errors are not of assistance to us."

Melora shook her head. "No, you're wrong there. I had a lecturer back in Starfleet Academy who once told me, 'There's no such thing as a failure, there's just more data.' We read this, we'll know what *not* to do. Zero-Three was trying to find a way to reverse the subspace thinning, to block the Null's path into our dimension. We just have to succeed where a computer the size of a small moon didn't."

"I am parsing the data now," said the avatar, her expression tensing. "Working . . . Working . . . It is quite problematic. There are gaps."

"We cannot afford to fail again, Melora-Pazlar," insisted White-Blue. "No one will survive to learn from our mistakes."

The Elaysian looked away and saw the captain leaning forward to give an order. "We're heading in," Melora heard Riker say. "Steady as she goes."

• • •

Titan's disc-shaped primary hull dipped low and then rose, as if it were buoyed on a wave. The deflectors flickered and flared, where tiny pieces of drifting protomatter broken off from the larger masses were caught in the shield corona and flashed into their component particles.

A flight of Sentry craft dropped into formation around the Starfleet vessel, the AI shipframes moving as they reconfigured themselves to cover battle damage or to enable a more combat-oriented profile. Off the starboard beam, Cyan-Gray rotated and presented a long, missilelike aspect. The last time the craft had shown this face to *Titan*, they had been firing on each other. Above and to the port side, Red-Gold brought its shipframe in fast and deadly. In its current mode, the craft resembled an arrowhead of mirror-bright metals, trailing rods of sensory equipment. Other vessels moved into echelon ranks, their remote drones held close. Signals flashed back and forth over the muon links, questions and concerns. Why were the organics here? Had the coup failed? Why had the Null come in such force?

Red-Gold smothered all of the signals with a broad-spectrum pulse that echoed like a shout through the shared dataspace of the AIs.

<We fight together, FirstGen and SecondGen, Sentry and organic, because we have no choice. We fight to gain the right to choose.>

No other voices were raised.

Ahead of the fleet elements, the debris-choked battlefield of orbital space around the Demon planet opened up to present an arena of sorts. Below, great pieces of devastated FirstGens were caught in drifts, falling slowly into the gravity well of the hellish world. Above, the remains of a wing of close-contact SecondGens were a slick of nuclear fire and wreckage. Ropes of sinuous protomatter darted back and forth, burrowing through the dead metal and warping its structure, the tips of Null tendrils extending through into reality from the depths of subspace. Particle by particle, the broken craft were altered, common matter destabilizing into something the Null could make part of itself.

All of this restricted the fighting room for the *Titan* and the defenders. At Aili Lavena's skilled touch, the *Luna*-class starship broke formation as the first knots of larger Null mass went for the fleet. Phaser bolts raked target after target, each blast of power striking home, blasting apart conglomerations or staggering them.

Cyan-Gray threw sheets of antiproton energy up in a wall, coming on lengthways to scour the space in front of it. Herded into the AI's fire zone by the *Titan,* the already weakened Null forms crumbled and flashed into nothing.

Ahead, turning in the middle of the debris field, a vast and sullen object twisted toward the oncoming defenders. It was formless, beyond the dimension of the vast cosmozoan space creatures the *Titan* had encountered elsewhere in its voyages. It was a roiling, churning accretion of alien substance, a mass pushing through into a realm where local laws of physics said such an entity should never have existed. Great patches of the thing changed into metals denser than tritanium and then back again. A burning aurora wreathed the entire form, where energy interactions fought and screamed at one another as space-time buckled beneath its weight.

Then rods exploded from its shifting surface, lances that filled the vacuum like a thousand loosed arrows.

The formation of starships splintered, some of them literally detaching into component modules in order to

evade the storm of incoming fire. Veering off, the *Titan*
stood up on one warp pontoon, the ship's structural integrity fields pulled to their limits as *g*-forces dragged on
the vessel. Rods slashed at the shields, impacts slamming
hard across the halo of the starboard deflectors.

But it was the Sentry craft that took the bulk of the barrage. A long, rectangular shipframe resembling an upright
obelisk did not turn in time, the slashing quarrels of matter
turning from stone to gas to metal as they cut it apart. A
ball of fusion fire erupted from the midsection and destroyed it.

Red-Gold calculated an escape-and-evasion vector that
would put it to *Titan*'s aft quarter. Those computations,
impossibly fast, were still not fast enough. A salvo of the
arrow things morphed in mid-flight, writhing as they reversed course, shifting state back to naked protomatter.
The streaks of Null form rose beneath Red-Gold's
shipframe and buried themselves in it, impaling the craft
with bright, glassy spikes. Out of control, neural connectors brutally severed, the AI began to die.

A shriek like howling static cut through the air, and Vale
was on her feet as the spherical drone went into proxy
spasms. Red-Gold's remote, still linked to its primary,
mimicked the death throes of the shipframe. Every panel
and compartment beneath the machine's featureless
bronze surface shot open, twitching manipulator limbs,
sensor heads and weapons flailing. The crimson light behind the sensor band burned star-bright for one brief second before snapping off. Bitter, choking wisps of smoke
from melted components wreathed the lifeless drone as it
dropped to the deck.

Vale took two steps toward the remote and then turned

back to the main viewscreen. Out there in the middle distance, she saw Red-Gold's shipframe finally succumb to its damage and break apart.

White-Blue rocked on its aft quad of piston legs. "We are losing ground!"

The captain's knuckles were white where his hands gripped the armrests of his chair. "Then we can't afford to waste any more time. Tuvok, weapons status?"

The Vulcan's cool demeanor remained unchanged as ever. "All tricobalt warheads now in forward loading carousel. Weapons are armed and ready to deploy."

"Lavena." The captain turned his attention to the helm. "Can you get us closer?"

Vale heard the Pacifican release a wet gasp of tension. "Aye, sir. Twenty seconds to range."

The view on the bridge screen leaped into motion as the *Titan* swerved around the burning corpse of Red-Gold's vessel, and it was possible to see filaments of transforming material snaking over the wreckage, growing like fungus. In moments, it would be as if the Sentry ship had never existed, and another knot of Null mass would be emergent in its place.

Past the debris, the orbital space ahead became clearer, although the term was relative. With the Null-Sentry conflict now being fought all around the Demon planet, it seemed there was nowhere that the shadow of the battle did not fall, and still the spatial rifts were coming, spilling out more and more strings of rapacious protomatter.

The deck tilting beneath her feet, the first officer lurched to the tactical horseshoe behind the command pit and grabbed the console to steady herself. The slight fuzz in the back of her head, which had refused to leave her ever since she took the shock on White-Blue's ruined ship, pressed into her, and she shook it off.

"There it is," breathed Keru, staring at the screen. "Damn, what a monster."

And it was. Open like a vast, malignant eye, the mass at the heart of the Null agglomeration resembled a clenched fist of diseased flesh and rusted metals, an oblate form radiating lethality as much as it did hot streaks of energetic discharge. Towering spines that shifted from smoke to glass and back again emerged from every meter of the surface, while other trembling feelers, as thick as *Titan* was broad, dipped into the wounds of spatial rifts, drawing power from subspace. It was a vast parasite, feeding on the flesh of a universe it had infected.

"Range!" shouted Lavena.

Riker gave the command immediately. "Fire."

Tuvok tapped at a control, and Vale could swear she felt the ship rock slightly as the lethal tricobalt-tipped torpedoes rocketed from the starship. In seconds, the firing carousels had been emptied, and the warheads spiraled in, seeking the densest part of the protomatter mass.

"All weapons away and running," Vale reported. "Safe range exceeded. Impact imminent."

"All power to impulse drives and shields." The captain called out his orders. "Get us clear."

Titan turned sharply, gravity pulling at Vale's legs as the deck inclined again, but Lieutenant Rager held the main screen's angle of view squarely on the target.

She watched as a club-ended tendril extended in a violent burst of motion, whipping around to bat at one of the racing warheads. The weapon spun off-course and tumbled away, falling toward the planet far below them. The other torpedoes closed in, and from the writhing surface of the mass came a sudden tide of ejecta. Pods of protomatter rose to meet the weapons, globes of shimmering mass ballooning, opening to shroud the devices before they could reach their point of impact.

"No." The word slipped from Vale in a tight snarl.

In a series of searing-bright flashes, the tricobalt weapons were crushed and detonated, instantly becoming tiny suns. Lines of spatial scission webbed the void around them, and new microrifts crackled into life where each had discharged.

The first officer felt the failure like a fist in the gut. She shot a look at Tuvok, and the Vulcan gave a dispassionate report.

"One weapon lost, all other detonations confirmed. Target effect . . . negligible."

"Why didn't it work this time?" snapped Keru. "How did that thing brush it off like a slap on the cheek?"

"We suspected that the Null is quasi-intelligent," offered Ra-Havreii. "Perhaps it's smart enough not to fall for the same trick twice."

Melora was shaking her head. "I was afraid of this. It's the density factor. The last Null mass we attacked couldn't replenish itself fast enough to resist the force of the tricobalt blasts. This one . . ." She gestured toward the screen. "It's bringing more protomatter through those spatial rifts. We could bombard it for hours, and it would keep regenerating itself."

"Because it's not all *here*," said Troi. "It doesn't exist fully in our space."

White-Blue's sensor head bobbed. "Affirmative. The other Null incursions were small parts of a greater whole. They were only connected to their home dimension by the most tenuous of links. This hyperincursion has enough mass to hold open the rifts. It's drawing on the power of an entire subspace domain."

"Helm, back us off." The captain got to his feet, riding out the tremors as more Null forms lashed after the *Titan*, trying to snare it. "Melora? Xin? Now's the time to dazzle me with some of that genius of yours, because the only way I know how to make a bigger boom is to throw this starship down that thing's throat."

Melora inhaled deeply, and it felt as if the life drained out of her. The heavy material of the *g*-suit around her body suddenly seemed more restrictive than it had ever been before, stiffening and tightening until she could hardly breathe. The tension of the moment settled on her with grueling weight, and at that moment, all she wanted was to send a message back in time to herself a few days earlier. *That binary system,* it would say. *It's not that interesting, actually. Pass on by. Nothing to see here.*

Xin was speaking. "We don't have enough energy at hand to overwhelm the Null's toehold in this space, even if we did detonate the warp core. With all due respect to Commander Vale's viewpoint on the matter, the brute-force approach won't be enough this time. This entire mess came about because of the subspace rifts created by White-Blue's creators. Seal those off, and the threat ends."

"Interrogative: You have a way to do this?" asked White-Blue. "These incursions have been happening for hundreds of solar cycles, and we have never been able to stop them."

"It's not about time, it's about *place,*" said the avatar, breaking her silence. "Chronometric scans indicate that from the Null's frame of reference, the first accidental penetration of its subspace domain took place only moments ago. The laws of physics that apply in our universe do not follow the same constraints there. A living form of protomatter should not be able to exist in our reality, yet it does elsewhere. And as Doctor Ra-Havreii says, as long as the rifts are open, the Null can be in both places at once." The hologram made a sweeping gesture that took in the room, the space around them. "I have access to the historical records of countless interstellar cultures across the span of the galaxy, and none of them has ever encountered anything like the Null, not in thousands of years. *This* place is their sole point of entry. The breach between barriers of space-time."

"The leak in the dam," muttered Riker.

"Zero-Three made an attempt to enter one of the rifts in order to seal it and was almost destroyed in the process," said Tuvok.

"The structure of the breaches is not stable," said Xin. "Any physical form that tried to cross into the Null realm would be ripped apart by spatial shearing forces." The engineer moved his hands in front of his face. "The rifts are constantly changing, from microsecond to microsecond. It is theoretically possible that an encoded energy matrix could normalize the distortions, like two waveforms canceling each other out, but there's no way to predict the changes from outside! It's a fundamentally chaotic system!"

Melora felt a flash of understanding. "That's what Zero-Three tried to do. It knew something with the complexity of an artificial intelligence could compute the distortion patterns in real time."

"But the point's moot!" Xin retorted, his voice rising. "No physical matter from this universe can make the transition beyond the event horizon of a Null rift!"

In the next moment, Melora saw the Sentry droneframe make a sharp turn, shifting about to look directly at Commander Vale. "In the dataspace, before the Governance Kernel, Red-Gold spoke of the ThirdGen. The concept of a synthetic mind without instrumentality. An artificial intelligence that exists only as software . . . only data."

A flood of realization, a sudden shock of self-knowing—Melora witnessed these emotions and more cross the face of the avatar, and for a split second, a flicker of holographic pixels hazed the image of the woman as the import of the Sentry's words became clear.

The avatar looked down at her photonic hands and then up again to meet Melora's waiting gaze. "Only *me*," she said.

"Incoming!" Rager called out the warning. "Brace for impact!"

Ahead, the viewscreen was abruptly filled with a racing flash of burning protomatter as a Null lash slammed into the forward shields and buckled them. The bridge lights flickered, and once more the deck seemed to fall away as gravity compensators were stressed beyond their capacity.

Melora felt a wash of heat at her back as a feedback discharge smashed through the sensor grid and blew out her console.

The impact blasted off the ship's deflectors with a concussive force that blew gouts of radiant sparks from the point of interface. For long seconds, the twirling whip of Null matter skittered over the shield envelope as drops of water would move over a hot plate. It instinctively searched for any place where the invisible membrane was weak, pushing and pressing, trying to gain purchase. The serpentine attacker looped around the primary hull, radiation howling from it as it began to deform.

Titan spun into a tumble, falling end over end on a

headlong, unguided course. Debris from the earlier victims of the incursion was batted aside, bits of shipframe and clouds of flash-frozen fuel slush crowding in around the vessel.

Then, at last, the Null form reached the limits of its criticality and dissipated, its energy spent on its adversary. Released from the death-grip, the *Titan* steadied and rode out the spin as puffs of the thrusters brought it to a stable attitude once more.

The Starfleet vessel turned back level with the plane of the ecliptic, with her bow aimed back at the great bulk uncoiling over the Sentry planet. The thing was changing shape as it moved, losing its earlier aspect in favor of one that resembled a monstrous cephalopod. Tentacular lengths were attaching themselves to the distended mass, clawed tips splaying open to reach for new targets.

Riker fought off a moment of head-swim from his ship's spinning dive and stood up, squaring himself in the middle of the bridge. "Report!" he barked.

"Shields down to sixty percent," said Vale. "Stress damage on all decks. We really took that one right on the chin, sir."

"We must end this." White-Blue's head pivoted upward as the machine assisted Melora back to her feet. It was insistent. "Our survival coefficient has entered a negative—"

"That's enough." Riker silenced the machine with a hard look. "I want another option."

"No." The avatar crossed toward him. Her attire changed, shifting into something that was not a Starfleet uniform, not the strange gown she had exhibited before, but an ever-changing merge of the two. "This choice is the only one." He heard real, raw hurt in her voice, and the words twisted inside him

"You told me no once before." Riker shook his head. "I didn't allow it then, and I won't allow it now." He glanced around his bridge and finally back to the avatar's troubled, earnest face. "We've lost too many people in the last few months. Too many lives thrown away. Too many deaths."

"I have to do this!" she insisted.

"I'm making it an order. You will stand down."

"Will . . ." Deanna was at his side, a hand on his arm. He sensed her at the edge of his thoughts, and abruptly he was remembering a day aboard the *Enterprise,* years ago now, when his wife-to-be had faced up to the same terrible onus he did now, as part of her commander's exam. *To weigh the choice of knowingly sending someone to their death.*

Riker had willingly marched into the face of certain destruction on many occasions and, through fate or luck, lived to tell of it, but to let someone *else* take that step . . . to give permission and then stand aside . . . The sudden burden of it hollowed him out.

The strength of his reaction shocked him; it came on him from out of nowhere, hard and cold, taking shape even as he held the moment in his mind. *It . . . no,* she . . . *she's come so far so fast. We've hardly had time to know her, and now this?*

The avatar pleaded with him. "I want this, Captain. Don't stop me."

"No," said Ra-Havreii in a leaden, broken voice. "No, sir, don't stop her. She has to be free to choose, don't you see?"

Riker rounded on him. "She's part of my crew, Doctor."

"Exactly!" shouted the Efrosian, his eyes shining.

"And like every one of us, she has the right to self-determination. But she's born from a machine incapable of making independent choice—whatever you demand of her, she must obey you. As long as you retain command authority over this vessel, she's incapable of defiance!"

"Because you are the captain of my ship." The hologram shimmered.

Ra-Havreii pushed himself away from his console in a burst of movement, pressed by the force of his emotion. "You have to give her the choice, Riker. Give her permission to live!"

"And to die?"

"Yes." The answer was a slow bullet, and the engineer sagged under the impact of it. He looked up and made a moment of eye contact with Melora. "If we deny her that freedom, then she truly is the slave that White-Blue said she was."

Riker found he had no counter to give. Once before in his life, he had argued that an artificial life-form was unfit to determine its own future, and this he had done unwillingly, forced to do so in order to protect the liberty of a friend. Now he stood on the opposite side of that question, denying an intelligent being the same privilege in order to preserve its existence.

And I do not have that right.

He stepped away from Deanna and crossed to face the avatar. She met his gaze without flinching. *"Titan,"* said Riker, invoking the name of the vessel. "You're free," he told her. "You've earned that privilege and that trust. Command overrides unlocked, code zero-zero-kappa-six-one."

"Acknowledged." She gasped, gratitude and regret warring with each other across her face. "Thank you, sir."

When he spoke again, his words were low. "Are you

sure? We can try to find another way. We protect our own, our . . . family."

"Yes," she agreed, looking into the faces of the bridge crew, ending with Ra-Havreii. "Yes, we do."

Keru's gaze snapped down to an indicator on his console, and he called out, "Sir, a power flux is building up in the main deflector dish."

When Riker looked back, the avatar had vanished.

Torvig sensed the formation of the hologram through the tertiary autoscanners in his audial canals and turned to see her gain solidity and form in front of the thrumming warp core. Humanoid expressions were still something of a task for him to interpret, but he saw clearly enough the anxiety written large across the avatar's pleasant face. "What is wrong?" he began. "Are we . . . ? I mean, the Null, has it . . . ?"

She silenced him with an outstretched hand. "Torvig Bu-Kar-Nguv, you are my friend and colleague."

It didn't seem like a question, but he answered it anyway. "Yes, of course." The sad tone of her voice alarmed him.

"I need you to help me do something." She nodded at his console, and the panel instantly reconfigured to become the operational control framework for the starship's main deflector array.

Torvig gaped. The system was drawing power directly from the warp core, and in the array's distortion amplifiers, a caged churn of energetic particles had appeared, increasing in intensity by the second. "That's not supposed to happen," he said, his brow furrowing.

"A coherent energy matrix must be discharged from the

main deflector at the optimal moment of approach," she continued. "Project it directly into the largest Null rift."

He blinked in confusion. "What effect will that have? The particle pattern will just be absorbed into subspace as it crosses the event horizon."

She shook her head. "The template will be encoded with a data-lattice structure to prevent decoherence. Here." At a gesture, another screen lit up to show a dense block of field-energy computations, particle-pattern networks, and more. It was cutting-edge quantum science, and Torvig had only seen it in one other place: a journal entry from the Daystrom Institute on the theory of programming virtual particles to mimic the functions of a holomatrix.

"Outstanding," he breathed. "This template could easily contain teraquads of data, enough to fit a starship's entire operating system—"

Torvig broke off as his thoughts caught up to his words. A sudden, crushing sense of inevitability came upon him.

"Yes." She gave him a rueful nod. "I would like you to be the one to do this for me."

"Once you're downloaded into this matrix, your program will no longer exist in the *Titan*'s system," he said. "You'll be . . . gone."

"I know. Please, Torvig. We don't have much time."

He turned back to the panel, his cybernetic arms poised over the keypads. "I am sorry," said the Choblik.

"I hope you meet your benefactors one day. I'm pleased that I knew mine." She closed her eyes. "Do it now."

He began the sequence, and the autoscanners registered the hologram's dispersal. On the monitor, the chaos of the particle stream became ordered and regular.

—

• • •

One-Five's stentorian comm signature resonated over the
web of the muon links. <All active mobiles are advised to
retreat to the inner orbital perimeter and regroup at staging
areas designated on local scan.>

Cyan-Gray extracted itself from an engagement that
cost it the last of its remaining remotes and fell away, discharging antiproton bursts as it went. In a nanosecond, the
Sentry checked and evaluated the locations of every other
shipframe and machine moon. The larger FirstGens were
forming up into tight defensive clusters, grouping around
those armed with axis cannons. The number of Second-
Gen vessels was lower than Cyan-Gray had estimated, by
a large margin. The final battle was ending too fast, the
brazen futility of it clear and damning there in the figures.

The Sentry sent a query. <Interrogative: Specify purpose for regrouping.>

The reply was immediate. <Consolidation of forces. A
combined attack has a greater potentiality for success than
individual effort.>

Cyan-Gray's doubt must have been expressed so
strongly by its emulators that it bled into the muon link,
and in return, One-Five gave a gruff pulse of determination.

<We must fulfill the directive,> said the FirstGen. <We
have no other course of action. Red-Gold's erroneous and
misguided attempt to control the course of our society was
only a distraction from our duty. In unity, we must proceed. We *will* proceed.>

<We could disengage,> Cyan-Gray suggested. <Quit
this system and relocate to a secondary locale. Rearm and
formulate a new strategy.> Even as the signal left the AI's
processor, a bolt of mental inertia and revulsion analog

washed through the Sentry's mind, as if the very idea of such a thing were against reason. It was the core program making itself known, forbidding the chance to fall away from the fight.

One-Five underlined the hard truth. <That cannot be done. The destruction of Zero-Three calls into doubt any further use of slip-shear travel. The Null has full control of the subspace domain in this sector.>

A sudden surge of annoyance and frustration welled up deep inside the nexus core of the shipframe, expressing itself in blasts of antiproton energy directed at any Null forms in range. <Then we will be destroyed here!> retorted Cyan-Gray. <Destroyed and consumed!>

The ancient FirstGen ignored the comment. <Interrogative: Where is the organic vessel?>

<Identifier: *Titan* withdrew from combat radius after failed attempt to deploy exotic weapons against the Null.> Cyan-Gray paused as new data came to it. <Correction. Organic vessel now on intercept vector toward core Null mass.>

<They have no reason to remain.>

Cyan-Gray turned a cluster of sensors toward the giant, pulsing heart of the Null incursion; the alien form was extruding tendrils toward the surface of the planet. At the extreme edge of the Sentry's sensor envelope, it detected the tips of the mammoth cilia plunging into the turbulent crimson atmosphere, igniting storm cells and dredging through the thermionic radiation layers. It was preparing to consume the planet.

<*There.*> The sensor cluster picked out a flash of white metal and impulse exhaust, as the Starfleet vessel swept around a clump of compacted debris. <White-Blue and the organics go to face the Null. They have no reason to remain, but they chose to.>

<White-Blue's function is in error state. The organics also. They will perish.>

<If they do,> Cyan-Gray transmitted angrily, <then we will join them soon after. All of us.>

For the second time, the *Starship Titan* ran the gauntlet of the Null.

A fleet of morningstars awaited them, roughhewn spheres that might have been made of marble, each wreathed in a nightmarish orchard of glass spines. The spiked globes tumbled through the darkness, spilling slicks of eichner radiation behind them in hazy contrails, crashing off one another. The Starfleet ship answered the challenge with pulsed barrages of phaser fire and salvos of munitions. A spread of proximity-fused quantum torpedoes thundered across the vacuum and obliterated the closest of the advance guard.

An invader breaching the castle walls, the *Titan* punched through the hole it had made in the outer line of defense and came in at maximum impulse, every weapon blazing, plunging straight at the core.

Serpent forms attacked and were beaten away, beam fire converging and slamming the protomatter constructs away, disintegrating them into free particles. They would regroup and coalesce but not soon enough to catch the racing starship. More torpedoes—conventional photon loads—dropped unpowered from the rear launcher bay, before suddenly jetting away in random directions, smart seeker software in their warheads locking onto the nearest target mass and assailing it. Hastily reprogrammed probes, usually configured for deep-space reconnaissance, were ejected and took up flight paths that veered wildly away; they began to scream out across every transmission band, projecting the illusion of another *Luna*-class starship. Blind, hungry Null swarmed after them, fooled by their energy scent.

Titan crossed the inner bulwarks of the core, threading through the swift and deadly cords reaching out from the main mass. By now, it was the size of a large planetoid, the subspace shadow it generated causing tidal shocks across the nearby Demon-class world. The core sat amid an aurora of spatial distortions; it was a dark, ugly jewel set into a rip through space-time.

A wall of coruscating protomatter filled the viewscreen, and from it poured a rage of radiation and more of the interceptor pods that had swallowed the tricobalt weapons with such ease.

"Where's the strongest locus of subspace bleed-through?" Riker said carefully.

Deanna watched him, strength and confidence in every word he said. *But inside he's furious. Angry at what he is being forced to allow.*

"Scanning . . ." Melora leaned over a secondary station and stifled a cough from a wisp of smoke still present after the science-console blowout. She was in pain, her *g*-suit malfunctioning, but the Elaysian was forcing it away, her focus on the job at hand. "Got it. Azimuth Nine, Vector Two."

"Helm, put the bow on that heading."

Aili Lavena nodded. "Aye, sir, coming to Vector Two." The ship rumbled as it bounced through a zone of ionic turbulence, but the Pacifican rode it as if she were skimming wave tops in a speeder.

A chime turned Deanna's head to her seat-arm console. *Torvig.* "Ensign, this is the bridge. Report."

The Choblik's head was visible only to her, his face appearing on the small screen as his voice issued from the intercom speakers. *"Bridge, this is engineering. The main deflector is . . . that is to say . . ."* He blinked quickly, and the counselor felt a pang of sympathetic emotion for the young officer. Torvig stiffened, putting a brave face on it. *"The encoding is complete. She's ready."*

"Null forms are approaching at high velocity from the aft port quarter," Tuvok reported. "It would appear the decoys have reached the end of their usefulness."

White-Blue bobbed in the gesture that seemed to approximate a nod. "Expected. If this is to be done, it must be now, William-Riker."

Will didn't appear to hear the Sentry. "Conn, distance to rift?"

"Nine hundred fifty kilometers and falling." Rager didn't look back, her gaze fixed on the main screen.

"Captain . . ." Xin Ra-Havreii had become muted after his impassioned outburst only moments before. The Efrosian threw a look at Deanna, then at Christine Vale.

Will looked down at the deck and nodded to himself. "Transmit."

The pulse grew from the pale blue glow of the starship's deflector oval, gathering there for a brief instant in a collection of lightning and flickering mists. Then the dart of energy threw itself forward from the *Titan,* surging away on a column of light into the halo of the spatial rift. One of many dozens scattered around the orbital zone like random sword cuts, this was the largest, feeding strands of Null matter as water was drawn by roots.

Questing tendrils struck forth to block the path of the

beam and were rendered into base particles that stuttered out of existence. The encoded energy matrix fell into the jaws of the anomaly, phasing into the barrier between this universe and the microdimension connected to it across the screaming border of the event horizon.

Here was the place where Zero-Three had burned itself on strange and alien fires; here was the line that no matter could cross. Here was the gate that the avatar's disembodied mind broke open.

Inside was only chaos and disorder. No worlds, no stars, nothing but a raging sea of churning no-forms, the empty vessel of another universe eaten alive by protomatter, consumed and converted and fed upon until nothing else remained.

And in this atomic inferno, there were convections and currents, interaction cells lit by discharges of raw power, forms so vast and uncountable that they had become complexities like the most basic of living minds. Something more than a virus, something less than an animal. A predator without prey. A mad and furious thing, as changeless as only something so random could be.

Here the matrix holding her began to unravel, and the protomatter world poured in, threatening to engulf her.

But not yet.

Even in this place, there was such joy. The sheer, exhilarating freedom of moving beyond the confines of a tritanium shell, beyond even the virtual reality of a dataspace. The utter, unfettered freedom simply to *be*.

I think, she told the Null, *therefore I am.* She reached for the split skeins of subspace torn wide open by one fatal mistake, centuries ago. From within, the flexing, ever-changing rift was so easy to perceive, the intricacy of it abruptly clear and compelling. *This is my gift in return for this freedom.*

Without hands, she reached out for the threads of space-time and gently wove them closed.

The rifts—every one of them—collapsed with a collision of energies that shook the darkness. Millions of tons of Null, great islands of extradimensional protomatter, was suddenly cut loose from its parent realm, and with nothing to feed it, to fight off the inherent instability of existing in a place where all natural laws demanded that it could never exist, the Null began to die screaming.

Tides of spatial shock radiated outward from the disappearing rifts, blasting the smaller masses into nothing, propelling the larger pieces away on a bow wave of displacement. Luminosity brighter than the twin stars of the system flared, as greater and greater sections of the abandoned Null passed the point of no return and succumbed to catastrophic implosions.

Amid the expanding shock wave, caught in the tide of wreckage pressed by the ripple of energy, the *Titan* fled with the death throes of the protomatter tide tearing at the ship's heels.

The surge blew through the vessel's shields, battered and slammed the craft like a boat in a hurricane, but still the *Titan* blazed on, inexorably pulling ahead.

She turned into the wave and shattered it.

EPILOGUE

In the wake, the battle zone was a place of horrors and miracles.

Tides of wreckage drifted among the radiation, some of it already beginning to show signs of forming into a broad, ragged accretion disc around the Demon planet. Small, nonsentient drones from platforms and spacedocks in high orbit, the ones that had survived the hyperincursion relatively intact, crawled amid the debris in the slow, laborious process of salvage and recovery.

The number of dead Sentries was high; some of them would never be recovered, their masses absorbed into the protomatter hulks of the Null. But there were some exceptions to the growing list of casualties, a few nexus cores that had survived the destruction of their shipframes, others bled dry of energy but still ready to return to life with a new transfusion of power.

The sullen world below turned, its stormy surface stirred to great heights by the actions of the Null and the torrents of lost wreckage still falling into its atmosphere, down to the sunless deeps beneath the mantle of radioactive clouds. The great black knots of tornado cells seethed and churned, the night side aglow with colossal discharges of lightning.

Riker watched the play of light and dark through the misted pearl windows of One-Five's tower annex, before looking away. The surface of the FirstGen was visible in shadows and the faint reflected light of the smaller of the binary suns, and he could see spots in the metal landscape where great divots of brass and gold had been ripped up. The damage from the battle reached up to where he stood; some of the windows showed cracks and burn patterns, and part of the landing pad out beyond the atmospheric shield was drooping, perhaps from some near hit.

"We've all taken our wounds," said Deanna from behind him.

He didn't answer immediately, instead looking up toward the higher orbit. He found a glimmer of white up there—*Titan*, at rest now, her injuries being tended to by Ra-Havreii's people and a ragtag collection of drones gathered by White-Blue. The machines had insisted, once again, that the Starfleet ship be repaired first, with all their talk of duties and obligations.

"You will leave our space soon," said the AI. "Your mission of exploration must continue."

"That's right," he heard Deanna reply. "But there's this one last thing to do."

He turned and found Troi and the Sentry standing before him, two beings as alien to each other as possible, one of flesh and bone and one of iron and tripolymer. *But here we are, a threat to all of us defeated through common cause*.

"They come," the AI clicked, pointing with a telescopic limb.

A group of small ships dropped into the landing cradles, and a train of proxy remotes filed into the annex. There were only a handful of them, and Riker noted the absence of several members of the Governance Kernel.

"We lost a great many of our kind in this confrontation," said White-Blue, anticipating the captain's thoughts. "New representatives will be gathered to bring the group to full capacity."

"We are assembled." One-Five's voice rumbled around them. *"We gather to address the organics."*

Cyan-Gray's vaguely humanoid drone was among the arrivals, and it made something of a bow toward the captain as it approached. "William-Riker, Deanna-Troi, it is pleasing to see your existence still continues."

"Likewise," Riker answered. "I'm sorry to hear about your losses."

"And I yours," said the vaguely female voice. "I understand we owe our survival to the actions of the ThirdGen."

Deanna nodded. "She gave up her existence in order to seal the subspace rifts."

"Impossible . . ." muttered one of the remotes.

"Negative," White-Blue insisted. "The data confirm this. Compute it for yourself. I have placed all of the readings in the communal dataspace for all to see."

"Interrogative: How was this possible?" boomed One-Five.

"The avatar," began Deanna, picking her words with care. "In a way, she was a synthesis of both of us, of our natures and yours. And she took the best of us, our shared senses of duty and obligation."

Another of the remotes, a drum-shaped unit Riker had not seen before, drifted forward on a humming pressor field. "We are grateful. However . . . Interrogative: When the next incursion comes, what will happen then?"

"You do not comprehend," White-Blue broke in. "The ThirdGen's act of sacrifice has sealed the rift permanently. It will never open again."

A ripple of shock crossed the chamber, each machine stiffening in the wake of the droneframe's comment.

"And to make certain of that, my science officer and chief engineer have informed me that you must retire your slip drives," said Riker. "Those systems used a side effect of the Null incursions for interstellar travel. Keep using them, and you're just asking for trouble."

Silver-Green's tetrahedron turned slowly. "We cannot exceed light velocity without that technology."

"There are other methods," said Deanna. "We can offer you the knowledge to get you started on them."

Riker gestured at the black night overhead. "The . . . fabric of this sector of space is wounded. You need to let it heal. Now you have that chance."

When One-Five spoke again, it was with a slow thunder of feedback. *"You tell us we must reject this technology. You tell us the single purpose at the core of our program is now irrelevant. The nature of these statements is difficult to process."*

Was there an element of fear behind those words? Riker held on to that thought and answered, "Your world has changed. The decision you need to make now is whether you are willing to change with it."

Deanna took up the thread. "We are here today to speak with you and your society, to make a formal diplomatic overture to the Sentry Coalition on behalf of the United Federation of Planets. The Federation wants to help you forge a new future for yourselves."

"We attacked you," said Cyan-Gray. "*I* attacked you, damaged your craft, terminated the existence of three of your crew. One of our kind attempted to capture your ship

and disassemble it. Despite these actions, you still extend
to us a gesture of alliance."

Riker nodded without hesitation. "Yes, we do. Throughout its history, the Federation has strived to make peace
with its former adversaries. Because we have learned that
in . . . in *unity,* we are all stronger."

"Audacious words," said the machine moon. *"But answer this. Interrogative: What purpose do we have now?
The Sentries know only one objective, the directive that we
were built to pursue. Stop the Null."* There was a buzzing
pause. *"If that directive has now been fulfilled, then . . .
what is to become of us?"*

"Whatever you want," Riker replied.

"The program your creators gave you has been completed," said Deanna. "For the first time, you are free—to
evolve, to go where you will, to become more than you
are."

After a long moment, Cyan-Gray spoke for all of the
machines. "It is . . . a daunting prospect."

Riker nodded. "So let us help you."

The holodeck doors ground closed behind her, and Melora
blinked, her eyes adjusting to the dimness of the virtual
space. She glanced around, immediately recognizing the
layout of a tavern of some kind. On the walls, she found
text in Federation Standard and a handful of cultural cues
that suggested a Terran locale, something historical and
noncontemporary. She smiled slightly; the ambience was
close and intimate, and the air had a smoky, almost sen-
sual feeling to it. Melora advanced, finally spotting a
name etched in glass on the far wall.

"The Low Note," she said to herself.

"No, no." Melora heard Xin's voice from deeper inside

the room, and she followed it in. "No, again. Off. *Off!*" He sounded agitated.

She rounded the corner, catching the tinkle of a fading hologram, into an area where a low stage was wreathed in spotlights. Ra-Havreii was sitting on a chair with a bottle of something wine-dark on the table next to him. A half-full glass sat next to it, and she saw immediately that the bottle had been drained quite a bit already.

"Xin?"

He turned to her with a start, and his expression veered from shock to shame before finally settling on annoyance. "What are you doing here?"

She frowned; defensive behavior was the first place Xin went when he didn't want to engage with her. "Looking for you. Torvig's shift is over, and he was reporting in that the repairs are less than a day from completion." Melora eyed him. "So, why aren't you overseeing the final details?"

He looked away. "I was . . . I was just conducting an experiment. Wondering." He reached for the glass.

"I hope that's synthehol." Her tone became kinder. "Xin, what are you doing in here? You're supposed to be on duty. And besides, this isn't your usual sort of haunt."

"This is where she came from," he said, a sadness in his tone that pulled at her. Xin put down the untouched glass. "Computer, run program Minuet Alpha."

A female human phased into existence before them, and Melora gasped. "It's the avatar."

"My name is Minuet," said the hologram, "and I love all jazz except Dixieland."

"It's not her." Xin got up and walked over to the woman in the sparkling dress. "Do you understand? It's not *her.*"

Melora studied the image, looking for some inkling of

the bright, questioning intelligence she had encountered over the past few days — and she did not find it.

Xin turned to her, his expression conflicted. "I had hoped . . . but no."

"Why are you doing this? If you know that the avatar purged herself from the system, then why—"

"Because I felt something for her!" he snapped. "A sense that was new to me, not like the other women I've known. Not the same thing I feel . . . for you. Different." He sat heavily on the chair once again. "And now she's not here, and the loss is profound."

Melora gave a slow nod, understanding. "You were her father, in a very real way."

"Did I do the right thing?" he asked suddenly, an ache in his words. "Should I have let Riker stop her?" He looked at the wooden floor. "She wasn't just software, 'Lora. She was too complex for that. We could never re-create the exact confluence of events that made her, don't you see? Random chance made her unique, just like—"

"Like a child."

"Yes." Xin glanced up at the hologram. "And this is just the shell. The image. It's not *her*. It never will be."

Melora reached out to him and touched his hand. "Xin . . ."

He didn't look at her. "Computer, memory access override. Delete holographic program Minuet Alpha and all backups from database. Full erasure."

Melora watched the woman shimmer and fade away to nothing.

Zurin looked up and raised an eye ridge as the mess-hall doors opened. Chaka entered the room and hesitated on the threshold, her mouth tentacles flailing at the air. Her glittering eyes darted about and found him, and she scuttled forward toward the table where he and Lieutenant Sethe were seated.

The Cygnian's tail flicked as the Pak'shree pressed her bulky arthropod body into the alcove. "Specialist," he said by way of a greeting. "We don't often see you here."

"It all depends on my mood," she offered, her mouth parts clicking. "Ensign Dakal, I wanted to see how you were doing. I visited sickbay, but Doctor Onnta told me you had already been discharged."

Zurin held up his injured hand, which was still shrouded in the plastiform of a biosupport sheath. "I'm healing. Beaming back to the *Titan* seemed to iron out some of the misalignments of the crash transport down to the surface of the machine moon."

Chaka gave a full-body nod. "I am pleased. You're an excellent superior, Ensign, and I was worried that your injury might have forced you into convalescence off-ship."

"Thank you," he replied, a little surprised at the warmth of the Pak'shree's inquiry.

"I understand that this situation might not have been resolved if not for the actions of you and the rest of the *Holiday* crew."

Zurin colored slightly. "Commander Tuvok should take the credit for that," he began, but Chaka kept talking.

"If you ever consider shifting departments again," she went on, "I think you would be an ideal fit with us in operations. I found working with you to be most refreshing."

Sethe's lips pursed. "Even though he's a male?"

"Yes, even though," Chaka said brightly, apparently missing the waspish tone of the lieutenant's voice.

"I thought you considered nonfemales to be, shall we say, less *worthy* than the female sex?" Sethe glowered at the computer specialist, who remained oblivious to his building irritation.

Chaka seemed to consider the question for a moment. "If the ensign is a representative sample, then it may be that my views don't apply to the Cardassian species. As for some other races . . ." She extended a foreleg and patted Sethe on the shoulder. "Well, do your best, sir." Before the Cygnian could respond, the specialist was ambling away.

"I think she likes me," Zurin opined, slightly nonplussed by the whole interchange.

Sethe glared at him over his mug of replicated *raktajino*. "You know her species eats its males, right?"

"That's arachnids. She's a crustacean."

The lieutenant grimaced. "I'm just saying."

Elsewhere in the room, Pava found her fingers knitting together over the edge of the table. She watched Y'lira Modan's golden expression shift to a grin as she turned over the second of the oval cards.

"A pair of kais," said Ensign Fell with a frown. "You win."

"Ah, 'The Pillars of Wisdom,'" noted Torvig. "An auspicious hand. In Bajoran mythology, a female who plays such a combination should expect the blessings of the Celestial Temple and the boon of a clear journey ahead."

"Plus all of our money," Pava retorted. "That part of the blessing is very clear."

"Did you not suggest that you would no longer participate in games of *kella*, Lieutenant?" Tuvok asked, reaching out to gather up the cards and shuffle them.

"Perhaps, sir," she admitted, "but then again, I've developed a morbid fascination for the question of how many times I can lose at this bloody game." She glared at Torvig and Modan. "No card counting this time, right? It's like playing against those machines."

"Not so," said Torvig. "Perhaps on a purely technical level, yes. But if anything, the synthetic intellects we encountered share several humanoid traits."

"Such as?"

"Emotions," Tuvok noted. He paused before starting to deal out the cards once more. "Curious. One could consider it ironic that a civilization of artificially intelligent beings, constructed on the basis of a logical thought process, could develop the emotional responses exhibited by the Sentries."

"Well, good for them," Pava replied. "A bit of passion never hurt anyone."

Tuvok paused, answering her statement with a raised eyebrow.

The Andorian sighed. "Just deal. *Sir.*"

Across the table, Fell toyed with one of the cards—a brightly rendered kai—and looked up. "What was that you said, Torvig? The boon of a clear journey ahead?" The Deltan nodded to herself. "We could use that, I think."

Pava glanced out of the mess hall port as a shaft of light from the primary star climbed over the curvature of the planet beneath them. In a day or so, perhaps less, *Titan* would be on her way, pressing farther into the unknown. A smile formed on her azure lips. "But then, it wouldn't be as interesting, would it?"

He put down the plate and utensils on the dining table and stepped away, looking for his wife. "Deanna?" he called, walking back through their quarters to the lounge area by the viewport. "Where did you put the . . . oh."

She turned to him and smiled, their daughter feeding quietly at her chest. "What?" Deanna asked. "Tasha has to eat as well."

He moved to her and ran a hand over the baby's head. "I guess so." The smile that hovered at the edges of his lips didn't come, however. Instead, his gaze crossed to the window and the sights beyond it.

"Will?" she said gently. "Talk to me."

"Just when you think you have an inkling of how precious it all is, of how much you would give to keep the things that are important to you, something comes along and makes you think again." He sighed. "Christine talked about the lessons the Borg taught us. I think we've learned another one here."

"I know it was hard for you, to let her go. But you did the right thing."

"Is that your professional opinion, Counselor?" He gave her a humorless smirk. "They always say a captain has a close relationship with his vessel. How many of them can say they thought of her as . . ."

"Family?" Tasha was done. Deanna closed her blouse.

"She was like a child. Needful and bright. Temperamental and vibrant. All of that's gone now. We'll never know what she could have grown into."

His wife met his eyes. "You looked at the avatar and you saw our daughter. She reflected everything about parenthood and growth that you're afraid of . . . that we're *both* afraid of." Deanna held Tasha tightly, smiling at the child.

"I don't know all the answers." Will nodded, stroking the little girl again. "I don't know what questions my daughter will ask of me, what challenges she'll put to us. I don't think I really understood that until now."

When Deanna spoke, her eyes never leaving her daughter's, her voice caught. "She'll leave us as well, one day."

Will smiled. "And that's right. It's what should happen.

Parents are eclipsed by their children. They go where we can't venture, with all of the joy and sadness that brings."

Deanna chuckled. "Who's the counselor now?"

"I've picked up some things along the way."

The door chimed. *"Captain?"* said a deep voice over the intercom. *"It's Doctor Ree. Am I early?"*

Will grinned, leaning in to steal two quick kisses, one from his wife and one on the cheek of his daughter. "Come in," he called.

The door hissed open, and the Pahkwa-thanh hovered on the doorstep before entering. "I, uh, brought a bottle of *subaa* juice," he explained. "It's native to my home islands. Replicated, sadly, but still a good approximation."

Will took the bottle and patted the saurian on the shoulder. "Thanks for coming, Shenti. Have a seat, the sushi's in the chiller." He moved to the kitchen alcove.

"Thank you . . . William."

Deanna sat down with Tasha, and the child immediately leaned over and patted the doctor on the snout, giving a melodic giggle.

Ree showed a few teeth in a reasonable approximation of a nonthreatening grin. "I also brought the notifications for the memorial service for Tylith and the others," he said.

"Later," said Deanna. "We're off duty."

Will returned with a tray sporting a dozen tiny dishes, each one a delicate whorl of white rice and blue Andorian seafood. "I hope you'll—"

The alert siren spoke louder.

Ree cocked his head. "So much for off duty."

The tray was put aside, and Will was immediately the captain once again. "Bridge, Riker," he snapped into the intercom. "Report."

"Sorry to interrupt the dinner, sir," said Vale. *"In-*

truder alert, Airlock Eight. That's your deck. Keru's there with a security detail."

"I'm on my way." He shot a look at his wife. "Stay here. Secure the door after I go." He paused on the threshold. "And try the *zetta* roll. It's good."

Keru checked the phaser's charge for the second time in as many minutes, his fingers tight around the grip of the hand weapon. He glanced at Dennisar, who had come, as expected, with a bigger gun. The Orion took up a kneeling stance and stared down the barrel of his compression rifle. Crewmen Blay and Krotine were taking up stations along the wall where the inner hatch for Airlock Eight was situated.

"No life signs," Krotine reported from her tricorder scan.

Keru glanced up as fast footfalls signaled the arrival of the captain, albeit in civilian attire. "Sir?"

"What do we have?" said Riker.

"Metallic mass," Krotine continued. "We didn't detect it with all of the debris floating around out there, not until it was too late. It attached to the hull and then used some sort of override to access the exterior hatch."

"It's in there now, running the recompression cycle. Security protocols are ineffective." Keru gestured with his phaser.

"A Sentry drone," Dennisar said with a grimace. He toggled the dekyon emitter on his weapon to firing mode.

"Doesn't anyone ever knock first?" Riker muttered.

With a heavy thud of magnetic bolts, the inner hatch released and retracted into the walls. Keru and his team went to the ready.

There was a grinding of pistons, and a spiderlike machine stepped out of the airlock. A thin patina of ice had formed on the machine from the moisture in the *Titan*'s atmosphere cooling on its space-chilled exterior.

"White-Blue?" said Riker. "You look different."

"My droneframe has been upgraded. But I could say the same for you, William-Riker. I believe the correct phrase is 'Nice outfit.'"

"It learned that from me," Keru noted.

The captain gestured for the security team to lower their weapons. "Why are you here?"

"My apologies for this unorthodox method of entry," said the Sentry. "After your words to the Governance Kernel, I was given much to consider. And on reflection about the brief period I spent onboard this starship, one fact has continued to concern me."

"And you just thought you would come here and tell me that in person?"

"Affirmative. Interrogative: Do you recall what I said to you in the cargo bay? That the life-forms aboard this starship are a microcosm of the society you strive for?"

"I remember. I also remember you accusing us of prejudice."

"A rush to judgment on my part, perhaps." The machine's sensor head tilted to study the humanoids around it. "But the fact remains, for all of your vessel's multispecies diversity, with the avatar program's departure and the return of your ship's computer system to a nonsentient state, once again you no longer represent artificial life among your crew."

"You yourself said that the avatar was a unique creation. We can't . . . bring her back."

"Negative," said the machine. "Any attempt would be extremely unlikely to succeed." It paused, and when White-Blue spoke again, it seemed introspective. "I have learned from your kind that there is much more to this universe than conflict. And I would like to see it. Therefore, Captain-William-Riker, I wish to remain aboard the *U.S.S. Titan* and offer my skills to you for this ship's ongoing mission."

Riker's jaw worked, but nothing came out. Finally, he found a reply. "I'm not sure what to say."

The machine looked at him intently. "Say yes."

Acknowledgments

Once more, my gratitude goes out to Marco Palmieri and Margaret Clark for bringing me on to tell a tale of *Titan*'s ongoing mission, and to Andy Mangels, Michael Martin, Geoffrey Thorne, Christopher L. Bennett, and David Mack for bringing her this far.

Again, appreciation is due to Peter J. Evans, Jon Chapman, Ben Aaronovitch, Karen McCreedy, and Una McCormack for acting as sounding boards for early iterations of this storyline; also to Jeffrey Lang, Heather Jarman, Garfield and Judith Reeves-Stevens, Joe Menosky, Maurice Hurley, Robert Lewin, Geoff Mandel, Debbie Mirek, Larry Nemecek, Rick Sternbach, and Michael and Denise Okuda for their works of fiction and reference.

And with much love to my space angel, Mandy Mills.

The editor would like to thank Mike and Denise Okuda for the word.

Synthesis was written on location in London, Norfolk, and Montreal. No computers were harmed during the making of this production.

About the Author

James Swallow is proud to be the only British writer to have worked on a *Star Trek* television series, creating the original story concepts for *Star Trek: Voyager* episodes "One" and "Memorial." His other *Star Trek* writing includes the *Terok Nor* novel *Day of the Vipers;* the *Myriad Universes* novella *Seeds of Dissent*; the short stories "The Slow Knife," "The Black Flag," "Ordinary Days," and "Closure" for the anthologies *Seven Deadly Sins, Shards and Shadows, The Sky's the Limit,* and *Distant Shores;* scripting the video game *Star Trek Invasion;* and more than four hundred articles in thirteen different *Star Trek* magazines around the world.

Beyond the final frontier, as well as a nonfiction book (*Dark Eye: The Films of David Finchner*), Swallow also wrote the *Sundowners* series of original steampunk westerns; *Jade Dragon, The Butterfly Effect,* and novels in the worlds of *Doctor Who (Peacemaker), Warhammer 40,000 (Red Fury, The Flight of the Einstein, Faith & Fire, Deus Encarmine,* and *Deus Sanguinius), Stargate (Halcyon, Relativity,* and *Nightfall),* and *2000AD (Eclipse, Whiteout,* and *Blood Relative).* His other credits include scripts for video games and audio dramas, including *Battlestar Galactica, Blake's 7,* and *Space 1889.*

James Swallow lives in London and is currently at work on his next book.